FUGITIVE COLORS

FUGITIVE
COLORS

A Novel

LISA BARR

Arcade Publishing
NEW YORK

First Edition
This is a work of fiction. Names, characters, places, and incidents are either the products of the author's imagination or used fictitiously.

Arcade Publishing books may be purchased in bulk at special discounts for sales promotion, corporate gifts, fund-raising, or educational purposes. Special editions can also be created to specifications. For details, contact the Special Sales Department, Arcade Publishing, 307 West 36th Street, 11th Floor, New York, NY 10018 or arcade@skyhorsepublishing.com.

Arcade Publishing® is a registered trademark of Skyhorse Publishing, Inc.®, a Delaware corporation.

Visit our website at www.arcadepub.com.

10 9 8 7 6 5 4 3 2 1

Library of Congress Cataloging-in-Publication Data
Barr, Lisa.
  Fugitive Colors : a novel / Lisa Barr.
    pages cm
  ISBN 978-1-61145-894-7 (hardcover : alk. paper)
  1. Artists—France—Paris—20th century—Fiction.   2. Art—France—Paris—20th century —Fiction.   3. Americans—France—Paris—20th century—Fiction.   4. Nineteen thirties—Fiction.   5. Nazis—Fiction. 6. Suspense fiction.   I. Title.
  PS3602.A777434F84 2013
  813'.6—dc23

                                    2013012206

Printed in the United States of America.

To David—My Love, My Passion, My Secret Editor

&

To My Beautiful Girls—Noa, Maya, and Maya (xoxo *Always & Forever*)

. . . .

"Color has taken possession of me; no longer do I have to chase after it. I know that it has hold of me forever . . . Color and I are one. I am a painter."
—Paul Klee, artist

"Anyone who sees and paints a sky green and fields blue ought to be sterilized."
—Adolf Hitler

. . . .

Prologue

CHICAGO, 1926

Yakov Klein slowly ran his finger over the cover of the art book he was about to steal from the library, as a burglar would a precious jewel just snatched from a glass case. Pressing the book to his face, he inhaled the familiar dusty scent of his latest prize: *Gustav Klimt*. It was a delicious moment, but one he would have to savor later, in the secrecy of his bedroom once the lights were out and his parents were sleeping. Right now, he had to get out of the library without getting caught.

Shoving the thick book inside his overcoat, Yakov quickly made a beeline from the art collection toward the exit, one floor down, and across the long vaulted hallway. The linoleum floor squeaked loudly as he neared the sole librarian bent over a bottom shelve next to a pile of just-returned books. He paused briefly and stared at the librarian's large buttocks straining too tightly against the cheap material of her royal blue skirt. If only he could paint her like that—compromised, determined to get the book alphabetized and in its place—but he kept walking. Thirty-two more steps until he was safely out the door.

From the corner of his eye, Yakov saw a little girl, no more than five, holding her mother's hand and watching him. He knew what she saw—what everyone saw when they looked at him—the long black wool coat, the tall black silk hat that was still too big, and the *payis*—long sidelocks—that Jewish custom had required him to grow his whole life. It was a uniform borne of a different century. Yakov, son of Benjamin, raised as an Orthodox Jew, wore some version of the same clothing every day—black and white, a wardrobe devoid of color or change—and he hated it.

That's why he stole the art book. If truth were told, that was why he had been stealing art books since the week after his bar mitzvah, nine months earlier. He desperately needed color. This desire was apparent at age seven when he discovered his mother's special pale pink lipstick stashed in the skinny wooden drawer in the nightstand by her bed. It was the same color as the covering for the *challah* on the Sabbath table. It was also the same color as the fancy napkins his mother put out on Rosh Hashanah. Yakov took the lipstick. He knew it was wrong, but he had to have it. Pink, he thought with excitement, was also the color of the forbidden pig—that un-kosher swine his father always ranted on about.

Yakov thought a lot about pigs, perhaps because he wasn't supposed to think about them. At first he felt guilty as he began to draw, but once the lipstick met the paper he could not stop until he was finished. Holding the paper to the light, Yakov felt an indescribable thrill—the plump curly-tailed *treif* animal was now his. He hid the drawing inside his bedroom closet. And it was on that day that he discovered the joy of art, and when the lying began.

In time, Yakov became more sophisticated in his art. Using a pencil, he drew everything around him from memory: his mother, his father, books, food, *Shabbos* candles—everything he'd see would soon find its way onto paper and then into the secret box hidden in his closet. No one knew. Just him and God. And that was more than enough.

One day, after Yakov's father left early for the synagogue, his mother came into his bedroom, closed the door, and gestured Yakov to join her on the bed. They faced each other in silence, the kind of stern cross-armed quiet that meant he'd done something wrong. He waited.

"Yakov, I know."

She knew.

Yakov, ten years old, was his mother's only child, in a world where only children simply did not exist, unless there were problems. And there were definitely problems. Yakov would hear his mother cry at night through his bedroom wall, telling his father that she was half a woman because she could not have more children. She would go on about her sister Channa with six kids and pregnant with the seventh, and why was it God's way that she should only have one? And all the babies she lost before and after Yakov. Five, she would cry, five. At dinner, Yakov would see the disappointment unveiled in his father's eyes when he'd look at his wife across the table, and then Yakov would see his mother's fallen face. But right now, his mother, angry and sad with five dead pregnancies, *knew*.

"Are you going to tell him, Mama?" Yakov asked quietly. He was not scared of his father, just terrified of losing his collection of artwork.

"No," she whispered, gently wiping away a wisp of light brown hair from his forehead. Her green eyes welled up. Yakov thought, if only he could draw her like that: the loose hair falling out of her bun, her head tilted just so, her beautiful wet green eyes that were the same color as the sofa.

"I'm afraid for you, Yakov."

"Don't be," he said, sitting up straight, knowing she hated when he slouched. "I'm not afraid."

"But your father . . . and the rabbi. It is forbidden. The drawings. You need to study your Torah." His mother's tone was stern but her gaze was milky and far away. "You are too young to understand. But passion, dreams of something else, something better—can destroy." Silent, slow-moving tears began to fall lightly against her cheeks.

Are you still talking about me, Mama? Yakov wanted to ask, but knew better. Instead, he reached for his mother's trembling hand and held it tightly, protectively, inside his own.

"I won't tell him," she promised through her tears. "But you must stop. You must . . . " Her voice trailed away.

That day, his art and his lies became hers; an umbilical cord of shared but necessary silence.

What Yakov's mother did not know was that the pencil and paper were not enough. Yakov knew that only he could answer the voice nagging deep inside him: *More*.

More began with stolen crayons and paints from a nearby hardware store. More led Yakov to the Chicago Public Library, with its treasure trove of art books on painters, paintings, technique, and even lessons. He could not just borrow those books. That would leave a record. His father would somehow find out. At first Yakov thought that one book on Michelangelo would be enough, but it simply whet his appetite. Soon, one book became two; two became five; five turned into ten. Today's book marked eighteen—the most significant of all biblical numbers, he thought. Eighteen was *chai*—life.

These books give me life. Surely God understands, Yakov rationalized as he closed the heavy library door behind him.

Holding the book close to his chest, he ran the eight blocks from the library to the *cheder*—the dank, windowless classroom where he studied six days a week with the rabbi and other boys from his community. If only the rabbi could know that Yakov cared nothing about Abraham, Isaac, and Jacob—except to paint them. If only he could paint the sacrifice of Isaac in Abraham's hands. If only he could paint the beautiful Rachel with her long, thick, black hair and those full breasts that tempted Jacob, making him work seven years, day and night, like an ox, just to "know" her. How many times did Yakov paint that scene in his head at night, or daydream in the classroom while the rabbi droned on? If only he could paint all of his favorite biblical stories, but it was as forbidden as worshiping the Golden Calf. The images were allowed only in his head, and in his heart. His hands were bound and restrained. Painting was breathing, and Yakov was suffocating. But one day, he knew, things would be different.

Yakov told no one about the art books. He had friends, boys he grew up with, but none could be trusted not to tell the rabbi that he broke the Eighth Commandment eighteen times. Nineteen, if you counted the pig. He patted the treasured book inside his coat as he nervously opened the classroom door, knowing before he crossed the threshold exactly what was waiting for him.

"Yakov Klein, you are late again!" the rabbi shouted when he entered the room, six minutes after the other boys.

"I'm sorry." Yakov kept his gaze glued to the scratched-up wood floor.

"You're always sorry."

"I'm really not sorry," Yakov muttered under his breath.

"What?"

"Nothing."

As Yakov walked over to his desk, a leg stuck out into the aisle and tripped him on purpose. Yakov went flying, and so did *Gustav Klimt*. The boys laughed until they saw the rabbi bend over and pick up the stolen book, then there was dead silence. Yakov Klein, the class trouble-maker, was in big trouble.

"What is this?" the rabbi demanded, his eyes blazing as he held up the book. "And where did you get it?"

Yakov knew better than to speak.

"Answer me!"

Yakov stared up at the rabbi, who was tugging angrily on his long, scraggly beard, waiting. He stole a glance at the boys around him, who were half worried for him and half thinking, *better him than me.*

"It's a book," he said slowly.

"Don't tell me what I already see. Tell me what I don't."

Yakov paused, long enough to muster his courage. "It's a book about art."

"It doesn't belong here!" The rabbi wagged an angry finger, the same angry finger he used whether he was discussing Commentary or Torah or doling out discipline. That finger was loaded.

Eyeing the finger, Yakov whispered, "I don't belong here, Rabbi."

"Don't belong here?" mocked the rabbi who was nearing eighty or ninety—no one knew for sure. He opened and quickly slammed shut the book on Klimt, the loud clap echoing throughout the musty room. His dark eyes behind thick glasses blazed as he wagged that finger in double-time. "Barely fourteen years old. You think you know about life, but you know nothing."

Yakov quickly glanced at the other boys, his friends. No one said a word. He saw the terror in their eyes, but suddenly, strangely, he felt none inside his own body. He took a few steps forward and stood defiantly before the rabbi. "I will show *you* something about life."

The rabbi's eyes widened with disbelief at his insolent student. But there was something else in those black eyes that Yakov saw immediately, which the rabbi could not conceal: curiosity. The rabbi, a teacher, a father of eight and grandfather of thirty, was only a man after all.

Yakov did not wait for a response. He quickly reached inside his desk and took out the piece of paper that he had been hiding for several months. He handed it to the rabbi. "This, I drew for you."

The rabbi took the paper and held it with both hands, first at arm's length and then up into the light. Slowly, he brought the drawing close to his face. It was a picture of the rabbi, alone, praying in his study. His large white *tallis*—a hand-woven shawl with thick black stripes—was draped like a cape over his shoulders, his *tefillin*—phylacteries—were wrapped tightly around his forehead and arm. His heavy-hooded eyes bulged not with the wrath of a dissatisfied teacher but with the joy of Morning Prayer. It was an intense, intimate moment that Yakov had captured.

The rabbi tore his gaze away from the image and stared at Yakov. Known as a man who could scold like a snake and reduce a boy to tears with a mere glare, the rabbi was, for the first time, speechless, that finger hanging limply at his side. There was well over a *minyan* of witnesses as the rabbi stood in silent awe of his worst student's God-given talent.

That look was all Yakov needed to confirm what he already knew: *He was chosen.*

GREEN

"Great art picks up where nature ends."
—Marc Chagall

Chapter One

PARIS, 1932

Julian stepped off the train platform at Gare de Lyon and onto the cobblestone street. Clutching his suitcase, portfolio, and new identity, he drew in a deep, satisfied breath.

I'm here, finally.

Sharp fumes from passing cars and garbage rot were certainly not what he expected. Somehow, the air in Paris should be savory, sweet, musky, or wine-scented, not ripe with urban odors. As Julian waited for a taxicab, a stylish young woman with long auburn curls walked toward him with an airy bounce, quickly making him forget the stench. Her dress was clingy and floral. Blooming red roses gripped her curvaceous body like a silk glove. Julian smiled at her. She paused, and he knew what she saw: the white even teeth and boyish dimples—a smile that could sell anything, his mother used to say. But this girl wasn't buying. She rolled her eyes, giggling, and kept walking. Julian realized he had a large baguette crumb hanging off of his lip. He heard her still laughing as she crossed the street.

"Where to?" The driver leaned out of the Renault window, speaking without even looking at him.

Julian knew he should go to the university to get situated. His first class started tomorrow, but the day was still young. He hesitated, but only for a few seconds. *Why not?*

"Where do the artists hang out?" he asked in broken French. He understood the language much better than he could speak it.

"The Left Bank," the driver said gruffly. "Get in."

Café de Flore at the corner of boulevard Saint Germain and rue Saint-Benoît was crowded. The outdoor seating area was packed with young people drinking, talking, and smoking shoulder to shoulder. No one seemed to mind the sardine-like arrangement. On the contrary, Julian noted, as he approached the restaurant, they appeared to revel in it.

When he entered the two-story café, he was struck by the expensive décor filled with large mirrors, mahogany furniture, and candy-apple red-cushioned seats lining the walls. Julian was used to cheap crummy diners with scattered old newspapers left behind on the seats and cracks on the walls that no one bothered to fix. This place, in comparison, was immaculate, and probably too pricey. He patted his coat and felt the comforting thickness of the wad of money concealed inside a sewn-in pocket. He must have checked the pocket a thousand times on his long journey to Paris. This money was all he had to get by. He had to pace himself. He was hungry, but a cup of coffee and bread would have to do.

He scanned the room. Tiny round tables were brimming with young people. He saw dozens of large portfolios leaning against chair legs. *Artists.* Julian's heart beat fast. So this was it. Paris—home of Picasso, Braque, Chagall, Monet, Manet, Renoir, Cézanne—every artist who mattered. *And now me.* It seemed only yesterday that he had left his parents' home in Chicago for New York. Left? Julian shook his head at the innocence of that word—more like *ran* for his life.

As he stood near the door waiting for a table, Julian tried not to think about the past, but no matter how hard he pushed away those thoughts, they continued to haunt him. *Don't go there,* he warned himself. *Not now, not today.*

Instead, he focused on the pretty brunette sitting alone at a table in the center of the room. She caught his eye and smiled. He guessed she was his age, around twenty, perhaps a few years older. He smiled back. The girl laughed and lit a cigarette. Her exhale was long and seductive; the smoke, a smooth, thick line in front of her face. As the smoke cleared, she leaned back and assessed him daringly. *Was that an invitation?* Julian wondered if he should join her, when suddenly two men pushed past him and walked over to her table.

Damn. The girl stood and kissed them both warmly. Who were they? While she was talking, Julian took the opportunity to get a better look at her. She was medium height, very slim with small curves, like a teenager. He studied the way her hands moved as she spoke, animated like a conductor, and how her long dark ponytail swished behind her as she laughed at something one of those guys said to her. Her lips were full and sensual, slightly duck-like with gleaming white teeth that lit up her whole face. Julian had known women in New York—mostly artists' models—who were, perhaps, more blatantly beautiful, yet none exuded the instant vibrancy of this girl. Her presence seemed to fill the room.

If only she would sit still, Julian thought, then he could paint her— first in his head, and later, on canvas.

"*Monsieur*, your table is ready." The waiter tapped his arm, interrupting his thoughts. He led Julian to a table near the girl. He felt self-conscious as his shabby suitcase bumped several people along the way. Everyone seemed to be watching him. From the corner of his eye, he could see her eyes on him too.

"Hey—just get off the boat?" one of the two guys sitting at her table called out in harsh-sounding French. Julian turned around.

"Leave him alone, Felix," the girl scolded. Then Julian heard her whisper, "Besides, he's quite attractive."

"Just having a little fun, Adrienne," the guy she called Felix said. "And for the record, he's not as good looking as I am."

Her name is Adrienne. It fits.

"You mean not as good looking as you *think* you are." She squeezed Felix's arm affectionately. *A friendly squeeze,* Julian noted. He was certain that Felix was not her boyfriend. Must be the other one then. Julian sat back in his chair, stretched his legs, watching the trio from the corner of his eye. *And, she thinks I'm attractive.*

"Let's settle this, Adrienne." Felix turned to his friend. "René, who is better looking? Me, or the guy with the suitcase?"

René laughed. "Von Bredow, you never change. Always competing. Hate to say it, but Bag Boy wins hands down."

"Bastard."

"Truth hurts."

Felix leaned forward. "So do lies."

Adrienne laughed hard, and then their conversation quickly changed from Julian's looks to politics. Julian readjusted his chair to get a better view. He could not help but stare at René, whose hair was thick with jet-black waves that nearly reached his shoulders. His blackish eyes were deep-set, and his strong, straight nose flared slightly at the end like a Greek warrior's. He was pretty, like a prince in a fairy tale. As René spoke, he lightly stroked Adrienne's upper arm. *Definitely the boyfriend.* Julian knew he could not compete.

"So, where are you from?" Felix called out, catching Julian staring at them. "America, right?"

Julian felt his cheeks heat up. Conversations seemed to have stopped.

"New York," Julian answered quietly.

"Long way from home," Felix announced loud enough for his attentive audience. "Get lost?"

He was exactly the kind of guy Julian hated—the loudmouth who demanded constant attention.

"I'm an artist," Julian mumbled, not sure why he even bothered to answer.

The spectators at the surrounding tables burst out in allied laughter. Julian cringed, wishing he could disappear. But the waiter brought his coffee and he was stuck.

"An artist?" Felix arched a thick black eyebrow. "A true artist drinks wine in the afternoon and coffee after midnight. You call yourself *an artist*?"

Julian's fists curled tightly. *Ignore him*. He sipped his coffee and focused on the street-side window in front of him, but he could still hear Felix going at it, enjoying himself at Julian's expense.

"Leave him alone already, Felix. You never know when to stop." It was Adrienne rushing to Julian's defense.

Felix, who clearly did not like to be ignored, responded by getting up and walking over to Julian's table. "I didn't mean to offend you," he said, his breath reeking of wine. "I'm just having some fun. Look, we don't bite. We're artists too." He extended his hand, but Julian pretended not to notice. "Felix Von Bredow."

"Julian Klein." He stood and assessed Felix, who was taller than him, but less muscular. His hair, black and slicked back, set off a wide forehead and large eyes that were a startling shade of blue. His pockmarked cheeks marred what might have been a perfect face.

"Have a drink with us." Felix gestured toward his table.

Julian met Adrienne's sparkling almond gaze. She smiled warmly, and he felt himself blush.

"I can guarantee we'll insult you," Felix added wryly, "but we won't bore you."

Julian wanted to tell Felix to go to hell, but Felix had already grabbed Julian's bag without waiting for an answer.

~✺~

"*Garçon*, another," Felix shouted out in French, lifting a just-finished bottle of Beaujolais high overhead. He then raised his still-full glass and said in German, "A toast to the tortured memory of my father. May Baron Wilhelm Von Bredow forever rest in peace, and remain far away from me."

"But your father is alive and well," Adrienne objected in English, for Julian's benefit.

"There you go again." Felix playfully kissed her cheek. "Trying to ruin my day."

Julian glanced at his watch in shock. It felt like minutes since he'd sat down with them, but he had been drinking for almost three hours. The traffic outside was dying down, and the bustling afternoon had transformed into a lethargic dusk. He was tired from traveling and light-headed from listening to his new friends switch languages as easily as they changed their drinks.

"So, how do you know French and German so well?" Felix asked Julian, as he downed his glass and opened yet another bottle of wine. "Europeans converse easily in at least three languages, but most Americans I meet can barely speak one."

"Very funny." Julian deemed Felix an asshole but figured he'd never see him again after today. "I had a neighbor who was French," he explained. "And a cousin by marriage who was German. But if I were you, I wouldn't brag about your English."

Adrienne laughed and punched Felix's arm. "No wonder René and I are the only friends you have left."

"Not true," Felix countered, nudging Julian. "I now have him too."

Adrienne rolled her eyes and leaned forward. Her blouse opened slightly and Julian forced himself to look away. "We've been talking nonstop. Tell us more about you, Julian."

For the first time since Julian had joined their table, Felix actually stopped talking and gave Julian the floor. The three of them were silent and waiting. Julian was not prepared to talk about himself, but knew he had to give them something. He skipped the part about Chicago and instead told them how he had lived briefly with his cousin Sammy in Brooklyn while taking art classes at night. During the day, while Sammy ran his bootlegging business, Julian spent time with his cousin's German-born wife Gertrude, who modeled for him as he painted her, cooked for him, and taught him the language. Julian omitted telling them how Gertrude had tried to seduce him one afternoon and that he quickly packed up his belongings and left Sammy's home that night. Instead, Julian told his new friends that he needed a change and moved into a ramshackle apartment in Manhattan with five other young artists whom he had met in his classes. By day, Julian painted houses to make money. On those nights he did not have art classes, he painted on the street with his new friends, mostly portraits and landscapes of local tourist attractions, particularly tacky renderings of Yankee Stadium and the Statue of Liberty.

Julian quickly understood that while his subjects were uninspiring, his work sold faster than any other artist's paintings on the street. He heard the same comments again and again. "You are better than this, Julian. A natural. Go to Paris, that's where the real artists are."

An elderly French woman who lived in his apartment building encouraged Julian to send his sketches to her brother, an instructor at the École des Beaux-Arts, to get an opinion of his work. When Julian received an invitation to attend the famous Parisian art school, he knew that what they had said about him on the street must be true. He happily painted the French woman's portrait in exchange for French lessons.

Six months later, after he had saved up enough money for travel expenses, Julian returned to his cousin's home, asking Sammy if he could borrow money to move to Paris to study. He showed Sammy the letter from the École des Beaux-Arts and promised him a return with interest on the investment.

Sammy brought Julian into his office and opened up the safe, which was filled with more money than Julian had ever seen. He handed Julian several stacks of bills and a bottle of whiskey, and hugged him tightly. He then looked his cousin squarely in the eye and said, "I trust you, Julian. If it's what you really want, then go to Paris and paint, but when you become the next Picasso, don't forget your cousin Sammy."

Felix listened to Julian's story as he finished off the last of the wine. "A bootlegger, huh? My kind of guy. The École des Beaux-Arts part—not impressed." He glanced at Adrienne and René, then lifted the almost emptied bottle of Beaujolais to get the waiter's attention. Julian had never seen anyone drink so much, and so fast.

"Go easy, Felix," René warned him, giving the approaching waiter a no-more signal. He turned to Julian. "Don't get Felix started on the Beaux-Arts, or we will be here all night."

"You think I'm drunk, René? You have no faith in my true calling." Felix grabbed René's half-full glass of wine and finished it, slamming down the glass against the table. "But you're right. Let's get out of here. I say we paint. My creative juices are flowing. Let's go now before I piss it all out." He draped his arm around René's shoulders. "My place this time. Why don't you join us, Julian? You have nothing better to do."

Julian knew he should get to the art school to settle in. "I've really got to go," he said reluctantly. "Classes begin tomorrow, and I can barely see straight."

"The goal here is to *not* see straight." Felix wiped his wine-drenched mouth with his sleeve. "I almost forgot. École des Beaux-Arts's students need all of their energy to stomach heavy doses of academic rubbish."

René and Adrienne exchanged knowing glances. "Here we go," René said, rolling his eyes.

Julian turned to Adrienne. "What's his problem with the École des Beaux-Arts?"

"You have to understand, we were all once students there," she explained. "We're dropouts."

"That place is a death warrant for artists." Felix leaned in close to Julian. His breath was sour. "A bunch of cookie-cutter instructors out to destroy any independent creative thinking."

René nodded vigorously, and Julian noticed how his black hair had a deep blue sheen under the glow of the overhead light. "A couple of years ago we all left the school together for Léon Dubois's studio," René explained. "Way back, Dubois taught at the Beaux-Arts. He was considered one of their star painters until he declared himself to be independent of the Establishment."

Julian listened as René described how their mentor had been fed up with the school's stringent rules and had decided to break free. As René spoke, Julian gazed at his hands, which were slim-tipped and delicately carved. They did not seem to match the rest of René, who was powerfully built, like an athlete.

Adrienne lit another cigarette and blew smoke over Julian's shoulder, interrupting his thoughts. "Dubois challenged the powers-that-be by joining up with the German Expressionists and flaunting it," she said. The stream of her breath felt warm near Julian's mouth, and he inhaled it guiltily.

"It was a slap in the school's face," she continued. "The French hate the Expressionists because their technique is considered formless, excessive, and wild—totally unsophisticated."

"But brilliant," René added, as he lightly stroked her shoulder again. She looked up at him, and they both smiled intimately, as though they would rather be in bed than at the café. Julian felt an unexpected pang of jealousy.

"Yes, the Expressionists are brilliant, German, and barbaric—like me." Felix laughed heartily, joined by the others. He stood. He was done talking, done drinking. He threw money down on the table and pulled Julian up alongside him. "Tomorrow, you will be stuck in a classroom, my friend. But tonight, you're coming with us, and we will show you what you will never get at the École des Beaux-Arts."

Chapter Two

The group left the boulevard Saint Germain and headed toward the rue Mazarine to drop off Adrienne, who claimed she was too tired to paint. As they passed several bookstores and art galleries, Julian caught the inebriated group's reflection in the succession of sepia-tinted glass panels. *Paint?* he thought. *We can barely stand.*

They stumbled along chipped cobblestones, and Julian concentrated hard to keep one foot in front of the other, balancing his body with his bag and portfolio. Julian stopped moving when he spotted a group of vendors gathering across the street with their wooden carts filled with leftovers from the day—bread, fruit, and vegetables. A full-bearded young man stepped away from his cart and seemed to be looking directly at Julian. He was wearing a long black jacket, white shirt, and tall black silk hat. Julian rubbed his eyes. *Here it is. Can't get away.*

Julian tried to walk forward and ignore the man, but then he saw the small, black prayer book in the man's hand, and he froze. Squeezing his eyes shut, Julian remembered the feel of that book; the rough texture of the worn-in binder, the yellowing pages crammed with thousands of tiny black Hebrew letters—words that were pounded into his head, day after day for eighteen hellish years.

"Do you know that guy, Julian? He seems to know you." Felix pointed across the street at the man facing them. "That's not your cousin Sammy, is it?"

"Felix, enough," Adrienne reprimanded him, glancing at Julian.

But Felix kept going. "See, what I don't understand is fine, be Jewish, but not *that* Jewish."

Julian's face turned red. He should leave now.

"Ignore Felix. He drank way too much," Adrienne said in a way that Julian could tell she was used to apologizing on Felix's behalf.

Be Jewish, but not that *Jewish.*

Felix's words weighed heavily on Julian's mind, and he knew that no matter how hard he tried to get away from being *that* Jewish, he could never escape. Not in Chicago, not in New York, and not here in Paris. There would always be reminders of Yakov Klein, the part of himself that was dead, but not buried.

The afternoon heat in Chicago was particularly brutal *that* day. Yakov had been standing by his father's rickety wooden cart in the Maxwell Street market since dawn. He felt weary, sweaty, and bored, as usual. *I hate my life,* he thought. He glanced around at the dull cast of characters who showed up every day at the outdoor market, selling the same goods, wearing the same black and white clothing. *Nothing ever changes. I hate that most of all.*

It was too hot and muggy to be stuck wearing the same black wool overcoat and matching trousers. How he wished he could break free from the confining layers and wear a short-sleeved shirt and light khaki pants like those boys who attended the nearby college. But he was trapped, in these clothes, in this damn market, in this life.

Glancing down at his cart, Yakov stared with contempt at the bottomless pit of men's black socks that never seemed to diminish, no matter how many pairs he sold. He knew he should be soliciting potential customers, but instead he remained silent, gazing at the tall woman nearby who had just arrived in the market. She was new. A potato peddler. She saw Yakov watching her and turned away self-consciously. Yakov took a few steps closer. Now *she* was interesting.

He studied the back of the woman's head, imagining the look and feel of her hair beneath the confines of her faded yellow scarf. He envisaged the flowing blond locks, the same flaxen color as the wisps that rose delicately along the slim line of her exposed neck, but his gaze was forbidden by the laws of the Torah. The woman, he knew by the ring on her finger and the two kids tugging at her skirt, was married.

Yakov forced himself to look away, but could not stop himself from imagining the woman at night, shedding her soiled clothes, flinging them to the floor. Her long fingers would unknot the scarf, undo the bobby pins, and shake out her hair. She would walk toward her tub. A breast, a thigh, the swell of buttocks froze in Yakov's mind like a still life. But at almost nineteen years old, he had never seen a woman naked, only in pictures.

"Excuse me—you—I said how much for a bundle?"

The man's voice was intrusive. And for a moment Yakov forgot where he was. He glared at the customer. *How much for men's black socks? Who cared?* He wished he could ignore the man and leave the market for good, but his cart overflowed with the nearly two hundred pairs of socks that his mother had spent all night rolling. He kept hearing his father's bullying voice: *You can forget about dinner, Yakov, if you don't sell the socks.*

"For you, eighteen cents," Yakov mustered, barely looking at the customer.

The man threw down the socks and stomped off.

Yakov knew he was supposed to follow the customer and offer fifteen cents. The man would counter with ten. A deal would be struck at thirteen. But Yakov let the man walk.

Instead, he stole another glance at the woman. She was moving about now. Through her drab dress, he could see the bouncing silhouette of her full breasts. She was not young, at least ten years older than he was. She was not beautiful either. Her eyes were closely spaced, her nose was too narrow, and her lips curved into a natural frown. Yet, it was the way she held herself, proud and haughty, as though she were a princess and not a peddler.

The woman began shouting at potential customers; her voice was shrill and slightly irritating as she tried to sell her grayish-looking potatoes. Yakov wished she would be quiet. He just wanted to look at her, to focus on the subtle curve of her neck. He could practically feel the smooth flesh as though it were silk rubbing against his fingertips. And so many colors at once—white, peach, gold with flecks of rose. He squeezed his hands into tight fists to prevent himself from reaching out to touch the moistness of her skin as the sun danced over it.

Someone was tugging at the back of his coat, demanding *two* bundles of socks for twenty cents. The same guy again. Yakov dismissed him with a sharp flick of his wrist. Couldn't the man see that he had no time for socks? No time for bargaining games.

Not anymore.

Yakov's heart pounded beneath the thick layers of his dark clothing. How he longed to tear off the binding uniform—the overcoat, the jacket, the white shirt, the *tzitzis*, the vest—the same colorless uniform day after day, season after season. How he yearned to stand beside the woman as she stood naked in her tub. Not to touch her. Simply to paint her.

But that, too, was forbidden.

The urges lately had become unbearable, and he could no longer sleep through the night. Yakov felt he was losing his mind. He had to paint out in the open, freely, or he would die. It was not just this woman that Yakov yearned to paint. It was many women—old, young, fat, ugly, beautiful—it didn't matter. Each had some unique quality that stuck in Yakov's head. He would see these women on his way to the yeshiva, at *Shabbos* dinner, at weddings and bar mitzvahs, at the grocer, on the street. Faces, postures, looks, and gestures—all of them passing through his head day and night, so that he was on the verge of exploding.

The woman turned slightly, peering quickly over her shoulder at Yakov, as though she understood. His mouth dropped open. How could she possibly know what he was thinking? No one in the market understood him—his unquenchable desire to paint not peddle, paint not study, paint not pray. He shook his head. No, she could not know any of that.

He squinted back at her, and she smiled. Was she teasing him? Had he imagined that too?

His heart raced, and Yakov knew if he did not do something immediately, he would erupt right there in the middle of the market, against the hated bundles of black socks.

He pushed the cart forward, looked around, and then reached inside his overcoat. He pulled out a charcoal pencil and the special prayer book that he had received from his parents on his bar mitzvah. The items trembled in his sweaty grasp. He could have found something else to use, or even another place to do this where no one would see him. But then, he thought, nothing would change. He knew that once the pencil left the camouflage of his coat, there would be no turning back.

After all these years in hiding, it was time.

Exhaling as though each escaping breath were his last, Yakov opened the prayer book and began to sketch the woman's image right there inside the slim margins where the Hebrew letters ended and the white margin of space began. It was the worst kind of sin: desecrating God's name inside the Holy Book. But if there were indeed a God, Yakov reasoned, He would understand why it had to be done precisely this way.

It was his farewell sin.

People began to surround Yakov as he drew, and the woman looked frightened, yet she tilted her head slightly, posing in full view, defying them. But why, he wondered? She owed Yakov nothing. Perhaps deep down she, too, must want something more out of life than potatoes.

All around him, Yakov was being assaulted by shouts and threats to tell his father, his mother, the rabbi. Yet nothing mattered to him but the drawing. He drew voraciously, until everything—including the woman—lost all shape and form, until the surrounding sounds melded into one long, abstract, meaningless drone.

Suddenly, a rough hand clasped like pincers onto his left shoulder. Yakov glanced briefly at the hairy knuckles squeezing his jacket. An angry mouth then pressed against his ear, shouting in Yiddish to leave the market and never come back. Then came the tomatoes, potatoes, onions, carrots, and fruit being thrown at him from all sides.

It didn't matter. Yakov understood their anger and took it. Despite the attack, he kept drawing and did not move—even when someone began throwing his own rolled-up black socks at him. He welcomed it all, because this was the day that Yakov Klein would officially cease to exist.

When the food throwing subsided and he was fully covered with tomato juice and slop, Yakov quietly placed the Holy Book on top of his father's cart as evidence. Tears of relief ran down his face.

What was done was finally done.

The enraged crowd opened up for his exit, shouting that he was a *gonif*—a thief—who had stolen their honor and rejected their cloistered, predictable world for the one outside. But as he slowly moved through the mud-caked aisle, Yakov held his head high even as more tomatoes were flung at his back. He was free, that's all that mattered. The chains were now severed, and he was no longer a prisoner, but a fugitive—on the run from a life he never should have been born into in the first place.

But there were still more sins to come.

Later that night, gazing up at the familiar cracked ceiling of his bedroom, Yakov reflected on what had happened in the market, and knew that he had brought dishonor upon his family. When he had returned home, his parents would not speak to him. His mother did not offer him dinner, did not look at him. Instead, his father had handed him a suitcase, and then both watched him pack in silence. His mother's bright green eyes were red, her face splotchy from hours of crying. She could not hide her shame at having been betrayed by her only child before the entire community, before God. She had always known about his art, but their unspoken deal was that it was to remain a secret. Yakov knew that what had happened in the market was unforgivable. But he would do it all over again. In that single moment, his life had finally become his own, marking his true bar mitzvah—his passage into manhood.

Yakov punched his pillow and sat up, deciding there was no point in waiting for morning. He would leave now. It would be easier on everyone.

He rose from the bed, put on his trousers, and opened his suitcase. He gazed at the bundle of drawings that had once been concealed beneath his floor, but was now neatly organized on top of his clothes. He would no longer have to draw in secret. He gently lifted the bundle. Under it was a small black leather case. Inside was a razor that he used periodically to trim his hair. He removed the razor from the case, walked toward the small mirror hanging on the wall, and stared at his bearded reflection. He tried to picture the smooth skin under the thick light brown facial hair and *payis*. He imagined that he might be quite handsome without all the hair. He had seen the way the secular girls eyed him at the market, especially when he smiled. And he had heard through friends at the yeshiva that the religious girls were always discussing his potential as a husband. The thought had embarrassed him, but now he was excited to see what all the fuss was about.

He dipped the razor into a cup of water that had been left out on his desk, and then pressed the blade against the dangling six-inch lock of hair and cut it off. First the right side, then the left. He stuffed the two sidelocks into his pocket, sparing his mother the additional pain of finding them in his garbage once he was gone. He stared at his new self in the mirror and admired his changed reflection. He felt new, different. He smiled guiltily: *Goodbye, Yakov Klein.*

He packed up the razor and a few scattered belongings, picked up his suitcase, and closed his bedroom door behind him. Tiptoeing through the kitchen, he paused before a wooden cabinet in the far corner of the room. He knew that in the back of the cabinet, hidden behind the meat dishes, stood a large pickle jar in which his mother kept money that she had been saving for him since the day he was born. She was planning to give it to him on his wedding day.

Yakov knew that exactly three hundred and sixty-two dollars were stuffed inside that jar. His mother would announce the weekly accounting every Sunday night with pride. He carefully opened the cabinet and reached in back of the dishes for the jar, promising himself that he would take only half the money and return it as soon as he could.

As he counted out the bills and change on the kitchen table, his heart beat heavily. He suddenly felt guilty about all the socks his mother had to roll to earn the money. He tried to push the feeling away. He was just borrowing the money, he reminded himself, not stealing it.

Stuffing the wad of bills inside his coat pocket and replacing the jar, he picked up his suitcase and headed for the door. The train station was half a mile away. The night was warm; it would be an easy walk.

He took one last look around the small dark kitchen. He should leave a note—something, he thought. He found a pencil and paper and started to write, but then tore up the paper. What could he possibly say to his parents? Instead, he opened up his suitcase and pulled out the bundle of drawings. He sifted quickly through the artwork until he found the picture of his mother that he had sketched over a year ago from memory. In the image, she was standing over the stove cooking *Shabbos* dinner, wearing her fancy lace apron over her good black *Shabbos* dress. Her face was peaceful, her shoulders and body relaxed, her lips were closed, but she was smiling.

Yakov kissed the drawing and then left it on the table. He felt a lump forming in his throat and swallowed hard as he quietly shut the front door behind him.

Don't look back, or you will turn into a pillar of salt.

As he approached the end of the street, he could sense his mother behind him, feel the weight of her presence pulling at him.

Keep going, he warned himself, but knew he would turn around.

And there she was, his mother, standing at the kitchen window, the streetlight illuminating her presence. She wore her white nightgown, only without her robe. The gown was unbuttoned at the top, revealing her neck and the top of her chest. Her hair was disheveled, hanging loosely around her face. Yakov had never seen her look like that. Even at breakfast, she always remained modestly dressed in front of him, her long dark hair always pulled back into a bun. He could see that she was holding his drawing and the pickle jar. She then touched the window with just her fingertip, moving it slowly along the glass, as if to trace the image

of a son she would never see again. Her hand dropped, and the drawing was gone from his view. She then pressed her face hard against the
glass, her mouth and nose flattening violently against it. She opened her
mouth wide—a silent scream. It was too much for him to bear. Yakov
tried to look away but could not stop staring. If only he could paint her
like that—her green eyes wet and glistening with fear, her pale forehead
pleated with worry, her full lips opened and filled with blackened words
that no one would ever hear.

Yakov reluctantly turned away and moved forward, a skinny shadow
against the night, just as his mother began to cry.

"Julian, are you okay?" Adrienne squeezed his arm and pulled him away
in the opposite direction of the vendors. "You're Jewish, right? I am too,
and so is René—although no one would know it."

"That's because I've never stepped foot inside a synagogue." René
pulled Adrienne in close. "Besides, art is my religion, and Adrienne is
my goddess."

"Oh, please. Haven't we all had enough stupidity for one night?"
Adrienne pointed across the street and looked at René lovingly. "Well,
we're here, and I'm exhausted. I hope you understand that I need a good
night's sleep." She touched his arm. "I'll see you and Felix at the studio
tomorrow."

René tenderly kissed the top of her head. "Of course I understand."

They followed Adrienne inside the exquisitely manicured courtyard
of an ornate gray stone building covered with ivy, and Julian understood
that his new friends were not starving artists like himself.

Adrienne kissed Felix goodnight and then turned to Julian, clasping
his clammy hand inside her soft, cool one. "It was lovely meeting you,
Julian. We must do it again."

"I would like that," he said, trying to keep his face blank, but he could
feel his cheeks redden at her touch. He quickly released her hand and

walked back toward the gate where Felix was standing. But from the corner of his eye he watched René kiss Adrienne passionately at her doorstep. The kiss was long and hard. Adrienne's eyes were closed. Her skin was illuminated by the moonlight. Julian tried to look away, but she was so natural and beautiful.

"Don't get too attached," Felix commented sharply from behind him. "They are planning to marry."

Was he that obvious? "René is definitely a lucky guy," Julian said.

"More than lucky," Felix said tersely, and Julian caught a fleeting spark in Felix's cobalt eyes. "Adrienne and I were together for a short time, that is, until she met René. Just a warning, my friend: Never bring your girlfriends around René. They all fall in love with him. He's too pretty."

Julian eyed Felix closely as René slowly walked over to them. "That must have been hard."

Felix's gaze became cloudy. "It took a few models at the studio and I was cured."

Before Julian could respond, René joined them. "Well, my muse is off to sleep." He patted Felix on the back. "What'll it be, Von Bredow?"

"The usual. Paint, drink, paint, and drink some more. Are you game, Julian?" Without waiting for an answer, Felix snatched Julian's portfolio out from under his arm and started to run.

"Hey, give that back!" Julian chased after him.

"I want to see your *oeuvre*—what you're made of," Felix called out into the wind, and then he slowed down.

"Damn you," Julian said, as he quickly caught up with him. "That's personal."

"Nothing's personal." Felix walked briskly toward a nearby bench and sat down.

Julian knew he had a choice: rip the portfolio out of Felix's hands or let it pass. He walked toward Felix, and then stopped. Why should he feel ashamed? It shouldn't matter what Felix thought about his work. He was good enough to get into the École des Beaux-Arts. But as Felix turned each page, Julian stared down at the ground, anxiously awaiting a verdict.

"This one isn't bad," Felix proclaimed finally. "It is kind of surreal. Nice use of color. What is this, anyway?"

"A baseball field."

"What? No flowers or fruit in a bowl? So this is what they teach in America?" He held up the book. "René, have a look."

René joined Felix on the bench, and Julian was forced to watch them both sift through the pages. After ten minutes, Felix looked up with a taunting grin. "What do you call this one—*Man On Blue Mound*?" He indicated another of his many drawings of Yankee Stadium.

Julian lunged for his portfolio and snatched it out of Felix's hands.

Felix kicked up his feet onto the bench. "Sensitive, ay? I like you, Julian. And your work is good."

Julian started to walk in the opposite direction when René grabbed him by the sleeve. "Ignore him. Felix acts like a child—but he's right. Your technique is *really* good, Julian. But if you want to know the truth, you don't go far enough."

Julian stopped in his tracks. *What made René an expert?*

"Really?" He turned angrily. "And how far is that?"

René shook his head. "The portraits are exact, but there is no emotion. The baseball players, for example, look like statues. And the field is precise but empty."

"Empty? I bet you have never even seen a baseball field." Julian knew he sounded defensive, like someone's kid brother out to prove himself.

"Actually, I have. My father is an art dealer. I have traveled to America with him on several occasions," René said. "Look, the field is geometrically correct. Perfect, actually. The colors work. But I want to *feel* the game, not see it. I can't feel it at all."

Julian turned once again to go, but René stopped him.

"Paint with us," he insisted. "One night. It won't kill you, I promise."

"I make no such promise," Felix declared, and then gestured across the street. "Anyway, here we are."

Felix and René entered the apartment ahead of Julian, who stopped at the doorway and stared inside in awe. The room was an enormous studio apartment that was at least five times the size of the hole that he had lived in back in New York. And it was a pigsty. Hundreds of jars of paint, clusters of easels, half-finished canvases and stretchers were strewn about the hardwood floor. Clothes were everywhere, covering the bed, the couch, and the large desk. Dirty coffee mugs, wine bottles, and paint rags claimed any leftover space. The whole place reeked of turpentine.

"Get the hell inside, Julian, before my neighbors complain," Felix yelled from the kitchen area. "And lock the door while you're at it."

Julian entered the apartment, placing his things near the door, and then slowly walked around the room. He noticed Felix watching him with interest.

"So, you like my apartment?" Felix asked. "My ancestors are probably rolling in their graves. As you can see, I'm not only the cursed second son, but a slob as well."

Julian walked toward the couch where René was sitting. He gestured toward the painting hanging over René's head and whispered, "Van Gogh?"

"A self-portrait," Felix answered nonchalantly from behind him. "It belonged to my grandmother." He strolled over to the painting, cocked his head to the side, and then removed the picture from the wall.

Julian could not believe that Felix possessed an actual van Gogh. He stared at the painting, which was now on the floor. He longed to pick it up and protect it somehow.

René smiled at Felix, as if they both shared an inside joke. "Not the wall again, Felix. How unoriginal of you."

"Julian is new to my antics, so everything I do is highly original." Felix turned to Julian. "I once painted an entire wall of my governess's room with fat naked ladies on her day off. My father, of course, was livid. I tried to explain that I was merely copying the Botticelli hanging in the library. The servants loved it." Patting the wall like an old friend, he said, "A wall, Julian, is a splendid medium to release pent-up energy. You will never do a wall at the Beaux-Arts. Any objection?"

Julian shook his head, unable to take his eyes off the van Gogh. He wanted to touch it.

"Good. Now grab the paints over there. The brushes are drying on the rack in the kitchen. Would you mind?"

As Julian walked toward the kitchen, Felix playfully flung a balled-up sweater at the back of his head. It nipped him, but Julian did not turn around.

"Nice reflexes," Felix teased when Julian returned with the brushes.

René ground out his cigarette into an overflowing ashtray on the floor. Julian noticed that several butts were stained with pink lipstick. He wondered if they had belonged to Adrienne. Stretching his arms, René walked across the room and turned on the radio, which was playing Verdi's *Nabucco*. René's eyes met Felix's, and they locked.

It was strange, Julian thought uncomfortably, the intense way they were looking at each other. He wondered if he should leave. Then, as if someone had given René and Felix their cue, they removed their shirts and turned together toward the bare wall. Julian pushed some magazines off the couch and sat down to observe.

René landed the first stroke. This caught Julian off guard. He assumed that Felix, who had been boasting all evening, would claim his stake as the leader. But Felix stood back and waited.

René began to caress the wall with midnight blue pigment, lightly dragging his brush across the white plaster, creating an undulated effect. He added in light dabs of orange, and the texture changed completely. Julian had never seen anything like it. As the music picked up, René's body began to twist as he painted. He swept from left to right, blending in various shades of yellow, green, and red into the blue. Each stroke, each poetic movement, was mesmerizing. Julian felt dizzy.

He did not know where to focus first: René's hands, his chest, the shuffle of his bare feet, or the wall itself. He settled on René's face. His full lips were parted, his breath was heavy, his eyes opened and closed rapidly as if surprised. His neck muscles seemed to be bursting through his skin. René looked at once monstrous and inhumanly handsome. He did not paint. He *was* the paint.

Julian tore his gaze from René and turned to Felix. Tiny bubbles of moisture had gathered at Felix's temples, and his lips were pursed so tightly that they had all but disappeared. Felix seemed daunted by René as well. But there was something else, something Julian could not put his finger on. He did not really know Felix, except that his moods, his expressions, his drink, seemed to change by the second.

"How does this work?" Julian asked Felix, wanting to know exactly when he was supposed to join them. But Felix feigned deafness, firmly concentrating on René's brushstroke. As far as Felix was concerned, Julian was invisible.

Felix finally walked toward the wall with his brush thrust forward like a tomahawk. It was his turn now. Julian leaned forward with great expectation. *Let's see what this guy can do.*

Felix's gaze never deviated from René as he painted. Only he was not painting, Julian realized. He was copying René. Felix's strokes were surprisingly timid and awkward. And René, oblivious or used to being imitated, pranced around Felix. It was a dance of sorts. Julian was baffled by their role reversal. He grabbed an uncorked bottle of Bordeaux from the floor and swigged hard. The music was swirling around him. He closed his eyes, feeling his body sway to the rhythm.

Opening his eyes, hours or perhaps minutes later, he glanced over at the wall. René and Felix were now intertwined, painting over and under one another. Julian gulped down the rest of his drink, which no longer had a taste, just wetness.

Suddenly, it didn't matter—none of it—except for the burning inside him. He knew he should stop the drinking now and leave this place while he could still stand. He rose from the couch, willing his body toward the door. Instead, he ripped off his own shirt and flexed his fingers. He had waited long enough for the invitation that had not come. They had invited him here to paint, but what they really wanted was an audience. To hell with them both, Julian thought. It was time to crash the party.

When Julian approached, they both stopped painting briefly to admire the image of the woman on the wall.

"She's ugly as sin, isn't she?" René pointed to the mural.

"I wouldn't sleep with her," Felix said.

"You'd sleep with anyone." René laughed as he waved his brush. "What do you say Julian tries his hand at fashioning our duckling into a swan?"

"That's much too easy." Felix turned to Julian. "The object is you cannot recreate what we have already done. You have to work around it. Remember, it's not a baseball field, Julian. Think you can handle it?"

Julian wanted to tell Felix that he had been watching him mimic every stroke of René's, but he held back because he wanted to paint, *had* to paint, with them. Without responding, Julian took the brush and the palette that René offered him and began to work.

A streak of daylight seeped through the window, landing next to Julian on the floor. Staring at it with half-closed eyes, he reached out to touch the slim golden ray.

"You're not going to the École des Beaux-Arts," René declared sleepily from his corner of the hardwood floor. "What you don't need is more theory, Julian. You need freedom to paint—to feel, not to be muzzled by lectures and useless technique. Join our studio."

Julian traced the sunbeam distractedly.

"You'll move in with me," Felix announced as he struggled to sit up. His voice was heavy. Even from across the room, Julian could smell the Bordeaux on his breath, like rotting grapes.

"I don't have the kind of money—"

"I have plenty to spare," Felix said, as he reached for a cigarette, and then threw the pack to René. "I don't like to talk about it, because I detest my family's ridiculous obsession with titles, but my father is a baron. My grandfather was a count, and the list goes on. I may live like a bum, but my blood is fucking blue."

Julian began to perspire. He looked at his wristwatch, and then at Felix. His first class started an hour ago. "I couldn't possibly touch your money."

"With your ability, I would be honored to have your hands all over it," Felix said.

"I couldn't," Julian said slowly, not convincing either of them.

"Von Bredows don't beg. Move in," Felix insisted. "And I'll even clean off the couch."

"He doesn't do that for anyone," René affirmed with a half smile. "Now you have no choice but to stay."

Julian gazed at the fiery brushstrokes covering the wall. A woman's enormous face stood out from the muted background like a full moon. Her lush mouth was painted every shade but red. From one angle, her features were contorted, jaundiced, and she appeared to be crying. From another angle—the one he had painted—she was blushing, crimson and joyous. Julian felt the sensual movement of her drying lips and smelled the vibrant hues of yellow and orange gleaming from her sun-streaked hair. Her slim body seemed to writhe before him as if she were still under his fingertips.

He, like René, had become the paint, the brush, and the wall. Nothing like that had ever happened to him before, and he realized that it would likely never happen again if he went to the École des Beaux-Arts. He would come out with more baseball fields—or worse, fruit bowls.

"Yes," Julian whispered, as he watched Felix sweep debris off the couch and onto the floor. "I'll stay."

Chapter Three

Léon Dubois's studio was located in the heart of the Latin Quarter above a small bakery, and Julian could smell the aroma of fresh bread through the walls as he painted. The studio, which also doubled as Dubois's home, was ornate, with two large floor-to-ceiling windows and exotic plants scattered throughout the room. The walls were painted a shimmering aquamarine, the ceiling was coral, and the antique furniture was upholstered with various patterns of green. Nothing matched, yet somehow everything blended brilliantly. Dubois boasted that nothing in life was black or white, except, Julian quickly learned after a few months in his studio, his attitude toward his students.

Dubois played favorites. It was a perverse little game. René was his pet student, followed by Adrienne. Dubois seemed indifferent about Julian, neither criticizing nor complimenting his work. Felix, on the other hand, could do nothing right, and Dubois seemed to relish letting Felix know it. And today was no different as he stood over Felix's shoulder with a pointer, rapidly tapping his unfinished painting.

"This is amateur, imitation!" Dubois's mood was particularly foul. "I've told you a hundred times, Felix, I don't want to visualize the sea. I want to *smell* it. I want to feel the heaviness of the waves, the texture of water. Use color and contour." Five taps. "This is a postcard, not a painting."

"But it is my interpretation," Felix said meekly, using his body to conceal his canvas from the others.

"Interpret all you want, but not like a child," Dubois countered. "Ernst Ludwig Kirchner, the greatest German Expressionist, did not allow his emotions to knock his brush from his hand. Look at René's canvas. The strokes are natural, not contrived. You can practically taste the salt in the water. That is why *he* is exhibiting at Charles Ferrat's gallery next month."

Julian glanced quickly at René and Adrienne. They nodded back. Brutal.

Felix squeezed his brush so hard that the wood cracked. The sound was faint but audible. Aware that everyone was watching him, he released the brush just before it broke.

"Get to work!" Dubois shouted when he noticed that the other students had stopped painting. He straightened his coat and tugged at the drooping end of his reddish-gray beard, jiggling his excess chin in the process. Julian could not help but think how much he resembled a walrus. He laughed to himself until Dubois met his gaze angrily.

"You, Klein, are fortunate even to be here." Dubois's heavily hooded pale-blue eyes narrowed in. "Stop gaping and paint, damn it."

Dubois left Julian, sauntered over to Adrienne, and glanced down at her canvas. "Interesting. Now go and get Charlotte. Tell her we are ready."

Adrienne glared at Dubois, and Julian could tell by the way her shoulders tightened that "interesting" didn't quite cut it. She then proceeded toward the studio's small adjoining dressing room and emerged with Charlotte, the new model, by her side. Felix and René exchanged looks. Charlotte was beautiful.

The model, holding her head high, advanced slowly toward the podium. The slightly tattered hem of her peach silk robe skimmed the floor. Julian watched Dubois, who was moving toward her almost hypnotically from the back of the class. He seemed to light up as she walked by. It was the first time Julian had ever seen a sign of life in his instructor, and it was almost embarrassing to watch. The guy was so old, and she was so young. The girl paused momentarily in front of Dubois, and then she smiled as if no one else existed.

"Lucky bastard," Felix whispered to Julian as Charlotte stepped up to the podium and dropped her robe. "He's sleeping with her."

"Clearly." Julian nodded as he closely studied the model. Her golden hair was pulled back into a tight chignon, emphasizing the perfect lines of her oval face, high cheekbones, and full lips. Her breasts, round and ample, were tipped with dark pink nipples. With only his eyes moving, Julian followed the smooth line of her torso, leading to a blonde triangle. She was physically perfect, but something was missing, he decided. It was in her eyes. They were clear and blue, but vacant, lacking warmth and vibrancy. Somehow he would have to convey that flaw on canvas.

Dubois was now circling the model, stopping behind her. He reached for her right breast and lifted it with his hand. He then took her free arm and placed her palm over her forehead. Pleased with the pose, he rested his hands on her generous hips.

"Pain and longing," Dubois announced in a deep, eerie voice. "Experience the energy, the vibration of this woman's beauty, its hidden life."

Julian scoffed inwardly at the melodrama. Dubois cleared his throat as if to say more, but then seemed to change his mind. He descended the podium and returned to the back of the studio. Julian glanced at Felix, who was gently stroking his broken paintbrush. Next to him, René sketched ardently, mesmerized by the model, unaware that Adrienne was watching him angrily. She, too, had seen the lustful look that he'd exchanged with Felix.

Adrienne turned and saw Julian observing her. He quickly averted his gaze and tried to focus on the model. He began to dissect the girl's perfect features, hoping to find inspiration, yet he felt nothing. She just stared forward blankly, unblinking.

Closing his eyes briefly, Julian's mind wandered, hoping something would inspire him. He began to sketch aimlessly. When he examined his work, he saw not Charlotte but Adrienne. He paused, realizing what he'd done, and then he felt a surge of fire in his fingers. He wanted to keep going. Dipping greedily into red paint, Julian began to create Adrienne's mouth: wide, toothy, and inviting. He applied twin marks of gold to the canvas and shaped them into delicate almonds, envisioning the glow of her eyes when the sunlight hit them. Julian painted zealously without looking up, experiencing the energy of Adrienne's beauty, which had the hidden life that he longed to explore on canvas, *and* off.

Julian knew he had to cut off those thoughts—that desire. Adrienne was not his to think about. Yet, as the hours passed, he felt an overwhelming connection to his painting. Across the room, however, the real Adrienne was not smiling, nor was she painting. Her own brush had disappeared inside a full jar of black paint, as if it drowned. Her arms were folded tightly across her chest as she watched René. The model, Julian knew, was about to become a problem.

Julian felt a tug at his sleeve as he packed up his brushes. "Wait for me," Adrienne whispered, as she put away her supplies. Julian noticed that she did not say good-bye to René, nor did he seem to notice that they were leaving the studio.

As they exited the building, Julian felt the silent sting of Adrienne's emotions. She walked ahead of him, mumbling something. Her jacket collar was turned up, concealing her ears and most of her face.

"Is everything okay?" Julian asked softly, catching up to her.

She stopped walking and looked at him as if he were an imbecile, her acerbic tone taking him by surprise. "You saw René. Don't pretend you didn't." She searched Julian's eyes for truth, but he averted his gaze. "I'm not imagining it," she said, giving him a look of disgust—as though he, too, were guilty.

"She is just a model. I am a painter," Adrienne declared as they continued walking.

Julian did not want her to hurt, but he had seen what she saw. "Adrienne, listen to me. There is no comparison to you. The model is pretty, but after a few days she will blend into the woodwork—like all of them. You know exactly how it works."

He didn't have to explain to Adrienne the unwritten code about most artists' models: After a few days of modeling, they quickly transformed from real to inanimate. Once the artist's brush grazed the canvas, the model became no more lifelike than a ripe red apple in a fruit bowl, a blossoming rose in a garden, or a fading sunset over water. She ceased to be a woman and instead became an object of interpretation. And those models who became muses, ending up in bed with the artist, were quickly discarded once a new model entered the studio and a new painting was ready in the wings.

Adrienne nodded. *She knew.*

Julian wanted to make her laugh. "How about Dubois and his 'pain and longing' act."

Adrienne did laugh despite herself. *How he loved that smile.* "Not to mention the model's mysterious 'hidden life.' Truly pathetic."

"But it was definitely the first time I have seen the old goat come alive," Julian said.

Adrienne's smile quickly disappeared, and Julian knew that he'd said the wrong thing.

She turned away and kept walking, leading them past several of their favorite cafés. She ignored the familiar faces, the waves, and the shout-outs to join them. He should not have said that, Julian thought, as he watched her weave through the streets, the color drained from her face.

After ten minutes of silence, Adrienne stopped mid stride. "Yes, Julian, Dubois came alive when the model walked in, and so did René. There have been so many models, but this was the first time I've seen that look—" She paused. "A look that belongs to me."

"She is pretty, Adrienne. But you know damn well it was nothing." Julian tried to sound convincing.

Adrienne clearly wasn't buying it. "But did you see her eyes?" Her voice was shaky. "Empty and callous. You could sense that immediately."

Julian grabbed Adrienne by the shoulders as they cut through an alley and made her face him. "You are taking this too far. It was one night of painting. René is not an idiot."

There is no comparison to you.

"I just know him too well," she whispered, blinking back tears, and he wanted to hug her.

Admit it, you want to kiss her. But she's not yours.

"The model was beautiful but lifeless. I saw what you saw. And I'm sure René did too," Julian said. *Couldn't Adrienne see herself? She was beautiful. She was worth painting. She had hidden life. He had never seen eyes so goddamn alive.*

Adrienne shook her head with disbelief. He wanted to lace his fingers through hers and protect her somehow. Instead, he led Adrienne back in the direction—the distraction—of the Latin Quarter, more for himself than for her. He had to stay in control.

"How about we let it go for now. Coffee's on me," he said lightly, pointing to one of their nighttime haunts in the distance.

"But you have no money."

Julian held out a handful of francs. "Courtesy of the Baron Wilhelm Von Bredow trust fund."

Adrienne reached for his other hand, and Julian wished she would never let go.

Late the following evening, Felix pranced around the apartment in his underpants. He kicked empty wine bottles and paint jars out of his way. "All I could think about was fucking her. I forced myself to think about my father. I pictured his ugly face so I would not explode right there in the studio while I was painting Charlotte."

Julian laughed and picked up yesterday's copy of *Le Figaro* off the couch, beginning to peruse the headlines. Felix immediately snatched the pages out of his hands and faced him. "Are you even listening?"

Julian kicked his feet up onto the coffee table. "You have my undivided attention."

Felix smiled and sat down next to him. "Tell me, was it my imagination, or did you see the way Charlotte was staring at me today while she was modeling? It was as if we were one person."

Julian sighed. "Give it up, Felix."

"Admit it, Julian, you're jealous because she wants me."

Julian shrugged. "She's all yours. I don't know her. You don't know her."

"Who needs to know her?" Felix flicked his hand dismissively. "I know what I feel, what I see."

"Well, then, if my blessing is what you want, then go for it, my friend." Julian reclaimed the newspaper. "Now, do I have your permission to indulge in the petty world of politics?"

Felix threw up his hands, stood, and headed toward the kitchen. "You are a complete bore. Trust me, that girl will be in my bed by the end of next week."

"I trust you," Julian shouted after him, thinking that the model hadn't been staring at Felix—she had been staring at René. "But I don't trust her," he whispered under his breath.

Julian attempted to read an article about the political turmoil in Germany, how the National Socialist leader Adolf Hitler had won over the nation with his unyielding stance against the leftist Weimar government. But the letters soon began to blur and then fade. Instead, he pictured the droplets of coffee wetting Adrienne's lips the previous day. He felt the soft texture of her slim fingers against his palm when his hand had grazed hers in the café. Had she felt it too? Then the guilt quickly set in. He put down the newspaper. Adrienne was not his to fantasize about, nor did she think of him in that way. He was merely a shoulder to cry on. It was all about René.

Don't forget that, he reminded himself. *A shoulder.* He had to somehow get Adrienne out of his head.

Felix returned to the room with clean brushes, a wine bottle under his arm, and a half eaten loaf of bread. He nodded conspiratorially. Julian stood. The newspaper, Hitler, and the thoughts of Adrienne fell away. It was time to paint.

Chapter Four

Julian glanced at the large clock on Dubois's wall as he was packing up his supplies. Nearly eight at night. They had been there since morning. Everything ached, his neck, his shoulders, but in that good way from a full day of hard work. His new painting was finally progressing. Dubois had challenged them to paint a portrait of someone, anyone, they desired. The key to the exercise was to paint the emotion *not* the image.

"Adrienne, I have no doubt that you can do this." Dubois lit his pipe as he eyed his second favorite student. His eyes narrowed. "But you, Julian?"

But you, Julian?

Dubois was an ass. But the challenge was interesting. Anything to take a break from painting Charlotte. One month of trying to find something inspiring about that woman was more than enough.

Julian decided to paint a scene of a painter alone at work in his studio, standing before an unfinished canvas. He tried to convey the painter's frustration, anger, and loneliness, particularly in his eyes. The colors were precise and the form was good—exactly how he'd envisioned. Julian stood back, folded his arms as he scrutinized his painter. Something was missing. The emotion. The intensity. Damn. He shook his head. No matter how many times he repainted it, he could not get the face right.

"Let's get out of here, take a break," Felix announced.

"I'm in." Julian put down his brush. He needed a breather.

"Me too," said Adrienne, standing back from her painting. Julian glanced over. It was an abstract—a woman's face from one angle, an artist's palette from another. The colors jumped angrily off the canvas, smearing her beauty, roiling in anger. The woman's eyes were fiery blue, and her hair was a riotous tangle of gold and red. The colors of the palette on the other side of her face were painted various shades of orange, red, gray, and purple; tints of rage and passion. The woman was both beautiful and terrifying. Julian's eyes met Adrienne's and locked. *God, you're brilliant.*

Adrienne turned and Julian followed her gaze. René was staring at Charlotte, neither hearing nor seeing anything around them. Adrienne slammed her portfolio shut.

"René," Julian said loudly. "We're heading to Les Deux Magots for a drink. Now."

René turned slowly. "What?" He saw the others staring at him, and he tried to recover. "Yes. I could use a glass of wine."

"Well, I'm not going for drinks. I'm going to the market on rue de Buci. And Felix," Adrienne announced, not looking at René, "you're coming with me."

Her hazel eyes were now dense, dark, and unforgiving—a dagger-like pierce that left no confusion. Adrienne had become her painting.

The truth loomed there at a corner table just outside Les Deux Magots, obvious and unavoidable, like a Rodin sculpture perched in the middle of a room filled with watercolors: René *was* fucking Charlotte. And by the way René was fidgeting with his wine glass, tilting it up to the point that wine may or may not spill over, Julian knew the truth was making its way out. Glancing at his watch, Julian gave his friend five minutes. Tops.

"So, how does it feel having your first real exhibition?" Julian asked, trying to get the conversation going in any direction. "Ferrat is definitely big time."

But René was deaf, lost in his own world.

"René?"

He looked up, startled. The wine spilled.

"Are you with me? Or, am I drinking alone here?"

René laughed tensely as he mopped up the table. "I'm sorry. I just have a lot on my mind."

Here it comes, Julian thought, *the big confession in less than two minutes.*

René paused and twisted his head in the same way he assessed a painting. "Julian, I know this may sound odd, but what do you think about Charlotte?"

I hated her on sight.

"What do I think about Charlotte?" Julian repeated, buying himself a few moments to figure out how he was going to handle it. He could not stand to see the sudden animation in René's eyes. He didn't know why he disliked Charlotte so intensely, except that she reminded him of the seductive snake in the story of Adam and Eve. She was Delilah putting one over Samson. Julian didn't know her, but he knew instinctively, the way a painter exposes a hidden flaw or a mother knows her child is lying, that Charlotte, with all her God-given beauty, was ugly on the inside.

"Charlotte is pretty. No one can deny that." Julian eyed René squarely, seeing the twisted agony in his friend's face. He was on the brink of exposing his secret and nervously testing the waters. "But, when I paint her, I always find myself thinking something is missing."

"I've never been so inspired in my life," René murmured.

Julian tried to control his eyes from rolling. "Inspired by what?"

"Tell me, have you ever seen anyone more beautiful?"

Yes. The woman crying on my goddamn shoulder over you.

Julian leaned forward. Enough games. "Where are you going with this, René?"

René inhaled deeply, squeezing his eyes shut, as if he had been asking himself that same question. "I'm not sure."

Julian was used to studying faces. René was *definitely* fucking her. About that, he was sure. But was he actually falling for Charlotte? Julian

thought of Adrienne's painting. The raw anger. He thought of her sadness. Those lovely eyes wet and pained.

"Whatever you're doing, René, just stop, okay. It's not worth it. She's
not worth it."

René didn't answer. He took a long look around the café and
waved at another table. They both knew practically everyone there—
painters, sculptors, writers, students, as well as a few sketchy characters from around town. "Damn it, Julian," he hissed, slamming the
table louder than he'd intended. "See, that's the crazy thing. It just
may be worth it."

Julian had seen their stolen glances at the studio, the exchange of
secretive smiles. He had been listening to Adrienne go on about nothing else for the past few weeks. Only Felix didn't seem to see any of it.
He believed that those lingering looks were meant for him. René was
waiting for him to say something, but Julian didn't know what to say.
He felt like hitting René, waking him up. Christ, he had Adrienne. Why
would he want anyone else? Julian shook his head in dismay. "Adrienne
suspects something's going on between you two."

René's dark eyes were wide open, as though innocent. "I know. We've
been fighting. But I've been careful."

So, that's what guilty and stupid look like.

"I'm not going to tell you what to do, René, but just don't hurt her.
She deserves better than that."

René arched a dark eyebrow into a perfect curve. "Perhaps you think
she deserves you."

Julian froze. Did he know? Was he that obvious? Each man contemplated the other in silence.

"She loves you, René," Julian said quietly. "You."

"And you, Julian. Who do you love?"

Julian exhaled deeply. There were certain codes a man—a friend—
never breaks, no matter what, even if his own heart was at stake. He
pictured the rabbi waving that loaded finger. *Thou Shalt Not Covet Thy
Neighbor's Wife.* He refilled their glasses.

"All of you," Julian answered almost honestly. "I've never had friends like you. This will change everything, you know. And I don't have to tell you about Felix. He has been going on about Charlotte nonstop."

René sat back in the chair, folding his arms defensively. "Felix has been my closest friend for years. You don't know him like I do. He finds a girl and obsesses until he gets her in bed. Seconds later, he's onto the next victim. Charlotte is simply his target fuck of the week. It's all about conquest. It's different for me."

"So, you are fucking her." Julian didn't know why he said that. The truth had already been established.

René sighed deeply in response. It was not a yes or a no. It was the sound of a man who could have any woman he wanted, and it was obvious who that woman was. Of course he was fucking her. That was not the question. It was what should he do now?

"It's much more than that, Julian. You don't know her." There was anger in René's voice.

"Do you? Do you really know her?" Julian realized he was yelling and toned it down. "She's a model. And she probably slept with Dubois to get the job."

"Whose side are you on here? I told you the truth, Julian, because you're my friend, and I need your help."

"No, you told me the truth because I'm not Adrienne, who loves you, or Felix, who trusts you. You told me because I'm goddamn neutral. Your only option."

René nodded. The truth was the truth, no matter how you twisted it.

"As your friend, I'm telling you to get out of it. And if you can't, then you really need to deal with Adrienne right away and talk to Felix. Target fuck or not, Felix is your best friend. This will kill him."

René looked tormented. "You think I don't know any of this? I love them both, Julian. But you don't know Felix the way I do. He appears easy-going, funny, the life of the party, but he has a dark side. You have to understand that when Adrienne and I got together it was difficult for him. He took it badly. It was a long time before we could all be friends again. And you and I both know that the Ferrat exhibition is eating him up alive." René stared intently into his emptied glass, as if the answer were somehow stuck to the bottom. "There are wedges between us. Jealousies." His gaze was far away. "Divides, Julian, that you don't understand."

Julian thought back to that first night when he'd met them all. Felix warned him that René had too much, that he got whatever he wanted. He wanted to tell René that perhaps it was *he* who set up the divides, but he chose to stay silent.

René reached over and grabbed Julian's arm too tightly, like a man clinging to driftwood. "I need just one thing from you."

Julian paused. René, like Felix, had become more than his friend in the short time they had known each other. They painted. They talked. They drank. They laughed. They spent countless hours day and night together. They were never apart in nearly four months. It wasn't a lifetime. It wasn't history, but René had become the brother he never had. And . . . Julian looked away, fearing René would see it. They both loved the same woman. At the very least, he owed him for that.

"Name it."

"Time. I need time, Julian."

Julian shook his head. "I can't give you that."

"All I'm asking is that for a few days you keep everybody occupied until I figure out what I really want. I just need more time to think it through."

"What the hell am I supposed to do? Lie for you?"

René's eyes became filmy, like an Impressionist's painting. Monet at Giverny. Degas in the ballet studio. Dreamlike beauty; strokes of deceit.

"Yes, Julian. Just this once, lie for me."

Chapter Five

Julian entered the courtyard of Adrienne's apartment building. He was a few minutes early picking her up for René's opening night exhibition at the Galerie Ferrat. As he fiddled with his tie and waited, Adrienne walked out of the building toward him, and his breath was taken away. *God, she's beautiful.* He was so used to seeing her casual attire of slim black pants and a large man's buttoned-down shirt, but tonight she looked radiant. Her black dress was long, strapless, and form fitting. She smiled, obviously pleased by Julian's reaction.

"Wow," he whispered.

Beaming, she planted light kisses on his cheeks, then wiped off her lipstick marks and straightened his tie. "And you look handsome, Julian-gelo." She called him by the nickname Felix had given him. He glanced down at the dark suit and tie that Felix had lent him. She knew the suit.

"Felix's," Julian said sheepishly.

"Don't tell him, but it looks better on you."

He laughed. "Are you kidding? I'm going to tell that cocky bastard first chance I get."

They both laughed. Her fingertips still rested against Julian's neck, and he wished she would just leave them there. But she quickly grabbed his hand and led him down the walkway.

Julian said, "I thought we'd take a leisurely walk to the Galerie."

Her smiling face instantly turned solemn. "It will not matter whether I am early, late, or don't appear at all."

Julian said firmly, "It matters."

"She'll be there," Adrienne said. Both knew exactly who *she* was. "I wish Dubois would just get rid of her."

Don't hold your breath, Julian said to himself, as he squeezed her hand and closed the courtyard gate behind them.

They strolled past Carrefour de Buci, the bustling market in the heart of the Rive Gauche, which was still busy with vendors trying to sell the last of their remaining pastries, flowers, and other wares for cheap. Rounding the corner, they saw that the Galerie Ferrat was lit up with dozens of people swarming the entrance, smoking, laughing, drinks already in hand. Julian pulled Adrienne close to him and whispered, "It's going to be a big night for René."

He could feel her body become tense and she wriggled away from him, just as the doorman ushered them inside.

Entering the crowded foyer, Julian and Adrienne surveyed the walls of the gallery, which were filled with René's artwork. Julian recognized each canvas. But away from the studio and framed so elegantly, the paintings took on a new, more significant tone. The colors seemed brighter, more challenging.

Julian steered Adrienne toward his favorite painting, a medium-sized oil framed in cherry wood. It depicted a pale, almost translucent old man standing naked and alone in black and white despair in the Latin Quarter. Surrounding him was a colorfully painted café crowd, laughing, vivacious, and celebrating, clearly oblivious to the man's isolated, somber existence.

"It makes such a social statement," declared an expensively clad woman standing next to them. She wore a highly floral fragrance, the kind that would linger long after she left the room.

"And the colors, the contrast with the black and white. It is frightfully exciting. Definitely a find," her friend responded.

"But really, Ines, would you want to see that depressing thing hanging in your salon every day?"

"Of course not." They sniffed and moved on. Julian glanced at Adrienne and they both burst into laughter.

Appraising the crowd, Adrienne said, "Well, the entire circle is here."

Julian stood on his toes, trying to find René, and finally spotting him on the far side of the room surrounded by a dozen people. Everyone wore jackets, except René, who looked elegant and relaxed, wearing a cream-colored cashmere scarf wrapped loosely around his neck, which emphasized the blackness of his hair. Felix stood next to René in a navy corduroy jacket and burgundy ascot, a pipe dangling from his lips. Julian was surprised. Felix seemed to be playing up the son-of-a-baron thing, when he had nothing but contempt for the French elite.

"Let's go over there," Julian said to Adrienne, until he saw Charlotte approaching René's circle. She was stunning in a low-cut emerald silk dress that left nothing to the imagination. Felix and René simultaneously turned away from their small talk and vied like swordsmen for Charlotte's attention. Julian felt suddenly guilty, especially concerning Felix. He had known the truth for more than a week now, and Felix's feelings had heated to the point of explosion for Charlotte. He glanced at Adrienne. Her lovely mouth tightened as she saw René kiss Charlotte on both cheeks and then press her tightly against him. It was more than a thanks for coming. It was a promise.

"I could use a drink now," Adrienne said angrily, turning in the direction of the bar.

"I'll come with you," Julian said, following her.

As they walked, someone grabbed Adrienne's arm and stopped her. Julian felt an acute pang inside his chest. The man holding her appeared to be in his mid-forties, compact and handsome, wearing an expensively tailored pinstriped suit. He pulled Adrienne close, then he whispered something in her ear, causing her to throw her head back with laughter.

"Not to mention that you look fabulous," Julian heard him say.

Adrienne, clutching the man's arm, turned around. "Julian, meet René's father, Jacob Levi."

Jacob Levi. He sighed with relief and extended his hand. "Truly a pleasure, Mr. Levi. "

Jacob assessed Julian from head to toe. "You are the American fellow, right?"

"Am I that obvious?"

They all laughed.

"I've heard a lot about your gallery, Mr. Levi. It's supposed to be the finest in Paris." Julian paused. Every time he asked René to visit the gallery, there was always an excuse.

"Well, then, you must come and visit." Jacob glanced briefly at a group gathering nearby. "Lovely to finally meet you. Adrienne, it's wonderful to see you. Excuse me." He turned with a slight bow, moving swiftly toward the other circle, which opened up for him like an oyster.

"It must be very difficult for Jacob to be here," Adrienne commented under her breath. "Charles Ferrat steals clients from him left and right. From what I hear, Jacob is livid that René is making his debut here. He feels betrayed. He and René are not speaking, you know."

"No, I didn't know. René never mentioned it," Julian said, thinking that he and René had not spent any real time together since their discussion about Charlotte at the café. "Neither did Felix. I'm surprised."

Adrienne laughed. "Oh, please. Felix cannot get over that René is having his own exhibition. He could care less about Jacob's feelings."

She pressed her mouth against Julian's ear as she spoke, and the sensation was moist and tickly. "Jacob is no saint. He can be ruthless and is quite the ladies' man. I'm sure he came tonight only because the gossip would have been fierce had he not shown up for his son's debut."

"Why am I hearing about all of this just now?"

Adrienne ruffled Julian's hair as though he were a child. "Don't you think I know how we all unload everything on you? You came to Paris to paint, not to solve our silly problems."

Julian smiled. *She knew.* And then he felt the guilty lump rise again in his throat, reminding him that what she didn't know was that he was lying to her as well. Those late nights René spent with Charlotte. The lies. When Adrienne had cried to him, asking him if she was crazy when he knew first-hand that she wasn't. After the exhibition, he would tell René that he was done covering for him. He'd give him tonight, and then the lying was officially over.

In the distance, he saw Charlotte leaving René's entourage. He counted the near-dozen double takes she chalked up as she moved through the crowd.

"Charlotte is finally gone," he said. "Let's go over there."

Adrienne watched Charlotte work the crowd and shook her head. "I'm not crazy, am I, Julian? You see what I see. I know you do."

Julian didn't say anything. He squeezed her hand tightly and pulled her in the direction of René. "You're not crazy. C'mon, Adrienne."

"Look, I'm just not up to seeing him right now," she said, the tears welling up as she pulled her hand away. "But you go. I will meet you later, okay?"

Julian was hesitant to leave her.

"I'm a big girl. Twenty-two next month. I don't need a bodyguard. Besides, there are a few people I must say hello to." Adrienne took Julian's hand inside hers and lightly kissed his fingers. The kiss sent shockwaves through his body, and he was afraid to look at her. He felt her eyes on him, and then she turned and left.

He watched the rustling back of her dress as she disappeared into the next room, and he yearned to follow her. Instead, he smoothed down his jacket and slowly walked over to René and Felix. Dubois was there, too, taking full credit for his pet student's success.

René wrapped his arm around Julian's shoulder. "Do you believe this?"

"You deserve it," Julian said. "Everything looks fantastic."

René beamed. He scanned the room and whispered, "Where is Adrienne? I thought you two were coming together."

Julian looked him in the eyes and said quietly, "She saw you with Charlotte and left the room."

René's brow crinkled with comprehension, and then he turned to shake the hand of someone joining the circle.

"Georges Wildenstein," Felix grumbled under his breath. "Is there an art dealer in this town *not* here?" He lifted his empty glass. "Refill time. I've had enough of these pint-sized portions. Be a good friend, Julian, and bring us a goddamn bottle."

Julian wanted to tell Felix what he could do with his goddamn bottle, but the dejected look in Felix's eyes forced Julian to let him off the hook, albeit not entirely. "In exchange for you doing this week's laundry," Julian said evenly.

"Make that two bottles."

"Done."

Julian pushed through clusters of conversation, catching scraps of airborne commentary as he proceeded toward the bar. He paused when he overheard a familiar seductive voice somewhere to his left.

"He is much better than you on your best days," she whispered huskily.

"Don't be a bitch, Charlotte," a male voice hissed. "You know damn well I can never leave Sofie."

Julian whipped his head around in disbelief and saw them. Charlotte and Jacob Levi? *How many men were under this woman's spell?*

"You are the most important art dealer in Paris. The Great Jacob Levi," she said mockingly. "You can do anything you want, have anyone you want." She paused. "And you do—including me. But not anymore."

"So, now you're punishing me by sleeping with my son," Jacob whispered angrily. "You really are a whore."

"No more than you are. We both sell our goods for the right price." She smiled through her teeth. "You may sell Picasso. My body *is* a Picasso."

"Stay away from René," he warned.

"No one owns me, Jacob. But don't feel so bad." Her voice dropped. "At least I'm keeping it in the family."

Julian practically ran to the bar, feeling overwhelmed with secrets. He asked for two bottles of wine, but hardly heard himself speak. Charlotte's voice was still ringing in his ear.

A hand brushed against his shoulder. He could smell the familiar lilac scent and knew it was Charlotte without even looking. That scent seemed to fill the studio.

"Hello, Julian," she said demurely. "Having fun?"

"Yes," he said stiffly. "Great."

She studied his face. "You look a little disturbed."

Julian was unable to contain himself. She was so damn sure of herself. "Look, Charlotte, I don't know what you are up to—but be careful with my friends."

She faltered for an instant, then her eyes smoldered. She straightened to her full height, assuming the pose he had studied for weeks. Taking one of the bottles from his hand, she examined the label. "Château Lafite Rothschild." Charlotte smiled broadly as she pivoted on her heel. "I'll bring this to René. It happens to be his favorite."

Chapter Six

It had been a long day at the studio and Julian needed a good night's sleep. He trudged toward the apartment, his portfolio and supplies weighing him down. From more than a block away, he spotted a fancy car parked in front of his building and as he moved closer, he saw the foreign license plate. The sleek Daimler-Benz, with its long louvered hood and rear-mounted spare tire, postured like a queen among the queue of Peugeots, Renaults, and Citroëns. As Julian approached, he noticed a chauffeur guarding the vehicle and staring up at his building.

No one Julian knew had a driver or a car like that—except maybe for someone in Felix's family. Julian stopped in his tracks. By the way the man was staring at his building, Julian knew something was definitely wrong. Quickening his pace, he passed the driver without making eye contact and flew up the two flights of stairs to his apartment. He paused breathlessly outside the door, about to insert his key into the lock when he heard Felix engaged in a shouting match in German. He slid the key back into his pocket and waited.

"Damn you, Father. Why didn't you contact me first before coming?" Felix demanded.

"So, this is what I'm paying for, Felix? You're living here like a pig in shit. I can't even breathe in this place. If your mother saw—"

"Leave Mother out of this!" Felix shouted.

"Look, I did not come here to argue. I came here to discuss an important issue concerning the family."

"Discuss?" Felix laughed contemptuously. "As in exchange words like human beings? Please, Father, we've been down that road before, and it's a dead end."

"I see," the baron said coldly. "Then I will get to the point. You have lived in Paris for five years. I have allowed you to play around with this painting hobby."

"You've allowed me?" Felix countered. "What the hell—"

"Goddamn it, Felix, you are going to listen to me!" Baron Wilhelm Von Bredow's deep baritone bellowed down the hallway. Julian expected Felix to strike back, but he heard nothing in return except for heavy breathing.

"Now, as I was saying," the baron continued, "your brother is not well."

"I could have told you that," Felix said.

"Damn you, Felix. Hans is very sick. Do you understand me? He is no longer able to work. You will come home."

"What? No, Father, I am not going anywhere."

Julian pressed his ear hard against the door. Silence.

"You are coming home," the baron repeated. His voice, though calm, was on the verge of eruption, like the stillness just before a storm. "You will run the company while I take care of political affairs. The situation is changing quickly, to our good fortune. Enough playtime, Felix. You will pack up your things. We are leaving here in two days."

"I am not a child, Father. I don't pack up my things because you say so. And why the hell do you want *me* to run your company? What about your puppet, Rolf? He's been waiting for years for a chance like this. Let him do it." Felix sounded bitter. "Look, I'm not leaving Paris. My life is here. I am an artist, not an accountant."

"You have responsibilities to our family, whether or not you recognize them," the baron said sharply. "And I'm sorry, son, to break the news, but you are by no means an artist."

"Get out of here!" Felix yelled.

Julian heard a rush toward the door, so he hustled up one flight of stairs. The apartment door flung open violently. The baron was now standing in the doorway.

"I am not giving you a choice, Felix," he said. "I am prepared to cut you off from your allowance unless you return to Berlin."

"So cut me off," Felix retorted.

"Don't test me." The baron laughed scornfully. "You haven't worked a single day in your life. Let me put it in a way that even you can understand: I am not leaving Paris without you."

The door slammed shut. Peering through the wrought-iron baluster, Julian saw the shiny bald top of the baron's head as he descended the stairs. He was a big man, taller than Felix, and was wearing a large wool overcoat and holding a matching gray fedora. Each step pounded oppressively against the thinly carpeted wood. Julian heard the closing of a car door outside and pictured the dour-faced driver behind the wheel, his face fixed forward, awaiting instructions. Julian stayed where he was until he heard the roar of the car engine and then the dwindling sound as the vehicle sped down the street.

Entering the apartment, he found Felix sitting on the couch with his head buried in his hands. Suddenly, the room seemed smaller. Julian walked over to Felix and put his hand on his friend's shoulder, but Felix did not look up.

"I was standing outside the door, Felix. I heard everything," Julian said quietly. "I'm so sorry."

"You have no idea what he is like." Felix was fighting back tears.

Julian had never seen him like this, so broken. He opened the nearest bottle of wine and even managed to find a clean glass. He offered it to Felix, who took it without looking up.

"What are you going to do?" Julian asked, sitting next to him.

"I have no choice."

"Forget your father, Felix. Let him stick around Paris all he wants, but you're staying here."

Felix swigged hard. "You don't understand, Julian. He is a very powerful man."

"So hide," Julian said. "We'll all help you. You don't have to do this."

"There is nowhere to hide. My father's friends are everywhere. The political situation in Germany is changing rapidly, as you know. And my father—" Felix paused, about to say something, but stopped himself. "We have never agreed on anything, especially politics."

Felix got up from the couch, walked to the window, pulled back the curtain, and peered out at the street below. His gaze was distant, frozen in time like a court portrait. "All I ever wanted was to paint, Julian. But my father is right. I don't have it."

Julian walked over to him. "You don't have what, Felix?"

Felix turned to face him. "What René possesses. I have the passion—" He shook his head sadly. "It just doesn't translate. Even Dubois says I paint like a juvenile."

"Dubois is an idiot."

"Look me in the goddamn eye, Julian, and tell me I am wrong."

Julian knew he could not do that. Felix was not a good artist. But it didn't matter. For all of them, painting was breathing. That is what mattered—the desire, the need to paint no matter what. He grabbed Felix by the shoulders. "Listen to me. No one can take away your love of art. Don't let him do that to you, Felix." Julian paused, thinking, *I did not let them do it to me.* But Felix did not know about that part of his life. None of them did.

Felix's eyes were watery, and this time he didn't fight it. "Did you know that growing up I ate dinner at a table larger than this entire room? I could have had any damn thing I wanted, and all I have ever wanted was to be an artist."

"And you are."

Felix shook his head despairingly. "No, I'm not. I paint. I know art. I love art. But I was born with the inclination, not the talent. I'm a painter, not an artist. There's a difference." Felix pushed past Julian and began pacing around the couch. His red eyes were now wild and accusatory.

"René has it. You see him work. You know what I'm talking about— the demon that possesses him. The world could fall on René's head, and he'd still be painting amid the rubble. I love René, Julian, but he has something that I will never possess, no matter if I paint day and night. That is why I need him—to learn from him, to take from him what I lack. But I will never be an artist like René . . . or like you." Felix looked away, ashamed. He picked up the opened bottle of wine from the coffee table and waved it. "My father knows how important art is to me. Throughout my childhood he cut it down. I pretend it doesn't hurt, but it still hurts like hell."

"I'm so sorry, Felix." And Julian truly was. He understood the pain, the internal hell, more than Felix could ever know. He thought of his own father, of the horrible day when he had discovered Julian's artwork hidden in the closet. He was fifteen years old, and by that time, Yakov Klein had become a skilled thief. What began as bi-monthly stints of stealing art books from the library turned into a full-time occupation of weekly pilfering. By day, Yakov sat long hours in the *cheder*, barely listening to the teachings of the rabbi, daydreaming about painters. At night, instead of reviewing his Talmud studies, he'd teach himself how to paint and draw. He had no real teacher to work with—only thousands of pages of masters to guide him. But Yakov took what he could get. He studied art with the intensity and dedication he should have been giving to the Torah.

That fateful night, after dinner, Yakov was helping his mother clean up, not knowing that his father was busy scouring his bedroom. When he emerged with a stack of the stolen art books and drawings and stood there in the kitchen, glaring with raw hatred at him and his mother, Yakov knew that the worst was about to come. His father violently dropped the books at Yakov's feet and lunged toward his mother. It was the first time that Yakov had ever seen his father strike his mother. It was a hard slap across the face, a swift whip-like crack that drew blood from her mouth and nose.

"It's your fault for spoiling him, indulging his sins in my own house. Damn you." His father, ranting in English and Yiddish, blamed his mother for the transgressions of their son, *the artist*. He spat out the words "the artist" as though Yakov were "the murderer." But there was more to it. Yakov knew that slap had dual meaning, and in his father's eyes, it was a long time in coming—payback for all of the babies his mother was unable to give him. And what she had given her husband was Yakov, the artist-murderer, the disappointment—the *cheder's* worst student who cared nothing for his studies.

Yakov, who was taller and stronger than his portly father, immediately wrestled him to the floor and pinned him down with his knees.

"I hate you!" he shouted, staring into his father's dark cowardly eyes. "If you ever hit her again, I will kill you!"

But his mother, still bleeding, pulled her only child off the man she did not love but had been taught to revere no matter what. Yakov stood and released his father—for her. He knew he might have killed him in that moment. Perhaps he was a thief. Perhaps he was an artist-murderer. But his mother had kept his secret all these years, and he owed her. Someday, he vowed, he would get out of this place, away from that bastard, but she was stuck with him until death.

"Julian? Did you hear what I was saying?" Felix repeated.

Julian nodded, but was still caught in his childhood memory—that night still too fresh in his mind. He remembered his father's face later that night, the mask of cruelty, as he'd lit a match to each drawing, each page of each precious book being thrown into the fireplace, slowly, meticulously, with madman relish. Julian saw his mother cowering in the corner with the bloodstained kitchen towel pressed against her swollen mouth. They both stood in silence, watching the man they hated destroy everything, the only real beauty in their home—the sketches, the paints, the pencils, the art books, all gone—a burning bush of color against the blackness of night. What he lost, she lost. Never again, Yakov swore to himself. He would find his time. He would get out one day and never come back. His mother met his hardened gaze, and he saw the fear in her eyes. In her husband's burning of their son's art—the essence of his young soul—she knew she had lost him for good. Yakov's green eyes blazed silently, lovingly, into hers. *I have no choice now, Mama.* She blinked back tears. *I know, Yakov, I know.*

Felix took another long, hard swig straight from the bottle, his eyes fastened on Julian. "As I was saying, my mother would support my father while he was in the room, but as soon as he left, she would be right there with a new set of paints for me. She used to take me and my sister Isabel on visits to modern art museums in Germany and Paris. My father loved the Old Masters, but my mother showed us only the most contemporary exhibits. It was our secret. The Masters were too cold, too dark, too much like my father. Van Gogh, Munch, Matisse, and Gauguin represented freedom to me."

"Then don't give it up now," Julian said. "Don't let him control you."

"You just don't understand. It's not that simple. His friends are—" Felix averted his eyes. "Dangerous."

Felix threw the empty bottle at the wall in the corner, causing the glass to shatter everywhere. "You know what I'm going to do, Julian? I'm going to run his goddamn company into the ground." He smiled painfully, eyeing the broken glass as though justice had been served.

"You don't have to go."

Felix shook his head as if his fate were already sealed. "When I leave, you're keeping the apartment. I will make that bastard pay for it. You will stay here, and then I'll come back. It will be as though I never left."

They stared at each other, knowing it was a lie. If Felix followed his father, he was not coming back.

"I don't care about the damn apartment." Julian looked around the pig-in-shit apartment that they both loved. "This is crazy. You are twenty-three years old. To hell with him."

"It's a done deal. It was done the second he walked through that door, Julian. That's how it works in the world of the Von Bredows. With all of our money and fancy titles, there are no choices, only obligations." Felix looked more depressed than before but he hid it by changing the subject. "Did you see the way Charlotte flirted with me at René's exhibition? It is finally starting to happen, Julian. Damn it, what do I do about her?"

Julian wanted to tell him everything about Charlotte—about René and Jacob Levi. But he realized that the truth would be too much for Felix to handle at that moment. Besides, it was up to René to tell Felix, not him. But, would René tell him? Julian stared down at his damp shoes, uncertain as to what he should say or do. But now was not the time, he decided. Felix couldn't handle it.

Felix stood, then paced across the room, finally stopping beneath the van Gogh. He stared up at the painting in stoic silence, then turned around with a satisfied look on his face. Julian knew that look.

"This may be crazy, but what if I bring you all to Germany with me?" Felix smiled.

"That is crazy." Julian began cracking his knuckles. He knew Felix was serious. But there was no way in hell he was being dragged to Germany too. He'd read the newspapers. He listened to the radio broadcasts. He knew what was going on there. Everyone did.

"Just hear me out, Julian." Felix's eyes were wide open and devious. "What if I could set you up in a studio there? Would you come? Just for a short time? I will make a deal with my father. He knows he'll have to cough up something to get me to come home."

Julian shook his head no. "Forget it. The political situation is out of control."

"Believe me," Felix pointed out, "it is no crazier than Bastille Day here."

Julian spoke slowly. "You have a life there, a home, a history. I don't want you to leave, but I sure as hell am not going there." He eyed Felix closely. "And I'm a Jew, remember? It's not safe."

"Is the situation really any different here in France?" Felix retorted.

They both knew it wasn't. Julian conceded. "The difference is, there aren't anti-Semitic thugs on every corner here."

"You're right, Julian, because they are all inside the cafés. Look, the Nazis are a handful of lowlife extremists, buffoons," Felix continued. "No one pays attention to them, except perhaps my father and his ridiculous friends. But you will be fine if you are with me."

"I'm sure your father would just love me tagging along." Julian laughed, and Felix joined him.

"That's the beauty of it, isn't it?" Felix picked up a new bottle of Bordeaux, clearly next in line of what would be a long night of drinking. "Let me ask you this: How many times have you said that painting with Dubois is a waste of time?"

Julian shrugged. "About a thousand. What's your point?"

Felix grinned with buoyed confidence. "I have a close connection with Ernst Engel, you know."

Julian leaned forward. "*The* Ernst Engel?"

"Yes, the one and only," Felix boasted. "He is a friend of my mother's. What if I can arrange a spot for both you and René in Engel's studio while I do my father's shit-work?" He paused. "And believe me, René will not refuse. I know after his exhibition at the gallery things are happening for him here, but he has been begging to meet Ernst Engel for the last five years. Given the opportunity to paint with Engel, you can bet René will be in Germany before my father can pick up a prostitute at Le Panier Fleuri."

They both laughed at that, picturing the baron heading over to Paris's infamous brothel.

"Are you serious about Ernst Engel?" Julian stared at Felix, imagining what it would be like to paint alongside one of the world's most innovative Expressionist artists—the leader of the entire new movement in Germany. Julian tried to shake the thought. Engel or no Engel, he knew he should not be traipsing anywhere near Germany right now.

Sensing Julian's hesitation, Felix continued, "Look, this is not just about painting with Ernst Engel, Julian. It's about me. I know you have a certain view of me here—but around my father, back in Berlin, I'm different. It's hard for me, and that's why I left. And I can't go back there alone. I really need you with me."

Julian took a deep breath. He picked up a pinkish cigarette butt that was hiding near the base of the couch. It must have been Adrienne's. "What about the others?" he asked, staring down at the lipstick marks.

Felix eyed Julian closely. "Look, if you and René both come, Adrienne will come too. We will all be together."

Julian recalled the harsh slam of Adrienne's portfolio the day before as she watched René and Charlotte talking quietly in the corner of Dubois's studio. "I'm not so sure."

"I know Adrienne and René have not been getting along lately, but whatever it is, she'll get over it," Felix assured him, rubbing his hands together. "And maybe I can somehow convince Charlotte to join us, and then Berlin really will be a party."

"I don't think that will happen," Julian said hesitating. *Tell him now.*

Felix tapped his stomach. "Look, my gut speaks to me, Julian. Charlotte is not planning to pose forever. That girl will seize any opportunity to elevate herself. We both know that she is probably screwing Dubois, foolishly thinking *he* is her meal ticket. That doesn't bother me, Julian. You know I want her." He smacked his fist into his hand. "Let her see my life in Berlin and that girl will come running to me."

Julian hated Charlotte more than ever at that moment. Felix was right. She would not only come running, but also surely come between his friends. This was going to be bad. Julian cleared his throat. "Felix, there is something you need to know."

Felix looked intently at Julian, not hearing him. "What I need to know is if you will come with me. It will only be for a short time and then we'll return to Paris and pick up where we left off." His voice cracked. "I'm not asking you, Julian. I'm begging you. Come with me. I love you like a brother. I don't want to do this alone."

Julian lost himself in the assorted shades of Felix's eyes. The inner ring was yellowish brown, merging into a thinner circle of sea green, and the outer ring was so blue that it was practically violet. Perhaps he would paint those eyes—they were so volatile and strong. Felix was his friend who needed support. After everything Felix had done for him— free apartment, free food and living expenses—so he could paint without having to get a job, Julian felt he owed him something. And how could he pass up the opportunity to paint with Ernst Engel? The move would be temporary. What could really happen in a few months? He'd get called a kike? Big deal.

Julian took a deep breath and Felix was embracing him even before he said yes.

Chapter Seven

Julian and René walked hurriedly down the rue de Seine on their way to Jacob Levi's gallery. They were close to the École des Beaux-Arts and for a moment Julian wondered how things might have turned out had he attended the famous art school. Surely, by this time, he would have accomplished something more than he had so far. His days spent painting with Dubois were uninspiring, a disappointment.

Digging his hands deep inside the pockets of the thick tweed overcoat that he had borrowed from Felix, he glanced over at René, who, despite the cold, somehow managed to look like he had just stepped out of a magazine. The blustery wind against René's face accentuated his deep olive skin, and the tears forming in the corners of his eyes provided a shimmering onyx veneer.

"You really should do this alone, René," Julian said. "Your father hardly knows me. I will just be in the way."

"But I want you in the way," René insisted. "I know my father. He won't explode if you are there. You don't even have to say a word. Just act as a buffer."

Julian glanced angrily at his friend's flawless profile. "A buffer? That is all I've been doing since I got to Paris—shutting up about *your* secrets. You have to tell Felix about Charlotte—even if he is leaving in a few days. It has pushed me into a corner. I feel like I'm lying every time I see him. You know damn well he's completely infatuated with her."

"I planned on telling him earlier this week." René slowed his stride. "And then his father showed up. I just didn't want to make the situation any worse for Felix."

"Bullshit, René. You're stalling, and I get it, but he's going to find out. Better that you tell him first." Julian stopped walking, and they turned and faced each other. "Look, I don't want to be caught in the middle of this any longer."

René nodded, but said nothing. He gestured to the corner market right across from where they were standing. "Cigarettes. I'll be back."

Julian watched René give the vendor's pretty daughter a confident smile as he paid her, and the girl blushed as René pulled out an expensive leather wallet. The bundle of cash seemed to float in his elegant hand. Julian could not help but think that René had been given too much—exceptional looks, talent, money, charm, confidence. *And Adrienne.* Julian pretended to peruse a shelf of fresh vegetables, chastising himself for feeling so jealous—for being in love with her. It wasn't fair.

René returned with a cigarette already in his mouth. "Much better now."

As they walked away from the market, Julian said, "You have to talk to Adrienne about Charlotte too. I can't cover for you any longer. She knows." He paused. "I can't lie to her, René. She's too smart."

René threw up his hands, and the cigarette went flying. "Damn it, Julian, I've tried, but she refuses to speak to me."

They walked toward Jacob Levi's art gallery in silence. As they crossed onto the rue Jacob, René stopped in the middle of the street and turned to Julian. "I know I've put you in a bad position, and I'm sorry about it. But I said I would take care of things. We won't have to discuss any of this again."

"Fine," Julian said.

"Fine," René responded.

Julian decided this was the time to tell René about the conversation he'd overheard at Ferrat's gallery. No more secrets. "Listen, René, there is something else you need to know about Charlotte."

"Hold it for later, Julian, because we're here, and we're late." René scurried up the marble steps to his father's gallery and Julian followed. He would have to tell him about Charlotte and Jacob Levi after the meeting. He glanced up at the impressive four-story gallery with the fancy coral-tinted stonework and Art Deco stained-glass windows. Although he had passed by the landmark building dozens of times, this was the first time that René had ever invited him inside.

"Those are incredible." Julian stood in awe of the windows.

"Yes, incredible," René responded without affect, as though he'd heard the same thing repeated a thousand times before. "My father acquired them at the Paris Exposition of 1925—the so-called birth of Deco, as he calls it." He paused. "And once my father calls the trend, the trend is then established."

"Is your father really that influential?"

"Yes," René said as he slowly climbed the steps. "Just ask him."

Julian took a deep breath and stood next to René at the entrance. He thought that the simple, tiny gold-scripted engraved sign reading GALERIE ROHAN-LEVI hung almost too modestly over the doorway.

"Who is Rohan?" Julian asked.

"Nobody." René rolled his eyes as he opened the door. "My father thought that Galerie Levi sounded too Jewish, too déclassé. So, he threw in Rohan, an aristocratic Parisian name, to offset Levi. We French tolerate Jews but don't accept them—even if we are one."

Before Julian could respond, an elegantly dressed young woman rushed toward them with outstretched arms as they entered the foyer. "René!"

"Françoise, you look wonderful." René brushed his lips gallantly against the woman's hand.

She blushed and rearranged the lone curl shining against her forehead. "I haven't seen you in months. Where have you been?" Françoise turned to Julian and smiled seductively. Her teeth were almost unnaturally white, sparkling against her fuchsia lipstick. "And who is your friend?" she asked in English, clearly pegging Julian as American.

"You're good, Françoise," René laughed. "Julian Klein, meet the lovely Françoise Marceau." He turned to Julian. "Françoise is not only easy on the eyes but also incredibly intelligent. She is my father's secret weapon, the sole reason he has so many clients." René paused. "And she is a classmate of mine. Actually, two years ahead of me. I had a crush on her my whole life but lost out, of course, when she chose my father."

"René, please." Françoise beamed, and then quickly averted her eyes. "Your father is expecting you, but he is still with a client who came all the way from Barcelona to see him."

"So, Spanish is the language du jour," René snickered, glancing at Julian. "My father speaks seven languages fluently. You should spend a day with him when he's on the phone with clients. You feel like you have traveled around the world. It's exhausting."

Françoise smiled. "Why are you complaining? I am the one who has had to master all seven languages to keep up with your father! How about a drink while you wait?" She offered them each a glass of Moët.

René declined and waved his hand. "It's not even half-past ten, Françoise. I've barely digested my croissant."

Julian surprised himself by taking the glass, but something told him that he might need it. Over Françoise's shoulder, he noticed an enormous crystal chandelier hanging in the next room. "Would you mind if I have a look around?" he asked.

Françoise took Julian's free arm. "Better yet, allow me to give you a quick tour."

They walked slowly into the opulent room, with a golden spiral staircase at its center. Julian took silent inventory of the exquisite oils and watercolors on the walls. On one side of the room were the Impressionists—Cézanne, Pissarro, Renoir, Monet, Sisley. The opposite wall was occupied with a selection of Picassos from his Blue Period. All of the artist's works were suffused with monochromatic blues and blue-greens, conveying a sentimental, albeit melancholic, tone. Julian found these paintings to be among Picasso's most intense work, a powerful reaction to the artist's close friend's suicide.

On the far wall was a selection of paintings by the French Fauves—Braque, Matisse, de Vlaminck, Derain. Unlike the whimsical brushstrokes of the Impressionists, or the somber blues of Picasso, the Fauves' paintings roared with color and vivacity. Julian examined each brilliant canvas and thought excitedly that perhaps one day it would be his time, his work hanging on a prominent art dealer's wall.

Françoise led Julian into another room filled exclusively with German Expressionists and Julian stopped in his tracks, stunned by what he saw.

"Jacob Levi has the largest collection of Expressionists in Paris," Françoise explained, as she noted Julian's startled reaction. "They are selling fast, but under the table, of course. Foreigners are buying up the paintings. They are too abstract, considered too emotionally charged for our more conservative local clientele."

Julian barely heard her as he moved hypnotically toward the paintings. His head was spinning. He had never seen anything like this before. He had seen images in books, but never the real thing. The colors on these canvases jumped out unapologetically. Unlike the Impressionists' neat and organized style, these paintings were violent, brusque, and chaotic. The brushstrokes were wide, exaggerated, and undisciplined. Red skies, blue buildings, yellow people. It was all wrong, madness, yet the result was extraordinary.

Julian walked slowly past each painting, and then back again. He could feel Françoise's eyes on him, but he didn't care. Everything else he had been exposed to at this point was pure technique. It meant nothing. *This* was art.

He perused landscapes in watercolor by Erich Heckel, oils by Ernst Ludwig Kirchner, vibrant flowers by Emil Nolde. Julian was dizzy, in the lightheaded way he had felt that first night painting with René and Felix. He realized that as much as he had tried, he had never been able to recapture that feeling. Until now.

When he spotted Ernst Engel's work, he had to make a conscious effort to keep his hands at his sides. He leaned forward and read the plaque: *Women Bathing*. It was gorgeous, sensual, and forbidden. The colors were shocking. The lake was pinkish, the sky golden, the naked bodies free-flowing with burgundy and splashes of indigo. Julian yearned to touch the painting, to feel the depth of the texture against his fingertips. If only Françoise weren't breathing down his neck, he might have lightly grazed the canvas.

"Incredible," Julian said, his breath dry, his throat parched.

"Yes. Ernst Engel is clearly at the forefront of the movement," Françoise whispered, as though the information were top secret.

Julian did not respond. He just wanted to experience the art. He imagined what it would be like to work in the shadows of Engel's sheer brilliance. He gazed at the nude bathers, seeing not their nakedness but instead every stroke adorning their bodies. This was not a painting but a sign, telling him that it was the right decision to go with Felix to Germany. Dubois was stale. But with Ernst Engel . . . his mind raced with the possibilities.

"René," a deep voice called out from the top of the staircase, resounding through the room. "I'm sorry to have kept you."

Julian looked up. Jacob Levi, in a stylishly tailored gray three-piece suit, stood his ground, not moving an inch toward Julian or his son. He was clearly the kind of a man who expected others to walk his way. As Julian slowly followed René upstairs, he noticed that father and son shared the same chiseled profile.

"It is truly a pleasure to see you again, Julian," Jacob said eloquently, but something in the way he glanced coldly at René caused Julian to believe that perhaps his unexpected presence was not a pleasure at all.

"Likewise, Mr. Levi." Julian felt ill at ease and prepared for his exit. Clearing his throat, he said, "What if I wander around the gallery so you two can talk?"

René shot Julian a warning look. "That won't be necessary."

"Join us, please," Jacob said firmly, and Julian understood that Jacob Levi was actually relieved to have a buffer between him and his son.

Jacob ushered René and Julian into his office and immediately took his place at the helm, sinking into his roomy chocolate-brown leather chair. Behind him, a Picasso dominated the entire wall. It was an abstract of a woman sitting alone in a chair. The large slabs of muted color felt both bold and disruptive, as if the artist wanted to display anger, boredom, and sorrow all at once.

Extending his hand toward the painting, Jacob explained, "The image is the highlight of Picasso's pre-Cubist period. I acquired it last week."

"Take a long hard look, Julian," René interrupted. "You won't see that painting again. In fact, my father is probably on his way to selling it, or perhaps it has already been sold. His tactic is to hang a major work behind his desk before a meeting and gauge his client's reaction to it." René paused. "Usually the client does not leave the building before buying the piece directly off the wall. Isn't that right, Papa?" he said icily.

Jacob responded just as coldly. "Why yes, René. In fact the client who was just here purchased the piece, as well as another Picasso. But that is not why you're here, is it? To critique my selling abilities. In fact, I have not seen or heard from you since the Ferrat gallery fiasco."

"Fiasco." René laughed with blunt hardness. Julian had never heard that spiteful tone from him before. "Yes, I suppose you would see it that way. Let's not waste each other's time with small talk." René gestured in Julian's direction. "We intend to travel to Berlin for a few months or more. I thought you should know where I am."

Jacob sat silently for a moment, then slammed his fist against the desk. "Germany! Are you mad, René? Now? That will kill your mother."

René did not say anything at first. Julian could see that the mention of his mother made René twinge. "Yes. We are going," René said calmly. "And you of all people have no right to talk to me about 'killing' Mother."

Jacob walked around his desk and stood in front of his son. "Why now?" His tone softened. "Your reviews at Ferrat's were superb."

"Superb? I thought it was a fiasco." René's voice rose. "Was it too much for you to even congratulate me? The fact is you were so angry that I made my debut with Ferrat that you couldn't even look at me that night. It killed you that Ferrat recognized my talent before you did. No matter what you feel about Ferrat, you should have been at my side, not hiding in the crowd."

Julian ground his toes into the plush oriental rug, yearning to run out the door. He started to stand, but Jacob pointed his finger accusingly. "Are you part of this idiocy as well?"

"It—it's only a short time," Julian stammered, sitting down. "We plan to paint with Ernst Engel. He agreed to take us on."

Jacob was visibly surprised. "Ernst Engel? I have no idea why he would possibly encourage this. As if he doesn't have enough problems of his own. At a safer time, fine, go, René—but now?" He walked to the far side of his office and poured himself a drink without offering anything to Julian or his son. Staring into his whiskey glass, he said, "You're not children, but you obviously don't read the newspapers. My clients in Berlin tell me the situation worsens by the minute. That fascist Hitler is gaining power and has an excellent chance of capturing the chancellery." He put down his drink and threw open his appointment book. "You need a change, René, is that it? Go to Tuscany or Costa del Sol. I have clients all over Europe who would be happy to let you stay in their villas and paint anytime."

"I am not even going to respond to that," René said.

Jacob began to lose his composure. "Well, you'd better respond!" he shouted. "Germany is an economic catastrophe. And I don't have to tell you who is being blamed for the government's follies. Anti-Semitism is rampant. In case you have forgotten, you are a Jew, René. And you, Julian, are as well, if I'm not mistaken. Now is certainly not the time for young Jewish artists to go there to try to *find* themselves."

"I'm not in the mood for your 'Jewish victims' speech." René stood, towering over his father. "As if Judaism ever mattered to you. What commandment *haven't* you broken?" He turned to Julian. "If we stay here one minute longer, we will have to listen to the Spanish Inquisition story, the tale of why the persecuted Levi clan fled to France. Besides,

Papa, I didn't come here to be convinced otherwise. I came merely to inform you that I am leaving."

Jacob blocked Julian from moving from the couch. "Is this Felix's idea?"

Jacob was shorter and slimmer than Julian, and it would have been no problem to push past him. But the man's gaze was so sharp and over-powering that Julian felt trapped. He managed to say in a small voice, "Felix needs to return to Berlin to help his father run his company. It's only for a few months."

"His father's company!" Jacob exploded. "Wilhelm Von Bredow is leading the anti-Semitic pack of businessmen funding Hitler. Look, I have nothing against Felix. He is a little misguided, but he seems to be a good kid. His father, however, is dangerous. His wife was a client years ago . . . " His voice trailed off.

René shook his head with disgust. "What is it, Papa? Did you sleep with Felix's mother as well?"

"Damn you, René. This is not a game."

René walked toward the door, then stopped and turned. "All I want to do is to paint. And I won't pass up the opportunity to paint with Ernst Engel. I don't care about Hitler, politics, or religion. Let's go, Julian."

"Is Adrienne going as well?" Jacob called after him.

René did not face his father. He stared at Julian. "No, she is not."

"I've always said she is too smart for you."

"Yes, you did always say that." René turned slowly toward his father. "We are bringing a model. You don't know her."

Julian let his hands sink deep in between the couch cushions. *Here it comes.* He should have warned René earlier, but how was he to know things were going to be this bad?

"Charlotte Béjart?" Jacob's voice was barely audible.

René looked surprised.

"Julian," Jacob said slowly, gesturing toward the door, "I need to speak to René alone."

Julian rose quickly from the couch. The tension in the air was unbearable. He was only too happy to escape. "No problem. René, I'll wait for you at the bookshop around the corner. I'm sorry, Mr. Levi."

"Don't feel sorry for me. Watch yourself."

Julian practically ran down the stairs. He waved good-bye to Françoise, who had a worried look on her face, and raced out the door.

Chapter Eight

René, Felix, and Julian walked toward the Latin Quarter for drinks. Felix was laughing and joking, punching René, who also seemed to be enjoying himself. But in-between the jibes, there were fleeting moments when a wounded look crossed René's face. Julian knew he was hurting. It was unspoken, palpable, between them: René now knew the truth about Charlotte and his father.

"Hey, why are you so damn morose, Klein?" Felix asked, sidling up to Julian. "Wake up, man. We've got a long night ahead of us. My last night on the town before my father kidnaps me. I need you on board."

"No worries, Felix. I'm on board."

But the truth was Julian was lost in thought. Jacob Levi's words had been haunting him all afternoon: *In case you have forgotten, you are a Jew, René. And you, Julian, are as well, if I'm not mistaken . . .*

Yes, he was once a Jew. Yet in Paris, art was his religion. But was he even an artist? Right now he had nothing to show for himself but a series of forgettable paintings. He told himself to ignore Jacob's warnings, that he had already made the decision to go to Germany with Felix. It was a done deal. So what if Germany was unstable. Many of the greatest artists throughout history produced their finest work during political unrest. Perhaps Berlin would be an inspiration to him. Julian shook his head, wishing Jacob's words would just disappear.

As they made their way down boulevard Saint Michel, Julian half-listened to his friends' heated debate on Cubism. Felix was arguing that

Georges Braque was the true Cubist and Picasso a mere follower who took all the credit. René countered that the two artists were clearly a team—Cubism was a simultaneous intellectualization by both painters.

Felix turned to Julian. "Settle this. Who came first—Picasso or Braque? You know it is Braque all the way."

"Don't lead his answer, Felix." René grabbed Julian firmly by the arm. "Besides, unlike you, Von Bredow, Julian has a brain. He knows Picasso had equal billing with Braque. Isn't that right, Julian?"

"If Julian's brain is working, then he will tell you that Braque is the man," Felix countered, laughing. "C'mon, Julian, settle this. Tell René I'm right."

Each man waited for Julian to choose—the same tie-breaking scenario that occurred nearly a dozen times a week whether it was Bordeaux or Burgundy, oil or watercolor, Adrienne or Charlotte, and right now Julian felt tired of being a pawn for them. He was done being their middleman.

"It was neither Braque nor Picasso. They both merely picked up where van Gogh left off." He crossed his arms defiantly. "In fact, name any contemporary artist, and I will trace you a direct line to van Gogh. No one before or after him possessed the intensity of his stroke, or his mastery of abstract color." Julian smiled, enjoying this. Let them sweat it out. "The Cubists, the Surrealists, the Symbolists, and the Post-Impressionists, for that matter, can all thank our friend Vincent. So, if you are asking me which of you is right—" he scratched his head in mock consideration, taking an extra long pause for effect—"I'd have to say you are both dead wrong."

"You can do better than that." Felix was not ready to concede defeat.

"That's as good as it gets, I'm afraid." Turning away, Julian walked ahead of his friends. He'd had enough, his patience for their constant competition had worn thin. He needed a strong drink to clear his head. But when he heard Felix say to René, "What the hell is wrong with him? Oh, I almost forgot—how did Jacob take the news that you guys are joining me in Berlin?" Julian immediately slowed to listen.

"Very badly," René said. "I wasn't going to spoil our night by rehashing the conversation with my father. But he thinks going to Germany right now is a major mistake. A suicide mission for two Jews with a paintbrush."

Felix leaned against a parked car and lit a cigarette. "Look, I know the move is not ideal. But it's temporary, and it means a hell of a lot to me that both of you are coming."

René laughed nervously. "Now don't go soft on us, Von Bredow. It's not like you."

Julian knew exactly what would follow, and he could practically hear his heart pounding beneath the thick layers of his clothing, as he back-tracked to where his friends were standing.

"Now, if I can just convince Charlotte to come," Felix continued, inhaling his cigarette slow and hard. "René, you have got to help me on this one. Between the two of us, I'm sure we can convince her to leave Dubois and join us."

René grinned uneasily. "Just turn on that Von Bredow charm."

Julian glared at René. *Don't be a bastard. Come clean. Tell him now.*

"Believe me, I've been working the charm, but that woman is playing too hard to get, even by my standards."

René adeptly avoided Julian's searing gaze. "I was just thinking, let's skip the Quarter. Too many people I have no interest in seeing will be out tonight. Why don't we go to Dubois's studio—just the three of us—and paint and hang out? Dubois is not coming back from the South until tomorrow night." He draped his arm around Felix's neck and pulled him close. "What do you say we pick up a few good bottles on the way—my treat? And if we're still up to it later, we can catch some late night jazz in Montparnasse."

"Free wine? On your tab? I'm in." Felix glanced over at Julian, who was busy flicking a broken piece of cobblestone from one shoe to the other. "Hey—you've been acting strange. What the hell is wrong?"

I'm angry. René is going to let you go to Berlin without confessing the truth about Charlotte. I can't keep up this charade much longer. "Just tired," Julian responded.

"Well, wake up." Felix kicked the stray cobblestone piece out of Julian's reach. "We're just getting started here."

The wine, of course, took precedent over painting. The trio lay sprawled across Dubois's large cushiony couches with two empty bottles of Bordeaux between them.

Felix raised his glass lazily. "Here's to Dubois, a pompous ass, whom I despise, but he has the best damn couches in town." He patted the cushion beneath him. "I could die right here, right now."

René, also lying down, raised his glass high. "I hate Dubois too, but here's to the couches."

Felix shook his head, not buying it. "Hate him? Please. Dubois worships the ground you walk on."

René sat upright, placing the glass on the coffee table. "You mean he worships the ground *my father* walks on," he corrected Felix. "Dubois only kisses up to me to get to the Great Jacob Levi—like everyone else."

Felix threw a pillow at René. "Don't underestimate your talent—even if Dubois *is* a suck-up to your father."

René stared at the pillow, and then up at Felix guiltily. Julian could practically read René's mind: *How do I possibly tell him about Charlotte?*

Julian took a deep breath. *Just tell him, damn it.*

Felix pushed Julian's feet off the couch with his own. "Okay, out with it, Klein. You're not yourself. So morose and depressing that I could kill myself."

Julian was always amazed that Felix was his most perceptive when he was drunk.

"Well?" Felix's dark eyebrow was raised, framing his eye like a bow to an arrow.

Julian cleared his throat. "I actually agree with both of you," he said, making a pathetic attempt to shift the subject away from his melancholy.

"Dubois is a waste of my time too. I feel like I've learned nothing here. Maybe I should have gone to École des Beaux-Arts."

"Blasphemy!" Felix's whole body ejected from the couch. "No way, Klein. You made the right decision. You wouldn't have had us. Who would you have found more entertaining than me? Or duller than him?" He pointed at René, who had a fearful look on his face. "The more I think about it," Felix continued, "perhaps our time in Berlin may just be what the doctor ordered."

He made a panoramic sweep of the room with his arms. "Maybe we're finally done here. Between me, you guys, Adrienne, and our friends—we can start our own studio, develop our own style when we come back." He began counting off his fingers. "There's Impressionism, Surrealism, Fauvism, Expressionism, and—"

"If it's *your* studio, Felix," René interrupted, "we can teach Drunkenism."

"Fuck you!"

"If only you could."

Using all of his weight, Felix fell backward onto the couch on top of both his friends, tackling them and laughing, and it felt good. Felix was the life of their party, always. And suddenly Julian missed him. He missed knowing that tomorrow Felix would be whisked off to Berlin, and though they would follow in a few weeks, Julian had not slept a single night apart from Felix in the apartment since he'd arrived in Paris. Julian watched his friends taunt each other, and he wished that all the other stuff—the hovering black cloud called Charlotte—would just disappear.

A few minutes later, Felix loudly clapped his hands together; his signature move indicating a new activity was up on the agenda. "I'm drunk." Felix stood and stretched his arms high. "I'm horny, and I want to paint." He laughed hard at his own joke. "And not necessarily in that order."

Walking over to the canvases drying against the far wall, Felix surveyed the various images of Charlotte. Julian put down his wine glass and eyed the paintings from his vantage point on the couch. Charlotte's poses seemed to fill every wall of the studio. *They love her and I hate her,* he thought. *I hate her for ruining this, ruining us.*

Felix pointed at the paintings accusingly, and announced, "He's fucking her, you know."

"Who's fucking her?" René called out.

Why was he keeping this up? Julian thought angrily. It was only going to make the truth worse.

"Dubois, who else?" Felix responded before Julian could interject. "It sickens me to think of that pig ruining something so beautiful."

René was silent and unblinking. Julian shot him a final look: *Tell him immediately, or I will.*

But Felix clapped his hands loudly and headed toward the kitchen. "Well, Dubois has got to have some more wine hiding somewhere." He began ransacking the cabinets, the loud clanking noise echoing throughout the studio. "And here we are." He emerged triumphantly with a bottle of red tucked under each armpit.

Humming an unrecognizable tune, he refilled Julian's glass first, and then topped off René's. Felix sat down between them, and as usual, swigged straight from the bottle. "This is shit," he announced, spitting it out. "But I'm not surprised." He leaned sideways into Julian. "It's time for your confession."

"My confession?" Julian pulled away.

"Yes. Wine and women go together. If you haven't learned a thing in Paris, know that." Felix crossed his arms and then his legs, cocking his head as though he were the supreme expert on both subjects. "Tell me, how many have there been, my friend?"

"How many *what* have there been?" Julian's face turned red.

"Women, you idiot. You're so damn secretive. And what about that gorgeous redhead at Deux Magots?" Felix asked, followed by another long swig of Dubois's cheap wine. "She practically throws her body across the table every time you walk into the café. And you never give her the time of day." He pointed the bottle accusingly. "Are you a virgin, Julian?"

Julian looked away. How could he admit to them that his life had only begun a few years ago.

"I knew it!" Felix slammed down the bottle against the table like a gavel. "So that *is* the problem."

No. Adrienne is the problem, Julian thought uneasily. "Not a virgin," he said quietly. "Three women. Are you happy, Von Bredow? Or did I ruin your theory?"

Felix laughed. "Three? Well, then, you are practically a virgin. I'm three times ten," he boasted. "So, who was your first?"

Julian was too tired to play Felix's stupid games.

"C'mon, I'm waiting."

Julian took a deep breath followed by a swig from his glass. This was going to be bad. "It was Gertrude," he whispered, plus two one-nighters with women who meant nothing—that he'd felt nothing for.

"You fucked Gertrude?" Felix howled with joy. "Your cousin Sammy's wife? The same cousin who gave you money for school? I didn't know you had it in you. Honestly, Juliangelo, now I'm impressed."

Julian rolled his eyes. Felix was loving this.

"The gory details, please," Felix pushed.

"Leave him alone, Felix," René said, sitting up. "You should have been a lawyer. No one can interrogate like you."

"You mean no one can get out a confession like me." Felix pounded his chest proudly. "To most, I seem dumb, drunk, and arrogant. But it's just a front, because I'm smart, drunk, and arrogant." He leaned forward, reclaiming his bottle. "Now, back to Gertrude, the unfaithful slut, and Julian's deeply guarded secret."

"You don't stop, do you?" Julian laughed despite himself.

"Why should I?"

"It happened while I was painting her." Julian avoided mentioning that he had never seen a woman naked before Gertrude. "I couldn't help it. I—"

"Couldn't help it!" Felix taunted. "An artist and a model. Hmm, how original. I love it!"

"You're an idiot, Felix." René shook his head.

Felix concurred, "Yes, and proud of it. Well, I fucked my nanny, which is equally unoriginal for the second son of a blue-blooded bastard. Everybody knows my father slept with every servant in the house, his own nanny, and probably mine too." Felix's face tightened angrily, and then whatever he was thinking seemed to pass. "Anyway, I had just turned fourteen, and in pure Von Bredow fashion I told Else that if she didn't do what I wanted, she would lose her job. Terrible, I know . . . " Felix shook his head, feigning disgust over his own transgression and glanced over at René. "And you, Don Juan? Can you possibly top that?"

René took a long sip of Dubois's bad wine. "Possibly, well . . . I wouldn't call her a girl," he began slowly. "Yvette was my mother's best friend—twenty-two years older than me. It happened in our country house in Saint-Paul-de-Vence. I was sixteen."

"In the country house with a bored married aristocrat." Felix rolled his eyes. "So typically French, but keep going . . . " Felix fanned his arms over the back of the couch. He could go on like this all night.

"It gets better, Von Bredow—even for your sick twisted mind." René was clearly enjoying himself too. "I began seeing the woman's daughter." He squeezed Felix's kneecap. "Get this. A few weeks later, I slept with her in the morning and then her mother at night. All in a day's work. Never forgave myself for that one."

"Pure poetry. Okay, you win." Felix shrugged. "And we don't even need Julian to decide who takes the victory. Your story earns top billing." He pointed to the pack of cigarettes near René. "Now fork one of those over as my consolation prize, and let's paint."

René tossed him the pack. "Paint? Look at Julian. Half dead. And I can barely move. I don't know how you do it, Von Bredow. The more you drink, the more sane and awake you are. It's either a blessing or a curse. Go paint for all of us."

"I think I will." Felix stood with the cigarette dangling from his mouth and walked slowly around the room, hands knotted at his back like an art critic. He stopped in front of his most recent painting of Charlotte on the far side of the room, eyeing it critically. They all knew that Dubois hated that particular canvas. He'd gone on about it for a good half hour earlier in the week, calling it juvenile and embarrassing. He said each feature of Charlotte's was out of proportion and the colors were wrong—loud and buffoonish—a prime example of "what not to do."

"He's right, you know. It is awful, isn't it?" Felix said quietly, as though Dubois's words were echoing in his head just then.

Julian and René said nothing as Felix walked past his painting and pointed at Julian's image of Charlotte. "I see where you are going here. But where are her damn eyes? You painted them blank, like an alien or an albino. Her eyes are clear blue. No color, nothing?"

He waited for a response, but Julian was too drunk to argue that the blankness was painted on purpose. The blankness was what he really saw in Charlotte. Her eyes revealed who she really was—inarguably beautiful on the outside, the ugly on the inside emanating through that vacant translucent gaze. After studying every inch of her for weeks, Charlotte's eyes gave her away.

But Felix had already moved on to the next canvas. It was René's: a charcoal drawing of Charlotte. The lines were so simple that it was, in a way, very complex. Felix turned on his fake French accent, imitating a pompous art critic. "Hmm, I see . . . simplicity meets intricacy, hints of Matisse. Look at the detail, the definition of the model's face in just a few curious lines." He peered up at Julian, snapped his fingers. "Now *these* eyes are alive, Julian—clearly an exploration of emotion and passion, beauty and grace." He clasped his hands together dramatically. "Perfection, René, as always."

Suddenly, Felix saw something else. He stopped the acting, took the canvas off the easel, and brought it close to his face, as if some hidden truth was there all along inside the image and he'd just discovered it. As if the reason why Charlotte had not succumbed to his advances was secretly drawn inside the lines of her torso, the curves of her breasts, and he'd somehow—inexplicably—missed all of the cues.

Felix's voice began to slur, and his light mood thickened. His whisper was barely audible. "So realistic, and believable, that I could actually fuck this canvas." He looked up at both of them, his gaze resting heavily on René. He walked toward him, still holding the canvas. Looking completely deflated, he said, "You're fucking her."

René took a deep choppy breath. "Yes, I, well . . . I have been seeing Charlotte."

The silence in the room was so heavy that Julian was afraid to breathe.

"Seeing, René? Seeing, as in painting her? Or seeing, as in fucking her?"

René stared hard at Felix, their eyes locking like they did on Julian's first night in Paris. René's mouth fell open like a guilty child's, but nothing came out.

"How long has this been going on?" Felix demanded, and then he angrily turned to Julian. His eyes were blazing an unforgiving blue hue. "And how long have you known?"

Julian tried to look away, but he couldn't. He was no less guilty. "I wanted to tell you, but—"

"But you didn't, goddamn it!" Felix shouted, cutting him off. "The two of you have been laughing yourselves to sleep every night about what an ass I've made of myself. A drunken dumb ass, right?"

"Not true—" Julian started to object.

"Don't talk to me about truth." He turned violently toward René. "And tell me, how is Adrienne taking this so-called truth? Have you even told her? Or are you fucking Charlotte behind her back and weighing all of your options, as usual?" Felix kicked an empty wine bottle out of his way, his eyes bulging at Julian. "You have listened to me go on about Charlotte every goddamn night. I trusted you. Every time you walked into our apartment, you lied to me. You, of all people, Mr. Holier-Than-Thou. Damn you, Julian—" His voice was shaking.

"It's not Julian's fault," René interjected. "It's mine. He pushed me to tell you, but I held back, trying to find the right moment."

"The right moment? Ha!" Felix laughed contemptuously, squeezing his eyes shut as if to ward off the images invading his mind—a whirling blackened vision of Charlotte and René intertwined, laughing behind his back, mocking him as they rolled around in bed. "You swore this would never happen again." He circled René. "Remember when I told you I had feelings for Adrienne? And then suddenly the two of you were in love. You swore you would never deceive me again."

"I'm so sorry." René tried to break out of the circle, but Felix blocked him, then turned away and stood still. René walked in front of him. "Felix, you have to believe how much I struggled inside about this. I just didn't know how to tell you."

"You struggled?" When Felix looked up his face was tear-streaked. His wet cobalt eyes darted from René to Julian, as if to ascertain which friend was worse—the liar or the enabler. "How could you guys do this to me?"

His voice sounded so small. He stared down at the floor as though he had no one else to trust but the wooden planks beneath him.

"Felix," Julian whispered painfully. "I'm so sorry."

When Felix finally looked up, his face seemed to be twisting, as if each feature were physically fighting against the others. Julian took a step backward from the sting of his gaze and leaned forward. *That's it!* he thought, taking a mental snapshot of Felix's face. *That's the exact expression I want to use for my faceless painter.* Julian looked away guiltily, surprised by his own selfishness.

Felix said coldly, "Now I understand why you both are coming to Germany. Out of pity. Out of guilt."

"You're wrong," Julian countered softly.

"I have never been more right in my life."

Felix stepped forward and rapped his finger hard onto René's chest, and René stood there and took it. "The only thing you care about is painting with Ernst Engel. You get everything, don't you? Every god-damn thing you want. Well, I have no use for you anymore."

Felix's hand dropped limply to his side. He was standing motionless, eyeing both men with naked hatred. "This is goodbye, then. Don't even think of stepping foot in Berlin. Your father was right, René. Two Jews and a paintbrush have no place in Germany."

He walked over to the couch and grabbed the second unopened bottle of Dubois's cheap wine and headed toward the door.

"Felix, don't go," René pleaded. "Let's work this out."

Felix stopped in his tracks at the doorframe and faced René. His eyes were crazed, the colors of his pupils seemed to be changing by the second—shards of blue, gray, violet, and green—blending and separating like a kaleidoscope. "There's nothing to work out because whatever it is, it only works out for you. You have everything. Adrienne, talent, money, looks. Every goddamn thing you want at your fingertips. I never faulted you for it. I forgave you even after you knew how I felt about Adrienne and you still went for her. I forgave you for being a greedy bastard, because somewhere down deep I always believed no matter what that you had my back. But now I know that I was mistaken, simply deluding myself. There was a knife there all along. You pounced on Charlotte without a second thought about me. One day, René . . . one hellish day, you will learn that those who have everything end up with nothing. Someone will teach you."

He stood frozen before them like a Roman statue—hooded eyes, fierce mouth, prepared for battle. Exhaling deeply, Felix took one last look at his best friends, then slammed the door.

Julian and René stood staring at each other, listening to the residual echo of the door's closing, trying to digest the magnitude of what just happened. Something within Felix had changed before their eyes. Something, perhaps, Julian thought fearfully, as he listened to the fading pound of footsteps down the staircase, that had been there all along.

Chapter Nine

Tiny embers scattered in Adrienne's fireplace as she handed Julian a cup of hot cocoa. She joined him on the velvet cushions on the floor and together, in silence, they watched the fire. Julian's gaze shifted, following the long line of her leg. Adrienne was barefoot. Her feet were slim and delicate. He looked away before she caught him and instead focused on her paintings, which surrounded the large living room of her parents' luxurious apartment like spectators.

The dozen or so canvases were a series of faces. Each portrait was different, yet there was a common thread. Within the eyes of each image, Adrienne depicted a deep yearning, as though her subject was hungry and restless for more out of life. Julian's gaze fell on the painting directly across from him. He had not seen that one before.

The young woman's eyes were half closed, her lips parted. Though the light in the room was dim, Julian could see the subtle wetness, the shimmering lacquer of the woman's tongue. Her caramel-colored hair was pulled away from her face, emphasizing the pale bareness of her neck. He could feel Adrienne watching his reaction to the painting. He knew it was a self-portrait. He could tell by the soft abstract angles of the woman's face, the almond shape of the eyes. He wondered when she had painted it. What had she been thinking at the very moment she added oil to give the tongue that glistening effect?

"So, that's it," Julian said, tearing his gaze away from the canvas, and turning toward Adrienne.

She shrugged. "Yes. I'm going to paint on my own. No more studios. No more instructors. I'm done."

"I mean about René."

"Honestly, it doesn't even have to do with Charlotte anymore. René has changed, and I refuse to stand by and watch it." She stretched out catlike, and Julian again had to look away to keep himself from reaching out to touch her.

"How did Felix take the news of the happy couple?" she asked. "Knowing how he pants every time Charlotte enters a room, I'm sure he was not exactly thrilled."

"It was worse than that," Julian said. "Felix refused to speak to either René or me before he left for Germany. He threw my things out of the apartment, got into his father's car, and drove off." He stared at the logs as they snapped apart in the flames. "Felix told us to forget about coming to Germany, but René and I are going anyway. We will do whatever it takes to fix things." He leaned forward. "Come with us, Adrienne."

She shook her head no. "I can't bear the thought of painting next to René and knowing that's where it would end." She sat upright, locking her knees to her chest. Her voice was fragile. "René willingly gave up everything we had for a stupid model, someone who does not create a damn thing."

Julian sipped his drink, thinking how lovely her eyes were as the reflection of the flames sparkled inside them.

"Look, I am not naive," she continued, moving her hands rhythmically, as if sculpting the air. "Many artists fall for their model. After hours of immobility, she transforms from a live, breathing object into an ideal, a goddess. But the infatuation passes quickly because there is always another model waiting in the wings, another portrait to be painted. Models are expendable. I always thought that René would never trade talent for beauty. But I was wrong, and that's what hurts." She averted her eyes. "Charlotte is beautiful."

"So are you," Julian said softly.

Adrienne turned, placing her fingertip against Julian's lips. "You have been my friend. So please respect that the only ego I want to stroke these days is my own. I need to paint in isolation, to heal."

"Adrienne, I didn't mean to hurt you." Julian's gaze bore into hers. "I wish I could have told you about René and Charlotte. I didn't know what to do, so I made the mistake of agreeing to keep it secret. I should never have done that."

She laughed sadly. "It's ironic how you seem to know all of our secrets and yet we know nothing about you."

Julian shifted uncomfortably against the pillows. "What do you mean?

Leaning forward, she said, "I mean, where is your family? You never talk about them or anything about your life before Paris. I know you're Jewish, like me and René. We're not religious at all, but we are not ashamed of being Jewish either."

"I'm not ashamed," Julian said defensively.

"But you never discuss it." She pointed an accusing finger at him. "In fact, when we were walking through the Marais last month I remember wondering why you couldn't even look at the beautiful synagogue there, even when I pointed out the gorgeous stained-glass windows. You kept your gaze fixed to the sidewalk, as though you were afraid of even looking, as if you were guilty of something."

"I don't know what you're talking about." Julian could not believe how she saw right through him.

"You know exactly what I'm talking about," she continued, her voice softening. "You see, in Dubois's studio, I studied you the way you studied me. I knew that you were painting my image when Charlotte was modeling. Everyone else was painting her, drooling over her. But not you, Julian." She sighed deeply. "I know you better than you think. So, tell me your secret . . . *before*."

Julian put down the cup and stared at the rug, too overcome with emotion to look at her.

"Before what?" he mustered, lifting his head slowly.

She lightly touched his cheek. "Before we make love."

~⁀⁀~

Julian told her everything. He lay back on a pillow, staring at the ceiling, and shared his past, relieved to release it all to her. Only Adrienne could understand that day in the market, the woman selling the potatoes, the forbidden drawings in the Holy Book, the tomatoes thrown at his back. He told her about the art books from the library and how he had stolen money from his mother's pickle jar. He recounted the night his father burned all of his artwork and about Sammy and Gertrude. He told her how Gertrude had seduced him. He talked without stopping, confessing all of it, until he could feel the wetness of Adrienne's tears against his cheek and the warmth of her arms around him.

"Now I understand," she whispered. "Have you contacted your parents since you've been in Paris?"

"No," he replied curtly, and she did not push him. He pulled back slightly and studied the smooth contours of her face. "After what happened that day in the market, I am dead to them."

He then closed his eyes, feeling the heat of Adrienne's body against his, and could not believe that she was in his arms. He did not want to move, did not want to breathe, too afraid this moment would be gone, or worse, that he was only imagining it. She lifted her face, and Julian could practically taste her breath. If he stuck out his tongue, he could touch her lips. And he knew those lips, as though they were a part of his own body. Red tinged with pink, turning slightly brown when they were cold. Right now, they were a moist, hot pink. Glistening like the tongue in her painting.

She extended her neck and pressed her mouth firmly against his. Julian closed his eyes. René's face flashed before him but disappeared as Adrienne's tongue darted inside his mouth. Her lips traveled, planting delicate kisses along his throat. From somewhere in the room, Julian heard loud moans, and it took him a few seconds to realize that they were coming from him.

Adrienne's eyes shone. It was a look that he'd seen her give René on numerous occasions. He almost turned to see if René was there, standing behind him, but caught himself. Instead, he held Adrienne even tighter, torn between wanting to rip off her clothes and remembering that she was not his.

"Do you still love him?" Julian asked under his breath, because he had to.

She did not hesitate. "That doesn't go away. But I want you."

It was enough.

Adrienne fastened her slim body onto Julian's and arched her back. He reached under her sweater and felt her small firm breasts. He gently stroked the velvet of her skin, feeling the hardening of her nipples against his fingers. He had never felt anything so exquisite.

She savagely tore open his shirt, as if she, too, had been waiting months just to touch him. The buttons popped off, and Julian groaned as her light brown hair journeyed down his torso. Her hand lingered between his legs, and then her mouth. Julian willed his body to not let go too soon.

And then he couldn't hold back. Everything inside him seemed to crush and expand simultaneously.

As he lay on the floor breathing heavily, Adrienne slowly made her way back up his chest. "You are beautiful, Julian." She played with his chest hair and then nestled into the crook of his arm, fitting inside like a puzzle piece. "I'm going to miss you terribly. I only wish I had time to paint you."

"I always paint you," Julian confessed, not caring what he said anymore. "In my head."

"Kiss me everywhere, and then paint me once more," she whispered huskily, placing his hand between her legs. She was warm and wet.

Pressing his mouth deeply into hers, Julian felt the sharpness of her teeth against his lips, her breasts locked into his chest. He turned her over on her back. His muse belonged to him, finally.

Even if was only for one night.

BLUE

"If you see a tree as blue, then make it blue."
— Paul Gauguin

Chapter Ten

POTSDAM, GERMANY, 1933

Icy rain pounded against the roof of the car. The driver René had hired was concentrating on the winding road and getting them to Potsdam safely. Julian could barely see out the fogged window. He glanced over at René, who was drawing on the steamed glass with his finger. He had created a young girl holding flowers. Julian could not believe it. His friend managed to make something beautiful even out of mist.

Using his sleeve to wipe off the window, Julian pressed his nose against it. The view was hazy, but they had entered what appeared to be a royal complex.

"René, look over there." Julian pointed toward the sprawling residence perched on a hilltop. A giant turquoise dome stood at the center of the structure, surrounded by layers of snow-covered terraces.

René tapped the driver's broad shoulder. In flawless German, he asked, "Where are we exactly?"

The driver glanced into his rearview mirror, raising an excessively bushy brow. "Potsdam," he answered gruffly. "Schloss Sanssouci. Where Frederick the Great lived."

Julian glanced down at the map in his hand. "I think we're getting close."

René looked tense. He rubbed his temples with both hands. "What if Felix slams the door in our faces? He practically threw me down the stairs when I tried talking to him again."

"My standing with him isn't much better." Julian recalled Felix tossing Julian's clothes out of the apartment. He paused and couldn't hold back what had been bothering him the entire trip. "Is Charlotte still planning to come?"

"Maybe." René shifted uncomfortably in his seat. "We've got to settle things with Felix first."

"You should really rethink this. Charlotte's presence is not going to help our cause in any way." Julian could not believe that after everything, René still wanted her to join them. Julian couldn't stand her. And there was no way Felix would forgive them if Charlotte came to Germany. Julian stared angrily at the back of the driver's jug-shaped head, thinking René a fool. He turned when he saw René observing him.

"Why don't you just get it all out, Julian," René said coldly.

Julian eyed him evenly. "Break it off, René. She is trouble. And you're insane if you think Felix will be okay with her coming here. That's why he ran off in the first place, because we both lied to him about her. Charlotte is manipulative and a user. You, your father, probably Dubois—who's next?" Julian realized he was practically shouting and tried unsuccessfully to tone it down. "Really, how could you love a woman like that?"

"You don't know her," René said defensively. "She's made mistakes, but she's had a rough life. She has had to make it on her own since she was a teenager."

"My guess is that Charlotte couldn't care less who she hurts along the way."

"Who the hell are you to judge?" René countered, turning away.

Julian looked out his window thinking, *Who am I to judge? I stole money from my own mother. I slept with my cousin's wife. I slept with Adrienne. I lied to Felix by keeping my mouth shut when he trusted me.* He glanced sideways at René. "You're right. I'm sorry," Julian said guiltily.

René rested his arm on the back of the cold leather seat. "We are both on edge. I'm sorry too. Right now, the most important thing is to work things out with Felix. Everything else comes later."

René returned to the window and doodled with the vapor, his face transfixed, as if he were creating a masterpiece and not something that would soon return to mist. Julian could not help but wonder if it was Felix's friendship that René wanted back, or rather salvaging the opportunity to paint with Ernst Engel.

They drove another twenty minutes along the Berlin-Potsdam Road. The driver slowed down at the end of a long secluded driveway. He stopped the car, turned around, and announced brusquely: "*Schloss* Von Bredow."

Julian glanced out the window in awe. The estate was an ornate three-story monstrosity. He could barely see where it began and where it ended. "How the hell did Felix go from the Von Bredow cathedral to our trashy apartment?" he whispered.

René laughed nervously. "He loved your trashy apartment. This place gave him nightmares."

"I can see why."

The driver slowly made his way up the long, white, paved driveway, which could easily have encircled Julian's entire Chicago neighborhood. He glanced at René and saw that the color had drained from his friend's face. The drawing had vaporized into a clean slate and René did not seem to notice.

The driver stopped just short of the entrance. René told the driver to wait for them no matter how long it took.

As they walked together toward the entrance, René ran his fingers through his wet, glossy hair. "I've heard about this place a thousand times, but I had no idea."

"Don't tell me the size of this fortress intimidates you," Julian said, slowly walking forward. "You've spent your life vacationing in European villas and chalets."

"It's not the exterior, Julian," René said quietly. "It's what's inside that makes me want to run."

Julian agreed. The castle looked like a haunted house. The entrance was safely ensconced behind enormous dark pillars, and the front door had to be nearly fifteen feet high. Breathing deeply, Julian reached for the knocker, an oversized gargoyle. He held the intricately carved iron beast in his hand, almost afraid to let it drop back on its head against the door.

The butler, a frail-looking man, opened the door immediately, as though he had been waiting for them. He wore a starched tuxedo with tails and his hands were knotted behind his back. He gave both men the once-over with a frown and then shut the door in their faces.

"What was that?" Julian couldn't help but laugh.

René laughed too. "That must be Walter. Felix told me about him— the walking corpse who has served three generations of Von Bredows."

The door reopened and Walter's pruned face peered out. "Yes."

Julian cleared his throat and glanced at René. "We came to see Felix."

"I see," he said dryly. "Follow me."

They were led in silence through a domed, dark hallway lit with ornate sconces. They passed a smoky, wall-sized mirror in which Julian caught a glimpse of himself, and the image was not pretty. The guy looking back at him needed a bath. He should have worn his good blue sweater, not the frayed second-hand shirt he had on. He should have put on a tie and gotten a haircut at least.

They followed Walter through another seemingly endless hallway. Along the wall, dozens of powder-wigged, dour-faced court portraits were interspersed with dozens of paintings by Old Masters. Julian half expected the gray, stern faces to jump out at him. He could not believe that Felix had actually grown up in this place. As they proceeded down the corridor, war scenes began to dominate the walls. Angry infantrymen seemed to be storming straight out of the canvases; their cannons, swords, and muskets aimed at Julian's head.

Feeling the security of René's shoulder pressing against his, Julian apprehensively turned a corner leading into yet another hallway filled with rows of gilt-framed paintings. He immediately recognized the dark, realistic detailing of Cranach and Dürer, as well as a few Rembrandts, Rubens, van Eycks, and El Grecos.

"It's a fucking museum in here," René whispered.

"Unbelievable." Julian could barely get the word out. He could not believe the art surrounding him. No wonder Felix's grandmother had tossed a van Gogh Felix's way as though it were extra furniture.

The hallway ended and burst into a short, bright foyer. The effect was staggering, like that of blinding light at the end of a tunnel. Walter stopped in front of a set of French doors. He grasped the gold knobs with both hands and dramatically flung open the doors.

Julian bit down on his tongue and entered first, then stopped in his tracks when he saw Felix.

Wearing a dark pinstriped suit, Felix stood next to the fireplace, an elbow resting on the mantelpiece as though he were one of the Von Bredow portraits in the hallway. The baron, staring coldly at them, sat erect behind his desk. Felix seemed to be trying to imitate his father's controlled stance, and for a moment, Julian longed to tackle Felix to the ground, rip off his pretentious jacket, drag him back to Paris, and shake the Von Bredow out of him. But Felix's face remained stony, guarded.

Who was this imposter?

"Hello, Felix," Julian managed.

"Julian," Felix responded blankly, ignoring René altogether.

Taking a step forward, Julian said, "Baron Von Bredow, would you mind if we had a word alone with Felix?" He glanced boldly at the baron, who was watching them with an amused half smile.

But the baron said nothing, dismissing Julian entirely. Felix nodded collaboratively to his father. Julian yearned to remind Felix of the hostile exchange between the two men in Paris just days ago, but Felix brushed past Julian and walked out the French doors. René dipped his head meekly in Felix's direction and followed him. So did Julian.

Felix led them into a large two-story sanctuary, sweetened with the rich scent of tobacco and filled floor-to-ceiling with thousands of leather-bound books. A heavy velvet tapestry depicting frolicking angels and shepherds occupied an entire wall.

Julian was careful to circumvent a stuffed bearskin rug with glassy egg-shaped eyeballs. He walked to the far corner of the room only to meet up with an enormous boar's head suspended from the wall. Picturing the baron hunting the animal down, his bald head projecting forward while wearing that cold half smile, Julian suddenly felt afraid as he turned toward Felix. They stared at each other in silence. The man standing before him was not the Felix he knew. Not the same Felix who slept in torn underwear, who got drunk and acted stupid on a hundred occasions.

"Felix," René began slowly, "we came because you are our best friend and things ended badly."

"I *was* your best friend," Felix corrected him, his face remaining stony. "And *you* ended things badly."

"You have every right to be angry," René said, trying to be conciliatory.

Felix wasn't buying it. He folded his arms against his chest and leaned forward. "And you have no right to be here."

"We took our chances," René continued. "We hoped we could work our problems out."

"Work our problems out—ha!" Felix mocked. "I bet Julian pulled you here by your socks."

René shook his head. "Felix, what can we do to make it up to you?"

"Nothing. The damage is done," Felix retorted. "How many times over the past few months did I tell you how I felt about Charlotte? Did that make it more exciting? Didn't our friendship mean a goddamn thing to you? Didn't you learn anything after Adrienne?"

At the mention of her name Julian looked away, just as Felix turned his anger on him. "And you, Julian, I took you in like a brother. Christ, I wouldn't even take in my brother. But, like everyone else, you, too, chose René."

"I did not choose anyone, Felix," Julian countered. "I was caught in the middle. I didn't want to hurt you. I knew how you felt. But I was wrong. I should have told you the truth right away, no matter what. I'm truly sorry."

"It wasn't Julian's fault," René interjected. "The blame is mine."

"How noble." Felix's focus shifted from René to Julian, sizing them up just as his butler had. Felix's polished leather shoe traced the stuffed bear's paw and then he stepped on it hard. "And Charlotte?" His lips were pursed tightly as he spoke. "Is she still coming, René?"

"That depends on you."

Felix crossed the rug and stood inches from René. "I want her."

"I love her," René replied evenly.

"More than you love me?" Felix demanded.

René shuffled his feet. "It is different."

"More than you love your art?" Felix took another step forward.

"No," René answered without hesitation.

The three men stared at one another, and then Felix broke the silence with unnaturally loud laughter, followed by his signature clap. "Well, then, winning her over won't be too difficult."

"That's not what I meant, Felix."

Felix looked at Julian. "Nothing comes before René's art." He pointed an accusing finger. "Not me, and not you, Julian. Don't forget that."

Felix turned toward the large Palladian window looking out onto the garden. He stood there staring for what seemed like an unbearably long time. Julian studied his back, the strain of Felix's neck muscles against his starched shirt collar. They should leave. Coming here was a mistake. Felix clearly needed more time to cool off.

But as Felix finally turned toward them, a wide grin stretched across his face. René grinned back, thinking the smile was meant for him, relieved at having been forgiven.

"Then it's settled," Felix said, as he served up a round of brandy.

What is settled? Julian wondered, but said nothing.

"Charlotte is welcome to come." He raised his glass. "Here's to moving forward."

Raising his glass high to match Felix's, René said happily, "To friend-ship."

"To friendship," Felix repeated as he lifted the decanter in Julian's di-rection. The smile was chilling. "And, of course, to Ernst Engel."

"To Ernst Engel," René toasted. Julian nodded, but his glass remained frozen at his side. Felix's smile was clearly a lie. Nothing was forgiven.

Chapter Eleven

THE GRUNEWALD FOREST, BERLIN

There were those nights when Julian would lie awake and think how far he had come from his old life in Chicago, where he had once been trapped. He would think of his mother, envision her stirring soup alone in the kitchen, the sadness filling her beautiful eyes—his eyes—and the guilt would set in. No matter how far he'd gone, she would always be with him, reminding him of the life he'd left behind but could never really escape. He recalled her face that very last time, the silent scream in the window as he was making his getaway. Were the tears meant solely for him? Or for her lost life as well? How his mother would have loved it here in the Berlin countryside, he thought. It was winter, but he imagined how beautiful the forest would be when the snow melted, revealing the wildflowers, the birch trees, the rare birds, and the small lakes. He remembered how his mother would sit on his bed and stare at his paintings, especially the landscapes—as though she were wishing she could jump inside the canvas for a day, for even a minute. *If only.*

I miss her, Julian thought sadly, as he buttoned up his coat and stared out at the endless birch trees surrounding him. *One day I'll go back. One day I'll take her away from there, and show her everything—another life, a different life. My life.*

Julian now understood how constrained he was by Dubois's limitations and apathy, a different feeling of being trapped. Over the past month, under Ernst Engel's guidance, Julian had learned the new language of color. Painting, he discovered, began not with the canvas, but with the power of his mind. Engel taught him how to envision his finished painting, and then to close his eyes as he painted. And Engel was right. Every stroke that he imagined in the night, in his dreams, would soon make its way onto his canvas. It was as if he had no control over what his hands did. For the first time, Julian knew he was no longer simply a painter. With Engel's mentorship, he was becoming an artist.

It was late in the afternoon, and today Engel insisted that he and René paint outdoors, even though it was cold and wet. He encouraged them to be as unconfined as the woods surrounding them—to forget everything they had learned up until that moment: technique, method, even the dire political situation in Germany. Hitler's rise to power, Engel emphasized, had no place in his forest. Here, they were safe, sheltered, and free. Never mind the cold.

Engel jumped around Julian and René like a man half his age, pointing at Charlotte, who was posing for them in the distance. "Now, close your eyes and paint, my friends. Don't even look at her. Instead, visualize the colors—the whites, the grays, the browns—surrounding her." He laughed, as though enjoying an inside joke. "And then, when I tell you to open your eyes, I want you to paint with every color *but* white, gray, and brown."

"Is this a test?" René called out.

"Yes, you might say that." Engel thrust his hands forward. "Remember, it is color, not the subject, that must fight to stand on its own. The impact of your work is determined by the contrast and tension between complementary shades.

"Painting," he continued, "does not have to be object-related. Things are obsolete; it is the emotion that is essential. Lose your perspective. It isn't necessary. You are not describing reality, my friends, but interpreting it. Do you understand? Smell the cool forest behind Charlotte. Sharp like menthol. Listen to the sway of the trees. Experience the wind tickling your skin. *That* is what I want you to paint—the emotion, how it makes you feel. That is why I brought you here to my home, to my forest. Now, make it yours."

Julian glanced at René and saw the heavy contours, the flat, unbroken stripes of color gracing his friend's canvas. His eyes were closed as he painted. Julian looked up at Charlotte, who stood in the distance between the trees. She never blinked. *What was she thinking? Did she even think?* Every day, he wished she would just go away. Yet, Charlotte seemed to hang on tighter. She and René had become inseparable, and strangely, Felix seemed to accept their relationship. *Too easily,* Julian thought anxiously. In the first few weeks after they'd arrived, Felix would paint with them, but soon that stopped. Now he spent all of his time with his father, making occasional visits to Engel's second studio in Berlin. Not to paint, just to observe. He would stand near the door with his arms crossed, say a few words, make some lame excuse, and then leave—but not before Julian caught glimpses of a well-concealed rage in his eyes as he watched Charlotte and René together. He couldn't hide that emotion. Julian knew those eyes, like he knew his own. His gut warned him that perhaps he and René should think about returning to Paris.

Soon, he told himself. *Just not yet.* Not when there was still so much to learn from Ernst Engel. Once he left Engel, Julian knew he would never get this precious time—this genius—to himself ever again.

Don't think about Felix now. Focus on Charlotte, and just paint. Feel. Follow your hands. Julian decided to ignore Charlotte's face and concentrate instead on the thick sheath of muslin wrapped around her body like a toga. The cold wind billowed through the loose material and clung to her generous curves. She was clearly freezing but held her pose. He studied the determined swing of the leafless trees behind her. Stalwart trunks of birch and pine extended out like attentive guardsman. He stared at Charlotte until she lost form and merged into the natural background, becoming a series of bold slabs of color. His fingers were numb, yet surprisingly nimble. Inhaling deeply, Julian drank in the dense woodland musk and began to paint.

Hours later, after they had all moved inside Engel's home to continue painting, Julian heard the front door open and Engel talking to someone.

"We're done for today," Engel called out merrily as he entered the room. "René, Julian, I want you to meet a close friend of mine."

An elegant gentleman with bright red hair and graying sideburns entered the room behind Engel.

"Max Kruger is one of the founding artists of the motley crew of Expressionists fondly known as *Die Brücke*," Engel said, with a gallant sweep of his arm. "We have been painting together for thirty years."

Julian perked up as the renowned painter moved toward them.

"Please, Ernst, you are giving away my age," Kruger chuckled.

"Sadly, Max, I think our age has given *us* away." As Engel laughed, the many lines on his face deepened. He turned to Julian and René. "We were quite the bohemians back then with crazy ideas. You see, our parents wanted us to become architects—to achieve a respectable profession. We spent three painful semesters at the Technische Hochschule in Dresden. But a group of us painted in secret." He turned to Kruger. "Remember skipping our final exams, sneaking off to the Moritzburg Lakes and painting all day? Simply the best time of my life."

"Come, Ernst, let's not bore these young people with 'remember when' tales." Kruger made a beeline for René. "You are Jacob Levi's son?"

"So I've heard," René laughed, extending his hand. "Mr. Kruger, it is truly an honor."

"Your father is a good man and an excellent art dealer. He sold several of my paintings. Quite well, I might add."

"For much more than they are worth," Engel piped in. They all laughed.

"And for the record, no one calls me Mr. Kruger. That was my father. It's Max, please. We are painters, not bankers." Smiling at Julian, Kruger said, "Ah, the American."

Julian glanced down at his baggy gray pants and faded green sweater, self-conscious of his lack of style, and smiled back. "Guilty as charged." He extended his hand. "Truly a pleasure—" he paused—"uh, Max."

"Don't worry. I make it my business to study all types." Kruger, still grinning, glanced at the others. "It is the way you hold yourself. Like this." He thrust his chest forward like an ape and everyone laughed. "Ernst told me about his new students from Paris. And who, may I ask, is that lovely woman?"

"Charlotte Béjart," Engel answered, following Kruger's gaze across the room. "Our resident model, straight from Paris."

Charlotte had been observing the scene from where she stood, but as soon as her name was mentioned, she quickly put on her robe.

"Simply exquisite, Ernst. I must borrow her in Munich."

"She is on loan from Léon Dubois."

"Léon Dubois?" Kruger smiled. "It's been years. How is the old boy?"

"Not too well, I'm afraid," Engel said. "His best students and favorite model deserted him to study under me."

"Excuse me." Charlotte walked past them haughtily, the robe sliding off her shoulder, exposing her creamy skin. "I'm going to sleep. I am totally exhausted." She stopped in front of Kruger. "And please, if you want to 'borrow me in Munich,' you must ask me. I make my own decisions."

Kruger's already reddish cheeks turned a shade darker. "Forgive me if I insulted you. It was the opposite of my intent. You, my dear, inspire men like myself to paint. Allow me to rephrase my offer." He swept his hand graciously through the air like a royal suitor. "It would be my honor to have you model for me in Munich, if you would agree to it."

Charlotte smiled demurely as she headed for the stairs. "I'll consider it. René, darling, are you coming?"

René threw up his hands and cocked his head innocently to one side. "As you can see, gentlemen, I have no choice in the matter. Will you be joining us tomorrow, Max?"

"Bright and early," Kruger said. "And you'd better hurry, René. She is not the kind of woman one keeps waiting."

Everyone exchanged goodnights at the base of the staircase. Julian hesitated, thinking he should probably leave Engel and Kruger alone. But Engel grabbed his arm tightly as he took the first step upstairs.

"No, Julian," his instructor said with a strange look. "I want you to come with us."

They entered the library and Julian stood near the doorway, shuffling his feet, unsure of what he should do as Kruger made himself comfortable on the couch.

"Brandy? Cognac?" Engel called out, as though Julian were a colleague.

Julian walked in slowly, nodding to both offers, not believing that he had Ernst Engel and Max Kruger all to himself. What could he possibly say that would be of interest to them? With a fixed smile, he sat on the edge of the couch next to Kruger, hoping that something remotely witty would emerge as Engel handed him a brandy.

Pouring Kruger a cognac, Engel said, "Well, what do you think, Max?"

"Julian could be an excellent choice." Kruger lit his pipe, then tilted his head in Julian's direction.

"For what am I being chosen?" Julian asked anxiously, inhaling the bittersweet scent of the pipe.

Dismissing the question with a wave of his glass, Kruger leaned back on the couch and said, "Tell me, Julian, why did you become a painter?"

"Why did I become a painter?" Julian repeated.

"Yes, tell me."

Julian fidgeted nervously. Kruger was eyeing him strangely. *How could this man possibly understand his childhood?* The prayers, the rules, the guilt, and the peddling of black socks to put money on the table. Art had been his escape, the only thing that kept him alive, breathing. Instead, he responded with a banal quote he had read somewhere: "There is no higher form of existence."

Kruger shook his head, clearly disappointed. "That does not answer my question. Why did *you* become an artist?"

"I didn't become anything, Mr. Kruger—Max," Julian blurted out. "I was born that way."

Kruger laughed. "What if you had been born a plumber?"

Julian crossed his arms. "I would paint the pipes."

Engel and Kruger exchanged approving glances.

"Excellent," Kruger whispered, then raised his voice. "Stand, Julian. Now. I want to have a good look at you."

Julian stood uneasily—so did Kruger, who began to assess him from head to toe, as though he were livestock. "Excellent shoulders, athletic build, strong back. Hmm, straight nose and squared chin. Green eyes with hints of gold. Clear, fair skin. Thick, light brown hair with no sign of curl or premature balding. Doesn't talk with his hands. No effeminate traits whatsoever. You don't look Jewish at all," Kruger declared happily.

Julian felt the heat rush to his face. If only they had seen him with the beard, the *payis,* the *tallis*, and the *tefilin*. He couldn't hold back from saying angrily, "What is Jewish supposed to look like?"

"Not like you," Kruger said quietly. "Please, sit down."

Julian remained standing. "I presume you are not interested in my entering a beauty contest."

"No, not exactly."

"Well, then, what is this about?"

"How far would you go for your art, Julian?" Kruger's tone had become almost threatening.

"Ernst, please, what is going on here?" Julian demanded.

"Just answer Max's questions," Engel said somberly. "Then I will explain everything."

Kruger moved past Julian and pretended to study Engel's book collection. He downed his cognac in one swig. Turning, he eyed Julian fiercely. "What if all of your art supplies were suddenly confiscated? What if your best works, your favorite pieces, were taken away and destroyed and you could do nothing about it?" He began to shout. "Tell me, what would you do, young man, if you were told that you could never paint again?"

"I would find a way to paint," Julian responded, confused by the interrogation. "I would paint up in a damn tree if I had to."

Kruger wiped the sweat off his brow, then tossed his handkerchief to the floor. He nodded at Engel, who said, "Julian, if you saw all those things happen to someone else, what would you do then?"

"You mean, would I fight his battle?"

His instructor nodded. "That is exactly what I mean."

They both closed in on Julian. Their features became magnified, and Julian took a step backward.

"How far would you go, Julian, if I asked you?" Engel's voice was low and shaky.

Julian took a deep breath. "I don't know where you are going with this, but you know damn well I would do anything to continue painting with you, Ernst."

Engel turned away, dewy eyed.

Kruger glanced at Engel but kept his focus on Julian. "Are you aware of a man named Joseph Goebbels?"

"Of course," Julian said. "He's Hitler's second-in-command."

"To be precise, he's the Third Reich's minister of propaganda and public enlightenment," Kruger explained. "Ernst and I have received a copy of Goebbels's secret art report, which will be released to the public shortly. It is a five-point manifesto stating what German artists can expect from the new government. Basically, it is an attack against the avant-garde movement. You see, Hitler and his gang of third-rate artists have made it a political priority to get rid of us."

Engel cut in. "Nearly everyone involved in the Reich's Chamber of Culture, including Hitler himself, has been, at one time or another, rejected by a prominent art institution—schools, museums, and galleries. Up until now, their artwork has been labeled uninspiring, behind the times. They were scoffed at by galleries that preferred artists like us; those who experimented with new styles over those who copied worn-out classical influences. So, these tiresome artists sulked until the Nazis lifted them off the street and gave them power and acceptance in return for absolute allegiance."

"Now that they are in power, it is payback time," Kruger added, suddenly looking older, his bright red hair clashing with his pale face. "How vindicated they must feel, creating new laws designed to throw us out while they bask in their newfound celebrity."

"But what does all this have to do with me?" Julian asked with escalating discomfort.

"Everything and nothing." Engel joined Kruger on the couch. "How did you feel when you painted today, succumbing to no one's set of rules but your own?"

"Fantastic," he answered truthfully. *I wished I never had to leave this place. Until now.*

Engel's voice dropped. "Yes, Julian. And all that is going to soon change. I find I am constantly paranoid, looking over my shoulder. I know I'm being watched, perhaps followed, by these Nazis. And it is not just me. My colleagues seem to be distancing themselves from one another out of self-protection. No one knows who is on whose side anymore. We are in very dangerous times."

Kruger nodded. "It's not just happening in Berlin. It is the whole damn country."

Rubbing his forehead as if to erase the image, Engel said, "First, the Jew auctions."

"Jew auctions?" Julian moved slowly toward his instructor.

"Yes, those bastards in the Chamber of Culture are planning hundreds of them," Engel explained. "We've learned that wealthy Jews will be forced to sell their art collections at a fraction of their value."

Julian felt ill listening to these two men talk. All he wanted to do was paint. He felt like screaming at Engel: "I thought you said that Hitler had no place in the Grunewald Forest!" Yet it was a moot point. Hitler's presence seemed to be rapidly filling every crevice of the room.

Engel poured himself another drink. His voice was shaky. "This is only the beginning, Julian."

Kruger removed his jacket, and large perspiration stains were visible under his arms. "We've had our day in the sun. We are not afraid for ourselves, but for young artists like you, whose ideas will be destroyed before they have a chance to bloom. Do you understand me?"

Julian felt uncomfortable under Kruger's penetrating gaze, as though he were under a microscope. He didn't understand either of them, but clearly they wanted something from him.

Engel wrapped his arm around Julian. "We need protection. Information—someone positioned inside to give us advanced warning. I've turned it over in my mind many times, and you fit the bill."

"What bill?" Julian pulled away from him. "And why me, Ernst?"

"Because of your relationship with Felix. His father and his friends are at the forefront of Hitler's art policies. They are the ones plotting against us." Engel glanced at Kruger, who nodded. "We believe Felix has been recruited by the Reich. He is in on it."

Julian sunk back onto the couch. He tried to catch his breath. "Look, I know there are problems here. I'm not a fool. But Felix is not a Nazi. He is simply helping his father run his company. In a few months we're all going to return to Paris and pick up where we left off."

Even as he said it, Julian knew it wasn't true. He pictured Felix standing cross armed at the door of Engel's studio in Berlin. That lying smile. Felix was not going anywhere.

"Surely you don't believe that, Julian." Engel bent down and lightly ran his hand under Julian's chin, lifting his student's distraught face toward his. "Why would I lie to you?"

Julian pushed away his hand. "You brought Kruger here, putting on an old buddies act, when in fact the sole purpose of his visit today was to see me. Isn't that right? Well, I may not look like a Jew, but I think like one, and I'm not stupid."

Engel stared hard at Julian. "In the entire time that we have been here, Felix has come to my studio to paint exactly twice. All of the other times he has just stood in his damn suit and observed us, taking notes. Mental notes." He paused. "I knew exactly what he was doing, but I played dumb. Felix is not your friend."

"You don't know him like I do, Ernst. There were things that happened … but it was never like that," Julian protested. "Look, I know that whatever friendship Felix and I once had is nearly gone, but I still want to save it. And so does René. Our problems are over a girl, not over art. It can be fixed."

But even as he said it, Julian knew deep down that it wasn't true.

Engel took Julian's cold hands inside both of his, warming them as a father would. "Julian, you are young. You are smart, but not smarter than *they* are." He glanced at Kruger. "Neither are we, I'm afraid. We chose you to help us because you are our only shot at getting close to the source of our problems. I know this is hard to comprehend, but you could also be instrumental in saving some of history's most important art by penetrating Wilhelm Von Bredow's inner circle, especially if Felix is involved. You could get us information we need in order to survive what we believe is coming for us."

"Penetrate Baron Von Bredow's inner circle?" Julian laughed at their naiveté. "Did you forget the small fact that I'm Jewish?"

Kruger shook his head dismissively as though that small fact was incidental. "They hate the avant-garde more than they despise the Jews, trust me."

"Think of the art," Engel persisted. "You can do this. We are talking about the survival of an entire movement."

"Ernst, I don't know how you believe that any of this can work." Julian shook his head, thinking that if he was their only hope, then this art movement had no chance of survival. "What would you have done had I never come here? And why not approach René? He has the contacts. He's everybody's star painter. Who the hell am I?"

Engel seemed to weigh Julian's words. "René is extremely talented, but selfish. He would sacrifice only for his own art. But not you, Julian—there is something about you that is different. I saw it the first time I met you. My sense is that Felix trusts you over René, and for good reason. You, I believe, would sacrifice for art as a whole—given the opportunity. Am I right? You would go to any distance for art."

Julian thought of the stolen art books from the library, months and months of thievery and sin just to be close to the Masters, just to glimpse a forbidden world that he had no right entering. He would have done anything back then just to have a paintbrush in his hand. Engel somehow knew this. Engel, like Adrienne, could clearly see through him.

"I really don't understand any of this, Ernst."

Engel held his large nose inches from Julian's. "Then let me be frank. You are American. You've never had an exhibition. No one knows anything about you. And you have a connection to one of the most powerful and influential families in Germany—in fact, that's the reason why you're here." His voice became distant, almost mystical. "Perhaps you landed on my doorstep, Julian, for this very purpose. Do you believe in fate?"

Julian held his breath as they stared at each other. *Yes, goddamn it. You know I do.*

"All we are asking is that you consider it," Engel said carefully. "You wouldn't have to do much except to stay close to Felix and keep your eyes and ears open for us. I'll understand if you decline. I never thought I'd be in this position, Julian. We are artists. The only laws we know are those of nature. But now we are left with no choice. We have to protect our art before those savages destroy it."

"Just to help you along with your decision," Kruger added, "we thought you should attend a lecture next week given by Professor Friedrich Fricke at the Academy of Fine Arts. He is working hand-in-hand with Baron Von Bredow. Hear him speak on his favorite topic, 'Art and Race,' and then give us your final answer."

"That's all you have to do," Engel said slowly. "Go and listen. But no matter what you decide, Julian, no one is to know about this." Engel's tone was unyielding. He had never sounded like that before. "Everything must continue as if this meeting never took place. I must have your word."

Julian walked toward the bar, dragging his feet. He could feel their eyes watching him. He turned and saw Ernst Engel and Max Kruger for what they really were: two great artists, two desperate men.

Chapter Twelve

BERLIN

The assembly of students at Berlin's Academy of Fine Arts quieted down as a heavily-guarded man was led up to the podium.

"Today we have a special guest," announced the speaker, his voice resounding throughout the auditorium. "Renowned art professor Dr. Friedrich Fricke, who chairs the German Renaissance Department at the Academy, is considered one of our nation's finest painters. Professor Fricke will be leaving us to serve as the head of the painting, sculpture, and graphics division of the Reich's Chamber of Culture. Our esteemed colleague will oversee everyone connected with the arts, and will work to eliminate those artistic styles that do not conform to the Reich's ideals. A great honor for this institution."

The last bit earned a loud round of applause. Julian squirmed in his chair.

"Without further ado, please welcome Professor Friedrich Fricke."

Fricke, accompanied by two of his four bodyguards, stepped up to the microphone. He was around forty years old, wiry, with close-cropped dark hair and tiny round spectacles. He wore a gold swastika on the lapel of his dark suit. He stood in silence until the long applause died down, eyeing the hundreds of students with approval.

"Today, my friends, I will speak about degeneracy in art," he began curtly. "There is no question that we Germans are a superior race. But there are those among us who intend to bring us down. Scores of warped artists, writers, philosophers, and actors have infiltrated the Academy and other universities throughout the country, calling themselves educators. I have taken it upon myself, with great support, to lead the nation's campaign to remove these destructive forces."

More applause. Julian glanced at the pretty girl clapping next to him. She was wrapping strands of her long blonde hair around her finger. Her full lips were parted in awe.

"Look around," Fricke said, making a panoramic sweep of the room. "You are the new generation, the nation's elite. They, by disguising their distorted ideas under the rubric 'avant-garde,' are corrupting the Fatherland. Our beloved Germany is being lost to Jews, Bolsheviks, degenerate artists, and immoral writers. It is up to us, together, to put an end to this travesty and take back our country." He signaled to a young man sitting in the first row. "Allow me to present you with an example."

On cue, the student handed Fricke three large posters. Fricke smiled at him. The students struggled to obtain a better view, but Fricke held the posters tightly against his body.

"First, a bit of history," he said. "It all began and ended with the Versailles Treaty of 1919, when we, the citizenry of Deutschland, were exacted the harshest penalties of any country in history. Who among us can forget? The international community rejoiced in our downfall. They celebrated until we believed them, until collective guilt became our national symbol. This enabled the degenerates of today to prosper from our pain and to modernize—bastardize—what was still good and pure."

Fricke, still holding the posters, walked around the podium and stood at the edge of the stage, shouting, "With what are we left? The likes of Kirchner, who has the audacity to call himself an artist, instead of the great Cranach? What happened to the appreciation of our Masters—Holbein, Baldung, Dürer? Impostors who call themselves artists buried them. Expressionist murderers!"

The crowd whistled, and Fricke continued to shout over their calls: "Corrupting our culture with their elitist poison. But we will not allow them the pleasure, will we?" Fricke was perspiring profusely. "Repeat after me: We will not allow them the pleasure!"

Fricke broke into a wide smile as the students stomped their feet while parroting back his words.

"He is magnificent," the girl next to Julian beamed at her friend.

"Pieces of filth like these I have in my hands," Fricke indicated to the posters which he still had not revealed, "should not, will not, be tolerated." As he cleared his throat, the student lackey in the front row ran up to the stage with a glass of water. Fricke drank the water and continued. "Look at these images, my friends. Study them hard."

Slowly turning the posters toward the audience, Fricke revealed enlarged photographs of a Mongoloid child, a man with one eye, and a partially bald woman with a deranged expression.

He snapped his fingers. Immediately, the same student brought forth a series of contemporary paintings by local artists. Fricke and the boy placed each abstract depiction next to a poster of the deformed. A buzz broke out among the audience.

"These so-called artists use diseased and genetically degenerate examples of mankind as models of their physical ideal," Fricke continued. "I ask you: Is this what Germany has come to? I believe that, with your help, we can eradicate the inferior elements infecting our people, not celebrate them through artistic perversion."

His voice echoed throughout the assembly hall. The students stood on their chairs and cheered. Julian closed his eyes and listened to the vibrations as they struck his ears. At first he felt nothing, as if caught in the quiet space of an ocean just before the waves crashed; then he was swallowed in an undertow. Suddenly, he was gasping for air.

Pulling himself together, Julian looked up as Fricke bowed. Fricke snapped his fingers and the bodyguards seated behind him immediately jumped up and led him off the stage, toward the nearest exit. The applause heightened as Fricke walked down the aisle like a celebrity, shaking hands with students reaching out to touch him.

Julian sat in his chair, stunned by what he had just seen and heard. Engel was right. The Nazis were engaging in an all-out campaign against artists, and they cleverly knew exactly how to do it: Get the young generation on board, believing their lies and fighting their cause, and then the chips would fall naturally into place. Julian met the mesmerized gaze of the lovely girl next to him, and made a split-second decision to follow Friedrich Fricke out of the hall.

Lowering his hat to cover his face, Julian maintained a good distance behind Fricke and his entourage who were walking down the street less than a block ahead of him. They stopped in front of an expensive-looking restaurant with a gold awning, sleek double mahogany doors, and three imposing doormen. Julian also stopped where he was, lit a cigarette, and tried to appear as though he were mingling with a group of nearby students.

Fricke nodded at his bodyguards, who waited by the door as he entered the restaurant alone. Julian lingered a few minutes, then gathered his nerve and walked slowly past the restaurant's street-side window, peering inside.

He froze. Waiting for Fricke at the center table, with outstretched arms, was Felix. He watched Fricke walk straight into Felix's open embrace. Julian was stunned. He yearned to storm the restaurant and demand an explanation from his friend. But, from the corner of his eye, he glimpsed a guard's suspicious glare and willed his body to move forward. Walking without thinking, without turning around, Julian headed quickly toward the nearest alley. He kept a steady, unassuming pace until he was certain that the area was deserted. Then he gathered up his strength and ran.

In the distance, he spotted a crumbling shed jammed with large rusty garbage bins and occupied by a noisy band of stray cats. He advanced toward it, shoving his way past the debris, then crouched in the far corner of the shed between two smaller cans. He needed to hide, needed to think. *Goddamn it. Felix* was *one of them.*

Engel and Kruger must have known exactly where Fricke would be headed after that vile speech. And they must have predicted how Julian would react. It was one thing to see a Nazi like Fricke spew his venom, but Felix? Julian curled up and wrapped his arms around himself. He needed to get out of Berlin. To leave now. To take René and return to Paris. To let someone else do Engel's dirty work.

But after listening to Fricke, how could he just walk away? Engel's voice reverberated inside his head: *How far would you go for your art, Julian? How far would you go to save the art of others?*

How far would I go? Who the hell am I to save Germany's artists? And yet, Engel, the artist had showed him how to paint, how to see and feel color, how to believe he could somehow make a difference. Julian, the Jew who gave up his religion for art, was now being chosen for something bigger.

The cats, clearly disturbed by Julian's presence, formed a scraggly defensive line in front of him. He concentrated on the night's shadows darting along the far wall. Felix's silhouette seemed to emerge from one of them.

Closing his eyes, Julian recalled the old Felix welcoming him with open arms into his Paris apartment, stuffing money into his hands without ever asking for it to be returned. That Felix would always buy doubles of everything—paint, shaving cream, milk—just so Julian would not have to go wanting. That Felix never wore a suit and laughed boisterously as he spun tales of his womanizing, both real and feigned. They laughed together, they bonded, they drank, and they painted.

What about that *Felix?* Julian demanded of the shadow.

Closing his eyes, he pictured the Other Felix tantalizing René with the opportunity of working with Ernst Engel. He saw the triumphant look on Felix's face after René had taken the bait. And now, there was the firm wrap of Felix's arms as he embraced Fricke in the restaurant: matching smug smiles, shared conceit. This new Felix was toasting the demise of modern art, and Julian could practically hear the loud clink of Felix's raised glass next to Fricke's. Julian wanted to ignore the menacing shadows and to go on as before, but he realized he could not. Opening his eyes wide, like shutterless windows, he knew what he had to do.

Hours passed before Julian left the shed. Then, stretching his arms high overhead, he squinted into the dusky obscurity. Tones of brown, gray, and olive green.

No stars. No moon. Just murk.

Chapter Thirteen

THE GRUNEWALD FOREST

Charlotte opened the picnic basket slowly, then smoothed her long floral skirt around her ankles. The lake sparkled behind her as the sunlight hit its glassy azure surface. Julian noticed that the color of the lake matched her loose-fitting blouse almost too perfectly. She set the platter of sliced veal loaf, smoked turkey, and liver pâté on the blanket. She smiled knowingly at Felix as she placed a bottle of Bordeaux in front of him. But he looked away, sullen and detached. They hadn't seen him in weeks.

René stretched out his legs alongside Julian's. "Glad you finally joined us, Felix. Your father has been keeping you much too busy."

"Engel is constantly asking when you're going to come out to the house," Julian added carefully.

"I'll bet," Felix said, staring out at the lake, not looking at any of them.

"We've missed you, Felix," Charlotte added softly, leaning over and touching the top of his hand.

Felix pushed her hand away and stood. "Let's not pretend here, okay? We all know things have changed."

Julian thought Felix looked like hell. His eyes were bloodshot, and his face was swollen from drinking. "You look overworked, like you could use a little break," Julian told him.

"You have no idea how hard I am working or what I am working on, for that matter," Felix countered.

Julian sat up, seizing the opportunity. "Every time I've asked, you change the subject. Why don't you talk to us?"

"You want to talk?" Felix leaned over and grabbed the bottle of Bordeaux, waving it angrily. "My brother Hans is dying. My mother has already made the funeral arrangements. I heard her ask Hans the other day if he prefers a mahogany or an ebony casket."

Felix closed in on Julian, casting a cold shadow over him. "I have not picked up a paintbrush in months," he said. "And you know what? I don't even miss it."

That's because you have been too busy dining with Nazis, figuring out ways to destroy art, you asshole. Julian looked away quickly, hoping Felix couldn't read his mind.

"What is happening to you?" René asked, exchanging a worried glance with Julian.

Felix laughed. "My father tells anyone who will listen that 'Felix has finally grown up.' Imagine that, the old bastard is actually proud of me."

"What exactly is he proud of?" Julian tried to sound natural.

"Put it this way, he certainly wouldn't be proud of this little get-together." Felix waved the opened Bordeaux threateningly, not caring that he was spilling the remaining alcohol onto the blanket. "Picnicking in the country like a bunch of dandies. Do you have any clue as to what is happening outside of Engel's domain, beyond your sheltered little world? Want some inside information? Artists are first on the Reich's hit list. It intends to stop you from poisoning the country with your ideas. And you, the Jewish artists, will be hit twice as hard."

"Poisoning the country?" René shook his head with disgust. "You should definitely slow down on the drinking."

"And you, René, are oblivious as usual. *They* think because of my so-called extensive art background that I can help them." Felix began to perspire.

"Who are *they*?" Julian asked, trying not to sound pushy.

"Shut up, Julian. *They* are my father and his merry band of co-conspirators. Who else?" Felix slurred. "All I can tell you is that *they* want me to be part of 'The Big Plan.'" He laughed scornfully, and then opened a second bottle. He was drunk, obviously having been drinking prior to their gathering at the lake. "Hans is useless, a walking dead man. So my father has decided that I am to be groomed for Von Bredowhood."

"Then why are you here with us today?" Charlotte asked quietly, as though knowing anything she said could set him off.

He turned to her. "You mean, why am I cavorting with two Jews and a prostitute?"

"Take it back now!" René shouted. "Apologize to her."

Felix eyed them with contempt. "You had better get used to it. That is exactly how you are going to be perceived from now on." Felix swigged some more wine and stood over Julian. "Don't take it personally, Julian-gelo, but I came here today not because you begged me to, but because I wanted to paint with René. One last hurrah."

Julian tried to just let Felix talk, knowing that he wouldn't shut up the more drunk he became. "Just like old times." Julian couldn't help himself.

"Old times?" Felix scoffed. "Wake up, Julian! These are new times. New fucking times. Get used to it."

"You're stinking drunk, Felix," René said angrily. "You don't even know what the hell you're saying."

"I am most sane when I'm drinking, you all know that." He reached over to Charlotte and ran his hand seductively along her exposed shoulder. "I don't have a lot of time here. Take off that ridiculous hat and your provincial costume. Pose for us. Get naked. You do that so well."

René stood and grabbed Felix by the collar. "Goddamn you!"

Felix laughed and pushed René's hands off of him. "Can't take a joke? If we are unable to laugh at ourselves, then who are we?" He paused, as if waiting for one of them to deliver the punch line. "Our fathers! Didn't you tell me that on numerous occasions, René?"

Julian jumped in before he lost his opportunity. "You used to call your father an arrogant fool, and now you are following his orders like that half-dead butler. Why?"

"Why, Julian?" Felix's eyes were blazing. "I don't have to answer that. I am not interested in your adolescent philosophies."

"What philosophies are you interested in?" Julian pushed.

"Nothing you have to offer," Felix countered, as saliva dripped out from the corner of his mouth. "Here's what I do know. My father—"

Julian leaned forward, but René cut Felix off. "Leave Julian and Charlotte alone, you bastard." René's voice was hard but controlled, using a steely tone that Julian had never heard him use before. "Your problem is with me, Felix. You want to paint? So, let's paint." He turned apologetically to Julian. "Felix wants his last hurrah. Well, I'm going to give it to him good."

Felix looked momentarily taken aback by René's aggressiveness. René ignored him, grabbed two easels from the bag and pulled out a set of oils from a leather satchel, then tossed the bag back at Felix, who quickly took what he needed. They stood silently in front of each other with their sable brushes gripped rigidly at their sides, their gazes locked intensely. Several unbearable minutes passed between them, then René turned to his canvas. The duel had begun.

"Charlotte," René said tenderly. "Go stand by the water, near that rock over there, and pose for us."

Charlotte, her eyes never veering from either man, removed her hat and walked toward a large rock about ten feet from the shoreline. She sat down, focusing on the water, as though seeing something in it that only she knew existed. And then she began to unbutton her blouse.

Julian walked around his friends, not quite knowing what to do as they immersed themselves in their work. A small part of him felt badly that they had left him out of the last hurrah. Finally he sat back down on the blanket and watched as bullets of paint showered the air, the painters' clothes, and the surrounding tall grass. Their brushes slapped brutally against the canvases.

"She is beautiful," Felix commented.

"More than you know," René retaliated.

"Oh, I will know."

"What the hell is that supposed to mean?" René demanded.

"It can mean any damn thing you want it to."

There was no more discussion.

After four hours of playing audience, polishing off the picnic meat and nearly the entire blueberry pie, Julian knew that the competition was finally over. René and Felix had stopped painting almost simultaneously. Their faces were dripping with sweat. Their bodies were soaked with paint as they faced each other and crossed an imaginary line to inspect the other's work. Julian joined them, but neither seemed to notice his presence.

Within seconds, it was clear who had won. Felix's painting was laughable. His brushwork was childish. Charlotte was not a woman, rather a collage of oversized sexual organs. Her breasts dominated the canvas like two beige mountains. There was nothing left to the imagination, nothing to make a viewer think or feel. His painting was an infatuated schoolboy's doodle.

In contrast, René's oil painting was abstract and minimalist, the fine lines of color immediately evoked the bare image of woman against water, each blending into the other. Woman was water; water flowed into woman. Her raw beauty competed with nature's, yet on René's canvas, both were victorious.

Julian stared at Felix's and René's works and couldn't help but think that there was a different kind of division between the two; not of men but of talent—the have and the have-not—equally dangerous.

Felix, red-cheeked and silent, stormed away from the paintings and stood at the shoreline, near Charlotte but not looking at her. He then walked over to the tree by the picnic basket and pulled out a stylus from the bag and proceeded back toward the easels. He stood near René's painting, enraged. His eyes glistened as he raised the instrument high over his head and stabbed the canvas right through its center.

Charlotte screamed, and René stood motionless. Julian ran toward Felix to stop him, but Felix turned the instrument on him. Julian stood back, overcome by Felix's rage, and watched helplessly as Felix mutilated René's painting.

Felix turned to look at them all, resting his gaze on each face before him as though for the very last time. No one moved. Tears streamed down his face. Dropping the stylus onto the picnic blanket, Felix picked up his painting, the bottle of Bordeaux, and walked away.

Julian watched Felix's back until he dissipated into the forest, a black dot melding into the white birch. He observed the shreds of colored canvas that Felix had destroyed blowing swiftly toward the water until nothing remained of René's painting but an empty frame, through which Julian could see only Charlotte and the lake.

Chapter Fourteen

KREUZBERG

The outdoor café's tables were packed, and Julian was the only one sitting alone, except for an old piano player in the corner who seemed to be deeply immersed in his ivory world.

To his left, Julian noticed an attractive young redhead surrounded by three young men about his age. The woman said something that made them all laugh, throwing her head back flirtatiously, providing a moment of visibility into her low-cut blouse as she basked in their undivided attention. The confident way she carried herself immediately reminded him of Adrienne. Looking away, he wondered how she was, with whom she was laughing. He tried to push that night in Paris out of his mind, but he could not forget her scent, the taste of her, the way her velvety body slid over him, and hours later, how her strong hands had pulled him on top of her once again.

Squirming in his chair, Julian wished that the sunlight beating against his back were the heat from Adrienne's fireplace. He picked at the top layer of his chocolate cream cake. He checked his watch again. Felix was supposed to have arrived nearly forty minutes ago. Julian decided to give him another half hour. Busying himself with the newspaper, he repeatedly peered over the top of it until he felt a jab at his back. He turned and met Felix's icy blue stare.

"Just orange juice today, and coffee," Felix told the waitress as he sat down.

"What, no wine?" Julian ventured with a half smile, noticing Felix's tailored charcoal suit, starched white shirt, and navy blue tie with small white polka dots. His initials, FVB, were embroidered in royal blue on his shirt cuff. His hair was trimmed neatly, and he was clean-shaven. Felix looked like a different person from the madman at the lake the previous weekend; sober and business-like.

"I have a meeting this afternoon," Felix said firmly, playing with the tip of his tie. He glanced at Julian's plate, then called back the waitress and ordered the same cake. "I've got twenty minutes, Julian. What is so important that we had to meet?"

Julian took a deep breath, wondering how this would play out. "I'm very sorry about what happened at the lake," he said quietly.

Felix did not look at him. Instead, he focused on the redhead. She met his gaze, eyed the fancy suit, and lifted her chin invitingly, exposing her long freckled neck. Felix paused, raising his glass toward the woman. "Things just got out of hand, Julian."

"You got out of hand," Julian corrected him. "But that's not why I'm sorry. I realized after what happened there that our friendship is over. I asked you to come here so I could apologize once again for what a schmuck I was in Paris. I know that ruined things between us. It killed me not to have been honest with you." Julian took a slow bite of cake, allowing Felix time to digest his words.

"And your point is?"

"My point is that I'm leaving Germany. I called you here to say good-bye." Julian felt slightly off-balance at the thought of his imminent lies. "I have had enough of Ernst Engel and his flighty ideas. I am sick of his re-petitive lectures on color and spirituality, his flamboyance. Even Dubois gave me less of a headache. I am going back to New York, to do some real painting and to concentrate on art that actually matters."

Felix smiled slightly. "Like surreal baseball fields?"

Julian blushed at the comment but let it pass. "Something like that. Anything to get away from all the politics here." Julian watched Felix's face closely, but his expression betrayed nothing. Julian's feet began to feel hot and swollen inside his shoes. He would have to pull out the only card he possessed to somehow get through to Felix. "The truth is, I am sick of René's ego too. He is obsessed with the upcoming exhibition Engel is arranging for him. It's a good time for me to break away from all of it."

"What exhibition?" Felix slammed down his glass, and orange juice spilled over his fingers. He did not bother wiping his hand.

"Engel has not finalized the details, but it's some annual exhibition in Berlin where a new artist's work is showcased. Of course, they chose René. But you don't want to hear about this, Felix. You'll be late for your meeting." Julian stood, swiping crumbs off his trousers. "It is time to chalk up this adventure for what it was—just an adventure. All I want to do now is concentrate on *my* work. Enough distractions." Julian extended his hand, but Felix ignored it. "So, goodbye, Felix. I wish you well."

Tossing some change on the table, Julian left the café without looking back. His heart pounded as he crossed the street. His shirt felt wet against his back as he counted slowly to ten. On the count of eight, Julian felt the bulky hand grip his shoulder.

"Wait," Felix whispered from behind.

Three hours later, Julian entered a dank basement in a rundown building in the Wilmersdorf district of Berlin. As instructed by Engel, he did not turn on the light, nor did he say a word as he climbed down the creaking stairs. But the distinctive smell of Engel's potent cologne, like turpentine mixed with fruit salad, reassured him that his mentor was waiting for him at the bottom.

"Down here, Julian," Engel called out in loud whisper. "Watch your head."

Julian ducked, just missing an overhanging beam. When he reached the foot of the stairs, Engel grabbed his hand and pulled him toward his barrel chest, then turned on a light. "Tell me everything."

"Well, I did what you said, Ernst, and started out by trying to get our friendship back on track. It didn't seem to faze him." Julian took a few steps backward and relayed his conversation with Felix at the café. "Only when I mentioned René's name in the same sentence as the exhibition did I get his attention. Felix skipped his meeting, of course. He wanted to know everything about the exhibition, but he didn't want to seem too obvious. Until we started drinking, and then—"

"Did Felix bring up anything specific about his father's activities?" Engel interrupted.

"Not at first, and I thought it best not to push it, not to sound too interested in the work he was doing. I tried to keep the focus on our friendship. He asked me not to leave Germany—to stay on for a few more months and to continue painting with you until he wrapped up things with his father, and then we'd all go back to Paris together." Julian paused. "Of course he's lying. He has changed. I don't think he intends to go back to Paris ever. I can't quite figure out why it matters to him whether *I* stay or go. But I went along with it, agreeing to stay on the condition that he and I spend more time together, to repair things between us." Julian drew in a heavy breath. "I did this for you, Ernst. None of it feels right."

"Thank you, Julian."

Julian squeezed his instructor's hands, feeling the calloused, experienced fingertips, hard as seashells. "What worried me about our conversation is the more Felix drank, the more he ranted on about you and how the avant-garde has seen the end of its glory days. Felix didn't come out and say it, but he hinted that you and your friends are being watched closely. I think you should leave the country, Ernst. Get your family out while there is still time."

Engel sighed and his heavy breath smelled slightly of vinegar. "That is impossible. And they will only find someone else, another scapegoat. If we know they are following me, then at least we can manipulate them."

Julian shook his head. "What is not clear is why Felix wants you in particular. Why not Kruger or any of your other colleagues? He just kept talking about you." Julian studied Engel's face. His instructor's eyes were wide and unblinking, and he rubbed his lips together unnaturally.

Engel cleared his throat, and the loud disjointed sound resonated through the room. "About six years ago, Helen Von Bredow—Felix's mother—came to my studio. You know, there was a time when we were quite good friends. She had a penchant for modern art and she purchased fantastic pieces from all over Europe, keeping them hidden in her basement. Her husband forbade her from hanging any modern artwork in their home. Many times she called me for advice on not only which paintings to buy, but also to discuss her frustration with her husband's disdain for anything avant-garde."

He gazed down at his shuffling feet. "Her visit that day was unexpected, and I was under pressure for an upcoming exhibition. I was sleeping at the studio. I hadn't even seen my family for over a week. Anyway, Helen walked in unannounced, carrying a stack of paintings—Felix's work. She wanted me to critique them. I had no time, of course, but I would never refuse her. They were pathetic, Julian. A poor imitation of various artists."

Engel squeezed the back of his neck, as if to alleviate some tension. "I should have been diplomatic and advised Helen to encourage Felix to continue painting despite his obvious lack of talent. But I wasn't thinking. I told Helen the truth. I thought we were friends, that she could handle it, that she understood art. She just looked at me as if I had insulted her and walked out. I tried to get in touch with her, but she refused my calls and my letters. I heard that Felix left for Paris soon after.

"Then, several months ago, Felix called and asked if his two friends—students of Léon Dubois—could study with me for a few months, and if I was looking for a model. There was no sign of any bad blood. He sounded poised, mature, and friendly."

Julian interjected, "I'm sure he slipped in that one of the students happened to be Jacob Levi's son."

Engel smiled sadly. "Jacob Levi. You should know that it was rumored in certain circles that Helen Von Bredow was once his lover."

Julian nodded, remembering René's snide comment in Jacob's gallery about his father and Helen Von Bredow. He looked again at Engel. The sinister room seemed to magnify the contours of Engel's face, as though his features had lost all color.

"I said yes to Felix without hesitation," Engel continued. "Mostly out of guilt for what had happened with Helen."

Julian thought back to the conversation he'd had with Felix in their apartment, about him not having the natural talent to be a painter. Engel's rejection must have been just one of many that followed him to Paris.

"But no matter if he has real talent or not, Felix is a painter, and we have all had our share of rejections. That is normal," Engel said.

Julian shrugged. "I think Felix has been told by everyone that his paintings are not very good. René's work, on the other hand, has had the opposite impact on everyone who has rejected Felix." Julian paced the dusty cement floor then stared at the peeling walls. "What put Felix in my pocket today was not my apology, nor my agreeing to stay on and wait for him, but only when I mentioned René's exhibition."

"What exactly did he want to know?" Engel moved in closer, his voice suddenly sounding like an interrogator's.

"Who is sponsoring it, who is being invited, names. Felix kept pushing me even after I told him I didn't have any information. He got crazy. I don't know, Ernst. I think the exhibition is a mistake. You should cancel it."

Engel shook his head. "It has been an annual event here for the past fifteen years. I am not going to cancel it."

"It doesn't make sense," Julian said. "Why would you have this exhibition at all? Who cares if it has been going on for a hundred years? Right now, this type of event is begging for trouble."

Engel looked away. "Trust me, okay?"

"Then whatever you are planning, leave René out of it."

Engel shook his head innocently, as if that part of the plan could not be helped.

Julian pressed on, the reality of the situation becoming all too clear. "You and I both know how Felix feels about René. Jealousy is one thing. But for Felix, René is an obsession. I never really saw it before I came to Berlin, but René hinted at it when we were in Paris." He paused. "And the more I think about it, Felix does not give a damn about this Nazi art business. It's René's talent that he fears, that he hates. And now Felix is in a position to do something about it." He searched Engel's face for understanding but came up with nothing. Engel was silent.

Julian raised his voice. "We have to protect René and not put him out on a platter. Isn't that why I am here in the first place—to help safeguard the works of young artists like myself, like René? Or am I just caught in the middle of everyone's bullshit, Ernst? Tell me!"

Engel grabbed Julian by the shoulders. "René is French. His father is one of the most important art dealers in Europe. No one is stupid enough to touch him. The powers-that-be are expecting us to hold the annual exhibition, so we need to keep everything going on as usual. There is more danger if we cancel it."

Engel looked around the empty basement, then lowered his voice to a whisper. "I'm not naive, Julian. I know it's risky, but we have no choice. You see, that night, while the artists, my friends, are attending René's exhibition, their paintings—many important paintings—are going to be smuggled out of the country to safety, to friends in Paris and Spain. That is Max Kruger's end of it. The exhibition is merely camouflage. We believe that Von Bredow and friends have big plans for us not too far down the road, so we have to be one step ahead of them and act now. Let them monitor us at the exhibition. Let them try and scare us. They will never think that we are capable of outsmarting them, saving our paintings before they have a chance to destroy them."

Julian shook his head in disbelief. "I see. The goal is to save the art, but not the artist?"

"It is the art that matters to all of us. We come and go, but our art lives on." Engel's eyes welled up with tears. "These are madmen. Remember, Hitler is an artist, Julian. And like Felix, Hitler is a man obsessed with the desire to paint, but possesses no natural talent. Hitler's suffering is going to be the death of us."

Julian leaned unsteadily against a broken chair. "So, René is the sacrifice?"

Engel's eyebrows arched so high that they nearly met his hairline. "No, René is the diversion. But if it makes you feel better, I will tell him. I will give René the choice to exhibit and help us, or to pack up his supplies and run away."

Engel moved in so close that Julian could practically taste the sourness of his breath. "But that is all I will tell him. The rest has to remain between us."

Chapter Fifteen

THE GRUNEWALD FOREST

The bedsprings in René and Charlotte's room recoiled loudly like aching joints and could be heard throughout Engel's house. Julian punched his pillow against the headboard, sat up, and glanced at the clock on the nightstand. Nearly 2 AM. Fifteen minutes later than usual. He anticipated the forty bounces, three to four flip-flops interspersed with dirty French phrases, and the culminating screams of ecstasy. He could visualize their nightly acrobatics as though they were both lying in his bed with him.

Once the springs sprung into action, Julian sat up and stared at the wall, wondering if Engel, sleeping down the hall, could hear them as well. Their performance reminded Julian of how lonely he was, and how much he craved a warm body next to him. *Adrienne's body.*

"Why did you stop me?" Julian heard René ask Charlotte a few minutes later. "You are upset about something, aren't you?"

Julian pressed his ear against the wall.

"You keep mumbling Adrienne's name in your sleep."

Julian grabbed a pack of cigarettes from under the bed and lit one. So, he and René were both fantasizing about Adrienne. The warm smoke over his face began to cloud her image.

"I didn't know," René said softly. "Charlotte, I am so sorry."

"How can I ever compete with her?"

"There is no competition," René said. "Any feelings I once had for Adrienne are gone."

"But you were going to marry her."

"I chose you," René said firmly.

Julian heard nothing for a few seconds, just their heavy breathing and the shuffling of sheets.

"Don't touch me."

"Look, Charlotte, you are overreacting about nothing." René sounded angry.

"Go to hell!" she shouted.

"I am not going anywhere. You know damn well I came to Berlin for us," René retorted. "I knew it was important to get away from Paris and let the situation cool off with Adrienne so that we could be together without any pressure."

"Please, René, I'm not stupid. You came here to work with Ernst Engel."

"You're wrong."

"You can tell yourself that if it makes you feel better," Charlotte said coldly. "But Felix, crazy as he may be, is absolutely right. No one can compete with your work."

"You're wrong," he repeated.

"I want to leave this evil place, René, and go somewhere else. Anywhere else."

"Then let's do it. We'll leave after my exhibition."

"It is always after your exhibition," Charlotte complained. "All because Engel wants to show you off to his friends like a prized terrier."

"If you have not realized it yet, I am a painter and exhibitions are the only way to gain recognition," René argued. "Do you have any idea what this means to me, Charlotte? Engel's friends are important artists. And he is showing them *my* work. The Ferrat exhibition was minor compared to this."

Neither said anything. Julian heard René's voice soften. "After this show, I promise we will get out of here. But for now, you have got to understand and support me."

"What if I want to leave today?" she pleaded. "What if I say to hell with your exhibition and put me first? See, it's not just the ghost of Adrienne that gets between us. It's your work, René. You don't need me."

"What are you saying?"

"Why not just rub yourself against your paintings—what's the difference?"

Julian held his breath. He knew Charlotte had pushed René too far.

"That is just the cheap kind of thing you would say." René's voice was heated yet even, like a long growl.

"Now you are calling me cheap? I'm glad your true feelings finally came out. You are embarrassed by what I do, aren't you? You can't handle the fact that I model. And that men—many men—stare at my body and paint me," she taunted. "I am cheap in your mind because I am an art piece, an object."

"Keep your voice down, damn it! Do you want Julian to hear you?"

"I don't care who hears me," she shouted. "You know Julian can't stand me—the way he talks to me without ever looking me in the eye, like I'm not good enough. And when he does look at me, I see his contempt—he believes I stole you away from the perfect Adrienne." Her voice escalated, becoming shrill. "Well, I am not Adrienne, an artist—talented and ambitious like her. But I am so much more than she could ever dream of being. You just don't know it yet."

Julian pictured Charlotte standing next to the bed, her firm breasts erect, her dark pink nipples swollen with her anger.

"Unlike you," she continued, "I have had to work every day of my life to survive. You have had the luxury to do whatever you want. I don't have a rich father who fills my bank account every time it empties. I don't even know my father."

"You, of all people, have no right to discuss my father," René shot back. "Maybe I'm the one who needs to figure things out. I'm going to sleep with Julian."

"Maybe I should sleep with Julian!" she shouted.

"I'm surprised you haven't already!"

On that note, Julian moved to the far side of his bed, away from the wall. He did not want to listen to this anymore. He reached for another cigarette when he heard the phone ring down the hall. *Who could possibly*

be calling this late? He headed out of his room to answer it, nearly collid-
ing with René, who was wrapped up in his sheets.

"Door's open." Julian gestured toward his bedroom as he lunged for
the phone. "Hello?"

It was Felix.

"Talk louder," Julian shouted into the receiver. "I can't hear you."

"Hans died this morning." Felix's voice was muffled.

"What?"

"My brother had a heart attack while riding his horse. The guy was
on his deathbed. No one knows how the hell he got on that horse."
Felix's voice faded. "The funeral is the day after tomorrow, in the afternoon, at our home. Will you come?"

"Of course," Julian said. "We will all be there."

"No." Felix paused. "Just you and Charlotte. Not René, not now.
Come to the house. Plan to stay the night with us."

"Okay," Julian responded hesitantly as he put down the phone and
walked slowly back to his room. René was sitting cross-legged on the
bed.

"Who was it?" René asked.

Julian sat next to him. "It was Felix. His brother died. Hans was riding
his horse and had a heart attack."

"When is the funeral?"

"Friday."

René breathed heavily. "I presume Felix wants us there."

Julian put his arm around René's shoulder. "He wants me and Charlotte to come, but not you."

"He hates me, Julian."

"No, he hates your art."

René's jaw was clenched as he pointed to the wall behind him. "They
both do."

Chapter Sixteen

POTSDAM

The body of Hans Von Bredow, dressed in his Sunday best, was carried past the mourners in an ebony casket. He looked so much like Felix that Julian quickly averted his eyes.

Charlotte, who was sitting next to Julian, gasped loudly, drawing attention from those around them. Ignoring the stares, she looped her black silk-covered arm through Julian's, whispering, "It could be Felix."

Nodding, Julian glanced over at Felix, who was standing next to his father in front of the grave. He caught Julian's eye and observed Charlotte standing next to him. Smiling slightly, Felix turned back toward his brother's opened casket.

As the service droned on, Julian silently counted the mourners packing the grounds of the Von Bredow estate, estimating five hundred black hats of different shapes and sizes. A trumpet sounded in the distance, and a cavalry of soldiers approached on horseback. The noon sun was strong, reflecting off the woven gold Von Bredow crests draped over the horses. The soldiers, forming a half circle on the other side of Hans's grave, reined in the horses and awaited orders.

The baron stepped out from the front row and faced his friends and family. His eyes were heavily bagged. He appeared smaller and thinner than Julian remembered, almost ordinary, wearing the raw grief of a parent about to bury his child.

"My son Hans lived and died with his beloved horses," began the baron. "We believe it fitting that he should be buried here, outside the stables that he loved so much. Helen and I—" The baron looked directly at his wife who was crying inside her hands, balanced against her daughter, whose face was hidden by an oversized black veil. Even in her sorrow, the baroness was beautiful. She was slim, elegant, and more petite than Julian had expected. Her dark hair was swept up with a diamond and gold clip. Her skin, though tear-streaked, appeared lineless. The baron bowed his head briefly, turned to the cavalry, and nodded.

Raising their rifles toward the sky, the soldiers executed a ten-minute salute as Hans was laid to rest. There was an obligatory silence among the mourners, followed by soft hymns and loud sniffles. Julian closed his eyes, trying to feel, out of obligation, some kind of grief. He knew that for Felix, his older brother had been just like his father. Hans had scolded Felix with the same reprimanding eyes, had shaken his head with the same open disappointment. They had never been close, according to Felix.

Julian glanced again at Felix, unable to read him, though his cheeks were wet. Julian's mind wandered as he looked across the rolling hills and felt the cool breeze from the lake just beyond the stables.

Suddenly, shouting erupted from somewhere in the second row. A furious crescendo of "Heil Hitler" shook the previously tranquil grounds. Julian craned his neck to see what was happening, the sun-sweetened day instantly blackened once he spotted Professor Friedrich Fricke, his face inflamed, his high-handed salute slicing through the air like a conductor's. Rows of men in black hats followed Fricke's lead, their hands raised in unison.

The hair on the back of Julian's neck rose. How could this happen at a funeral? What was he, Julian, even doing here? A Jew among Nazis. He wanted to tell Charlotte that they should leave directly after the funeral and not stay the night as was planned. But the taunt of Ernst Engel's voice stopped him: *What kind of man are you, Julian, to let a few Heil Hitlers make you run away? Every prominent Nazi will be at that funeral. It is the opportunity that we have been waiting for.*

Charlotte latched onto Julian's jacket, whispering, "Do we have to stay the night? Let's get out of here."

She was scared too.

"We came for Felix. He needs our support." Julian tried to sound convincing. "One night won't kill us. We will leave first thing in the morning."

"It may not kill you, but my head is pounding from all the shouting." She gestured toward Fricke. "Just look at their faces—like animals."

"They are calming down," Julian whispered, and couldn't help but say, "Besides, Charlotte, you should be used to it."

She looked upset. "You heard my fight with René?"

"The entire country heard it."

She gripped his arm tightly. "You don't like me, do you?"

Julian met her hard gaze. "I don't like what you have done to my friends."

"At least it opened the door for you."

Blood rushed to his face. "What are you talking about?"

She smiled knowingly. "What do you think I do when I am posing for hours? Think about the weather? I study all of you right back. I watch your movements, the way you sit, the tension on your faces, the colors you choose from your palettes." A breeze blew Charlotte's hair from her face, emphasizing the gleam in her eyes. "When you looked at Adrienne, I saw hunger in your face. While everyone was staring at me, you were painting her, weren't you?"

Julian recalled that first day when Charlotte had entered Dubois's studio. He could still see the lustful looks on René's and Felix's faces, but he'd felt nothing. She was a woman used to men falling all over her. She must have known even then.

Charlotte breathed seductively into his ear. "Don't worry, Julian. Your secret is safe with me. I just wanted to point out that I am not the only guilty one here."

A few hours later, Julian was sitting with Felix in the library. Felix handed him a brandy. He had changed from his black funeral suit into a sporty green tweed smoking jacket. He looked intently at Julian. "Thanks for bringing Charlotte. It means a lot to me."

Julian nodded, though his gaze was downcast.

"Tell me, Julian. What did René say when you told him he wasn't invited?"

Julian was not going to give Felix what he clearly wanted by telling him just how hurt René was, so instead he said, "René was upset for you and your family. He genuinely feels bad about Hans and wanted me to relay his deepest condolences."

"Ha! I bet he did." Felix took a long hard guzzle, as if the brandy were water. "Why, then, did he let Charlotte come?"

"No one tells Charlotte what to do," Julian said. "She wanted to be here."

Satisfied, Felix rose and walked over to his father's desk in the corner of the room. He began thumbing through papers on the desk, not caring that Julian was watching him. Without looking up, he said, "My father is holding a meeting here at midnight. Imagine, my brother has not even been buried twenty-four hours, and my father is using the opportunity to bring his henchmen together."

Julian tried to keep his voice steady. This is exactly what Engel had been waiting for. He had to handle this carefully. "What kind of meeting?"

"The usual fare," Felix said nonchalantly. "How they plan to take over the world."

"Take over the world?" Julian repeated.

"That was a joke, Julian."

Julian laughed quickly. "I know that," he said, trying to be casual. "So, are you going to the meeting?"

"Why do you care?" Felix walked in front of the desk, leaned against it with crossed arms, and stared at Julian.

"I don't care about the meeting." Julian hesitated. "I just wondered what kind of time we would have together tonight, that's all."

Felix eyed him suspiciously. "We're spending time together now. But for your information, unfortunately, I do have to be at the meeting."

Julian nodded, took a sip of brandy. "I see."

Felix refilled his own glass. "I don't think you do. So much is changing, Julian, and so fast. It's overwhelming actually."

Felix appeared conflicted. Julian knew that now was the time to ask questions. He walked toward the desk and said slowly, "Why didn't you ever follow anyone's orders in Paris? If someone said black, you would say white, just to be different, just for the sake of argument. And the truth of the matter is that you used to scoff at the son-of-a-baron thing, hated it actually." Julian looked at him sincerely, hoping to reach him.

"You're right, Julian. Things changed, I've changed." Felix shrugged and looked away sadly, and Julian glimpsed the old Felix. "Paris was a different world."

Julian moved in closer. "You couldn't have changed that much in a few months."

Felix did not respond. He and Julian eyed each other in an awkward silence, and then Felix walked across the room toward a small cabinet. He opened a drawer, removing two cigars from an oriental box. He offered one to Julian, who declined. Stroking the cigar's plump skin, Felix sat on the couch, kicked his feet up, and smiled. "You are missing out on a Von Bredow tradition. Straight from Cuba, grown especially for my father."

Julian shook his head in disbelief. *Von Bredow tradition?* The glimpse of the old Felix was gone. "When did you start smoking cigars? Christ, Felix, what is happening to you?"

Felix contemplated Julian, lit the cigar, and sucked hard. "Nothing is happening to me, Julian. On the contrary, I am making things happen. All my life my father saw me as an embarrassment to the family. He would tell me that I had no natural talent for anything but trouble. He never hid the fact that Hans was his favorite and my sister Isabel came second. So, I left for Paris, to get away from him and to paint. When I

came back, it took my father's colleagues to recognize that I had something to offer, that my art background could be useful."

Now they are colleagues, Julian thought angrily. *One minute ago they were
henchmen.*

"My opinion actually matters to him. I've never had that before." As
Felix spoke about his father's newfound respect, Julian looked up at the
library's ornate domed stained-glass ceiling, thinking Engel was right.
Felix had crossed over. He was one of them. There was no going back.

"You know, Julian, it's too bad that it took Hans's death for my father
and me to come to an understanding." Felix lifted the crystal decanter
next to his elbow and examined it against the light before refilling his
glass for the fourth time. "Don't get me wrong. I still see through him.
My father uses people, controls them, and I hate him. But I don't feel
mediocre anymore, second to Hans or to anyone else. That's the difference." Felix kicked off his loafers. "And listen to this—my father even
asked to see some of my paintings."

"It doesn't get better than that," Julian mustered.

"Oh, I think a few rounds with Charlotte could top it." Felix laughed,
and then stopped himself abruptly when he saw Julian's unimpressed
look. "She has got to be one of the most beautiful women alive. How
come you never wanted her?" He smiled mischievously. "In fact, while
we are on the subject, I've never even seen you with a woman other than
friends. You sure you don't like boys?"

Julian sighed deeply, annoyed. "Last time I checked, no."

Still grinning, Felix said, "Perhaps Adrienne is the only girl for you?"

Julian froze. "What are you talking about?"

"I lived with you, Julian. I saw your face whenever she looked at
René. In fact, I saw it that first day when you arrived in Paris." He
pointed his cigar at Julian. "It has been Adrienne all along, hasn't it?"

"Maybe you should slow down on your drinking," Julian said defensively, hating Felix right then. He would get whatever Engel needed, and
then be done with all of this.

"Maybe you should catch up to me." Felix smirked.

Keep drinking, Julian thought wryly, *and by the end of the night I will have all of the information I need.*

"How do you plan to help your father's friends?" Julian asked boldly.

"Back to that?" Felix rolled his eyes. "If I didn't know better, I'd ask myself why you are pressing me on things that have no bearing on you." Felix slipped his loafers on. "It has been a long day, Julian. I am going to be an absolute gentleman and say goodnight to Aphrodite, who is lying upstairs all alone in her room. Perhaps I can get a little affection for my bereaved soul. Wait here. I'll be back, and we'll spend that quality time together that you seem to want so badly." He winked sarcastically, and Julian knew that he had made a major mistake pushing Felix about the meeting.

Felix gestured toward the bar. "In the meantime, Julian, help yourself."

"Sounds like a plan," Julian said with forced lightness. Bad move. What did Engel expect anyway? He wasn't a spy. He was a painter. All this was way over his head.

Felix walked to the far corner of the room and opened a second door, which was narrow and easy to overlook because it blended into the wall paneling. A hidden door, leading to the second floor guest chambers—probably where the baron stashed a maid or two. Julian watched his friend's departure from the corner of his eye as he refilled his glass.

Julian yearned to scour the room, to open every drawer, and to read through those papers that Felix had left spread across the desk so carelessly—purposely, perhaps? Julian restrained himself. Felix was not stupid. What if it was some kind of trap, leaving him in the library alone? What if the baron walked in? Julian buttoned up his jacket, deciding he had better sit on the couch and wait for Felix to return. But as he walked toward the couch, something stronger seemed to pull him toward the hidden door. He tiptoed over and pressed his ear against it. The acoustics were so good that Julian heard Felix climbing the stairs. He could even make out Charlotte's voice as she answered the knock at her door, and Felix's footsteps as he entered her room.

Chapter Seventeen

The wall clock in the Von Bredow guest room was about to strike midnight. Julian sat on the edge of the bed watching the clock through the flimsy gauze of the canopy. He pictured Felix, the baron, Fricke, and a cast of Nazis entering the library below his feet, finding their places, pouring drinks, and getting the meeting started.

He imagined how he would paint them. The canvas would be enormous—perhaps the size of an entire wall—and their dark-suited figures filing into the room would be done in shadowy tones. The baron would stand out from the others, his sepia suit the same burnished brown as the antique leather-bound books behind his desk. Torch lights would surround the men, providing just enough lighting to illuminate the conspiracy about to take place. It would be a kind of chiaroscuro, a bold contrast between light and dark, a technique mastered by Leonardo da Vinci.

He eyed the large bed. The crisp beige sheets surrounded him like a barren desert. The small mahogany nightstands on either side were draped with doilies. He got up and opened one of the stand's four narrow drawers: empty and dustless. No smell at all. The room was sterile, devoid of personal touches. Turning around, Julian faced the lone small portrait of a pointy-bearded, pallid fellow hanging on the wall. Like the room, the image was cold, stark, and unapproachable.

Returning to the edge of the bed, Julian picked up his wool slippers, wondering who had slept in this bed before him. No one important, he presumed. Perhaps no one at all. He glanced again at the clock.

Three more minutes.

He walked anxiously over to the small, gilt-framed mirror hanging over the nightstand and examined his face: same thick eyebrows, same green eyes sparkling innocently beneath them—as if those eyes were still innocent. Julian moved in closer. Something was not right.

His mouth seemed different.

He began stretching his lips, pulling them in opposite directions. They were curiously swollen, bursting with secrets. *Surely they will give me away.* The cold, sallow-looking fellow in the portrait seemed to be watching him with bitter suspicion, questioning his integrity: a friend who was not a friend; a painter without a palette; an artist turned spy.

He looked away from the mirror and glanced up at the clock. *No time to think about right or wrong. This is it. Go.*

Slowly opening the door, Julian scanned the empty hallway and tip-toed toward Charlotte's room. He leaned against her door and heard her soft, steady breathing inside. He eyed the staircase leading to the library. If he were caught, he would apologize profusely for interrupting the meeting, pretending to be sick, saying that he needed to speak to Felix urgently. The excuse was weak but was the best he could do.

Walking down to the third stair from the bottom, Julian held his slippers against his chest, eyeing the hidden door in front of him, and waited for the meeting to begin.

The baron's voice boomed with unquestionable authority, and Julian could hear everything perfectly. Gone was the baron's melancholic tone, the mawkish grief he had displayed that afternoon.

"Hartt," began the baron, "you will compile the lists of artists whose work we will confiscate and the museum directors who refuse to coop-erate with us. They must be dismissed from their positions immediately. Start with Berlin's Nationalgalerie, particularly the Kronprinzenpalais—it should be purged of all its modern art. Dismiss everyone who works there, effective immediately. Then go to Essen's Folkwang Museum. That should get things moving. And educational institutions, of course, start with Bauhaus. Then move on to the Berlin Academy of Fine Arts. Any director, curator, dean, or professor who refuses to toe the Party line must be removed."

"These lists are crucial, Hartt," Friedrich Fricke chimed in. Julian recognized the condescending tone immediately and suddenly the empty stairwell grew colder. "We are planning a series of major exhibitions throughout Germany that will showcase Reich art in its glory. We intend to teach the public what is and what is not acceptable under the Reich. Above all, there is to be no compensation for confiscation of any modern artwork." Something, probably a glass, was slammed down. "That is the official policy."

"Thank you for your enthusiasm, Friedrich. If I may continue," the baron said with a dry cough. "Hartt, I want an extremely knowledgeable team assembled. I will give you names and references. This team, under your direction, will undertake the enormous task of selection. I expect a full-scale plan on my desk at the end of this month. Do you see any difficulty in this?"

"None."

"Good. Streibel," the baron continued, his authoritative tone seeming to travel around the room, "you are in charge of the confiscation of this trash. Using Hartt's list, your team will find those degenerate artists who attempt to escape Germany with their paintings and expose those who are painting or sculpting illegally."

"I suggest we target the supply stores as well," Streibel interrupted.

"If you would let me finish." The baron paused and Julian pictured his feral face, the pierce of his glare, and the annoyance in his voice. "I want every art supply store threatened—they are not to sell to degenerate artists. An official list of the banned artists will be distributed throughout the country. Everyone must be registered with us, licensed to sell, licensed to paint. If someone is caught helping outlawed artists—no excuses—there will be immediate arrests. Make a few highly publicized examples so the threat is clear."

Silence followed, the baron's point sinking in.

"Exactly how far can we go?" Streibel piped up.

"Far enough," the baron answered. "The key to our success is to spread fear. Once there is real fear out there, I promise you it will perpetuate and do the work for us. I also want every gallery and every dealer who has represented modern art, observed. We will soon give the signal to legally shut them down."

"What about the meetings, Wilhelm?" Fricke jumped in. "My sources tell me the Expressionists have been holding secret meetings all over the country."

"I am speaking to Streibel now, Friedrich. So calm down and have another drink. As I was saying, Streibel, part of your responsibility is to raid any secret meetings. For now, threats and arrests should be enough. No deaths. We don't want the international community on our backs." He paused. "If, however, something happens in the process, the accident is to be publicized as suicide."

The baron offered refills and cigars. "Fricke will monitor your activities and report directly to me. Now, I will let Felix discuss his initiatives with the group. I am certain everyone will be as supportive as I am."

Felix cleared his throat. Julian recognized the sound, a late night noise from their apartment in Paris. He walked down to the last step, grasping the railing nervously.

"It is essential that we focus on the bottom line," Felix began. His voice was surprisingly clear and authoritative. "I am talking about the vast international market for modern art. I don't have to tell you that these works are in high demand. I propose we use this trend to our advantage. Don't you agree, Hartt?"

"Trend?" Hartt asked sarcastically. His voice was squeaky, girlish. "You mean trash."

"Let's not fool ourselves. This trash—Dali, Picasso, Engel—fetches big money, especially elsewhere in Europe. Why not sell what is valuable abroad, use the money for profit, and pour it back into the Party. We can utilize these degenerate paintings to bring the kind of art we really want to Reich museums of the future. We should sell as much of Germany's modern art as we can through auctions and dealers sympathetic to our cause, anonymously of course, particularly through our contacts in Switzerland, who as we know are discreet, reliable, and extremely competent."

Where was Felix getting these ideas? Julian stared intently at the wall panel, as if to find some hidden meaning in it. Felix had known nothing about money in Paris, except how to spend it. Julian no longer recognized the man on the other side of the secret door.

"The profit will be immeasurable because all the artwork will have been confiscated," Felix continued. "Not a single deutsche mark will have been spent on this venture, which should please Hitler's accountants. The money will benefit the departments of culture and defense—and whomever needs to be bribed at any given moment."

"Be careful, Felix," the baron cautioned.

"I am just stating the facts, Father," Felix argued. "From my understanding, this was to be an open and frank discussion."

"Leave the frankness to me," the baron replied. "Let's stay with the subject at hand."

There was a long silence, then Felix continued: "Without a doubt, as my father stated, we must take care of our own house domestically, then tackle the international markets. We need to find out where all the modernists are, where they are going, what they are working on, and, specifically, what they are hiding from the Reich. I have already recruited someone very close to Ernst Engel and his band of Expressionists to provide us with vital inside information. At this moment, he is perfectly positioned as a student of Engel's."

"Excellent," Hartt said.

"Who is the recruit?" Fricke asked.

Julian clung to the railing.

"His name is Julian Klein."

"Klein? German?"

"No, American."

Silence.

"Is he a Jew?"

Felix did not respond.

"Absolutely not. Not a Jew!" Fricke's voice rang out, and Julian felt lightheaded.

"Excuse me, Friedrich, but this has already been discussed at great length with my father, who trusts my instincts and has empowered *me* to handle the situation."

"When can we meet this Jew?" Fricke could not hide his contempt.

Julian's back dripped with perspiration. *This Jew, this pig.* He could visualize Fricke's look of disgust, as if his image were one of those posters of deformed individuals that Fricke had held up at the university lecture.

"You won't meet him," the baron said matter-of-factly. "Not yet, at least. He is Felix's Jew—his pet project. Felix has convinced me that this young man is worthy. I have met him on a couple of occasions. Apparently, this Jew told Felix he had even attended your lecture at the Academy, Friedrich—which is more than any of us could say." The baron laughed hard, joined mechanically by the others.

"I lived with him, Friedrich," Felix added. "I know everything there is to know about Julian Klein, and it is all quite simple."

Drops of warm urine trickled down Julian's leg.

"Klein's weakness, which works to our advantage, is that he is extremely naive and easily convinced," Felix explained dryly, as if Julian were a science project. "Too idealistic for his own good. Art is his religion—not Judaism. And he thinks we are close friends."

Julian felt as if he had been punched. He now clearly understood that Felix was using him to get to Ernst Engel. He swallowed hard. And Engel was using him to get to Felix. He was bait for both men, but he alone had allowed this to happen. He stepped backward up the stairs, but stopped, wanting to leave but knowing he had to stay. He would give Engel the information, and then tell him to find some other "extremely naive and idealistic young artist" to do the dirty work. After this, he was done.

Fricke snapped, "Have you considered the fact that this Jew is an American, and it is too risky? We don't want their diplomats meddling in our business."

"Let's look at the long term," the baron countered. "The fact that he is American may actually help us with our international activities in the future. But most crucial to our immediate success is maintaining Julian Klein's anonymity. The less he is known outside this room, the less chance he will have of being discovered by anyone in the art community. Though he does not know it yet, Klein will be our secret weapon. The unappealing fact that he is Jewish will not be revealed or discussed by anyone here again. Do I make myself clear?"

Nobody answered.

"What has this Julian Klein done to prove himself?" Hartt asked finally.

"I will answer that, Father," Felix jumped in. "Let me rephrase your question, Edmund. What *will* Julian Klein do to prove himself? Let's begin with the annual avant-garde exhibition being held at Johann Finch's gallery next week. An Engel protégé will be making his debut." Felix paused dramatically, like an informant about to divulge his source. "The artist's name is René Levi. He is French."

"Levi? Any relation to that French Jew art dealer?" Hartt asked.

"Jacob Levi. Yes, René is his son. In fact, it was Julian Klein who shared the exhibition information with me," Felix said. "I think we should make Levi's debut a night for Engel and his friends to remember, and a test for Julian."

Julian held his breath. *Those bastards are planning to destroy the Ernst Engels of Germany, and they are going to try to use me to help them do it. And Engel is using me to help save the Ernst Engels of Germany.*

With those odds, Julian knew no one would win.

As he closed the door to the guest bedroom and leaned against it, Julian realized there was only one choice left: He must get himself and René out of Germany immediately—*before* the exhibition—before this madness went any further.

Chapter Eighteen

THE GRUNEWALD FOREST

Airborne paint doused Julian's canvas, splashing his trousers and landing on the blades of grass between his toes. He looked across the spans of the Grunewald Forest. It was thick with birch and wildflowers, unscathed as far as the eye could see. Julian inhaled the fresh country air. The mid-morning sun warmed his back. Beads of sweat glided from his neck down to his tailbone, and he felt relaxed for the first time in weeks. It was all an illusion, but for the moment he did not care. He glanced over his shoulder at Engel's country house. A pageant of rare birds paraded freely along its rounded arches and through the ivy ornamenting the white paneling. Julian loved this place. It helped him forget about manicured lawns, confiscated art, and ebony caskets.

Today he would paint, and tonight he would tell Ernst Engel that he and René would be leaving Germany. One last hurrah, as Felix would say. Only René did not yet know it.

Julian glanced at his friend painting across from him. René was sucking on the slim end of his paintbrush while concentrating on his canvas. Julian watched him with admiration and envy. René painted as though he had no cares in the world. How Julian wished he could be that free.

In the distance, Julian heard Engel's voice. He looked up and saw his instructor leaning against a tree, quietly singing a German folk song, his rich baritone harmonizing with the high-pitched, drawn-out chirp of the birds around him. Julian observed the direction of the light as it angled through the trees behind his instructor. Julian's fingers tingled slightly as the tepid breeze rustled the branches and moved over him, running down the length of his arms, encouraging him to create. *Don't think*, he told himself. *Just feel. Give yourself the time right now because later it will all be over.*

Julian held out his hands, eagerly surrendering himself to nature, which demanded to be painted. He tried to block out thoughts of the meeting at the *schloss* the previous night and promptly dabbed various shades of blue into the green, adding traces of gold onto his canvas to reflect the color of the leaves. He tried but still could not concentrate. From the corner of his eye he could see Charlotte lounging lazily in the gazebo. Absorbed in a book, with her feet resting on the white wooden bench, she looked like a teenager.

He watched Engel take a cold drink from the nearby table and walk over to René. Engel examined René's painting and patted his back, then made his way slowly toward Julian.

Julian tried to ignore Engel's approach because he knew their relationship was no longer instructor to student, but artist to spy. And right now, he wanted only to paint. As he dabbed at the canvas, Engel leaned over and pressed his lips close to Julian's ear. "I have been wracking my brain all night wondering just what they are going to do at Johann Finch's gallery. You should have stayed until they finished the meeting, Julian. If only you didn't leave, perhaps we would know more."

The spell was broken. The various shades of the leaves faded quickly. The wet paintbrush in Julian's hand fell to his side. With clenched teeth, he hissed, "I told you several times, Ernst, that I left because I was afraid to get caught. I got as much information as I could, and I was lucky to even get that, and—"

"Hey, what are you two whispering about?" René walked over and surveyed Julian's canvas. "Ernst, I was thinking, why not put a few of Julian's paintings in with my exhibition?"

"No!" Engel and Julian said at the same time.

René laughed, threw his hands up as though surrendering. "Okay, I get the message. I thought you would be open to the idea, Julian. One big bang before the Nazis steal our artwork."

"That isn't funny," Julian retorted, realizing that there was no point in waiting until evening to break the news to Engel and René. He would tell them both right now that they were getting the hell out of Germany. "Ernst, it's not safe here for us anymore," he began. "You got your information, and now René and I need to go back to Paris right away."

"What are you talking about, Julian?" René demanded. "What information?"

"The exhibition is not a good idea," Julian began unsteadily. "Trust me, it is too risky for you, René, too dangerous."

René pointed to Charlotte. "You sound just like her."

Julian knew he couldn't tell René what happened the night of the funeral. Not yet. When they returned to Paris, then he'd tell him everything.

"You saw Felix that day at the lake, René. Like a madman," Julian said. "I don't think he can handle you having an exhibition here. It is one thing for you to show your work in Paris, but here?" He paused, noticing Engel glaring at him. "It is only going to ruin relations between all of us. Let's leave now before things get worse."

René rolled his eyes. "Don't be so dramatic, Julian. I know Felix has not gotten over that I am with Charlotte, and that's why he didn't want me to come to Hans's funeral. And I'm not an idiot. I was there at the lake. I saw what you saw. But Felix will come to his senses. He will meet someone else. You don't know him like I do. He will get over all of this. He always does." René turned to Engel. "As for the exhibition, didn't you tell me that we could not allow the political situation here make us run away from art? Explain to Julian that running away now because of Felix's jealousy or because of silly politics is ludicrous."

"Are you blind, René?" Julian pressed, not caring that Engel was clearly furious with him. "Or just too self-absorbed not to see what is really going on around you? It is not a silly political situation. It's real. You will have so many other exhibitions down the road. You don't need this. And we don't need to be here any longer. We are leaving tonight."

Before René could respond, Engel wrapped his arm around René's shoulders. His voice was controlled. "René, would you mind if I speak to Julian alone for a few minutes?"

René shrugged, then headed toward Charlotte.

"I thought we agreed to keep this between us." Engel angrily kicked at the grass. "Look, Julian, I am also having second thoughts about the exhibition. I had no idea that their plans were so advanced and intricate. Perhaps you are right. Too many people are at risk—not just you and René. But the exhibition is one week away. If we cancel it now, the situation could get much worse."

"They specifically mentioned my name and René's at that meeting," Julian argued. "We need to get out of here. It is too dangerous, Ernst, to stay and play this game. I'm sorry."

Engel held Julian's arm tightly. "And what if I said that I need you to stay, that this situation is bigger than you and bigger than René. Yes, it is dangerous." Engel's voice was shaky. "It is risky. But the process is already in place. More than one hundred important paintings will be smuggled out of the country that night."

"Then use another artist as the main attraction," Julian said through clenched teeth. "Just not René."

"Damn it, Julian, I have nowhere else to turn." Tears filled Engel's eyes. "These people, these artists, are my friends and colleagues. They trust me, and they trust Max Kruger to save their paintings. Without you and René, this will surely fall apart."

Julian gazed out into the woods, no longer seeing color but a vast emptiness. He did not know what to do.

Engel's voice was barely audible. "It's one night, Julian. I'm asking you—begging you—for just one night. Then go."

Julian glanced over at the gazebo. René was tenderly kissing Charlotte's forehead. Her eyes were closed peacefully. Julian began to feel guilty for hating her. Maybe they did belong together. He looked back at Engel and took a slight, surprised step backward. His instructor was also staring at the gazebo. His right hand covered his mouth, his neck muscles protruded through the sallow skin, while his other hand was curled into a fist at his side. Julian recognized that pose from Dubois's studio—*pain and longing.* He had painted it.

Julian sighed deeply. "We will stay through the exhibition, but you will arrange for us to leave the very same night. That's the deal."

Engel clasped both of Julian's paint-splotched hands inside his own and held them there, a silent promise.

Chapter Nineteen

BERLIN

Johann Finch's gallery was packed, and Julian nervously searched the candlelit room for Ernst Engel. He finally saw him off to the side, surrounded by a group of artists. His instructor's wide, toothy grin radiated as he shook hand after hand. An outsider would have thought that Engel was having the night of his life. Julian knew otherwise.

Engel anxiously brushed past Julian as he led a group of artists to a painting on a nearby wall. As he passed, Engel whispered through his pasted-on smile, "Talk about drawing a crowd, Julian. All of goddamn Germany showed up tonight, like it's the Last Supper."

Julian laughed nervously. "I thought the Last Supper was by invitation only."

"Let's just get this night over with." Engel shook his head, not finding any humor in the turnout. It was clearly not what he had planned. He left Julian and moved quickly toward René.

Julian nursed his drink. He was not important to anyone here, and no one spoke to him, for which he was grateful. He preferred to blend into the scenery. Besides, he was too nervous to speak, so he reached inside his coat pocket for a cigarette.

René stood in the center of the room, encircled by guests, who appeared to be vying to praise him. His smile seemed strained and Julian could tell by the uneasy way he conversed—his gaze darting around the room as he spoke—that he was distracted and edgy. Obviously, René was looking for Charlotte, who had yet to arrive.

Julian felt a tug at his jacket and jumped. He turned to face Max Kruger, and he instantly relaxed. Kruger's suit was a patchwork of lime-green fabrics. With his shock of red hair, he looked like a leprechaun. Julian tried to suppress a chuckle.

Kruger smiled and pointed to his suit. "My wife tells me it's loud."

"It's shouting." Julian laughed. "How are things going on your end?"

Kruger pursed his lips. "We will see."

Julian noticed a small group of artists standing to the right of Kruger laughing at someone's joke, but the collective sound seemed measured, a deception. One woman kept glancing over her shoulder, as if certain that someone was keeping tabs on her.

"What is going to happen to these people, Max?" Julian asked.

Kruger eyed him strangely. "Many will be banned from working. Their paintings will most likely be confiscated. Perhaps even destroyed."

"At least some of their paintings will be saved," Julian said, thinking about the one hundred paintings that were on their way to Paris and Barcelona for safekeeping.

Kruger stared hard at Julian, his eyes turning gray and filmy like a winter lake. "Once an artist's hands are bound, Julian, he is as good as dead." He smoothed his suit jacket, looked anxiously around the room, and then glanced at his watch.

"What's wrong, Max?" Julian asked.

Kruger sighed deeply, gestured toward the gallery's back exit. "Come with me. I need your help."

Julian was confused by Kruger's bizarre behavior, as he was led a little too roughly to the door. Kruger seemed distracted and jumpy, his eyes constantly darting around the room. Something was not right. Julian wished he could send a signal to Engel that he was leaving, but the artist was across the room, engulfed by a group of young admirers.

"What is going on?" Julian demanded once they reached the dark alley behind the gallery. Kruger ignored him, searching up and down the narrow street.

Julian turned in the direction of the gallery. "I'm going back inside."

Kruger gripped his arm tightly. "Julian, please, just cooperate and things will be better for everyone."

"What the hell are you talking about?"

In the distance Julian heard the approach of a car. Kruger pointed at the silver Daimler pulling up at the end of the alley and whispered firmly, "I'm afraid that you cannot go back inside the gallery just yet."

Julian recognized the car, and he was gripped with fear. *Was it possible that Max Kruger had betrayed them?* Two men in dark uniform walked toward them.

"Why, Max?" Julian whispered. "Why are you doing this?"

"Listen to me, Julian. There is no time." Kruger's voice was sharp yet shaky. "You are treading on dangerous territory. More than you know. Just do as they say. They are smarter than we are, faster. They have contacts everywhere. Someone turned me in." His breath was heavy. "Von Bredow's people found out about the paintings being smuggled out of the country. Those bastards have people planted everywhere. They came to my house last night, threatened my family. They said it was either me or Engel." Kruger choked back his words. "I chose me."

The same chauffeur who had been with Baron Von Bredow in Paris exited the Daimler, opened the back door of the car, and stared ahead, showing no sign of emotion.

"Be careful, Julian. Watch yourself," Kruger whispered quickly just before the two uniformed men grabbed Julian's arms, pushed him toward the car, and shoved him inside.

Felix was in the back seat, waiting for him with a broad smile and an opened bottle of wine. "I saw you taking a stroll with Max Kruger, so I thought I'd stop by and say hello," Felix said lightly. "Tell me, Juliangelo, how is René's big night?"

"Big," Julian said numbly.

Digging his fingernails into the leather seat, Julian stared out the window. He was too afraid to think. And then he saw Kruger being pushed into a vehicle that had pulled up behind the Daimler. *What did Felix know? What had Kruger told them? What would happen to Ernst Engel? And to René?* Julian thought of the paintings that would never see the lights of Paris or the cobblestoned streets of Barcelona. He thought of the artists who were now as good as dead.

He turned to face Felix, searching for any sign of the friend he had once known. "Felix," he whispered. "What is going on here?"

"Why don't you tell me, Julian?" Felix's mouth was locked into a false smile, the rest of him remaining frighteningly calm.

Engel's urban studio was located in the heart of Berlin, barely ten minutes from Johann Finch's gallery. The door had already been pried open. A guard stood close behind him, watching over the door. The room was completely dark, except for slim shafts of moonlight angling through the four large windows.

Julian felt chilled. Just yesterday, he and René had been here, wrapping up loose ends before the exhibition. This same room had been inviting, spacious, and airy. Engel called the sprawling studio his "urban sanctuary" because it seemed the entire city could be seen through its windows. Those windows now appeared dark and foggy, and Julian could barely breathe. The air seemed to be thickening around him.

Felix glanced at his watch then gestured toward the bench near one of the windows. Julian moved to the far end of the bench, but Felix sat right next to him, his arms and legs pressing against Julian's. He put his hand on Julian's knee and clasped it.

"Any moment, Julian. Sit tight. This is going to be interesting."

Julian stared at the thick fingers gripping his kneecap, then looked up. Felix's profile was taut with anticipation. Julian had had enough. "I don't know what you are planning here, but I won't be part of this, Felix. Take me back to the gallery, now."

Julian tried to stand, but Felix pushed him back down roughly.

"Relax, Julian," he said coldly. "Things are just getting started, and I'm afraid you are going to have to stay."

Before Julian could respond, the window behind them crashed and shattered. Shards of glass landed on the floor next to Julian's feet and two men jumped down from the windowsill.

"What the hell is going on?" Julian shouted, his eyes ablaze. "What is wrong with you?"

"Ernst Engel is being robbed," Felix said distantly, as the men stood before him waiting for orders. "I need to know right now—are you with me, or are you with them?"

Julian knew that whatever was happening, this *was* a test. He stalled. "With you? What does that even mean, Felix?"

"You know exactly what it means." Felix leaned in close, his chapped lips nearly touching Julian's. "The night of Hans's funeral. You were there outside the library door, weren't you?"

Julian froze, his fingers gripping the bench. Even in the darkness, Felix's accusatory eyes were fiery. *How much had Kruger revealed in order to save himself?* Everything was at stake now. Felix was dangerous. A wrong response could mean lives. René's. Engel's. Johann Finch's gallery of artists. Perhaps even his own. It was clear that Felix already knew the truth. *Lie*, he told himself. *Lie like you mean it.*

Julian said firmly, his gaze locking into Felix's. "Yes, I am with you."

Felix wrapped his arm around Julian's neck, and Julian cringed at his touch which had once felt brotherly. Felix said he knew he could count on Julian and that he always came through. They both knew Felix was lying.

Felix then stood and beamed his flashlight across the room. "Boris, those files over there—break them open but don't touch a damn thing. I know what I'm looking for. Ludwig, you destroy everything I point to. And move! There is no time. I want everything by the wall out of here now and into the truck."

Julian's heart sank. Engel's treasures—his *Brücke* works. His instructor had been planning to send those paintings out of the country for safekeeping. Kruger was supposed to have had the artwork picked up. Now it was too late.

The man called Ludwig began spray-painting swastikas over Engel's recent paintings, which hung on the far wall. Julian wanted to scream out "Those are history—irreplaceable!" but he knew he had to stay silent. *For Ernst Engel.*

A few of Julian's paintings stood on easels next to the bathroom. Felix waved his hand and told his men to ignore them. For a moment Julian could not help but feel insulted, as if his work was unworthy of being stolen or defaced. He then saw Felix's hoodlum eyeing René's paintings on a nearby shelf—his unfinished work. Shaking the can enthusiastically, Ludwig prepared for another round of destruction.

"No!" Julian yelled. He could not stop himself.

Felix rushed between Ludwig and René's paintings. "Leave those alone," Felix ordered loudly. "The others should be enough. You will put those paintings in the truck. I'll direct you from there."

In the truck? What was Felix planning to do with René's paintings?

Boris and Ludwig exchanged glances. Ludwig, the larger of the two, hesitated, then said with a slight lisp, "Your father said that everything is to be taken directly back to Potsdam."

Felix threw down the flashlight. "I don't give a damn what my father says. You are working for me."

From his briefcase, Felix pulled out an oversized envelope and thrust it toward Boris. "Open this, and hang these photos over there." He winked at Julian.

Boris removed a handful of enlarged photographs from the envelope and began tacking them onto the wall, singing to himself as though he were hanging holiday greeting cards.

Julian's body shook when he saw the images, and it required all of his willpower not to strangle Felix on the spot. The first photo was of Charlotte and Engel rolling naked in the tall grass behind Engel's house, next to the gazebo. The second showed Charlotte lying on her back as Engel knelt over her. Charlotte's mouth was wrapped around Engel's penis. Julian looked away from the last picture. It was all too much. The sky seemed to be degenerating into unrelated points of black, blue, and gray, as though a Seurat painting had been blown up above him.

Everyone was lying to him.

Felix laughed at Julian's reaction. "How is that for modern art?"

"Where did you get those?"

Felix smiled as Julian stepped backwards, away from the photos, realizing that Engel, his family, and his close friends would be coming to his studio after the exhibition.

"Everyone who matters to Engel will see the photos," Julian said under his breath.

"Ernst Engel should be exposed for the cheat he really is," Felix said indifferently. "Don't you just wonder how René is going to feel about this?"

Julian swallowed hard. "What about Charlotte?"

"She looks pretty good." Felix grinned.

"How do you think she will react to this? I don't think this will endear her to you, since that seems to be your grand plan."

"René might not get over it, which is a good thing, but she will survive it. Engel, though, has a lot more to lose. His wife . . . I hear she's a tough one." Felix leaned forward, lowering his voice. "Now, he has plenty of reason to hang from his own noose."

"Engel is stronger than that," Julian countered.

"I think losing his paintings will upset Engel more than these photos. They are just an added touch—insurance."

"Insurance for what?"

"You tell me, Julian," Felix hissed. "You were there, eavesdropping."

So this was the "accident" that the baron had discussed. Murder made to look like suicide.

Careful, Julian told himself. *Admit to nothing.* "Ernst Engel is useful to you—founder of the avant-garde, with connections from here to South America. He will lead your father's friends to all of the artists who matter—everyone the Reich wants." Julian paused with a deep breath. "Leave him alone, Felix."

Felix did not flinch. His thick black eyebrows were raised high, his mouth locked in a scowl. Julian wondered why he was going after Engel with such vengeance.

"There will be other sources," Felix said. "Kruger's own colleagues turned on him without even flinching. And Kruger handed us Engel on a silver platter."

"You are not a murderer, Felix." Julian tried one last time to reason with him. "You are not your father. You are an artist too. Don't forget that."

Felix lowered his gaze.

"Why Engel, damn it?" Julian asked.

Felix advanced toward the wall. He posed under the last picture of Charlotte straddling Engel's wide, bony hips. Her mouth was open wide with laughter, and so was Engel's. He crossed his arms and leaned forward.

"Because Engel chose René over me."

Chapter Twenty

Two hours after Julian's abduction from the reception, Felix delivered him back to the gallery. Felix eyed Julian squarely before he let him go. "Bring Engel back to his studio. You do this, and no one gets hurt."

Yeah, right, Julian thought as he slammed the car door and quickly walked up the flight of stairs leading to the gallery entrance. He stopped when he spotted Engel standing on the top stair waiting for him, cross armed and angry.

Engel rammed his finger into Julian's shoulder. "Not even an explanation, Julian? Not even so much as a good-bye before you ran out with Max Kruger? You know how tense I have been about tonight. Standing at the door, asking everyone if they saw—"

Julian grabbed the finger in mid-jab. "Kruger betrayed us. Do you hear me, Ernst? They got to him. The paintings were discovered. It's over, damn it."

As Julian quickly recounted the events of the night, Engel seemed to shrink before his eyes. "My *Brücke* paintings." Engel's voice was barely audible.

It pained Julian to look at him. The guests congregating above them appeared concerned.

"That isn't all of it." Julian paused. "Explain Charlotte."

Engel peered up at him like a guilty child and said nothing.

"How could that have happened?" Julian demanded.

"How did you find out?"

"After they destroyed your artwork, Ernst, they hung up naked photos of the two of you. 'Insurance,' Felix called it."

"They are blackmailing me."

"It is more than that." Julian could not believe that Engel was so naive. "Felix wants you dead."

Engel searched Julian's eyes. "Because I told his mother that his paintings were worthless?"

Julian nodded.

"Where is Max Kruger?"

"Forget him. He is not coming back. He drove off with them somewhere." Julian wanted to shake Engel. "This is about you. There is nowhere safe for you to go. They've probably ransacked the country house, and they will be waiting for you at the studio."

Engel held up his hands, as though surrendering. "What about you, Julian? Kruger knew everything."

"I don't know exactly what they got out of him. But Felix knows I was there listening in on that meeting. And only you and Max knew about that." Julian looked around. The guests were clamoring closer, as though sensing some imminent danger. There was no time to waste. "I came back to find you, Ernst, to tell you what happened. And now I'm leaving, getting out of this mess, and I'm taking René with me."

Engel rested his hands on Julian's shoulders, his voice barely above a whisper. "Charlotte seduced me in order to get René to stop painting with me. It was after that day at the lake with Felix. She knew René was no longer safe here, but he would not listen to her. She knew I wanted her, and she used it, making me promise to push René to leave Germany, to prevent him from exhibiting tonight. Instead, I told René that if he didn't exhibit tonight, he would be running away; I told him that all the artists who mattered would see his work, and in turn, he would be helping to save their paintings. It didn't take much to sway him. Like you—like them—" Engel nodded toward the group of artists watching him. "They trusted me. I agreed to whatever Charlotte demanded because I wanted her, Julian." Engel's eyes welled up. "I admit it, each time I painted Charlotte, I wanted her. I still do."

Engel yanked his hands away guiltily and stared at his calloused palms. "At first, I honestly believed that I could cancel René's exhibition and keep up my end of the agreement for her. Then you told me about Von Bredow's meeting, their plans for us, and I knew, no matter what, that I could not cancel tonight."

Engel made an expansive sweep with his hand, as if invoking a landscape ready to be painted. "For them. So *they* would remember what freedom looks like before it is taken away. That's why Charlotte almost didn't come tonight. I slept with her and lied. She is angry with me. It was all a big mistake."

Julian drew in a deep breath. "It is going to cost you everything."

"Perhaps I am getting what I deserve." Engel looked defeated.

Julian walked back into the gallery and Engel followed him. He saw René and Charlotte talking in the far corner. Julian started to move toward them. He had to get René out of there now. But Engel pulled him back by his shirt. "Don't do it. Look around you. We have to somehow get through this night, and then leave."

"The night is over," Julian said firmly. "We are going right now."

But Engel would not let Julian go. Julian could feel the sharpness of his fingernails through his shirt. "Julian, you have to pass their test."

Julian shook him off angrily. "What test? Didn't you hear a damn thing I said, Ernst? Felix knows I am lying to him. I flunked the test, okay?"

Engel dropped his hands to his sides. "You promised me the night. It is all we have left."

"Yes, I promised you, but that was before Kruger betrayed us. I am getting René out of here now." But just then, Julian saw Felix, flanked by Gestapo, standing in the doorway. Suddenly all conversation stopped, and Julian knew that he and René were not going anywhere.

Felix nodded in Julian's direction as he entered the room. It was a collaborative nod. Julian tried to ignore it, but the surrounding faces turned to look at him with accusing eyes: a traitor among them. Julian yearned to defend his innocence, but the secret police formed a phalanx in front of the door, and then they scattered throughout the room. Tables were turned over, chairs thrown through the air. People quickly forgot Julian and began to scream.

Over the chaos, he heard Felix's name being shouted, and then just moments later, an eerie silence washed over the gallery. The crowd slowly divided, and René moved toward Felix. Their eyes locked, and time seemed to stop, as it had that first night in Paris. Felix signaled his guards to stay where they were.

René looked at Felix, at the police, and then at the damaged gallery. "Thanks for coming tonight, Felix," he said.

Felix smiled broadly, his teeth flashing in the glare of candlelight. "I would not have missed it."

"No, you wouldn't." René pointed to the Gestapo, his voice resonating against the high gallery walls. "But you don't belong with them, Felix. You are a painter, not an animal. This—them—your father—none of it is you."

"It is all me now." Felix walked toward him. "You betrayed me."

"And now you are betraying yourself." René's voice echoed throughout the room. Despite the guns and the soldiers, René did not back down. "You are betraying art—the only thing that you ever truly loved, Felix. It's not about me, or her." He pointed to Charlotte. "It's about you. You should be here with us. Not doing your father's dirty work. He is using you."

"You used me, goddamn it!" Felix roared, then his face dropped hard, his broad shoulders sagged. He stared back at the fearful faces in the room, watching him, waiting for his reaction. He had been exposed. He was once a painter, and now he was a thief. He had crossed the line— from *us* to *them*—the worst of all betrayals. But Julian knew Felix well enough to read him. He was an artist who could not paint. There was no deeper pain, no greater personal disgrace.

No one dared move. Everything was at stake. Felix straightened his back, turned to his guards, and nodded. Instantly, the police scattered again, only this time they were more brutal. They clubbed anyone standing in their way. Artists lay face down on the floor, their arms beneath their bodies, preferring that their backs, their heads, their legs be harmed—anything but their hands.

Charlotte rushed forward to prevent René from being taken away. She stood in front of him, trying to block the police. Her red chiffon dress, partially transparent, made her look for the first time vulnerable, like a young girl. Several of the men laughed as they pushed her roughly out of the way, and it was at that moment that Julian felt sorry for her.

"Felix, don't do this!" she begged as they handcuffed René. But Felix shook off her shrill pleas.

As Felix passed Julian on his way out of the gallery, his arm touched Julian's gruffly, but he refused to look at him directly. He did not have to. Julian felt the hot sweat of shame seeping through Felix's sleeve.

Julian turned when he heard Engel's wife wailing as the police advanced toward her husband. Engel pulled away from her and rushed over to Julian.

"Don't run away," he pleaded.

Before Julian could respond, two men grabbed Engel's arms. Julian looked on helplessly as his mentor—the artist who had taught him to see the world through vibrant strokes of color—was pushed mercilessly out the door. Engel turned briefly and held Julian's gaze one last time: *My time is done, Julian. The rest is up to you.*

Johann Finch was handcuffed. Dozens of artists were too. Those who were fast enough had already fled from the gallery; those who were not were shoved into trucks. A dozen or so Gestapo agents re-entered the gallery for a final sweep.

Their commander nodded when he saw Julian standing alone in the corner of the empty room. It was the same allied nod that Felix had given him. The Gestapo must have been told that he was one of them.

Julian watched the men strip the walls clean of René's artwork. One by one, each painting was lifted and passed through an assembly line of careless hands until it was out the door and delivered, he presumed, to Felix's doorstep. Julian smoked cigarette after cigarette, not allowing his mouth to be free for fear of what he might scream out. He watched them steal the artwork until nothing remained of René's paintings but an exhibition of nails.

The Gestapo finally left, and Julian sank to the floor, staring at the dusty trail of boot marks. He surveyed the barren room and began to count each nail, each hook. He forced himself to remember the placement of René's paintings. Categorizing each piece in his mind, he tried to memorize their vivid compositions. When he had finished taking mental inventory, an emptiness like he'd never known overtook him.

He should have told René everything, from that first night when Kruger and Engel had approached him. He should have packed his friend's bags and taken him out of Berlin, kicking and screaming, after that day at the lake. At least he could be certain that René would be alive now. Felix did not care about his father's big plans for ridding Germany of modern art. He cared only about René's art, that René's genius was not his own. That the brilliant brushstrokes belonging to modern artists like Ernst Engel and Max Kruger would never come from Felix's own hands.

Someone touched Julian's shoulder, demanding attention, but he did not turn around. He knew who it was, and it didn't matter. She stepped in front of him. The light from the surrounding sconces seemed to bleed through the sheer red material of her dress, and Julian could see the outline of her long legs. When he finally looked up at her, he noticed that for the first time her eyes were not vacant. They were wide open and wet. Charlotte looked afraid.

Turning away from her, Julian glanced up at the ceiling, picturing the Gestapo hanging Engel from his studio rafters. His instructor's grin would be wide and toothy as blood sputtered from his mouth. They would call it suicide.

"Where did they take René?" Charlotte asked quietly.

Julian looked at her with open hatred. "Why do you care?"

"I love him."

"You love yourself."

"I hate you, Julian."

He laughed. "You love René enough to sleep with Ernst Engel? You love René enough to sleep with his father and Dubois?" Julian couldn't stop himself. "Is fucking the only way you know to get things done, Charlotte?"

Charlotte slapped him. The smack was firm and swift across his cheek, but the tears welled up in her eyes.

"Cry all you want," he said coldly. "I don't know where they have taken René, or if he is ever coming back."

"Damn you, all that whispering with Engel!" Charlotte shouted. "You know exactly what is going on."

"I thought you were the one whispering with Engel."

"Bastard."

"How could you hurt René like that?"

Charlotte's wet blue gaze was penetrating, like cobalt glass. "And I would do it again if I thought it would mean leaving this place. I wanted to stop René from exhibiting. I was willing to do anything. I did not want René burning at Felix's stake. And as it turns out, I was right to worry."

Julian stood up and faced her. Sighing, he said, "What about getting Engel back?"

"He lied to me."

"Because he had to."

"For what—art?" Charlotte hissed. "It is always the art. It has overtaken our lives."

"It *is* our lives." Julian went to the wall and yanked out a nail. "For your information, pictures of you and Engel will probably make the front page of *Das Reich*."

Charlotte's lips separated, but no words emerged.

Julian turned to her. "I don't care what happens to you, Charlotte, but my advice is to leave this hellish country while you still can."

Charlotte crossed her arms tightly, standing her ground. "What are you going to do?"

"I don't know." Julian shrugged. "Everything has changed. I can't leave until I know René is okay."

"Well, then I am staying with you." She glanced at the empty walls, at the nails, her voice distant. "All his beautiful paintings." Tears streamed down her face. "You know, I used to watch Felix paint when we were at Dubois's studio. He always had one eye on René's canvas. Without René's guidance, he was lost. Without the money, the title, Felix is nothing. But here in Germany, he is trying to convince everyone that he is something special. René's presence—his incredible talent—keeps reminding Felix that he is still nothing." She wiped her cheeks and pointed her finger. "It all came to a head that day at the lake, Julian. We should have left right then, and you damn well know it."

Julian said nothing, stunned by her perceptiveness.

She hesitated. "But Felix wants me, Julian."

"Do you think he wants you as much as he wants to destroy René?"

She smiled sadly. "I think the two go hand in hand."

"René is gone, and Felix is your golden opportunity. He will catapult you to high society." Julian raised his hands. "It's your big break. What are you waiting for, Charlotte? Jump in."

Charlotte pushed him away. "Felix repulses me."

Julian laughed sarcastically. "You are telling me that Felix Von Bredow, the richest man you will ever meet, repulses you? And Léon Dubois didn't?"

Her voice was faint. "Léon was like a father to me."

"I don't know many daughters who sleep with their fathers."

She fidgeted with her hair, which earlier had been pulled back into a tight chignon and was now loose and stringy. "Dubois may be ugly, but at least he is a painter I could respect. And I owed him." Pressing her lips tightly together, she said, "I want in, Julian. Whatever you are involved with, however you are involved with Felix, I know I can somehow help."

Charlotte was so close to Julian that her lilac perfume flooded his nostrils. Julian took a few steps backward.

That damn perfume.

"How far would *you* go, Charlotte?"

Charlotte's gaze was unrelenting; she looked much older than her years. "I am a whore, Julian, remember? A whore who fell in love. I would go even further than you would to get René back."

Julian searched her pained face. Perhaps if Felix could have Charlotte, it would quench his thirst for René. There were no other options. "Can I trust you, Charlotte?"

"Do you have a choice?"

RED

*"I sense a scream passing through nature. I painted . . .
the clouds as actual blood. The color shrieked."*
—Edvard Munch

Chapter Twenty-One

Julian re-read the small article headline buried inside *Völkischer Beobachter,* the Nazi-owned newspaper: "Ernst Engel, fifty-seven, found dead."

It had been almost a week since the raid at Johann Finch's gallery, yet this was the first time that Julian had seen anything acknowledging that night. The article was strangely short. No one was named. Not a word was written about the raid at the gallery, not even a photograph. The last line stated that Engel had been found dead in his studio, alongside his wife, a double suicide. The article was accompanied by a vicious opinion piece discussing the corrupt Judeo-Bolshevik influence of Germany's avant-garde.

Julian searched desperately for a clue, something more between the highly censored lines. He had expected to see photos of Ernst Engel's corpse splashed all over the front pages. He thought this would be used as an example of what would happen if an artist tested the Reich.

He read the piece again. Nothing.

Walking through the Brandenburg Gate toward the Tiergarten, he nearly bumped into a uniformed division of young boys crossing the street. Hitler Youth recruits. They gazed blankly at Julian, their new swastika armbands shining. They passed by him in a two-line formation. He watched their proud straight backs, the perfectly synchronized goose step. One of the boys had a runny nose, and Julian almost felt sorry for him: a toy soldier, fresh Aryan meat who would know nothing about choices. These boys should be out playing ball, staring at girls—not training to destroy the nation's Ernst Engels.

Julian kept walking. Charlotte should be arriving at the Tiergarten at any moment. She had gone to Felix's home and begged him for information on René's whereabouts. Julian had stayed in town, sleeping first on the floor of Johann Finch's gallery, and then the last few days he'd spent in the basement hideout in Wilmersdorf, where he'd met Engel secretly. Charlotte had contacted him there, and they planned this meeting. He prayed she was coming with information.

He picked up his pace and entered the garden. Strolling along the wooded parkland, Julian tried to lose himself amid the lush vegetation, the picturesque canal. But it all seemed false, like a film set. Everywhere he turned, he kept seeing faces nesting in the trees and bushes: René, Engel, Charlotte, Felix, the baron, Max Kruger, Friedrich Fricke, his parents.

He shook his head. He was hallucinating. He hadn't slept in days. Turning to a secluded section of trees, Julian leaned against one of them, the wool of his shirt catching on the bark. He knew he should leave Berlin. He was in danger. Engel was dead. But René was still here, alive somewhere, he was sure of it. Perhaps he should return to Paris and tell Jacob Levi to use his high-level contacts to deal with this, and then he'd go home. But he had no real home. And by the time he got to Paris, who knew if René would still be alive. No, Julian decided, no matter what happens, he was staying in Germany until he found René.

"Julian!"

He heard Charlotte call out to him. Julian turned, and she waved as she walked toward him. She wore an ankle-length lace dress and a matching crocheted hat that shielded her face from the midday sun. She looked elegant, high society. *Where did she get that dress? Did Felix buy it for her?* Julian imagined Engel's wife having seen the naked pictures of Charlotte and her husband before Felix's thugs killed her, and he could barely look Charlotte in the face.

"Nice to see you," she said with a strained brightness.

"You look well."

"And you don't."

Julian nodded, and then quickly scanned the grounds, feeling para-noid that Charlotte might have been followed, and he did not want to waste time. "Did you find out anything about René?"

Up close, Charlotte's face was pale beneath her hat. She, too, had one eye on what was going on around her as she quietly spoke.

"René is alive," she whispered. "They are accusing him of murder-ing Ernst Engel, and they took him to a prison called Sachsenhausen in Oranienburg, just north of Berlin. It is where they are holding hun-dreds of political prisoners, mainly government opposition leaders." She glanced quickly over her shoulder. "Felix promised he would do every-thing in his power to bring René back."

Julian leaned against a nearby tree. "He is lying, of course. He probably signed the papers to jail René."

Charlotte nodded, smiling sadly. "I put on a good show that I believed him."

"Doesn't Felix wonder why you are being so friendly when you know this is all his doing?" Julian asked.

"Of course he knows that I know." Her voice was hard. "But don't you understand that it doesn't matter. Felix is blinded, just like every other man who looks at me. They see only what they want to see. They hear what they want to hear, as long as they can get me into bed." She paused. "As you know, I have been staying at the house all week. I went there only for the day, but of course, Felix wouldn't let me leave. And I let him think it was his idea that I stayed." She pointed to her expensive clothes. "Yes, straight from the Von Bredow collection. This dress belongs to his sister. Anyway, I proved to Felix that I would be more than grateful for his efforts to find René. I am not stupid, Julian. I know Felix is lying, and that he has no intention of releasing René. But as long as I stay close to Felix, René won't slip out of our hands, and that is all that matters." She searched Julian's face. "You're not going to be happy about this, but he knows that I am here with you."

Julian slammed the tree with his hand. "Damn it, Charlotte, our meeting was supposed to be secret."

"Now you're the fool, Julian." She exhaled deeply. "There are no secrets in Germany. Not anymore. I thought honesty would be best. I told him that I was meeting with you today. For some reason, he thinks you and I are now close friends."

Julian laughed at that, then kicked a cluster of dandelions at his feet and watched the seeds go flying.

"I also told Felix that you are not leaving the country, but sticking around for any word on René." Charlotte leaned over and flicked the dirt from the bottom of her shoe with a stick. "He wants me to bring you back to Potsdam."

Julian shook his head. "No way."

She grinned uneasily. "Felix said he has a surprise for us."

"I hate surprises. Especially his." Julian looked at her intently. "Was that before or after you slept with him?"

"During," she said evenly, then added softly, "At least we know René is alive, Julian."

"Yes, but for how long?"

She bit down on her lip, fighting the tears. "I don't know."

"For God's sake, they've gotten away with murdering Engel. What now? We have got to think."

She studied Julian closely. "Have you told me everything?" she asked.

He squinted into the sun. "You are not going to like this, and I don't know if it means anything, but Engel once told me that Jacob Levi had an affair with Felix's mother years ago."

A slim vein appeared in Charlotte's forehead. He could not tell whether she was angry or indifferent, so he continued: "Felix told me while his father was busy grooming Hans, his mother used to take him and his sister Isabel to see the most important modern art collections all over Europe. That's probably how she met Jacob. Maybe you can feel out the baroness. Perhaps she has information that could lead us somewhere."

"Now, that's a thought," Charlotte mocked. "We can swap Jacob Levi bedtime stories, discuss his favorite positions over hot cocoa in the kitchen."

"Charlotte, listen to me." Julian leaned forward. "You cannot take this personally or we have no chance."

"It's all personal." She stared at the pale pink lacquer on her long oval fingernails. Her voice had an annoyed tone. "What else?"

"Felix's sister. Do we know anything about her?"

"All I know is that she is out of favor with the baron. Felix told me she dropped out of the university to become an actress." Charlotte laughed. "Another artist in the Von Bredow family."

"See what you can find out by snooping around the house."

"Fine." She paused. "We have to alert René's family somehow. We have to tell Jacob what happened. Maybe he can help."

"I've thought about that," Julian said. "But every move we make right now, I guarantee, is being monitored. We cannot risk any interference. It could mean René's life."

They stared out onto the vast, landscaped park without speaking. It was hard to believe that this beautiful place was part of the same Germany that was trying to destroy an art movement that aligned itself so closely with nature.

A group of young mothers pushing baby carriages strolled along the walkway in front of them. Charlotte's eyes followed the women almost longingly. "You are coming with me to Potsdam," she said firmly, once they passed by. "Felix insists."

Julian shook his head. "Don't be stupid. It's a trap. You in his bed and me under his control—don't you see what he's doing?"

"I think you're the one being stupid." She folded her arms. "You are certainly not going to find René by holing up in a basement in Wilmersdorf and reading the newspaper for information. We don't have time to play around, Julian. You said it yourself, every minute is crucial."

He started to walk away. "I said I'm not going."

Charlotte pointed to the sleek black Mercedes visible at the entrance to the garden in the distance, and Julian stopped in his tracks. He knew that what he wanted or said no longer mattered.

Chapter Twenty-Two

POTSDAM

Felix led Julian and Charlotte across the grounds of the Von Bredow estate toward the stables, stopping briefly at the newly erected monument under which Hans had been buried. It was a bronze sculpture of a headless horseman, his muscular torso riding a raging stallion as if into battle. The horse's saddle was draped with the Von Bredow coat of arms, representing Hans the Great Warrior, defender of the *schloss*.

Felix gauged Julian's reaction. "Well, what do you think?"

Julian cleared his throat. "Where is the damn head?"

"I asked myself the same thing, but then remembered that Hans—may he rest in peace—never had a brain. So why bother with a head."

Julian could not help but laugh with Felix. The release felt surprisingly good and nostalgic. For a moment he forgot where he was and why he was there and that he and Felix were no longer friends. As they walked toward the stables, even Felix's confident strut, a light, loose swagger that Julian had seen countless times on their way to Café de Flore, was reminiscent of the old Felix.

"Since neither of you ride," Felix said, turning to Julian, "Charlotte will ride with me and you will try out our beginner's horse." Before Julian could respond, Felix took Charlotte's hand and pulled her toward him. He tickled her playfully along her forearm. It was a silly gesture, but she looked at him and blushed. At that moment, Julian remembered exactly why he was there.

Unlocking the first stall, Felix gestured toward Julian's horse. She was camel colored with a creamy mane. *Beautiful, but probably a killer*, Julian thought, *like the rest of the Von Bredows*.

Felix helped Charlotte mount his horse and then mounted himself. The stable boy assisted Julian, who was still distracted by Charlotte's blush. It had seemed a little too genuine.

"We are having a picnic, and then I have a surprise!" Felix shouted excitedly as he galloped past Julian with Charlotte clinging to his waist. Her long blonde hair flowed with the horse's mane. The pair looked like a fairy tale gone awry: the princess taking off with the rogue while the prince rotted in jail.

The trio rode for about twenty minutes around the estate. Once Julian got the rhythm down, he found himself enjoying the ride. Felix stopped under a large lemon tree and dismounted with the kind of pedigreed flair that Julian knew, no matter how long he practiced, he himself would never have.

Felix lifted Charlotte off the saddle, and she slid against him as he gently set her down. She arched her back and pressed her breasts into his chest. Felix seized the picnic basket attached to his saddle and opened it. Five corks peeked out from the top, as well as a blanket. There was no food inside. He winked at Julian. "My kind of picnic."

"So, what's the big surprise?" Julian asked after he had dismounted.

"It has been a long, hard week. Why not indulge in the moment?" Felix opened two bottles.

Julian stood in front of Felix with crossed arms, letting the nostalgia fall away. "Let's cut the bullshit, Felix. I don't quite feel like indulging after Ernst Engel's death and René's disappearance. And I cannot imagine that Charlotte is feeling festive."

Felix glanced at Charlotte, but she turned her head, pretending to be busy straightening the edges of the picnic blanket.

"Drink with me." Felix gestured Julian to the blanket with a wave of the bottle. "Sit, relax, then we'll talk."

"I don't feel like sitting," Julian said, digging his foot into the grass, "especially when I am told to."

"Have it your way." Felix sat down, stretching out his long legs in front of him.

Julian hovered over him. "Where is René, damn it?"

Felix looked up, shielding his eyes from the sun. "You meant to ask, what has René done? I presume Charlotte has informed you that the authorities are investigating René, who has been accused of murdering Engel."

"Murdering Engel?" Julian spat in the grass. "What happened to calling it a suicide? Your people can't seem to get it straight. What a joke."

Charlotte cast Julian a scolding look that urged him to be quiet and let Felix talk. They both knew what happened to Felix's inhibitions when he drank.

"I'm no monster, Julian," Felix said. "I am doing everything I can to help René."

Like hell you are.

Felix sounded almost believably troubled. "But this murder charge has made any kind of release extremely difficult."

Julian wanted to strangle him. He couldn't play this game anymore. "Where is he, damn it?"

Felix drank his wine, staring up at Julian over the rim of the bottle. "First things first. We want you to go to Paris and bring Jacob Levi back here."

Charlotte and Julian looked at each other in alarm. Julian leaned forward. His body felt elastic, as if he were losing control, but he managed to sound firm. "*We*, Felix? Why do *we* need me to go to Paris, and why do *we* need Jacob Levi to be brought to Germany?"

Felix glanced down at his hands, at his immaculate nails. Julian recalled when they had once been stained with paint. "It's simple, actually. They want Jacob to select from thousands of paintings—the best of Germany's modern art—for a series of upcoming exhibitions," Felix said, as if he were an art curator and not a murderer of art.

Julian glared at him. "Don't patronize me, Felix. Surely there are enough experts here. You certainly don't need Jacob for that. You expect him to come here and decide which art is worthy of Nazi appreciation while his son's life is in jeopardy?"

Felix took off his shirt, lay back, and bunched it under his head. His manner was disturbingly relaxed as he stared up at the sky. His voice was cold and steady. "You need to tell Jacob that if he wants to see René alive, he had better come to Germany without alerting anyone. People here are willing to cut a deal—his son for his expertise. I volunteered you."

"Your volunteered me?" Julian laughed. Did Felix really think he was falling for this? "Is this another one of your tests, Felix?"

Felix sat up on his elbows, his legs still crossed comfortably, as if they were discussing where they were going for drinks later. "Look, Julian, this will buy us time. It will keep René alive."

You are lying to my face.

Julian knew he had to be careful. One wrong move could mean René's life, but he couldn't hold back. "So, what's the catch, Felix? Are you and your father's friends trying to put us all away in one shot, and throwing in Jacob Levi for a bonus?"

"Don't be ridiculous. They want Jacob Levi to choose the artwork. Everyone here knows he is the best," Felix said slowly, the words tumbling effortlessly out of his mouth. "I volunteered you to bring him here, because Jacob knows you are René's friend. He will trust you."

"He also thinks you are René's friend," Julian countered. "Why don't you go?"

Felix gnawed his bottom lip and shook his head. "That would be impossible right now. I am not asking you to lie. I want you to tell Jacob the truth—that René is being held for murder, and that his expertise is in demand. If Jacob does what the authorities want, then René has a good chance of being set free. But if Jacob alerts the French government or his influential friends, it could mean René's life. The situation is fragile. He will understand. You will tell him exactly that." Felix leaned back on the blanket with his hands folded behind his head. "And, of course, you will return with Jacob."

Julian could barely look at Felix lounging without a care in the world, like those mothers strolling along the Tiergarten with their children. All of this was a charade. Felix wanted to keep him at close range, but why? He searched Felix's face for answers and found nothing. This was surely another trap.

"This is what I have been told they want," Felix continued, as if reading Julian's mind. "I'm just the messenger."

Julian wished he could shoot the messenger. "Tell me, Felix," Julian asked, barely able to control himself. "How can you be René's best friend one day, then want him dead the next? Why? Because he lied to you about Charlotte?"

"You lied too, damn it." Felix clenched his fists. "But that doesn't mean I want René dead."

"You've gone too far. And it doesn't look like you are suffering with René out of the picture." Julian gestured toward Charlotte. "Was that the plan all along?"

"Don't talk about me like I am not here," Charlotte shot back. Julian was not sure if she was acting or was truly hurt.

Felix pointed the wine bottle at Julian. "You double-cross me every chance you get. Once again, you have chosen René over me."

"What are you, a child? 'Chosen René over me,'" Julian mimicked. "Damn you, Felix. René's life is hanging here by a thread. I was there, Felix. So was Charlotte. Don't act like we all didn't see what happened at Johann Finch's gallery. My question is why? Because René won Charlotte? And Adrienne? Because Dubois, that bastard, admired *his* work, not *yours*? Because Engel thought René was a genius?" Julian knew there was no holding back now. He was shouting. "Is that what's consuming you? Playing second to René? Is René rotting in jail because of your goddamn jealousy?"

Felix stood, throwing down his bottle. "Shut the fuck up! I'm warning you, Julian."

Felix was drunk now. Julian could tell by the way his saliva rolled out the corner of his mouth.

"Warning me?" Julian exploded. "You don't think I see what's going on here? By the way, I can paint too. Engel apparently admired my work. Why don't you put me in jail and frame me for murder while you're at it?"

"You will regret this," Felix shot back unsteadily.

Keep going, Julian told himself. *You are breaking him*. "But it is not too late, Felix. You don't have to do this. Free René, and free yourself. You can paint again. You don't have to be this monster, like your father. It's not you. It never was you."

Felix's face dropped. He was having trouble hiding his emotions. There were tears in his eyes, and Julian thought he had finally gotten to him.

"It is beyond my control, Julian. Can't you see that?"

Julian eyed him squarely. "Felix, it is all in your control."

"I wish it was that simple." He wiped his lips with his shirtsleeve. "Charlotte, pass over that last bottle. I have had enough of this."

Julian took a deep breath. "Get René out of jail, Felix, and you will never have to see any of us again."

"Go to Paris, Julian." Felix's voice had resumed its coolness, and his eyes had dried up. "My father and his colleagues want Jacob's expertise for René's freedom—that's the deal, goddamn it. Take it or leave it."

Julian stared at him. He knew how Felix and his father's men operated. If he went to Paris and dragged Jacob back, the odds that they would cut a fair deal—or any deal—were slim to none. But if, in fact, there was some truth in all of this, he had to give Jacob the choice. He could not make that decision for René's father.

Felix cleared his throat. "I have already taken the liberty of making arrangements."

Julian said nothing, weighing his options, the possible outcomes. Everything seemed bleak. Bring Jacob, or don't bring Jacob. Return to Germany, or escape to another country. René was a dead man either way, but could he live with himself if he didn't do everything possible to try to save his friend's life?

Felix turned to Charlotte, who was sitting quietly watching both of them. "I apologize," he said to her. "We have virtually ignored you."

She pouted. "You have."

"Well, maybe you will forgive me when I tell you about my surprise. Joseph Goebbels has commissioned Friedrich Fricke to paint a portrait of a woman. Not just any woman, but someone whose beauty is perfect. Her image will hang in the Reichstag foyer." Felix's navy gaze became milky. The change in him was sudden. "I suggested you, Charlotte. Fricke saw you at the funeral. And he was all for it. It has been approved. You have been chosen as the model."

Charlotte sat up on her knees. "I can't believe it. That's wonderful!" she exclaimed.

She would be with Friedrich Fricke day and night—the ideal insider's pose, Julian thought. Yet another man Charlotte could use to extract information from between the sheets—her expertise. He looked away. After the afternoon's all-too-genuine performance, he did not know who or what to believe. He thought of the blush, and the way Charlotte had pressed her body against Felix. It was real. He decided she was not to be trusted after all, as he'd suspected the first time she'd entered Dubois's studio. He eyed her, then Felix, and knew that René's survival was entirely up to him.

Chapter Twenty-Three

PARIS

Julian stood waiting for someone to answer the door to the Galerie Rohan-Levi. He glanced down the street at the immaculate row of art galleries lining the rue Jacob, the stylishly dressed pedestrians, the shiny cars. He breathed in deeply, the air an unfamiliar mix of fresh bread and tulips. Paris in the spring was too beautiful, as unreal as Germany. Julian felt disoriented. He did not belong here anymore.

Françoise answered the door, and Julian was shocked by the drastic change in her appearance. Her eyes were puffy, surrounded by dark circles. A shapeless beige frock hung loosely over her thin frame as though in mourning. *She knew.*

"Come in, Julian." Her voice was aloof, fearful. "I assume you are alone." She stuck her head out the door and surveyed the street before allowing him inside then quickly locked the door behind her.

No flirtatious welcome, no Moët this time. Julian followed her up the gallery's winding staircase in silence, observing each passing floor in disbelief. The vitality seemed to have been sucked out of the gallery. Like Françoise herself, it was depleted—of the Picassos, the Gauguins, and the Braques. The walls were bare, with only faint white rectangular shadows remaining. Only the ornate chandelier seemed to burn as brightly as before. *It doesn't make sense*, Julian thought. *Why were all the walls stripped of paintings?* He wondered if someone had already warned Jacob to take precautions.

Françoise stopped in front of the closed door of Jacob's office. She did not announce Julian's arrival but instead scurried away, her legs looking like twigs carried by the wind. Julian turned the doorknob weakly, his hand shaking as he entered the room.

Jacob's large leather chair faced the wall. Julian waited a few unbearable seconds, staring at the backs of the polished shoes under the desk. They seemed to be the only remaining sign of luxury in the office.

"Mr. Levi, I just—"

Jacob spun around. His once smooth complexion had a pale gray veneer. He looked tired, but was still handsomely groomed, and not at all surprised to see Julian. "My son first, Julian. Everything else can wait."

Julian exhaled deeply. He didn't know where to begin. It was all too much. "I believe he is alive."

Jacob shook his head, as if it caused him pain. "They say he murdered Ernst Engel."

Julian leaned across the leather-padded desk. "They lie."

"Of course, they're lying. I just don't know why. I told him not to go there. I warned you boys. Damn it, Julian, why didn't you listen to me?" Jacob stood, pounding his fists against the desk.

"There is no time," Julian whispered anxiously, nodding toward the window. "Felix's people. He is orchestrating the whole thing. They want you to come to Germany."

"Are you out of your mind!"

Julian's voice trembled. "They want to use your expertise to select paintings for an exhibition they are planning."

"Don't insult me." Jacob eyed Julian contemptuously. "You work for them, don't you? You, a Jew, it's a disgrace."

"I would rather die than work for them." Julian gritted his teeth to hold back his emotion. "I am doing what I can to save René's life. He is being held in a political prison." Julian grasped the edge of Jacob's desk, feeling as though he could break the wood in half. "I couldn't save Ernst Engel, Mr. Levi. But I will not leave Germany without René.".

Jacob searched Julian's face as he would an unfamiliar painting, try-ing to assess its authenticity. "So, they sent you, Julian, to obtain my expertise? They were unable to find an expert of their own in all of Germany?" He fell back into the cushy embrace of his chair. "I could name ten top people over there. It doesn't make sense, does it, Julian?" Jacob paused despairingly. "Do I get my son in return?"

Julian could barely speak. "That is the deal."

"What else do they want?"

"Names," Julian responded, his voice lifeless. "Lists of all your clients throughout Europe. I didn't know about any of this until right before I came. You have to believe me."

Jacob loosened his tie as if he were choking. "Should I include Bar-oness Von Bredow on that list? Is that what this is about? Wilhelm Von Bredow settling an old score?"

So Jacob had been with Helen Von Bredow. Julian could barely breathe. "They've given me twenty minutes to speak to you alone before they storm the place."

"Who are *they*, Julian?" Jacob demanded.

"A Nazi lawyer, an appraiser, three armed guards. They want everything you have," Julian stammered under Jacob's probing gaze. "The entire history of Rohan-Levi, including files of all the artwork you have collected, shown, and sold, especially to Germans Jews. Apparently, they have detailed reports about your state of affairs, your net worth, and your investments. These peo-ple are dangerous, sick. I didn't know what to do, but I knew that I could not make the decision for you, not with René's life on the line."

Jacob's frozen face appeared to crack into fine webbed lines, like a Rembrandt portrait.

"They know you are close to the Rothschilds, the Sterns, the most prominent Jewish families throughout Europe. And that you know ex-actly where all the major Jewish-owned works are housed." Julian low-ered his voice, glanced around the room. "Mr. Levi, this is not just about René, is it? I saw that your gallery has been cleared out. They will see that, too, when they come in. I take it someone has already warned you."

Jacob's gaze was stony, revealing nothing.

"It doesn't matter," Julian said nervously, not wanting to pry any further. "You just better come up with something. The information you give them will be carefully reviewed before they release René."

"I'll be betraying everything my family worked generations to build."

Jacob poured himself a drink. He slugged it down, and then hurled the empty glass behind him at the barren wall that once boasted a Picasso. Julian jumped at the crash, but Jacob did not flinch. "And Charlotte Béjart? I hear she is living with the Von Bredows. Is she in on this as well? I warned René to stay away from that whore. He should never have left Adrienne."

Adrienne. Julian wanted to ask Jacob a thousand questions: *How was she? Did she, too, know about René? Had she ever mentioned Julian?* He tried to conceal the blatant yearning in his face, for fear that Jacob would see right through him as the others had. *Don't think about her right now. You can't see her.* Clearing his throat, he managed, "Charlotte says she is doing everything she can to find René. But I don't trust her. The situation is complicated."

"By complicated, you mean she is sleeping her way through the jails to find him?"

"Something like that." Julian decided it was better not to tell him that she had been sleeping her way through Felix.

"And what happened to Felix? He and René were so close. We once had a long conversation about his father. He told me he hated the baron and especially his politics." Jacob patted his pocket in search of his handkerchief. Finding nothing, he wiped his forehead with the back of his sleeve, leaving a stain of sweat. "Julian, what exactly happened in Berlin?"

Squeezing his eyes shut, Julian realized he did not know anymore. He had lived it, but he no longer saw it clearly. It was as though the pictures of Paris and Berlin, once vivid images that he had assembled, had been thrown recklessly into the air like a delicate puzzle and all he could see was the gray undersides of the individual pieces. "Felix can't paint, Jacob."

Jacob sat back, perplexed. "Felix's father owns practically all of Potsdam and he has property all over Europe. All of that will go to Felix one day. What in God's name more does he want?"

"It is not the money," Julian lamented. "It's René's artwork, his talent."

"Tell them, I will sell Felix's lousy paintings. I will make sure they hang in the goddamn Louvre, if that's what it takes. Just give me my son."

"Felix knows his ability is inferior to René's," Julian continued, "that Dubois only accepted him to his studio because he is a Von Bredow. You know better than anyone that talent cannot be bought. With everything that Felix has, he wants what he can never have—René's artistic birthright. That's what this is about."

Jacob nodded with measured consideration. Sounding tired, Jacob said, "And what's in it for you?"

"All I know is that I have to do something," Julian said. "My friends are dying. Felix and his father murdered Ernst Engel. He was my friend, my mentor."

Jacob moved closer to Julian. "Go home. Go back to America. Get out of this. You are just a kid. I will take it from here."

Julian tried to stand firm, shoulders back, but inside he felt anything but confident. "I can't leave."

"What is happening there is unstoppable, Julian." Jacob's voice was tender now, almost fatherly. "Go home to your family."

I don't have a family anymore, Julian thought sadly. His determined gaze bore into Jacob's bloodshot eyes. "Felix is deeply involved, and his father is running the show. No one else can get through to Felix the way I think I can. I know who he once was in Paris. He wants me around him, to watch me, perhaps to use me. But it seems that as long as I am involved, René stays alive. And maybe I have a chance of helping to save some of the art that they want to destroy."

"This is too big for you, Julian. You don't know what you are up against. You will get caught." Jacob shook his head. "Let me handle this alone. Go home, save yourself. I believe your good intentions, but this could mean your life too." Jacob grabbed Julian's hands and held them inside his own, and Julian noted how small and slender Jacob's fingers were, like René's.

"I could not live with myself if I left." Julian knew, no matter what happened, he couldn't run away, not now. There was too much at stake.

Jacob looked at Julian with what seemed like a newfound respect, his hands falling to his sides. "I love my son, but how can I help those bastards destroy everything I believe in? They want me to feed them other people's lives. Because if I select which art survives and which does not, I am choosing which artists will live and which will die."

"It's either the lists or René."

Jacob stared at the floor. His words were muffled, as though he were talking to himself. "You know, when René left Paris, he walked out that door angry. Our last conversation keeps replaying in my head, and I cannot forgive myself. A journalist once asked me how far I would go for art. I said there was nothing that could stop me from pursuing the spirit of the movement. Now it is between the movement and my son."

Jacob stood unsteadily. Julian recalled that day in his office when Jacob's presence had seemed god-like. Now, his shoulders were hunched with an enormous weight, and his lack of stature seemed more pronounced. Jacob turned toward the door longingly, as if wishing he could walk through it and erase time.

Julian took a deep breath. The wall that had hosted the Picasso was now stained with the remnants of Jacob's drink. Suddenly, he pictured the baron's face there, cold and unforgiving, like one of his dour family portraits hanging in the Von Bredow foyer.

"That's not all, Mr. Levi. There is something else," Julian said hoarsely. He reached into his coat pocket and pulled out a letter, which was sealed with a royal blue Von Bredow crest. "I don't know what this is, but they told me to give it to you."

Jacob took the letter from Julian's hand and ripped it open. It was in German. He read it quickly. "This is . . . " but he couldn't finish the sentence. "You were wrong, Julian. It *is* about money. Von Bredow wants me to legally disown René and make Felix my legal heir. That man has ten times more money than I will ever have. I am a Jew, for God's sake. Why would he want Felix to be associated with me?"

Anger raged through Julian like he had never felt before. He hated Felix. He hated himself for being there, for agreeing to bring Jacob to Germany, for delivering that despicable letter and putting Jacob in this situation. He could no longer look at René's father. Instead, he went to the bar, found an opened bottle, poured himself a glass, and swallowed hard. It turned out to be scotch, and it burned through his whole body. How he wished it would make him melt.

Jacob's voice was barely a whisper, echoing behind him. "Von Bredow is demanding access numbers to all my accounts, all legal documents, and my will, Julian. He says if I choose to hold on to my assets, then I might as well come to Germany and bury my son."

Julian turned and saw Jacob holding onto the back of the couch for support. "What about my wife, Julian? My daughter? Will it stop here?" Jacob tried to steady himself. "All this, because of a brief affair years ago?"

Julian shook his head, unsure how to answer, how to console him.

Jacob moved from the couch toward the window and clung to the beige curtain. "They are out there. Look, that's their car down there, isn't it?"

Julian nodded, too afraid to speak.

They both heard the bell ring downstairs, then the approaching voices and footsteps.

Jacob leaned against the wall. "You can tell their crook of a lawyer that I will give them every damn thing they want. I ask only one thing in return before I sign their papers. I demand to see my son." He led Julian out the office door. "*Before* they kill him."

Chapter Twenty-Four

ZURICH

The Mercedes sedan headed toward the center of Zurich. Jacob Levi sat motionless in the backseat sandwiched between the Nazi lawyer and two thugs. Julian was in front next to the German driver, who had been smoking incessantly since they had left Paris twelve hours earlier. He glimpsed Jacob's morose reflection in the side mirror. He was barely blinking. He looked as though he had already lost everything.

They had refused Jacob's demand to see René before he signed anything. The lawyer said he simply did not have the authority to grant such a request. Jacob either came with them or he didn't. The lawyer added coldly, that unfortunately, his son would immediately bear the consequence of Jacob's refusal to cooperate. Jacob signed their documents.

They drove for another twenty-five minutes toward Zurich's business district. "And here we are," the lawyer informed the guards excitedly, pointing to an immense building. "Zurich's most prestigious bank."

From the car window, Julian studied the massive, dour institution, which resembled a medieval abbey. Busts of mythic Swiss heroes stared out from the base of the bank's large marble steps.

"Now, get out." The lawyer eyed Julian and Jacob contemptuously.

As they climbed the stairs toward the entrance, Julian saw a mousy, balding man checking his watch and pacing as if he had been waiting a long time. The man stopped in mid stride when he saw them approach the building, his lips puckering with impatience. The lawyer also saw the man's irritation, and with an outstretched arm he apologized profusely for being late.

The mousy man acknowledged the rest of the group with an indifferent nod and escorted them down a long, bright corridor lavishly designed with deep red marble. Julian thought the walls looked bloodied. The hall widened at its end, leading directly to the banker's office. Julian expected to enter a colorless, lackluster chamber. Instead, the large office, painted in various shades of yellow and gold, was surprisingly bright and grandiose, filled with enough furniture to seat a dozen adults comfortably. Julian saw Jacob glancing around the room and could practically hear his brain ticking off the artwork—a crucifixion scene by Cranach, the Virgin and Child by da Vinci, a portrait of a pope by Breughel, and Tiepolo's *The Immaculate Conception* hanging right behind the desk. Art fit for a king, not a dreary banker.

Julian brushed his shoe over the plush green carpet and wondered what he was doing there. The banker, with bulging eyes set behind highly magnified glasses, glanced at Julian with disdain. He gestured toward the chairs in front of his desk, and they all sat down silently.

The banker, whose name was Herr S. Holstrom as Julian had discovered from the plaque on his desk, did not smile or move his lips when uttering his curt German phrases. "Account number," he said quickly. "Documentation number. Credit list." Nod. "Thank you."

The lawyer eagerly handed Herr Holstrom each of the documents requested, along with a hefty file. Holstrom stroked its cover with his thin fingers. Everyone watched him with anticipation, as if he were about to perform some kind of bureaucratic piece by Beethoven. Finally, he opened the folder and slowly read through the pages. With a perfectly filed fingernail, he skimmed each line, each word, glancing up occasionally and clearing his throat.

Jacob stared straight ahead, dazed, as if he were not actually present in the room with the rest of them. Holstrom then handed Jacob a stack of papers to sign. Jacob barely read through the first page before he began to tremble. Julian turned away, unable to watch Jacob's elegant shaky hand as he signed away his children's trust funds and his wife's security to a dummy German organization headed by Felix Von Bredow. Jacob wiped away the tears that could not be avoided, and Julian blamed himself. He had brought him here. He had done this to the Levi family.

As the ink dried on the cover page, Holstrom arranged Jacob's papers into a perfect rectangle. The Jacob Levi file became the tenth such pile that Julian counted on the large Biedermeier desk. No one said anything as Holstrom tested the drying ink with his fingertip. Satisfied with its permanence, he stood and strode past Jacob and Julian as though they were invisible. The Nazi lawyer stood and gave Holstrom a firm handshake.

"Heil Hitler." The lawyer smiled broadly.

"Heil Hitler," Holstrom responded, pushing up his thick glasses and then raising his hand high in the air as he ushered everyone out the door.

Hours later, the same group disembarked at Berlin's Hauptbahnhof station on the eastern side of the city, only to be met by the same Daimler that had been following Julian around Germany like a silver shadow. The lawyer ran exuberantly down the steps of the platform and knocked on the car's tinted window. It lowered several inches and whatever the lawyer said was greeted with laughter in reply. Julian glanced over at Jacob. He looked worn and fearful, as terrified by the sounds emitting from the car as Julian was.

The driver opened the back door of the car, gesturing Julian and Jacob inside. The driver's face beneath his wool cap was sallow. Julian gasped when he made eye contact with the two men sitting in the backseat: Baron Von Bredow and Friedrich Fricke dressed in full military regalia. Julian's gaze was immediately drawn to their decorated chests—rows of colorful pendants, a large silver eagle, an ostentatious diamond-studded swastika, and a dozen other gold and platinum medallions.

"And who do we have here?" The baron eyed Jacob greedily and turned toward Julian. "Well done."

Julian clutched his stomach as if he had been punched. He kept his eyes averted, the patronizing voice becoming as distant as the sound of the passing cars. Jacob stared ahead silently.

"Does the Jew speak?" Fricke asked, pointing to Jacob. "Or do we need to dangle money in front of him to get a word out?"

More laughter.

Fricke slowly removed his black leather gloves. "Frankly, we brought you here, Levi, because we want to tap into that vast knowledge and experience of yours." He eyed Julian. "And from my understanding, our talented young man here has accomplished a lot on this little mission. Let's see . . . " He began to count his fingers. "We have your client lists, your assets, your artwork and—oh, we stopped your mistress from depositing that generous check you gave her."

Jacob's face went white. "What did you do to her, damn it?"

"Such impudence." Fricke was clearly agitated. "If you must know, she was roughed up a bit. Nothing extraordinary. Nor, I'm afraid, did she ever make it to Rothschild's office. I don't know why you bothered trying to warn him."

Jacob mustered his godlike voice, the same tone he had used months ago when he had called down to René and Julian from the top of the gallery's staircase. "I demand to see my son."

Julian held his breath as Fricke slapped Jacob's face with the back of his glove. It cracked like a whip. Jacob's fists were clenched and his face rapidly changed color. Fricke raised an eyebrow at the baron and smiled.

"Wilhelm, all of this drama has made me ravenous," he said. "What do you say we take Julian out for a victory dinner?"

"I'm not hungry," Julian mumbled, as if it were his mother telling him to eat.

"Of course you are." Fricke tapped the driver's shoulder. "Pull over, Horst. We will be dining there, two blocks down, that restaurant to the left."

Julian felt the depth of Jacob's probing eyes, and he wanted to scream out that he was not collaborating with these bastards; that everything he had said in Paris was true. But he held his tongue and focused on a spot on the rear window, over Fricke's shoulder, trying to maintain a blank face.

"Levi will wait in the car, of course," the baron said as the driver assisted him and Fricke out of the Daimler, and then signaled Julian to follow.

The moment they entered the dark, candlelit restaurant, Julian wanted to run out the back door. The room was dim, and long black velvet couches lined the mahogany walls. Waiters wore white jackets and black bow ties, but most of the guests were uniformed in starched gray wool coats with stiff black collars. The swastika armbands with their shock of red provided the only source of color in the room. The host, with a tiny gold swastika medallion pinned to his lapel, bowed his head as he escorted his high-status guests to the center table, having less than discreetly rid the table of the lower-ranking officers who had been sitting there. Four waiters quickly cleared the table for the baron and Fricke.

Once they sat down, the baron raised the basket of rolls in Julian's direction. "Congratulations. As of today, you, Julian Klein, are no longer a Jew."

Julian began to feel dizzy.

"After your Paris success," Fricke continued as a heaping plate of meatballs arrived, "you, young man, are one of us."

Julian watched them eat. He took a roll, just to hold onto something. He squeezed and ripped the bread into tiny pieces.

"Paris," the baron snorted. "I cannot stand the French. Austria is more my style." He turned to Julian. "Did Felix mention that we have a chalet in Innsbruck?"

Julian shook his head. There were many things Felix hadn't mentioned.

"Not surprising. He hasn't been there in years. He always preferred our place in the Swiss Alps. By the way, how was my man, Holstrom?"

Julian nodded, afraid of what his voice would utter were he to open his lips.

"Not the most colorful fellow, but a genius with numbers, and exquisite taste in art."

"Now, the most important task for us," Fricke cut in, "is how to deal with Jacob Levi. There is so much information to wring out of him. Levi's knowledge of contemporary art should prove extremely lucrative. And then there is the issue of what to do with him afterwards. But, we will worry about that later."

"I have a few ideas." The baron smiled. Julian clutched the corner of the tablecloth as the two men drank to one another's health and toasted the Führer's longevity.

"What about the deal?" Julian mustered.

"What deal?" Fricke said.

Julian looked to the baron for backup. "Tell him."

"Tell him what?" The baron raised his bushy eyebrows.

Julian's legs began to shake beneath the table. "About the exchange. Jacob Levi's expertise for René's freedom."

The baron leaned forward. "Wherever did you get that idea?"

"From Felix." Julian's heart pounded and his stomach rumbled loudly. "He said you agreed to it."

They both laughed.

"We do not make deals with Jews," the baron said tersely.

Julian could no longer disguise his hatred for them. He might as well have shot Jacob dead in his office and saved him the trip. He glared at the baron and Fricke, and with only his fork and knife to protect him, said slowly, "I brought Jacob Levi here. All of his assets now belong to you. The only thing he asked in return is that he be able to see his son." Julian should have stopped himself right there, but he added, "Before there is an afterward."

The two men looked at each other with amused disbelief. Fricke turned to the baron accusingly. "You gave Klein rope, and now he wants to hang us."

"Get a hold of yourself, Friedrich," the baron ordered, his voice rising. He pointed to the restaurant window. "Is that what happened in Paris, Julian? You made a deal with that Jew? My Jew. I own him now, remember."

"A Jew who has bought and sold the most offensive art of our time," Fricke added angrily.

The baron leaned toward Julian, and Julian saw the bearskin rug and the boar's head hanging on the baron's library wall flash before his eyes.

"I said, did you cut a deal behind my back, Julian? What authority do you have?" he demanded.

Julian wanted to remind him that Felix was the one who had cut the deal in order to convince him to go to Paris. But he stared back, meeting a furious torrent of blue, knowing better than to look away.

"Well, then, Klein, consider your deal null and void." The baron turned to Fricke and pushed his plate forward. "I have lost my appetite. We are leaving."

They got up from the table, and someone in the restaurant paid the bill. Glasses were lifted as they walked out of the room. Fricke clicked his heals and saluted. The baron ignored everyone. They returned to the car and Fricke tossed a roll onto Jacob's lap. "Here is your end of the deal, Levi. Knock yourself out."

Jacob searched Julian's face. Julian knew that Jacob was a professional at drawing answers from expressions, and he did his best to avoid eye contact. One close look and Jacob would surely know that Julian had failed him.

The car stopped in front of Ernst Engel's studio where Julian was now staying, where Engel had been murdered. From the car window, Julian could see the familiar stretch of a large, blank canvas leaning against one of the windows. He had put it there to block out the sunlight.

Fricke and the baron began discussing the upcoming Olympic games and Julian knew that he would not have another chance. "They lied," he whispered to Jacob without moving his lips. "They are going to use you and then get rid of you."

"Of course they are lying." Jacob's voice was so faint that it felt like air brushing against Julian's cheek. "But you brought me here, Julian. I am counting on you to get me to René."

He squeezed his leg against Julian's, as if to close the deal, just as the baron turned around and ordered Julian out of the car.

Julian waited at the entrance of the studio and watched the Daimler speed down the street with Jacob Levi trapped inside. He imagined the "afterward" that Fricke and the baron were planning for Jacob, and he could barely stand.

What was I thinking? There are no deals to be made in Germany. Felix was right all along. Julian had been too naive, too easily convinced—the perfect candidate to feed Jacob Levi to the lions.

He slowly entered the dark studio, not bothering to turn on the light. He knew exactly where everything was—the long wooden workbench in the far corner of the room where he slept, the small toilet in the back, the location of the eleven red and black spray-painted swastikas defacing the studio walls from the night of René's exhibition.

This was where Engel had been murdered. And this was now home.

Julian paced aimlessly around the studio, each thought darker than the previous one. He sat on the bench, curled his knees to his chest, and glanced up at the rafters. *Tell me, Ernst, what now?*

He waited a few unbearable seconds for the only answer he knew Engel could give. He lay down his head, bunched up the clothes he used as a pillow, and tried to ignore his dead mentor's advice.

Staring up at the ceiling until he could no longer stand it, Julian got up and went to the window, roughly seizing the large canvas leaning against it. He propped it on an easel, then headed to the storage room, which was still filled with art supplies. He removed half a dozen jars of paint and selected a few brushes of varying sizes and returned to the waiting canvas.

He eyed the canvas but felt paralyzed. He had not painted since that day in the Grunewald Forest, just before René's exhibition. The canvas stared back at him, blank and guilty, like a liar. Julian clasped the canvas by its sides and threw it to the floor. It had betrayed him—it had betrayed all of them—with its temptation and infinite possibilities.

Dripping with sweat, Julian ripped off his shirt and then the rest of his clothes. He stood naked, glaring at the canvas that had once been his lifeline but was now his adversary. It lay face down, but he felt no pity as he dragged it back toward the easel, enjoying its painful scrape against the floor. He opened all the jars of paint, flipped over the canvas, and dumped a bottle of red onto its center. Black paint came next, then yellow, followed by orange. Julian could feel the blood moving beneath his skin as he layered color upon color on top of the despicable canvas.

He got down on his hands and knees and stuck both palms into the deep puddles of paint, stirring the colors until they became a thick muddy shade of scarlet. Inhaling the sharp aroma, Julian added brown and green to the mix and watched the texture gel and curdle. Using his shirt as a whip, he lashed the canvas, swirling the paint with the wooly fabric.

He felt empty, washed up, defeated. He never should have brought Jacob to Germany. He never should have allowed René to exhibit at Johann Finch's gallery. He never should have trusted Charlotte. Who was he to be making these decisions? He did not even deserve to paint in Ernst Engel's studio.

And then Julian looked down, and his hot tears seemed to freeze against his face. He stared in disbelief at the image that had materialized before him. The worthless puddles of paint had morphed into a crushing inferno: a torrent of color so dynamic, so raging, that it seemed to move from side to side, up and down, taking on a tempestuous life of its own.

For the first time, Julian saw what his hands could do, and it was magnificent.

He raised the painting high above his head toward the rafters so that Engel could see what he had created. He stared at his work in awe. His breath quickened. He was the paint, the brush, and the canvas. He *was* the image in the painting—the man on fire.

Tears of hope replaced anguish as Julian realized that he had finally arrived at that mysterious destination where Engel had pushed him to go, but where he had never before now gone. It was an ethereal landing where art and artist became one, a place where René had so often traveled. Julian stared long and hard at his painting, then lay next to it, knowing that if he did not do something right away, he and René might never journey there again.

Chapter Twenty-Five

KREUZBERG

Charlotte moved confidently toward the entrance of the small beer hall. Julian walked behind her, eyeing the contours of her body, yet distrusting each fluid movement. But he needed her, and she knew it. She turned around as if feeling the intensity of Julian's doubt and whispered firmly, "I know what I am doing."

Julian nodded. They had little time. Charlotte told him that she had overheard Fricke bragging to a colleague about keeping Jacob Levi up day and night, forcing him to appraise hundreds of works of modern art that had been stripped from museums across the country. When Jacob became tired, they poured water over his head. When they thought he was lying, they beat him.

Julian lit a cigarette out on the street as Charlotte entered the pub. He stood back and waited. Their plan was shaky at best. He took long drags on the cigarette, giving her enough time to get situated before he walked inside.

When he finally entered the dark, rundown beer hall, no one noticed him. All eyes were on Charlotte as she moved through the smoke-filled room, and he made a low-profile beeline for the bar. There were enough women in the room, but they were cheap looking, their clothes seductive and their makeup heavy. Whores, perhaps. Charlotte, dressed in a conservative pale-blue silk dress, stood out, a delicate flower among the weeds. The men at the bar wiped the dripping beer foam from their lips as they watched her. *Don't be fooled,* Julian yearned to shout. *She, too, is a whore.*

Charlotte ordered a drink and casually scouted out the long tables until she spotted her target: Ludwig, whose exclusive assignment was to serve as Felix's lackey. He was the same man who had defaced Engel's studio the night of René's exhibition. He noticed Charlotte staring at him. She raised her drink in his direction, signaling him to come over.

He moved toward Charlotte at a slow pace. He wore tight trousers and an olive-green work shirt opened at the collar. His blond shaggy hair fell over one eye.

Charlotte whispered something in his ear, and then gently pushed the blond locks away from his face. Ludwig pulled back at her touch, conscious of the dozens of envious eyes watching them. He focused on the dusty floor, shuffling his feet. She ran her finger along his arm and he yanked it away. She lowered her eyes demurely, and then laughed as though he had said something funny. Ludwig scanned the room nervously.

"Do us both a favor, Charlotte," he said, loud enough so everyone could hear. "Stay away from here."

Charlotte twirled slowly on her cream-colored high heels, looking upset, and walked away. Julian watched the pub patrons take in her body as she exited the building. Only Ludwig did not look. He concentrated on the floor, as if trying to decide what he should do. Julian finished his drink, thinking that Charlotte had made too big a scene. He ordered another beer, nursed the foam for a good ten minutes, and then left.

The rest was now up to her.

Charlotte had a room ready at the Bristol Hotel several blocks away from the pub. She quickly changed from the pristine dress into a sleek russet-colored oriental robe, with splashes of yellow running through the fabric like raindrops. She applied reddish-brown lipstick and sprayed something floral, even stronger than her usual lilac scent, between her breasts. Sitting in front of the vanity, she brushed her long blond hair, which turned more golden with each stroke. She cocked her head to one side before the mirror, scrutinizing her appearance. She knew Ludwig would come to the hotel. She sighed deeply at the beautiful woman staring back at her. *They all came.*

Within fifteen minutes, there was a knock at the door, surprisingly delicate.

Charlotte took a knife from her purse and pushed it under the mattress, just in case things got out of hand. It would not be the first time that a man would have to be put in his place.

"Coming," she called out as she walked slowly toward the door.

She opened it and Ludwig entered the room, not looking at her. "I've got five minutes to hear you out," he said nervously.

Charlotte smiled to herself. This would be easy. She ignored him and turned toward the vanity, running her hands along the curvy sides of her silky robe. Ludwig would not be able to take his eyes off her body. She knew what he saw. It was what they all saw when they stripped her naked with their eyes. Her beauty had been a weapon since she was a teenager. The faces changed along the way, but the desire—that look— was always the same.

Except for René. He saw through her outer beauty, tapping into something she had never experienced before. He valued her opinion, not just her body. He listened to her. Unlike the others, he knew that she was intelligent—even with her lack of formal education. He knew that she understood art better than most and observed things on the canvas that others missed. When she would pose, every other artist saw only the fullness of her breasts, her ass, her legs, the perfect symmetry of her face. Not René. He saw inside her; he felt what she felt: the faraway pained gaze in her eyes, the clench of her hand, the light scar running along her thigh, the raw tragedy of a stolen childhood. To René she was real, three-dimensional. Fucking her was secondary to loving her, and she loved him for that. Whatever it took, she would find René for that.

Sitting on the vanity chair, Charlotte stretched out her long legs, allowing her robe to fall slightly open, and then covered herself shyly. "What do you think of me, Ludwig?"

"Think of you?" He stared down at the braided oval rug next to the bed. "You're with Felix. I don't think about you. I work for him."

"What if I told you that I am extremely attracted to you? And that every time I see you I imagine your arms around me? I knew you would be at the pub tonight." Charlotte's voice hovered in the air as she reached for an ashtray, purposely allowing one breast free from the robe. She closed the robe quickly, watching Ludwig rub his legs together with boyish discomfort.

"If Felix knew I was here, he would kill me, and I wouldn't blame him. I'm leaving." Ludwig got up and made his way toward the door.

Charlotte quickly approached him from behind and pressed her body against his back. "What if he didn't have to know? What if you could touch me now, just once, and nobody would find out?"

He did not respond.

"Just once," she whispered.

Ludwig grasped the doorknob. He turned one last time to look at Charlotte, who had dropped her robe. Without hesitation he moved toward her.

"I thought you would see it my way." Charlotte laughed, pulling his large body on top of her.

Two hours later, Charlotte sat up and lit a cigarette. She glanced at the clock. She had to leave. She nudged Ludwig awake with her foot. "Get up," she said icily.

He smiled lazily, and then reached for her breasts.

Charlotte pushed away the groping hands. "I did you a favor. Now I want one from you."

Ludwig's breathing became heavy. "A favor?"

She nodded. "You are in charge of monitoring René Levi at the Sachsenhausen prison, and you are also responsible for Jacob Levi's daily beatings, am I right? Well, you will bring Jacob Levi, wherever he is and whatever condition he is in, to see his son René."

Ludwig's face reddened. His hand rose as if to strike her, and then it fell limply against the sheet. He knew better. "You lying bitch. You know I can't do that."

Charlotte smiled slightly. "Put it this way. It is a lot less risky for you to sneak Jacob Levi to his son than to bear the consequences of Felix hearing that you raped me."

Ludwig jumped out of the bed, flinging away the covers as he reached for his pants. "He will never believe you. I've got ten witnesses at the pub to back me up." He pointed an accusing finger. "You came and searched me out."

Charlotte laughed. "I will tell Felix that you dragged me here. I will have ten witnesses at this hotel when I come out of this room with a black eye and my dress ripped and my arms and legs bloodied." She pointed to the slim, long scar lining her thigh. "I've done it before. Besides, you don't work for Felix and his father because of your keen sense of humor. Everyone knows you are a sadistic bastard, especially Felix."

Ludwig's gray eyes widened with fear. "You will do everything I ask, and if anything goes wrong, or if anyone else hears of this, I will go straight to Friedrich Fricke, who adores me." Charlotte reached for the oriental robe hanging over the vanity. Her eyes blazed. She hated him. She hated what she had done, but there had been no other way. "And from my understanding, if Fricke is crossed, his methods of punishment make yours look like a stroll through the Tiergarten."

Chapter Twenty-Six

Julian sat impatiently in the small café in Kreuzberg waiting for Felix. It was the same café where they'd met before, only this time there was no piano player or beautiful redhead surrounded by suitors. But none of that mattered. Julian saw nothing around him except the watch on his wrist. *Where was Felix?*

A half hour late, Felix finally appeared, visibly distracted. He sat down, ordered a bottle of expensive wine and a slice of fruitcake, and did not waste any time on small talk or even a hello.

"Damn it, Julian, you should not have mentioned to my father that I said Jacob Levi could see René," Felix scolded. "That was between us, Julian. Now I have to clean up your mistakes."

Clean up my mistakes? I should strangle you right now. Julian ordered a cup of coffee and tried to keep his voice even. "Well, are you planning to take care of it?"

Felix speared his cake with the fork and ignored the question. Julian watched him separate the fruit from the crust. His only goal was to keep Felix talking, anything to stall for time. *Ludwig should be on his way to Sachsenhausen with Jacob Levi by now,* Julian thought anxiously. *A thousand things could go wrong.*

Felix glanced at his watch. "Charlotte should have been here. Did she mention anything to you?"

"I know she is posing for Friedrich Fricke, and she said something about going out with Fricke's assistant, Eva, and then coming here to meet us. She said we should wait for her if she is running late."

Felix licked his lips. "Going out with Eva, huh? Was that her excuse?" He cleared his throat angrily and stood abruptly. "I'll be right back."

"Where are you going?"

Felix glared at him. "I have to make a phone call."

As Felix turned, Julian grabbed him by the sleeve. "Can't it wait? Charlotte should be here very soon."

Felix pushed away Julian's hand and stared him down. "You look nervous, Julian."

Before Julian could respond, Felix headed to the back of the café. Julian could barely breathe. *Who was he calling?* Julian watched his determined stride and felt that his feeble plan was about to fall apart. Using Ludwig as a middleman was much too risky. But Ludwig was the only person who had keys to both René's and Jacob's prison cells. He was the only viable option.

Felix returned, his arms stiff at his sides, his eyes blazing. "I'm cutting this short. I have to leave."

Julian's head began to spin.

"Jacob Levi is missing."

"Missing?" Julian's heart was racing.

Felix laughed contemptuously. "Don't tell me you're surprised."

"Where are you going?"

Felix leaned forward, eyeing Julian with hatred. "You know exactly where I'm going."

"Then I am going with you," Julian announced and stood.

Felix glared at him. "No, you're staying here. You've done enough, Julian. Besides," he gestured to the entrance. "We wouldn't want to miss Charlotte, now would we?"

They stood facing each other, the lies between them palpable.

Felix broke the silence. "You are playing both sides, aren't you?"

"I said I am going with you."

"For old time's sake, right?" Felix angrily tossed some bills onto the table, turned, and left the café. Julian followed him to his car. The young driver leaning against the door was smoking a cigarette and immediately threw it to the ground when he saw Felix approaching.

Julian got into the car and Felix did not stop him. They sat side by side in silence. Felix stared out his window. Julian also looked out the window as they weaved through the streets like rats in a maze. He saw nothing; his thoughts were muddled. He glanced sideways at Felix and noticed several cake crumbs stuck to his cheek. Julian concentrated on them for the rest of the journey, too afraid to think about anything else.

The guards waved Felix's car through the gate as they entered the prison grounds. An instant chill overtook Julian as he absorbed the desolate landscape of endless cement buildings—long, cold, windowless, gray blocks of monotony. He imagined René's creativity dying inside.

Felix ordered the driver to park in front of the farthest building from the entrance and to wait for him to return. Julian noted that Felix had not included him in that order.

Julian followed Felix through a wide steel door, opened by the guards who had seen them approaching. Felix began to run and Julian kept pace with him. They ran through the prison corridors, maneuvering through the serpentine configuration.

Slowing down, Felix stopped in front of the last cell, which was also the darkest. Julian stood next to him. Neither acknowledged the other's presence. They heard voices coming from inside. Felix immediately removed a Luger from his jacket.

"What the hell, Felix?"

"Insurance. Keep talking, Julian, and I use this."

Julian said nothing. What he was feeling did not matter. If Jacob was in the cell with René, he wanted them to have every possible second together.

"You've got a visitor, Levi," Julian heard Ludwig say from inside the cell. "But if you open your trap about who brought him, I will kill you."

Julian heard a loud kick, then an excruciating moan. It was René. Julian's entire body tensed, as though the painful cry had been released from his own throat.

"My God, Father, what did they do to you?" René cried out.

Felix was watching Julian's reaction, but Julian did not care. At least he had fulfilled his promise to Jacob.

As Felix raised the pistol, Julian shouted, "No!"

"What the hell is going on out there?" Ludwig opened the cell door to face Felix and Julian. He could not mask his surprise. His face reddened and his thick, pale neck began to splotch with hives. "Look what I found in here, Felix," Ludwig said unconvincingly.

"Shut up." Felix pushed Ludwig aside and entered the cell, Julian right behind him. René and Jacob were lying next to each other on the floor, both beaten beyond recognition. But Julian couldn't help himself—it was the cell that caught his immediate attention. The cement walls had been painted with a vibrant mural: children playing, lovers holding hands, friends toasting one another at a café, artists painting along the seashore, boats gliding over aquamarine water. Julian stood back, amazed. They were trite images, yet within this structure of doom, René had created hope, had surrounded himself with light—but how had he managed to paint?

What was going on in here?

He turned slowly toward René, who was gaunt and pale, but his charcoal eyes appeared invincible, filled with some kind of enduring strength. His eyes alone thanked Julian for bringing his father to him.

Julian gasped as he turned toward Jacob. His nose had been broken and both eyes were blackened. Jacob smiled at Julian through busted lips, and Julian held his battered, appreciative gaze for a few seconds, then quickly looked away. The debonair art dealer was gone.

A nauseating smile spread across Felix's face. "Welcome to Germany, Jacob."

"You bastard," Jacob squeezed out from his cracked lips.

"Father, don't," René begged Jacob. Turning to Felix, he said, "Leave him out of this, Felix. Haven't I painted for you day and night in here? Haven't I done exactly what you asked?"

Painted for him? Julian glanced at Felix with surprise. Felix's face became flushed, but he refused to look at Julian. René, using the wall to brace himself, now stood in front of Felix, trying to block Jacob, to protect him somehow. Despite his ravaged appearance, René held his head high and steady.

The tip of Felix's tongue was visible at the corner of his mouth, and then he bit down hard on it. Julian had seen him do that many times before, often when he was assessing his own artwork, likely disturbed by what he saw.

"See what my son can do, even in prison?" Jacob pointed a proud, swollen finger at the vibrant wall behind him. He took a deep, difficult breath and said, "Don't destroy him, Felix. Don't be afraid of René's talent."

For a brief moment everything stood still except for the flare of Felix's nostrils and the muscles tightening his face. His shame was overwhelmingly apparent.

The first bullet hit Jacob in the chest.

As René dove toward his father, Felix shot him in the leg. René cried out in pain. Julian tried to wrestle the gun out of Felix's hand, but Ludwig was quicker. He grabbed the gun first and then dutifully handed it back to Felix.

"Damn you, Julian!" Felix yelled, aiming the gun at him. "You set me up!"

Nothing mattered anymore. "Set *you* up, you bastard!" Julian shouted. "You lied to me so that I would bring Jacob here. There was never any deal, was there? All Jacob wanted was to see René, but you couldn't even give him that."

"Get out of here!" Felix roared.

"I am not going anywhere without René. You will have to shoot me too."

"Julian, stop! Just go!" René pleaded as he clutched his leg.

"I am not moving," Julian said firmly.

Felix called for the nearest guard then turned to René, "I am not finished with you yet."

Ludwig smiled approvingly.

"What's so goddamn funny?" Felix's voice was frighteningly controlled. "And what are you doing here anyway? You are not scheduled to be here until tomorrow. Or is that when you are fucking Charlotte at the Bristol?" Felix wiped his mouth slowly with his free hand, saying calmly, "Get over by the wall."

Ludwig sputtered an incoherent explanation.

"Save it!" Felix ordered, and then shot Ludwig in the back as he walked slowly toward the wall, toward his imminent death without a fight.

Julian dropped to the floor, next to Jacob, who was still breathing and trying desperately to say something. He pressed his mouth against Jacob's ear. "You saw René. He will be okay. I'll make sure of it. Go in peace."

Jacob began to pant, struggling for words. He pulled Julian to him. "Find Max Kruger."

Find Max Kruger?

"What? Why?" Julian shook him for more information, but Jacob Levi was dead.

Ludwig howled as the final bullet ripped through his shoulder, and then he, too, toppled over.

Felix stared at the bodies, at the blood, at René, and then at Julian. He turned and slammed the cell door behind him. Julian heard the pounding of Felix's boots echoing down the corridor as he shouted at the guards to clean up the mess.

BLACK

"All colors will agree in the dark."

—Francis Bacon

Chapter Twenty-Seven

DACHAU

Julian and René were taken from the Sachsenhausen prison in the middle of the day. The guards pushed them roughly out of the cement building and into the blinding light. Julian had no sense of time or season, but when he looked up, he saw amber and copper leaves adorning the few trees around the prison and knew it must be autumn. After so many months holed up in solitary confinement, the alien sunshine felt almost cruel against his face.

He concentrated on his shadow against the pavement. The charcoal image felt familiar and safe. He had seen the same shadow cast against his wall in the prison cell. It was the only friend he had known for a long time.

The guards had a good laugh watching René and Julian stumble along the walkway. Julian had not been upright in weeks, and his legs were almost too weak to hold up his body. He had not seen René since Jacob's murder. He had heard his friend's voice on several occasions, a vacuous echo through the prison corridor. Now, as René tried to walk with the shackles around his legs, Julian could see that he was limping on his bad leg, and he imagined that the bullet was still lodged inside the bone.

A dozen guards waited for them at the end of the road, surrounding a truck. As they approached the vehicle, René was pushed inside first, seated between two soldiers holding rifles. They placed Julian next to the door, seeming not at all concerned that he would try to escape.

Once the truck started moving, the driver opened his window, and a cool breeze washed over Julian. He distinctly remembered the feel of that gentle wind. Just right. Perhaps it was spring, not autumn. Maybe it was summer, not spring. It did not matter. There were no seasons at Sachsenhausen, just texture—the chronic feel of cold cement and the hollow sensation of cinder block. He tried not to betray his enjoyment of the breeze for fear of the guards noticing. He wanted to take pleasure in it for as long as he could.

Through the window, Julian could see a smattering of small red farmhouses surrounded by lush green meadows, stout cows roaming inside white fences. He heard the faint howl of a country dog and the distant neigh of horses. The scene reminded him of an oil by Engel's friend Erich Heckel, which had hung in the kitchen at Engel's country house. The painting depicted a flaming red sky, a cherry inferno accented with thick, heavy blue brushstrokes. The houses and trees were also abstract, the entire landscape weightless, like a dream. Who knew what had become of that canvas. Julian glanced at René, who had also admired that painting, but his friend's face was emotionless—he did not seem to notice anything.

"How long is the ride?" a guard shouted out to the driver. "These prisoners stink."

"Eight hours," the driver yelled back, rolling up the window. "We are heading about twenty miles northwest of Munich."

"Where is this place?" one guard whispered to another.

"No man's land. At least three thousand prisoners there, in a camp called Dachau."

The guard next to Julian elbowed him in the ribs. "Better do all your breathing now, Klein. I've been to Dachau. If you thought Sachsenhausen was bad, wait until you see this shithole."

A shithole would have been luxurious compared to this, Julian thought, recalling the guard's words a few months earlier, as he walked closely behind the other prisoners. Dachau was not simply inhuman. It was *Hell*. He gazed up at the sign suspended over the prison camp's entrance—his sign. He had painted it: DACHAU—ARBEIT MACHT FREI. *Work makes one free.* Julian nearly laughed aloud as he did every day when he walked past the sign. *Freedom? Ha!*

This so-called "freedom" consisted of slaving away eighteen-hour workdays in the "Pit"—a smoke-filled underground factory packed with political prisoners who built the Nazis' secret stash of ammunition and airplanes. None of the slave laborers were engineers. Most were once teachers, philosophers, writers, actors, musicians, or artists, like Julian.

He quickly looked past the sign, through the barbed wire at the forest just ahead, trying to decide exactly how he would paint Dachau. No greens, browns, blacks. His forest would be a collage of vermilion, lavender, orange, and turquoise, tucked under a shrill yellow sky. He would paint his forest in every shade not found on this side of the barbed wire: the colors of freedom.

"Klein, you are holding everybody up. Get moving!" shouted the guard walking behind him, gesturing toward the factory in the distance. "You've got planes to paint today."

The guard did not have to remind Julian. He'd heard of nothing else. This week was the general's monthly inspection: The planes had to be perfect, or else.

And painted black. *Only* black. Julian's brush had not seen color since the day he'd last painted in Engel's studio. René was the only artist in Dachau who was allowed to paint with color.

At the beginning of each week, René was handed a blank canvas with explicit instructions in Felix's handwriting. At half past five each morning, three guards would accompany René to a special building and watch him paint there until midnight. At the end of the week, the painting was collected and never seen again. René was forced to produce a painting weekly, or, under Felix's orders, he was to be beaten.

In the middle of the night, after the other eight men in their bunk were asleep, René would record what he had painted earlier that day, sketching the image in a small notebook he had found in the closet containing his paints and other supplies. He hid the book under a loose floor plank that he had dug out himself. Julian would cover for him, making sure that none of the other prisoners saw René sketch. At Dachau, trust and loyalty did not exist. Information could be bought or sold easily for an extra slice of bread.

Before closing the book, René would hand the drawing to Julian to study. He seemed determined that Julian not lose faith in himself as an artist, by telling his friend repeatedly that art existed no matter the circumstances. He taught Julian how to visualize a painting before it reached a canvas, to smell color before a jar of paint had even been opened—that way he could keep it alive in his head.

"Painting," René explained in a way that reminded Julian of Engel, "is how you use your mind *before* you land a single stroke. It doesn't matter that they forbid you to paint. They can control everything, Julian, but not your thoughts. Never forget that."

"Klein, goddamn it, wake the fuck up!" The guard shoved Julian forward into the Pit.

Julian, keeping his face blank, headed over to his designated spot. The ladder, the bucket filled to the brim with thick black paint, and a large brush were already waiting for him. A guard stood nearby with his gun pointed. He was small and scrawny, his uniform hanging loosely over his slight frame. Julian knew if the other guards weren't around, he could overtake that guy in less than ten seconds. They made eye contact. The guard nodded a Nazi hello, which translated to: *Do your work so I don't have to shoot you.* As Julian dipped the brush into the bucket, he tried to focus on the plane, but he couldn't get last night's conversation with René out of his head.

"Julian," René had whispered, clutching the notebook. "If anything happens to me, this book is our Bible of Proof. It is our only evidence that those paintings Felix is stealing are mine." He squeezed Julian's arm tightly, and Julian felt it to his bone. "Promise me, if something happens to me, you will do everything possible to save this book."

"Nothing will happen to you, René," Julian said, knowing it was a lie. They were all walking dead men.

"I love when you lie." René laughed sadly. "Keeps things light around here." The thickness of his breath was hot and rancid, but stench in Dachau no longer had impact. Anything that was sanitary or fresh was long gone, a distant memory belonging to another life.

Julian leaned in even closer to René. "We will survive this."

"What was it that Felix once called you, Julian—'naive and easily convinced'?"

"You're a schmuck." Julian smiled in the dark.

"Yes. At least they haven't been able to beat the asshole out of me. It's my secret weapon," René said, pausing. "If we do somehow miraculously survive this, we have to find Max Kruger. I know my father. He was trying to tell us something important. Don't you agree?"

Not Max Kruger again. René would not let it go. Julian nodded, thinking, *If we survive Dachau, René, we are getting the fuck out of Germany and definitely not going on a suicide mission to find Kruger.*

"The first thing I'm going to do is find a canvas and paint." Julian carefully changed the subject, glancing down at his calloused hands. "Any color but black."

"The first thing I'm going to do is head to Café de Flore and get a croissant." René pulled Julian's sturdy hands inside his delicate ones. "You will paint again, Julian, I promise. One day the world will see your brilliance. Your brushstroke is as good as mine, if not better."

Another lie. Mind games. But that's all we've got, Julian thought. *At least we have each other to remind ourselves that we are still men, not animals.*

René released Julian's hands, looked around the room to make sure everyone was still sleeping, then quickly slipped the notebook under the flooring. He pressed his mouth against Julian's ear. "We have no chance if we don't get out of here soon. You know that, right?"

Julian nodded. Dachau was a numbers game. Prisoners were dying daily from starvation, disease, beatings, and shootings. Their turn was simply a matter of *when*.

"I have a plan." René's voice was barely audible.

Julian leaned in closer, nervously scanning the room again to see if anyone was pretending to be sleeping. Two prisoners had been caught trying to escape a month earlier and were shot dead on the spot. "Tell me."

René shook his head. "Not yet."

"Don't be stupid."

René laughed. "Too late."

Chapter Twenty-Eight

René wiped his face with the least dirty part of his sleeve. Even in the obscurity of night, Julian could see that beneath the soot and grime there were deeply etched lines around René's eyes that belonged to a man at least ten years older than twenty-four. Julian felt sad and angry at the loss of life in his friend's face. Imprisonment had robbed René of his exceptional looks. His features were now hard and gaunt, his softness had disappeared the day Jacob Levi had been removed from the jail cell at Sachsenhausen, his body stuffed inside a sack and thrown out with the rest of the prison's garbage.

René pulled Julian toward him as they slowly walked toward the barbed wire along the outskirts of the camp. They were now so close together that René's features began to blur. This was it, Julian thought, the escape that they had been planning for months. They had timed it when they knew that there was one fifteen-minute period in the night, at exactly ten o'clock, when only one guard was on duty by the entrance and the other was taking a cigarette break. They had been scouting the entrance for eight weeks straight. And every night it was the same pattern. *That was the beauty of the Nazis,* Julian thought, *they never deviated from habit. It was the one thing you could count on in Dachau. You knew exactly what you were going to get at any given moment, and it never changed. The Nazis were human Swiss trains.*

Together, they would overtake the guard with a palette knife that René had stolen from the art supplies closet and hid inside his prison uniform. Julian did not want to think about the possible consequences. He did not want to think about killing the guard. But he knew that tonight it was either him or them. As he and René slowly rounded the outskirts of the camp toward the entrance, Julian recalled Max Kruger's words the night he had given up Ernst Engel to the Nazis: *It was either me or him, Julian, and I chose me.* For the first time, Julian understood.

Eyeing their target, Julian held his breath, feeling everything and nothing at once. There it was in the visible distance, his sign: DACHAU. And there it was, freedom waiting on the other side of the barbed wire. Twenty more yards. Fifteen. Ten. He could touch it, taste it.

"Don't move, Julian." René held him back, and then quickly pulled him down to the ground.

René's face was frozen and Julian knew without looking that it was over. Bright lights suddenly flashed over their heads, causing momentary blindness. He could hear footsteps fast approaching from behind.

"Don't turn around, Julian. Don't speak. No matter what," René hissed under his breath. "Let me handle it."

"Sons of bitches!" the guard shouted, running toward them with his gun aimed. "Get off the goddamn ground, Levi. I could kill you right here, right now, and not even think about it."

"Hermann, it's you." René breathed easier as he pulled Julian up with him.

Julian was astonished. *Hermann, it's you.* René actually looked relieved. And no one ever addressed any guard by first name. This particular guard was known to be one of the camp's most sadistic, turning daily prisoner beatings into sport. Julian stared at René. *What is going on here?*

"You have been gone twenty minutes," Hermann told René, ignoring Julian entirely. "They were about to call a hunt. But I volunteered to find you. Had a feeling you'd be out here. But I don't want to know why you're here, Levi, now do I?"

René said nothing. Hermann's face stretched with anger as he pressed his nose close to René's ear. "Take your sidekick and get to the Pit now. Use the sewer. I will cover for you and meet you down there. Now go!"

René thanked Hermann with his eyes and quickly led Julian in the direction of the underground factory.

"What the hell was that?" Julian whispered as Hermann watched them from behind.

"Hermann guards me most of the week when I paint. He thinks he is an art connoisseur and likes to make suggestions. I let him think that his opinion matters." René stopped to rub his bad leg. "My existence allows him to sleep at night. He beats up the others but watches my ass."

René scanned the area, and then removed a small potato from the inside of his pants, where he had tied a small pouch. "Here, Julian. I was saving this for later. Hermann gave it to me yesterday. Share it with me. Who knows what we will come up against."

Julian tore off a chunk and shoved it into his mouth, not remembering the last time he had eaten a potato that was not rotten. It tasted crisp, like a just-picked apple. He stared at the remainder in his hand, thinking that this was how the color white must taste. "Why didn't you tell me about Hermann before?"

René ignored the question and moved forward toward a small group of buildings. He then turned quietly and said, "I figured the less you knew, Julian, the less they could beat out of you. I didn't want you involved should something happen. See, Hermann and I have a mutual understanding. He protects me in small ways, and I keep my mouth shut. That is all you need to know."

"Tell me, then, what did Hermann get in exchange for this potato?"

René leaned against the corner of the building and took a quick peek inside. "I sketched his portrait. He wants to give it to his wife for their anniversary. Imagine, my Jew drawing will be the centerpiece of his SS-infested living room."

They both laughed under their breath, a much-needed release. Julian gestured toward the large block-shaped building about a hundred feet ahead of them, which housed the Pit. "This is it," René whispered anxiously.

They tiptoed around the back of the building, but Julian stopped and held René back when he spotted a half dozen guards congregating at the front entrance. And then he saw them immersed in a conversation with Hermann, who indeed seemed to be covering for them. He still could not believe it.

Lights blazed overhead and René dropped to the ground, again bringing Julian down with him. They slid across the gravel toward the sewer. René inspected the area quickly before lifting the large chrome-plated lid.

Julian looked inside, seeing only blackness and expecting to whiff garbage rot, but there was no smell, just cool nothingness, like the inside of a cave.

"It was built to look like a sewer, but it's not," René explained, pointing inside. "It is a tunnel leading straight to the Pit. Hermann told me that it had been built for emergencies—a bomb shelter."

"For them, not us," Julian said, stating the obvious.

"Of course."

René guided Julian inside first, then closed the lid over his own head. They slid straight down over small pebbles and other debris, landing underground in a small storage room filled with barrels of cement powder. They inched forward and walked toward an adjoining room, where they were noticed immediately.

"Halt!" the guard barked, running toward them with his rifle aimed.

They stood still as the guard pressed his gun under René's chin and held it there. René did not flinch. "As if you could just waltz right out of the Pit. You, Levi, are supposed to be painting here today, not having your usual privileges in Block Seven, you ungrateful bastard. I will string you both up myself, if I have to."

"I got him, Strunk." Hermann entered the room just as René's skull was about to get boxed. "Nice work. I will personally put in a recommendation. Now, go cover your post before any more assholes decide to wander off. I will take care of them from here."

Hermann pushed them both forward. Loud enough for the other guards to hear, he yelled, "I said, walk and shut your fucking mouths!"

Hermann kept up the charade as he escorted them through a long, musty tunnel, which opened up to the Pit. Julian's gaze was drawn toward the center of the room where six shiny black airplanes were perched on ramps, glowering over the laborers like giant black bats. Hermann took the two men to the officer in charge of the painting division, who slapped their faces hard. It stung, but Julian didn't flinch. "I would kill you if inspection wasn't this week," the guard shouted, making sure other prisoners standing nearby heard him. "Now, hoist your lazy asses up the ladder and finish the job."

René climbed up first, dragging his bad leg along the rungs. Julian stayed close behind to protect him from slipping.

"You were playing Russian roulette back there," Julian whispered. "You are a sick bastard."

"It is what I've become," René agreed.

They stood next to each other on the flimsy scaffold. Two guards positioned at the bottom watched them with pointed guns. René held the bucket of paint. "I will let you do the honors," he said gallantly. "Ladies first."

"Fuck off, René," Julian chuckled, as he dipped a large brush into the bucket. Using a metal stencil, he outlined a large circle on the plane's tail and filled it in carefully.

"Start painting, Levi!" the guard yelled from below. "Klein does not need you to hold the goddamn bucket! You were brought here for a reason. Final touches. Do it."

"What I would give to dump this bucket onto his face," René mumbled. "Now that would be a final touch."

"Don't, René."

"They are not going to kill me."

"Maybe they will kill me and make you watch," Julian said. "Do me a favor and just paint the damn thing."

René examined the paintbrush, stroking its wide wooden handle and running his fingers through its bristles. He then dipped it deep inside the black paint and dabbed it over Julian's circle. René concentrated, one eye closed, as he painted a large swastika onto the plane. Julian was reminded again of that first night in Paris. René's arm, though emaciated, still tangoed with the brush. His face, though hardened, still ignited as the paint hit the surface. His deep brown eyes, which had seen too much, still danced.

The escape had failed miserably but he doesn't seem fazed, Julian thought as he watched René absorbed in his work.

Nothing seemed to matter to René as long as he was painting.

Chapter Twenty-Nine

René glanced over at their bunkmates again, then triple-checked: All asleep. He exhaled deeply. "The day after tomorrow, Julian," he whispered. "At four o'clock." René closed the notebook, satisfied.

"In broad daylight? Are you nuts?" Julian whispered back. "No way."

René leaned close into Julian. "Listen to me. They are heavily prepared for night escapes. And now they've added another guard at the entrance. There is no way for us to overtake three of them, or two if one takes a break. But I've got a plan, Julian. This one is foolproof."

Nothing is foolproof.

René's eyes bulged like a mad scientist, and Julian grew afraid. Lately, René seemed to be losing it. He was no longer sleeping at night, just staring overhead with his eyes wide open, obsessively plotting their next escape attempt.

"The way I see it," René continued, "is that they would never consider that one of us walking corpses would have the guts to take off while the sun is shining."

"But why at four?" Julian shook his head. "I am still in the Pit. There is no way I can get out. They will know I am missing in less than three seconds." *Just like last time,* Julian thought nervously. It had been four months since their failed escape.

"I've thought about you in the Pit. I've thought about it all. In fact, that's all I think about these days." René stared up at the thatched ceiling as if it held all the answers he needed. "You are going to break my right hand, Julian."

Julian bolted upright. "What?"

"Quiet. You're going to wake someone." He pulled Julian back down next to him. "It is the only way."

"I am not breaking your hand."

"It is our only option," René said, his face was so close to Julian's now that Julian felt the stale breath of each word as if it were inside his own mouth. "I'm expected to finish one painting a week, right? A painting that under normal circumstances would take me months to complete. If I don't, the guards get punished, and I get beaten. But with my painting hand broken, everybody is in trouble. Naturally, they will bring you in to help, and from there we will make our escape. I estimate that it will be around four. It has to be around four."

"I can't do it," Julian said, shaking his head furiously against the slab of wood that was his mattress. "Goddamn it, René, you know I can't do that to you."

René flexed his painting hand. "It is our only chance to get out of here."

René was clearly going crazy, Julian thought. And this plan was even flimsier than their last escape attempt. He scanned the room again until he, too, was satisfied that everyone was still sleeping, then pressed his mouth firmly against René's ear. "Did you at least get the tobacco from Hermann?"

René shook his head yes. "He finally brought it today. I thought you would have noticed I put on weight." René lightly patted his pants. "That's why we're doing this tomorrow. I can't wait anymore, Julian. And neither can you."

René was right. They were both so thin and weak. "What did you tell Hermann it was for?"

"That I needed to mix the tobacco into the paint, to create a certain texture for a landscape."

"A landscape?" Julian laughed. "And he fell for it?"

"Of course. He thinks I'm Picasso."

It was hard not to laugh at the guard's sheer stupidity. They held their hands over their mouths as the guy sleeping next to Julian began to stir from his sleep. At least René got the tobacco, Julian thought with some relief. An inmate at Sachsenhausen, a well-trained communist, had taught René about the wonders of the Russian Machorka tobacco, especially that it had an odor intolerable to dogs.

"And get this, Julian. Hermann even brought me extra tobacco to paint a landscape of Dachau for his home." René rolled over onto his stomach. "Perhaps I'll paint him the Box."

Julian thought about Block Ten, which the prisoners called the Box. It was the prison camp's torture chamber, and he began to feel sick. The Box was filled with an average of two-dozen men daily, thrown inside the building once they were on the brink of death or when they were being punished. Very few came out alive.

"I will paint those men dying of thirst, rotting with typhus," René said distantly. "Should make a great visual. The last painting will show their lifeless diseased bodies tossed into a grave that they were forced to dig for themselves." René smiled to himself crazily and swept his hand through the air as if invoking the painting.

Julian eyed his friend sadly then looked up at the makeshift ceiling, at the loose straw pieces that occasionally fell on their heads during the night. Their sleeping quarters had been constructed for dogs, not humans.

"And if you doubt that we need to leave now, Julian, just remember that any goddamn day, one of those rotting stinking bodies lounging in the Box will be yours. You look like a walking skeleton and I should be so lucky." He watched Julian somberly. "That's why we need to break my painting hand. It is our only way out."

Julian shook his head, horrified. There was no medical treatment for prisoners. René's broken hand would never heal properly.

"You can do it," Rene said firmly. "My hand will eventually heal. Trust me. I've got it figured out."

"No, damn it."

"Yes, Julian. That's final." The crazed look in René's eyes evolved into something warmer, deeper. *You came back to Germany to save me, Julian. Now it's my turn.*

Chapter Thirty

Julian put down his paintbrush and measured each angle of the thick black paint with his bare hands. All four legs of the swastika were equal. The two prison guards who stood behind him with their guns aimed at his back were pleased.

The bell rang loudly, and Julian heaved a sigh of relief. He had a ten-minute break, the only rest period in the workday. The scrawny guard who looked like he was wearing his father's uniform pushed Julian forward. He moved quickly toward the factory's exit, trying to blend in with the other prisoners charging toward the door, toward food. He kept his head bowed, his gaze to the ground, as he collected his meal of salted lukewarm water called "soup." He felt the bony, angular shoulders of the others pressing against him on all sides, but no one dared speak. No one wanted to miss his only meal.

After he finished eating, Julian quickly headed back to the Pit. As he approached the door, a young guard, fat and bookish, grabbed his arm and stopped him in his tracks. Julian tried to mask any emotion he was feeling.

"Those planes are beauties, Klein," the guard said slowly, leaning forward. His breath stank of whiskey and meat. "The paint is perfect."

"Thank you," Julian said, without moving his lips.

"I wasn't complimenting you."

Julian's heart began to race. He knew immediately that something was wrong. But he also knew better than to turn around, even when he heard the pounding sound of black boots coming toward him just seconds later. Two sets of arms grabbed him. One of the guards belonged to Hermann's entourage.

"Come with us."

Predictably, at five thirty the next morning, the guards came for René and brought him to his painting quarters in Block Seven. No one spoke. When René entered the room, he saw Hermann standing with arms crossed, feet shuffling.

Please tell me Julian is alive, Hermann, René begged with his eyes. Hermann nodded slightly and gestured toward the door.

René turned, and before he could feel any semblance of relief, the door swung violently open. In walked Felix wearing casual trousers, a loose fitting shirt, and riding boots. He was suntanned and his hair was tousled, looking as if he had just returned from vacation.

"Good morning, René," he said, smiling brightly.

"Where is he, Felix?" René demanded. "Goddamn you, where is Julian?"

Felix checked his watch and signaled Hermann to open the door.

"Julian is on his way here," Felix said casually. "I thought we'd have a little reunion."

René knew all about Felix's reunions. But at least Julian was alive. That is all that mattered. The deal was done. René held his breath as the door opened several minutes later.

Julian was brought inside the room, and once the guards released his arms he fell to the floor. René closed his eyes, as though trying to ward away the image of his friend lying in front of him. "Julian," he whispered. Blood was everywhere. Julian's nose was broken, his lips busted open and swollen, and both of his eyes were ringed in black. At least he was still breathing.

"Hold Julian up, so that everyone here can see clearly what is about to happen," Felix said coldly.

One of the guards propped up Julian, who balanced against him like a broken marionette.

"Julian, is that you?" Felix laughed cruelly. "Or half of you?" He then signaled the other two guards over to René. "Hold his arms back," he ordered. "And bring in the other prisoner."

One of the guards left the room and brought inside a terrified-looking Peter, the comedian, their bunkmate.

"Tell them what you told us," Felix shouted at the man.

Peter spoke softly, his voice shaking as he glanced sideways at René, and then at Julian. Tears ran uncontrollably down his face.

"They were discussing how they could escape," Peter stammered. "That is all I heard."

Julian's eyes widened, shocked with the knowledge that it was Peter who had betrayed them. There were at least six others who might have done it, but not Peter, who usually kept up their spirits with his imitations and jokes.

"Yes, Julian," Felix said, as though reading his mind. "You were sold for cheap. The comedian turned you in for a half a loaf of bread."

René shouted at Peter, "You had Julian sent to the Box for fucking breadcrumbs!"

Peter, once a well-known comedian in Berlin who did a spot-on Hitler imitation, had tears in his eyes. "I'm sorry, René. I was so hungry. I—"

"Goddamn you, Peter. We're all hungry. Look at him. Nearly dead. You will pay for this!"

Felix glared at Peter. "Tell me, who is laughing now? Take him back to the factory." He then turned to Julian. "What exactly did you and René talk about?"

Julian said nothing.

"The loyalty between you two is touching." Felix eyed them both with raw hatred. "Let me make it easy on you, Julian. You are still alive, because last night René threatened that unless you were freed from the Box, he would no longer paint for me. So, here you are, Julian, alive and free." He made a panoramic sweep of the room with his arm. "Free to see the price of freedom."

Julian held his breath. He noticed Hermann's face turning white.

"Get me that hammer over there," Felix said calmly, directing Hermann toward the table of paints stacked up against the far wall. Hermann walked slowly, then froze briefly in his tracks.

"Move it!" Felix shouted. Hermann scurried toward the hammer, averting his misty gaze as he slowly handed Felix the tool.

Felix moved toward Julian. "Like I said, René cut a deal last night, Julian. Your freedom for his hands."

"That's not what I said, Felix," René blurted out. "I said I would stop painting unless you freed Julian."

"Exactly," Felix countered. "However, I am the one determining how you will stop painting."

Julian eyed the hammer, and then René, whose eyes were wide open, terrified.

"You need me, goddamn it." René argued, trying to maintain control.

"Not anymore. I've got everything I need," Felix said, nodding to Julian. "I kept up my end of the deal, and now, René, it's your turn."

Julian shook his head painfully. "No, Felix. It's enough. You won."

Felix's lips tightened. "Here's how it's going to go, Julian. *You* are going to hammer René's fingers one by one until I say stop."

Julian tried to speak, but nothing came out.

Felix circled Julian, waving the hammer, and then pressed it hard into Julian's hand. "It is either René's hands or his life. The choice is yours."

Julian stared at the hammer. He turned to René, but instead saw Jacob Levi's dead body flashing before his eyes, slumped against the Sachsenhausen floor. He then heard the sharp cock of Felix's trigger. Julian's broken gaze went as black as Dachau, as dark as the swastikas that he was forced to paint day and night in the Pit. But his own hands chose life.

Raising the hammer in the air with what little strength he had left, Julian banged the gleaming metallic against René's beautiful, slim fingers.

Fingers with souls of their own. He closed his eyes with each devastating crunch of bone.

With each slam of the hammer's head, Julian tuned out his own screams and those coming from the back of René's throat; the vacuous cries of two drowning men.

"Stop," Felix said finally, sparing two fingers.

The hammer dropped from Julian's hand, crashing against the floor. When he looked up, his tortured gaze met Felix's triumphant sneer. The icy expression had disappeared, and in its place was the punishing look of vindication.

And then Julian slowly turned to René, who was slumped over, a fiery palette of red enveloping him. He was alive, but his genius was dead.

Chapter Thirty-One

In the yard outside the Pit, Julian stood in line for a serving of soup and a slice of bread. He sat alone on the ground and dipped the stale bread crust into the soup to soften it. He brought the bowl to his lips, and over its wooden rim he saw René in the distance. He was walking alongside Hermann, and even from where he was sitting Julian could see the destroyed hands wrapped in thick gauze, like boxer's gloves.

Julian glanced around at the other prisoners, but their heads were buried inside their bowls. Julian slurped down the rest of his soup as Hermann led René by the elbow in his direction.

"Klein, get up," Hermann called out gruffly. "You are coming with us to Block Seven. You are going to paint."

Julian entered Block Seven, accompanied by René, Hermann, and two other guards. The smell of paint freshly ground in linseed oil was intoxicating, and Julian felt almost faint with yearning. He looked around. There was no trace of *that* day less than a week earlier—the hammer, the blood, Felix—the murder of an artist. Like everything else at Dachau, it had been cleaned out, disinfected, the evidence buried.

Hermann pointed to the unfinished canvas. "They want that painting, Klein. I have been given orders that you are to finish what René has started." He paused. "In fact, you will be painting in here from now on. Levi will be moved to the Pit."

Julian was shocked, and then he caught Hermann glancing quickly at René, who nodded slightly. No one else would have noticed, but Julian knew René's every nuance. Something was definitely up. He knew by the subtle way his friend's eyes shifted that there was more to this change in circumstances. He searched René's face for answers, but his friend quickly looked away.

Julian stared at the canvas, and his pulse began to race with uncontained excitement. After more than a year of painting black swastikas on planes, his brush would finally touch a real canvas. Gathering his breath, he could barely keep from taking the thin, half-finished painting into his arms and dancing with it across the floor.

René began to spell out what Julian was supposed to paint. His explanation was purely mechanical, clearly for the guards' benefit. Julian knew the composition from René's notebook. The image was of a woman, blonde and curvaceous, wrapped in a flowing dress, reclining on the top of a rock with a lake and passing boats as the backdrop—nearly the same scene that René and Felix had painted that fateful day at the lake. The woman, of course, was Charlotte. The notebook rendition was a mere sketch. The painted version was vivid and alive. And now, Julian thought guiltily, it was his to paint.

When the guards turned away, René pointed to the far left side of the canvas, whispering without moving his lips. "Take a good look inside the reeds, Julian. What do you see?"

Julian studied the composition. Inside the swaying stems, Julian deciphered the subtle swirl of René's signature.

In a low voice, René said, "I am inside every painting, Julian. No matter what Felix does with my work, I've signed my name in such a way that he simply cannot erase me. No matter what happens at Dachau, someone will eventually discover the truth."

"Stop yakking and finish it up!" Hermann shouted from the bench. "I have to bring that painting to the gate in less than five hours. Do you hear me? Five hours, that's it."

Julian began to paint, then stopped. His feeling toward the slim brush was so tender that it was almost painful. He glanced up at René, whose face was blank.

As the hours passed, strange looks passed between René and Hermann. No one seemed to notice the bizarre exchange but Julian. René said nothing. When the painting was nearly finished, René eyed it critically and pointed to the tall reeds swaying in the background and said, "It needs more red right here, Julian. This needs to be touched up, as in *now*. Do you understand me?"

"Now?" Julian repeated. René was clearly sending him a signal. Julian felt sick. *Not again.*

René tapped his belly. Julian could tell by the slight ripple of his shirt that something was beneath it. He glanced nervously at Hermann, who was picking dirt out of his ear with the end of a paintbrush.

"Trip the easel," René mouthed. "So that it breaks. Do it now."

Julian looked at the spindly legs at the base of the stand, and when Hermann turned to say something to the other guards, he kicked it and it snapped loudly. The painting fell, but René caught it with his good leg just in time, minimizing the impact of the fall.

"You idiot!" Hermann shouted at Julian. "You could have ruined the whole thing."

"It was my fault," René said. "I leaned against it by accident."

"Well, you can't just stand there holding the painting with your foot," Hermann said. "We need to steady it against something. Lean it against the damn wall!"

"Impossible, Hermann. Julian will not get the effect he needs. It must be propped up a certain way. He is almost finished. We need a new stand." René eyed Hermann in a collaborative way.

"What do you suggest?" Hermann asked in a measured tone.

"Why don't we throw together a stand out of some logs?" René suggested. "I saw a huge pile being brought in yesterday morning, near the entrance. Let's borrow some for a few hours. That should solve the problem. And it should take no time at all."

Hermann glanced at the other guards, who nodded their approval. "A piss first, then I'll take the prisoners out there."

As they waited for Hermann to return, Julian whispered, "What's going on?"

René ignored him and said loudly for the other guards to hear, "Julian, hold the painting upright for a moment. I need to make sure the canvas is stretched tight enough."

During the split second that Julian held up the painting, which blocked the guards' view, René stuck his finger down his pants, pulled out a canvas pouch, and shoved it against Julian, who quickly hid it inside his own pants. It was the Russian tobacco.

"As soon as we get out to the logs, sprinkle that all around the wood," René whispered. "There is a large hole in the ground. You cannot miss it. Put the tobacco all around it."

"What if Hermann sees me?"

"Hermann knows," René said calmly. "Don't ask questions."

At three forty-five, right on schedule, the painting was complete. Hermann took René and Julian outside the barbed wire to return the wood. Their backs were to Julian as he quickly sprinkled the tobacco around the logs and the large hole.

"Done," he announced to both men.

"Not yet," Hermann said quickly, his voice barely a whisper. "Put those logs over that hole, Julian, in a crossed formation. Leave some air in between." He scanned the area quickly. "Believe me, you will need it."

As they slowly made their way back to Block Seven, Hermann patted René on the back, like a proud father would a son. Julian noticed that René's emaciated shoulders buckled under the guard's touch. "The painting was right on schedule." Hermann tilted his head slightly, his eyes wide and unblinking. "Why don't you boys have a quick rest, and I'll come get you in fifteen minutes." Hermann grunted, then looked around nervously. "Fifteen minutes is all I can give you."

René smiled appreciatively. "It is all I need."

Then, looking at Julian, Hermann said, "You did a good job today."

Julian nodded, accepting the praise. Once they arrived at their barracks Hermann started to walk away, but then he quickly turned around, his eyes slightly watery. "Be careful, Levi."

As they entered the room, Julian wanted to ask René a thousand questions but held back. This was it. Hermann had allowed this to happen.

"We have less than two minutes, Julian," René said. "Look everywhere, over and under the beds. Check that no one is around."

Julian did as he was told. When René was satisfied with Julian's search, he pointed to the wooden floor plank, where he kept the notebook. Julian lifted it up.

"Now, lift the plank beneath that one."

Julian lifted the wood and peered into a large hole. "What is that?"

"That is how we are getting out."

Julian could barely catch his breath, thinking about how René's hands had been bandaged for nearly a week. He must have dug this before *that* day.

"The hole took me two months to dig," René explained. "Each time Hermann granted me a few minutes of rest after I finished a painting, I dug into that hole with the palette knife and a small shovel." René stared intently at the wooden floor. "I didn't want to tell you until it was ready. Until it was a real possibility." He paused. "Then I thought the hand plan was better, but I was wrong."

Julian felt light headed, imagining his friend working his way through the dirt like a mole.

René gazed down the hole. "We can do this."

"That hole next to the wood pile, and the logs," Julian said slowly, admiring the artistry of René's work, "that was no accident."

"Hermann helped me. He set up the logs himself, and the hole. He finished the digging for me, Julian. He said he could no longer sleep at night after what had happened to me. He heard from some of the officers that they plan to kill me soon. I'm worthless without my hands. And after that, it would only be a matter of time until they come for you." René pointed to a small sack inside the hole. "Take that, and grab the notebook. There is no time. Let's go."

Despite René's bandaged hands and injured leg, they crawled through the narrow tunnel, a good thirty yards. The hole was filled with insects. With each breath, Julian swallowed dirt kicked in his face by René's shoes. But he did not mind. His friend's torn soles were all the security he had right now.

When they arrived at the mouth of the hole outside the barbed wire border, they lay waiting, spooned around each other, inhaling the slivers of air that passed through the opened space between the logs.

Each passing minute felt ominously charged, like a time bomb. René squirmed anxiously against Julian, and then the siren went off. They both stopped moving.

Shouts erupted. Their names were called out repeatedly over a loudspeaker, then several loudspeakers, followed by the mad rush of the SS command with their long-leashed, growling dogs. Julian imagined they had just seconds before being chewed apart by those sadistic beasts. He had seen it happen dozens of times to other prisoners. Or, worse, they would be taken alive and tortured to death. The only tiny hope that he allowed himself was that the Machorka tobacco would actually work to repel the dogs, as the Sachsenhausen communist had promised it would.

The dogs charged in their direction. Julian envisaged their moist snouts glistening as their furious legs pounded the ground over their heads. Digging his nails into the dirt, Julian prayed—*whatever happens, let it be fast*—when suddenly the pounding halted and the dogs began to run in the opposite direction. They could not seem to get away from the wood fast enough.

The shouting, the gun-fired warnings, the graphic threats he envisioned—all of it—slowly faded away like the morning fog. And then, miraculously, it was over.

The tobacco had thrown off the dogs. The Nazis had not even bothered to explore the area themselves. Julian pictured Hermann leading the pack away from their hiding spot, feigning shock at having been deceived by René and vowing revenge.

Hermann, the brutal art-loving Nazi who had witnessed the destruction of his favorite artist's hands, had helped them escape.

The flutter in Julian's chest subsided, and an unexpected calm settled in as he and René waited for silence, followed by night. He pictured the forest just yards away as he had once yearned to paint it—a collage of vermilion, lavender, and orange tucked under a shrill yellow sky. He suddenly felt comforted, inside the cushion of soil, as though he belonged there. He took René's two remaining good fingers into his own hands. Julian held the slim tips against his cold lips for a long while, and then he kissed them.

GRAY

"Remember the enemy of all painting is gray."
—Eugéne Delacroix

Chapter Thirty-Two

MUNICH

Moving through the forest's thick growth of trees and underbrush, René balanced against Julian's arm. Peering over his shoulder, Julian kept seeing things in the darkness that were not there and hearing things that were, like the wind lashing the treetops and the ravenous howls of wolves, a reminder that he and René were not free—they were simply trespassers in the forest. Julian wanted to yell out that he was just a pile of bones, unworthy of any animal's appetite, but he remained silent.

Finally, after several hours of walking with a few breaks, they stopped. They were both exhausted.

"How far would you say we've gone?" Julian asked.

"Twenty miles, maybe more." René wiped the sweat off his forehead with the least dirty part of his sleeve. "Hand me a potato. We need to eat, Julian."

Emptying out the contents of the small sack René had stashed away, Julian knew that they did not have much to go on: two potatoes, a small jug of water, a handful of marks courtesy of Hermann, surplus Machorka, the palette knife, and an old, barely readable map.

He wished he could wrap a blanket around himself and sleep. Rubbing his eyes, he studied the faded colors of the old map, trying to make sense of the faint lines that seemed to blend together.

"Here's the way I see it," he said, handing René the less bruised potato. "We can skirt around Munich, head down along the Lech toward Füssen, and then out via the Austrian border, or we can cut southwest and make our way to Switzerland. But first, we have to somehow burn these prison pajamas and get cleaned up."

René scraped the ball of his shoe against a tangled tree root. "Julian, I have to go to Munich."

Julian stared up at him. "What?"

"I have to go."

"Are you mad? We can't go to Munich," Julian argued. "If they are not waiting for us at the end of this forest, then surely there will be a blitzkrieg welcoming us in Munich."

René gazed at Julian blankly. His dark eyes with coal circles beneath them made his face look ghostly. "You know damn well I can't leave Germany without finding Max Kruger."

This was too much for Julian; he couldn't believe what his friend was saying. He clasped his hands around René's shoulders, feeling the sharpness of the blades against his palms.

"We just escaped, and we don't know even know if we will make it to real safety." Julian softened his tone. "I know how you feel, but not now, René, not when we have a chance to live. Munich is suicide. Your father died so that you could live."

René pushed Julian away and stood. "You are free to make your own choices. But I have got to do this."

Julian glared at him. "And then you will be free? Why didn't we both just die in Dachau? Why did we even escape? Why did you dig a hole for months? Just to go back and get captured again?" Julian was shouting now. "Goddamn it, René—look at your hands! We are leaving Germany. We are going home, to Paris, and getting you the medical help that you need. Home, damn it! Do you even remember what that is?"

René stared at his limp leg, at his broken hands. "I want my paintings back, Julian. I want everything that Felix has stolen from me." His voice cracked. "Kruger knows something important. My father did not say those words in vain. Maybe Kruger can help me find my paintings."

Julian spoke quietly. "Look, we have a chance to start again. We will get you to a good doctor in Paris, a surgeon. Your hands will heal properly. We will both be strong again, and then we can search for Max Kruger, with help. We will contact your father's friends. Let's not do this alone."

"My fingers are deformed, Julian. There is no healing. All I have left of who I once was are those paintings." Tears welled in René's eyes, lending a faint sparkle to the turbid shades of brown.

Julian could not bear to see him this way. "You are a brilliant artist, René. Remember what you told me in Dachau? 'Painting is how you use your mind before you even land a single stroke.' You can learn to paint again." Julian, too, wanted to cry.

"Goddamn it, Julian!" René shouted painfully. "I will never land a single stroke again!"

Julian looked away. He knew it was true, that René would never paint again. He had been given a choice to let René die quickly, to spare him Felix's cruel vengeance. But instead, Julian had chosen life for his friend; a life that was really death in disguise. An artist who could no longer hold his own brush was as good as dead. Felix had taken everything from René: his father, Charlotte, his looks, his talent, and his inheritance. Julian stared deep into René's eyes and knew the unspoken truth: René had gotten them out of Dachau for Julian, not for himself.

Neither spoke as they gathered their meager belongings and moved forward in silence. The heaviness of Julian's thoughts weighed him down. If they went back to Munich, they would be sitting ducks. There was no way they could pull off another escape. He knew by the determined look in René's eyes, though, that he was going, no matter what. And how could he leave René? They had survived so much together. Julian glanced at the leg dragging, and at the bloodstained dirty bandages that needed to be changed. Max Kruger, who had betrayed Ernst Engel, was somehow linked to Jacob Levi. René had nothing left but the last words of a dying father and stolen paintings that were out in the world somewhere.

Julian peered into the forest, but it gave him no answers. Then, suddenly, he thought of the teachings of the Talmud: *If you save one person, it is like saving the entire world.* He glanced at René, hunched over, destroyed. If, together, they could find even one of René's stolen paintings, maybe it would bring his friend back to life.

Once they approached the end of the forest, Julian started to sweat, keenly aware of the danger they were in and amazed that there was any moisture left in his body. The guards must be out there somewhere. He nervously sprinkled a handful of Machorka around them, just in case the dogs were on their way.

He turned to René, but his friend's gaze seemed a million miles away. Julian knew it was up to him to insure their safety.

"Rest your leg," he whispered, noticing a large, sturdy tree up ahead. "I am going to climb that tree and scout out the situation before we move anywhere. Okay?"

René said nothing.

It took all of Julian's strength to climb to the lowest branch. "There's a farm ahead. Dogs, cows, chickens," Julian called down. "Would you look at that? Laundry lines filled with clothes just waiting to be taken."

"They are probably wet," René replied.

Julian began his descent. "Let's take the clothes, a bucket of water, whatever else we can find, and get the hell out of here."

At Julian's insistence, they stole two pairs of trousers and two long-sleeved flannel shirts, which were, as René predicted, still wet. The clothes felt ten sizes too big so Julian made belts out of twine.

"You still want to go to Munich and find Max Kruger?" Julian eyed René intently, already knowing the answer.

"Julian, I can go myself," René said weakly.

"Stop being a martyr," Julian countered. "We've been through everything together. But after Munich, we will never step foot in Germany again. That's final." Before René could respond, Julian pointed to a beat-up pick-up truck. "And we are going to Munich my way. We're not walking there. We are getting into the back of that truck and hoping that tomorrow morning the farmer heads to Munich. Maybe I'm crazy, René, but I want to get out of this place alive."

"What if the farmer finds us first?" René asked.

"Better him than the Nazis."

René, for once, did not argue. They climbed into the back of the truck and hid under a tarp. They were both so thin that they barely caused the thick canvas to ripple. Julian tried to fight against falling asleep, too afraid of the possibilities—but once René began breathing heavily next to him, the sound became hypnotic and soon he, too, fell asleep.

They woke to find that the truck was moving and that a woman, presumably the farmer's wife, was the driver. They could hear her arguing with a younger woman in the front seat. Julian made out that they were going to a hair salon in Munich in preparation for some kind of banquet. Or maybe it was a wedding. He assumed they were mother and daughter; the mother wanted her daughter's hair swept up, off her shoulders. But the daughter insisted on wearing it down, parted, with a single barrette. The argument ensued, and Julian was enjoying every minute of it. How long it had been since he had heard a simple, frivolous conversation? But all that really mattered was that they were on the right track—headed toward Munich.

"It's a good sign," René whispered.

Julian didn't answer, knowing that luck had a way of changing all too quickly, that good signs did not exist.

Pressing his ear against the cold metal bed, Julian felt the vibration of the wheels beneath them. Then the truck finally stopped.

Julian and René waited ten minutes before making a move. Julian lifted the corner of the tarp slightly and saw that they were in front

of a beauty shop. He signaled to René that the area seemed clear, and
they both jumped out as fast as they could, onto the narrow sidewalk.
They made their way to a small shop and the first thing they bought,
with Hermann's money, was a thick loaf of bread and a few wedges of
cheese. The sharp cheddar glided across Julian's tongue, and he kept it
there, savoring the taste. He then tucked a newspaper that he found in a
nearby garbage bin under his arm. They strolled along the street, passing
several guards. Julian held his breath. They were emaciated, bandaged,
and clearly strangers to the area. There was no point in hiding so they did
they opposite. They walked slowly, acting as if they had all the time in
the world. They made themselves so obvious that even those who took
notice dismissed them—as if they did not exist.

They hid in an alleyway while Julian studied the map. He determined
that they were in the center of Munich, and he noted that the university was only about eight or ten miles away. So they were not too far
from Kruger's home, which René remembered was near the university,
though he could not recall the street name.

"We will find it," René assured Julian. "The house is unforgettable.
Kruger's friend, the architect Erich Mendelsohn designed it. It's made of
glass, brick, and steel. You have never seen anything like it."

Julian nodded, but his thoughts were elsewhere. Kruger had betrayed
Ernst Engel. Perhaps he had also betrayed Jacob Levi. René seemed too
hopeful about their meeting. After Sachsenhausen and Dachau, Julian
knew they had to proceed cautiously, and that it was up to him to think
for them both.

They began walking, maintaining a leisurely pace for the first half hour,
trying to remain inconspicuous. With each step, Julian felt as though he
were in another man's body. As they strolled out of the city center, along
Odeonsplatz, north to Ludwigstrasse, he kept reminding himself that he
was free to actually choose which direction he wanted to go. He was so

used to receiving orders that he kept looking over his shoulder, waiting for someone to shout out: "Turn right, then left, Klein, you lazy Jew."

They picked up speed and concentrated on taking side streets, maneuvering through alleys until they found the university. They saw a group of students congregating outside the building, talking, laughing, eating at tables, their school books piled high next to them. They seemed so free, so normal. But Julian knew that appearances were deceiving. They, too, would soon be robbed of their individuality and idealism. Some of them, in time, would also become the Nazis' prisoners.

Moving quickly past the university, they turned down side streets, searching for the house. René was sure they were close, but nothing looked familiar. The sun was setting and they were both fatigued, but they were determined to find the house before dark.

"That's it, Julian!" René pointed to an elegant tree-lined street in the distance. "Do you see that house over there on the corner? It has a tree house in the yard, and I remember it. I remember thinking that my father had always promised to build one with me, but never got around to it."

"Then let's go," Julian said, brushing aside memories of his father, who had never promised him anything but work.

They moved quickly toward Kruger's property. It was a large flat-roofed structure with wide glass windows, steel beams, and brick, an anomaly standing out from the luxurious Tudor houses surrounding it.

Julian exhaled deeply. "That is the ugliest, yet most fantastic thing I have ever seen. It looks like a sculpture, not a home."

René nodded. "Now, we just have to hope that Kruger is inside."

They hid behind some tall bushes, then moved around the side of the house toward the backyard. A small light shone through the large center window on the first floor, near the back door. Julian moved in for a closer look. Peering inside, he saw Kruger seated alone in front of a fireplace, looking dapper and relaxed in a burgundy robe and slippers. He wondered if Kruger's family was also at home. Julian breathed deeply. Was this luck? A sign? He shook his head to himself. No such thing. They would do what they had to do, and get out.

Kruger was gazing into the fireplace, stroking the stem of a wine goblet. Julian watched him tap his free hand on the armrest, nodding his head from side to side. It looked like he was humming. *Bastard.* Julian recalled Kruger's words at Johann Finch's gallery just before he was whisked him away: *It was either Engel or me, and I chose me.*

"René," he whispered. "Don't trust him. Remember, we don't know whose side he is on. He may have betrayed your father too."

"We'll soon find out."

Julian signaled René to stay to one side of the glass door. He tossed a pebble at the window, hoping to get Kruger's attention. He ducked as Kruger walked toward the window, and then threw a second stone a bit harder.

Kruger shouted out, "Who's there?"

Julian waited a few more seconds before tossing the third pebble, then again repositioning himself across from René, waiting. "Maybe he's got a gun," Julian warned, hearing the shuffling sound of Kruger's approach.

As Kruger stepped out of the door, Julian grabbed him from behind and held the palette knife to his throat. While Kruger struggled to free himself from Julian's headlock, René kneed him in the groin with his good leg. Kruger cried out, and then a small pistol tumbled from his hand as he doubled over in pain. René kicked the gun over to Julian, who quickly retrieved it and aimed it at Kruger.

The artist looked disoriented, uncertain at first who they were. Suddenly, he covered his mouth in disbelief.

"I thought you'd be dead by now," he stammered through his fingers.

"We are," Julian said. "Look at us."

"Have they freed you?"

"Freed us?" Julian laughed.

"Is anyone else with you?" René demanded.

"I am home alone." Kruger held his throat, shaking his head.

"Don't move," Julian warned René. "It could be a trap."

"The neighbors will see you," Kruger said anxiously. "I can't discuss anything out here. "Please, let's go inside and we can talk."

Julian shook his head no to René. *Don't go inside. We don't know what's in there.*

"Please, believe me." Kruger searched the backyard. "It's too dangerous out in the open."

René pointed a bandaged hand at Kruger's eyes as Julian pressed the gun to the man's back. "Julian is the only person I believe," René said. "Now, let's go inside slowly, turn out the lights, and then we are going to talk."

Sitting on an upholstered chair in Kruger's living room, Julian could not believe where he was. Inside a real home, surrounded by a sofa, chairs with embroidered cushions, a loveseat, an oriental carpet, a fireplace—relics of humanity. Just a day ago he had been trekking through a forest, running for his life. He looked around the cozy room and realized with surprise that there were no paintings on the walls. *Strange,* he thought, *an artist's home without artwork?* And then Julian spotted the small black-and-white framed portrait of Adolf Hitler resting on the mantelpiece, and knew with certainty that they were not safe.

"Why did my father say your name before he died?" René demanded, also eyeing the portrait.

"I was the one who contacted him and told him that Felix had you sent to Sachsenhausen," Kruger whispered nervously. "Maybe he thought I could help you."

"But you didn't help us," Julian countered. "You must have known we were in Dachau."

Kruger shook his head.

"Liar!" Julian shouted, pointing to Hitler's portrait on the fireplace. "You work for them. You were responsible for Engel's death. I was there."

"Yes," Kruger admitted. "And I have paid the price dearly for saving myself and my family. Many of my colleagues are dead, jailed, or have fled the country, leaving their artwork behind. They were not given a choice. So much valuable work has been lost. And my students," Kruger could barely contain his emotion. "Several have been taken away to God knows where."

"But your art survived," Julian said accusingly.

"Many of my paintings have disappeared from galleries that have been raided," Kruger replied quietly.

"What does any of this have to do with my father?" René persisted.

Kruger exhaled deeply. "Once the Nazis rose to power, the French were concerned about the fate of their art in Germany. They contacted prominent artists and art dealers here, including Ernst Engel and me. They wanted us to help them obtain information on the fate of French artwork. In turn, they said they would help us." He leaned toward René, who was now sitting in a chair near the fireplace. "Your father, because of his connections to many of Europe's most prominent families—particularly in Germany—was part of this, even before you came here to study with Engel."

He pointed a shaky finger at René. "Jacob Levi helped his government. But the French did nothing to help him when he was captured and brought here. And they knew exactly what had happened to him— because I let them know. Still, they did nothing. Not even after they killed him. Silence. Typical of your countrymen," Kruger chided. "They take what they want and then discard you when you are no longer useful, even someone with the status of your father."

René looked physically sick. Kruger walked over and touched René's stooped back. "Your father was a brilliant man, René. He was loyal to his family, his friends, his government, and most of all, to art—even to the end. They beat him for days, but got nothing from him." He eyed René sympathetically. "You should know that."

Julian recalled Jacob's destroyed face, as René stood and moved to the other side of the room, his back facing them.

Kruger's compassionate gaze suddenly turned callous. "I don't care about France," he continued. "I did what I had to do for *our* movement. Once it was obvious what would happen, Ernst and I smuggled many paintings to France, even before the night of the exhibition at Finch's gallery. We needed protection for *our* art, *our* artists. We had friends in Spain, but France was our only real hope. The French are traitors, but we knew they would do anything to preserve art, especially where their precious Monets, Renoirs, and Pissarros are concerned." He reached for his pipe. "Unfortunately for France, many of those great works happen to be in the hands of prominent Jewish families here. So, the fate of many French paintings is, at this point, ambiguous."

"Engel was your best friend, a founding member of your movement," Julian said slowly, as Kruger lit his pipe. "If you truly cared about the fate of the avant-garde here, how could you let him die like that?"

Kruger's voice was barely audible. "I have to live with Ernst Engel's death every day of my life."

He tightened his robe around his waist, and Julian realized Kruger looked trimmer, more fit, than he remembered. His bright red hair was laced with gray. Apparently, the Reich had served him well.

"And what have you done to save the movement while we were rotting away in prison?" Julian demanded.

Kruger stared down at his black silk slippers. Then, looking up slowly, he stared at René's bandaged hands. "Follow me upstairs. First, we will change your bandages, and then you will get your answers."

Kruger said nothing as he cleaned René's deformed fingers, which were swollen and black. Julian had to look away as René stared down at his hands, tears streaming uncontrollably down his face.

After Kruger finished wrapping them, he held René's hands inside his own and whispered, "They will pay for this, I promise." He paused. "Now we must go."

He led them up a winding staircase, through several corridors to a part of the house that had no windows. He went to a narrow linen closet in the hallway, opened it, and quickly transferred piles of neatly folded sheets from a three-tiered shelving unit onto the floor. He then reached back into the closet's middle shelf and pulled a lever. The wall unit turned, and Kruger ushered them inside a small enclave.

He tugged at a string hanging from the ceiling, turning on a dim light. Julian saw that layers of artwork were stacked neatly against one wall. The opposite wall contained what appeared to be a small, intricate radio system. He counted four large cameras and dozens of rolls of film perched on a long makeshift shelf above a desk. Papers, files, and photographs were organized in another corner. Whether it was the Germans or the French, Kruger was definitely working for somebody.

Sitting down, Kruger quickly hooked up the radio system. Julian moved behind him as he pressed several buttons and punched in codes that Julian had no way of deciphering. He watched for a while, attempting to discern a pattern, then realized that Kruger was trying to contact someone. He quickly pressed the gun to Kruger's temple. "Turn the damn thing off."

Kruger swiveled around in his chair, ignoring the gun. "I have a direct connection to the Paris office. You wanted me to prove myself."

"How do we know you are contacting France?"

Kruger shrugged. "You don't."

"And what the hell is the 'Paris office' anyway?" Julian asked. Unused to the weight of the gun in his hand, he put more pressure on it, and Kruger turned off the radio.

Kruger reached inside a drawer and handed Julian a stack of photographs. "The Paris office is my source, who must remain anonymous, but take a look at these."

Keeping the gun aimed at Kruger, Julian passed half the pile to René, who sifted through images of unfamiliar faces and abstract paintings. Julian paused when he came across photographs of Friedrich Fricke, who was holding those same posters of deformed individuals that he exhibited during the lecture Julian had attended at the university. Another picture showed a fully uniformed Fricke standing alongside his car, arms crossed, watching approvingly as artwork was being removed from the

Folkwang Museum in Essen. There were close-up shots of famous artists and their work, many whom Julian recognized—Kandinsky, Nolde, Kirchner, Grosz, Beckmann, Klee, Marc, Heckel, and Engel.

Julian flipped further through the stack and stopped when he came to pictures of Felix and Charlotte out on the town. He could feel René's burning gaze over his shoulder. Felix was smiling for the camera, holding Charlotte's arm. She stared straight ahead, lifelessly. Another photo depicted Charlotte draped in a floor-length fur coat, laughing at something Felix was saying.

Kruger pointed to the photo. "Charlotte works for them. Trades art for them. She stopped modeling for Fricke and started working for the Reich's culture department." He looked intently at René. "The Reich's goal is to fill Germany's museums with the Old Masters, and to get rid of all modern artwork. They have people placed all over Europe, and Charlotte runs the Paris operation. Just last month, she obtained Cranach's *Portrait of Frederick the Wise* from dealers in Paris. Wilhelm Von Bredow presented that painting to Hermann Goering himself."

"She's in Paris?" René whispered.

Kruger looked at Julian and then at René. "I am sorry to tell you this, but Charlotte is not only trading art—she also oversees a group of German art historians who are roaming French libraries and museums, searching for all valuable works of art and objects that were looted by the French and stolen from us since the fifteen hundreds. The Reich's goal, of course, is to return to Germany what they believe is theirs."

Julian gestured toward the radio system. "Why don't the French arrest her?"

"She is too well protected. Anyone who could arrest her has been paid off handsomely. There are those in the French government who have been very cooperative with the Germans, for the right price. As long as Charlotte feeds the right people paintings by French artists, they let her do her business. They don't care if the artwork was confiscated from German homes or museums, as long as French artwork is back on

French soil." He paused, eyeing René closely. "Charlotte has become more dangerous, perhaps even more important to the Reich than Felix."

"No!" René yelled painfully, the sound from so deep a place that Julian could not bear it. René flung the photo of Charlotte and Felix to the floor.

Kruger watched, shook his head with pity, but did not respond. He went to a corner of the room and pulled out a thick file labeled in bold black letters: *Entartete Kunst*, Degenerate Art.

"This is my report," he explained. "It is going to those few in France who truly care about the fate of modern art. Not just French art, but German, Spanish, Italian." He stabbed a manicured finger into the file, and then dropped it onto Julian's lap. "Read this, and then tell me if I am lying."

Julian opened the heavy folder. Inside were photographs of hundreds of artists and their work. Paintings, drawings, sculptures, and graphics— all modern art. Everything was organized by the name of the artist, followed by the title and date of the work, the dimensions, and which gallery represented the piece or if it came from a private collection.

He sifted through photos of work by prominent German Expressionists and many foreigners including Picasso, van Gogh, and Dali. He paused when he saw the artist Marc Chagall's painting of a rabbi pinching snuff. It was a 1912 oil of an Orthodox rabbi with a long greenish beard and sidelocks. He wore a black suit, a yarmulke, and was studying the Bible, the Hebrew letters visible. A large Jewish star hung prominently in the background. It reminded Julian of the world he had left behind—he quickly closed the file, handing it back to Kruger.

"Why are you showing us this?" Julian asked faintly.

"Because that portrait of Hitler on my fireplace is just a cover, Julian," Kruger explained. "The Nazis think I am with them, while actually I am working with the most important galleries throughout Germany, whose art has been seized and whose brave directors and curators have been fired for trying to preserve the art. Together, we are keeping inventories, records of everything that has been expropriated and stolen by those bastards." He closed his eyes. "The art is still alive, but who knows for how long."

"Where are the Nazis storing all the artwork?" René asked.

Kruger lowered his voice. "More than a thousand of the most valuable paintings are being stored at Schloss Schonhausen in Niederschonhausen in Berlin." He wiped his hand over his lips. "Paintings by Gauguin, Picasso, Matisse, Klimt, van Gogh. The list is endless. And the remaining thousands of confiscated works that are *not* considered lucrative are being crammed into various storerooms throughout Berlin and Munich. We have friends working inside many of the facilities. Their hands are tied, but not their eyes. We know exactly what is going on."

Kruger walked toward the paintings propped against the wall and touched each one tenderly, running his fingertips along their delicate wooden frames. He drew one canvas toward him and looked at it as if seeing it for the first time.

Julian moved in closer and examined the painting. The brushwork was stunning. It was an urban scene of Berlin juxtaposed with Munich. Each recognizable building, each face, was luminous and strong, characterized by embellished abstract strokes, dense with color. Julian did not see the cities while gazing at the painting—he *felt* them, as if they were inside the tiny room.

Kruger looked at Julian sadly. "This was once my Germany, a place where individuality was unconstrained and full of passion. We had a drunken freedom back then that no longer exists and, I'm afraid, can never exist again."

Julian played with the trigger of the gun. Kruger sounded too much like Ernst Engel, he thought, and did not deserve to.

Kruger rambled on about the early days of his *Die Brücke* group and his friends in *Der Blaue Reiter*, the founders of German Expressionism. He did not seem to care whether Julian and René were even listening. He smiled to himself, indulging his memories. Julian realized that for Kruger, those memories were where it all ended. There would be no more inspiration, no more artistic refueling. His career was finished; his world had crashed and burned.

Kruger opened a small jar of paint and held it under Julian's nose. "Smell this. This is what yellow was like when she was alive. You have no idea all the things yellow could do." Kruger stroked the tiny bottle, and then quickly returned it to its spot. "There is no going back," he lamented, as he shut off the light and led them out of the room. "The past was glorious but the present is nonexistent as far as any real artist is concerned. There are no morals left in Europe, no muses. Just deals to be made between men, between countries. Germany's plan is to first rape Europe of its great art, and then to desecrate it."

He placed the Degenerate Art file back into Julian's hands, and Julian was disturbingly aware of the man's delicate fingertips, which were amazingly similar to René's before they had been destroyed.

"Read the file again, Julian. Carefully," Kruger urged. "Then, we will discuss what you are going to do."

Julian glared at him. He was done with doing. Kruger owed *him*, not the other way around. Now for their own safety, they had to get out of Munich.

"Before we leave, we also came for information about René's paintings," Julian said firmly. "Felix forced him to paint more than fifty paintings in Dachau and then stole them all. Do you know where they are?"

Kruger's grayish-green eyes hardened as he slowly descended the stairs. He turned and looked up. "You do something for me, and I will use my sources to locate René's paintings."

Julian laughed with contempt. "Do something for you? No way. No deal."

He was about to tell Kruger to go to hell. But when he looked to René for support, his friend was already following the middle-aged artist down the stairs, too closely, like a prowler's shadow.

~~)C~~

Over thinly sliced meats and sauerkraut, Kruger summarized the file. "Two days from now, on July eighteenth, there will be a major event here in Munich celebrating the opening of the Great German Art Exhibit, which is being displayed in Hitler's favorite new museum, the House of German Art."

Julian and René hardly heard Kruger as they slowly nibbled the turkey, roast beef, and fresh vegetables. Kruger watched them eat the meal as if each bite could be their last, and he shook his head with pity. "Hitler and his entourage are using the opportunity to exploit the growing public resentment against the avant-garde," he continued. "The celebration will be the official kick-off of a 'reeducation' program, following more than a year of planning by a committee of Nazi officials. Look at this list."

Kruger placed a document on the table and Julian studied it. Baron Von Bredow's and Fricke's names were on it, as were Hartt's and Streibel's—all those who attended the meeting in the baron's library the night of Hans's funeral. Julian stopped chewing. "Where is Felix's name?"

"Felix refuses to have his name printed anywhere, on any document," Kruger explained. "He wants to remain a silent player. Anyway, the most frightening part of this is that by the end of the summer this committee plans to confiscate upwards of sixteen thousand paintings, drawings, sculptures, and prints from galleries and museums throughout Germany."

Kruger paused. He leaned over Julian's shoulder, pointing at the list. "Hundreds of paintings have already been sold for hard currency to foreign buyers at private auctions, mainly in Switzerland. My source in Paris tells me that an important auction to be held in Lucerne is already in the works. The most valuable stolen works are going to be prostituted to the highest bidder. It sickens me."

"Where do we fit in all this?" René asked.

"Why do we need to fit in?" Julian countered, increasingly worried that their escape from Munich was never going to happen.

Kruger sat down next to Julian. "I need you."

"Need us? For all you knew before tonight, we were dead."

Kruger shrugged innocently. "But you're not, Julian. You came to find me."

Julian turned to René, his fists tightly curled at his sides. "I don't care if Kruger is spying for God. We have paid our dues. And you know that Felix will not rest until we are caught, and this time he'll want us dead, I'm sure." He stood. "Let's go, René. Now."

René pushed away his plate, but remained seated. "I want my paintings back!" he shouted at Julian. "They are all I have left. And what about all the other artists whose works have been stolen or sold against their will? If, as Max says, we can do something, then I'm in. My father would never have abandoned this cause." Veins protruded angrily from René's neck as he dared Julian to defy him or his dead father.

This is crazy. Goddamn it, René, don't do this. Julian clenched his teeth and turned to Kruger, "What exactly do you want us to do?"

Kruger began pacing. "I want you, Julian, to attend two exhibitions that are opening one day apart and report everything you see there at both. One is the Great German Art exhibit that I mentioned, and the other is what they call Degenerate Art."

"Why don't you go yourself?" Julian asked.

Kruger paused, his gaze intensifying. "Because something is wrong. My source in the culture department refused to take my calls this week. This has never happened before." Kruger walked around the large dining room table. "I think it is best for me to keep a low profile until I find out what's going on. I want you to go to the exhibitions in my place. We will then put together a detailed report for my contact in Paris that I will send with you." Kruger leaned over the table. "You do this for me and I will make sure both of you get out safely."

"Why me?" Julian complained, feeling in advance the emptiness he knew would come over him without René. "Why not—"

"My leg and my hands, Julian," René answered before Kruger had a chance to respond. "A dead giveaway."

Julian nodded. He turned to Kruger. "And René's paintings?"

Kruger looked at both of them. "As I said, I will see what I can find out."

"And how exactly do you plan to do that?" Julian demanded. "Knock on Felix's door and politely ask him to hand them over?"

"I will find a way," Kruger said confidently.

Julian glanced across the table. René's eyes were bright and optimistic, as if Kruger were *the* answer to his stolen paintings. Julian felt otherwise, but he had not seen that look on René's face in many months.

He looked at both men, who were waiting for him to decide. Julian stared at the empty white porcelain plate in front of him—a blank canvas starving for color. The brush was now in his hands.

Chapter Thirty-Three

Outside the House of German Art, Julian moved anxiously through the throng of excited spectators. He estimated that fifty thousand people were waiting to see the parade celebrating the museum's opening. He found a decent spot along Munich's Prinzregentenstrasse and studied the crowd. The street was lined with forty-foot high pylons crowned with an eagle and a swastika. The people seemed to be fighting over who got to stand closest to the displays. The sun beat down on Julian's back, yet he felt a shiver course through him. This was the last place in the world he should be standing. Adjusting his tie—rather, Kruger's tie—nervously, he hoped that despite his emaciated appearance, the glasses, blond hair dye, and fake mustache would disguise him thoroughly.

An orchestra began to play loudly and the extravaganza rose up before him, with ornate golden Viking ships moving down the street, bearing costumed priests and seers from European legends. He watched Charlemagne pass by on a float, ahead of Frederick of Barbarossa, followed by Henry the Lionhearted. Thousands of participants wore historical costumes. A procession of Germanic gods and goddesses passed by, and the noise around Julian heightened until he began to lose track of where he was.

He turned and tried to leave, but could not move. The crowd was so densely packed, and the summer heat so smoldering, that he thought for a moment he must be back in the Box. He looked around, frantically searching for some way out. If he could just push through several more rows, he would be in the clear, but an abundance of applause and locked shoulders forced him to stay where he was. Without will or effort, he turned and listened.

Adolf Hitler stepped up to the podium to speak. He greeted the spectators with a high salute, and then began to rant on about "cultural barbarism" and the need to eradicate those traitors who were using corrupt art to destroy Germany. His voice was slightly hoarse yet penetrating, demanding, larger than life, and Julian felt surprisingly sucked into the spectacle. Locking his arms at his sides, Julian tried to balance himself and defy the leader's magnetism. Yet, it was impossible. The people surrounding him seemed to be hypnotized. Their mesmerized expressions reminded Julian of the fresh-faced students mooning over Friedrich Fricke: one nation, one delusion.

The man was truly hateful. *If only I could paint him. Just like that, standing in a blaze of screaming reds, ardent oranges, and passionate yellows amid thousands of black stick figure followers, who are entranced by his fury and blinded by his spell.*

Julian closed his eyes and then opened them to thunderous applause. The painting in his mind quickly vanished and all that remained was reality—evil surrounding him on all sides.

This is what hell must look like.

Julian finally managed to push through the crowd toward the House of German Art, despising Kruger for sending him there, knowing that he had no choice now but to go deeper inside if he ever wanted to get home.

Battling his way out of the masses, Hitler's voice still pounding at his back, Julian finally stood in front of the House of German Art. The gleaming marble structure occupied an entire street, dominating like no other museum he had ever seen before.

It took over an hour to enter the museum, and the waiting intensified Julian's anxiety. He kept his head down, certain everyone must know who he was. When he neared the front doors, he merged into a large group and walked with them through an arched hallway leading into a spacious foyer. Potted laurel trees at the entrance surrounded an enormous, bronze bust of Hitler, an idealized, younger version of the man. The group stopped to pay homage, but Julian dodged the sculpture and moved toward a young, gold-braided attendant who was handing out exhibition brochures. He took one. He would see the museum's highlights, record what he saw for Kruger, and then leave as soon as possible.

The brochure echoed Hitler's words, emphasizing the need to eradicate the immoral forms of art that had attempted to claim Germany and contaminate it. The museum's display consisted of six hundred paintings and sculptures around Hitler's favorite neoclassical themes, each organized by category—portraits, nudes, landscapes, and military subjects.

Attempting to appear casual and anonymous, Julian moved at a leisurely pace through a wide, well-lit marble gallery. But he stopped in his tracks when he saw the life-sized portrait of *Heavenly Woman* framed in gold, an entire wall devoted to the single painting.

Christ, it's her.

The image of Charlotte, painted in a sheer white sheath, looked like a Viking goddess. Her full breasts protruded proudly beneath the scant material like seventeenth-century Venetian globes. Her creamy skin was tinged with a gold glaze and a wreath of miniature roses ran through her flowing blonde hair. Her azure stare was penetrating, unavoidable; a look so real that Julian was convinced she must recognize him. He glanced quickly at the bottom corner of the painting. It was signed in crisp, square script by Friedrich Fricke. The gold-plated plaque beneath the painting read: "Courtesy of the Reichstag."

Thank God René was not here, he thought. He would never be able to keep it together under Charlotte's painted Nazi gaze. People began to stare at Julian looking so intently at the painting. Time to move.

Proceeding quickly toward the sculpture gallery, Julian was taken aback by the giant, fierce-looking bronze nudes in the central gallery, designed to intimidate. Their perfectly carved gaze glared angrily like warriors. The Nazis' declaration was shoved down the viewer's throat with those statues: Erotica was extinct under the Third Reich; perversion was reserved for the modernists.

Hurrying through a maze of corridors, Julian began to slow down when he realized people were turning to watch him. He knew what he looked like—a skeleton wearing a suit three sizes too big. He moved past the portraits, paintings, and photographs of Hitler and other high-ranking Nazis. He stopped—he couldn't help it—when he saw Baron Von Bredow's gold-plated, egg-shaped bust. It was so real and frightening. This was not art, Julian thought, but a class reunion—a celebration of Nazism, glorified, sanctified, and feared, exactly as the curators had intended.

He moved past a series of paintings of young Aryan women—androgynous, almost indistinguishable from their male counterparts except for their nipples, which were long and thick. The models' breasts did not defy nor tempt like Charlotte's; they merely pointed forward, firm like a man's, sexless, and chaste, showing the indomitable strength of Nazism among both men and women.

He walked quickly through the rooms, digesting what he saw while searching for the nearest exit. Finally, he saw a sign in the distance. He had to get out of there, but his breath caught in his throat, and he stopped moving: Standing near the exit sign were Friedrich Fricke, Baron Von Bredow, and a group of Nazi commanders in full regalia. Fricke was leading the group into the gallery with his signature gold-tipped cane.

Julian realized that he was staring. *Leave now!* he warned himself. Julian turned quickly and merged with a group staring at a series of landscapes. As soon as Fricke and the others entered a side room, Julian went to the exit and slipped out of the House of German Art. He couldn't feel his body move, just the frenzied thump of his heart racing.

Julian felt anxious as he headed toward the second exhibition. After yesterday's fiasco of nearly running into Fricke and the baron, he was worried that he would see them again at this exhibition. *Don't think. Just get in and get out, and then you are done,* he told himself as he cut across the park toward the rundown, gray, windowless building in the distance.

Will Kruger keep up his end of the deal? Julian tried not to think about the alternative as he slowly approached the entrance.

The first thing he noticed was the large white banner hanging carelessly over the doorframe, like a large wrinkled cotton sheet. Its thick, uneven black letters reading *Entartete Kunst,* Degenerate Art, were scribbled carelessly. Julian was surprised to see that the line for this exhibition wrapped around the building. It seemed as though the number of visitors nearly tripled those who attended the Great German Art exhibit, yet the line here seemed to be moving three times as quickly, as though the visitors could not wait to get in and out.

When it was Julian's turn to enter the building, the entrance was narrow and confining. The exhibition planners clearly wanted visitors to feel uncomfortable from the start.

Once inside, Julian yearned to turn back. Unlike the other exhibition, with its daunting order and spaciousness, this place was cramped, barely breathable. The smell of mothballs overwhelmed the dim lobby, and there was a hollow clamor of whispers in the air, like that dominating a funeral parlor.

Julian followed a group of visitors who were being led by a guide. Before reaching the top stair, he heard a chorus of gasps. As he arrived at the landing, an immense wooden freak of a statue nailed to a cross greeted him. The piece was physically horrifying, deliberately placed as the premiere display to create a sudden, shocking impact.

Julian studied Ludwig Gies's *Crucified Christ* up close. The plaque explained that before it was confiscated, the sculpture had been a war memorial in the cathedral of Lübeck. It was indeed hideous, yet fascinating and powerful. The figure had horns, elevated ribs, angular knobby knees, a distorted face, and a deformed body.

"Gies destroys the image of Christ," one woman remarked contemptuously. "It's an abomination."

Others chimed in with derisive comments. Unlike the relatively silent appreciation at the previous exhibition, this place was buzzing with disgust. Julian left the group to browse alone.

He skimmed the brochure: Ten rooms crammed with six hundred and fifty pieces of artwork from Germany's great museums. *Nine more rooms to go.*

In the distance, he heard someone speaking and followed the voice into the next gallery. According to the sign, he was now entering Room Three. Adolf Ziegler, president of the Reich's Chamber of Visual Arts, was introducing the show to an exclusive group of Nazis. Behind him, nudes and war paintings hung on flimsily constructed walls. Julian recognized the artists immediately. It was like running into old friends, Ernst Engel's friends: Otto Mueller, Ernst Ludwig Kirchner, Otto Dix, Paul Kleinschmidt, and Karl Schmidt-Rottluff. Hanging sloppily over their artwork were epithets: "An Insult to German Womanhood"; "The Degenerate Ideal—Cretin and Whore"; "War Cripples."

Julian could not believe what he was seeing. It was despicable. He felt enraged by the twisted ideology that the Nazis were trying to implant in the public's mind. Paintings, carelessly attached to the partitions, were suspended lopsided and hung impossibly close together. Some pictures were frameless; others hung down by thick cords. Inflammatory language and distorted quotes were everywhere. The ceilings were extremely low and the lighting poor. The entire space was claustrophobic, designed to illicit discomfort, anger, and irritation.

He scanned the paintings. *Were Engel's paintings here?*

Julian stopped in front of Ernst Ludwig Kirchner's portrait of a nude woman combing her hair. It was brilliant. He could barely tear himself away from it. Engel had been right: An entire movement of art was being systematically destroyed.

As he turned to leave, Julian eyed the well-dressed crowd and nearly lost his balance: Felix and Charlotte were standing in Ziegler's inner circle. It was as though they had materialized from a bad dream. Julian looked around nervously. Surely they would see him. He had to get out of there immediately, but then he heard Charlotte's voice looming over the crowd, following him. This *was* a nightmare. There was no way he would escape discovery twice. If he ran ahead, he would be noticed. He stopped where he was, kept his head low, and waited.

"Would you look at that, Felix—a sculpture by Rudolf Belling," he heard Charlotte comment. "I thought I saw his work at the Great German Exhibit as well. How do you explain that? Can an artist be labeled both Degenerate *and* Aryan?" She laughed, seeming to provoke him. "Looks like someone made a major faux pas. What would Herr Hitler say now?"

As Felix turned to say something, Julian didn't hesitate. He moved quickly in the direction of the lone staircase, but heard Charlotte's voice drawing even closer. They were directly behind him. He quickly squeezed in with a group criticizing a work by Salvador Dali.

"And where are Ernst Engel's paintings?" Charlotte was now somewhere off to his right. "Shouldn't he be exhibited in Room Four with the other artists of the *Die Brücke* movement?"

"Of course not," Felix responded coldly. "Engel's grandmother was half Jewish. He's with the Jew artists."

"Well, where are they?" she persisted.

"You just love your Jews. Can't seem to keep you away," Felix said angrily. "Back in Room Two."

Julian knew he should leave—at any moment they would surely discover him. But as though lured by a magnet, he turned and followed Charlotte to Room Two—The Jew Room. He remained behind her as she moved into the crowded chamber, gently pushing browsers out of her path. She stopped once she reached a small painting hanging in the far corner of the room. Julian stood quietly. The painting belonged to Engel. Frameless and askew, the small image had been installed among works by Marc Chagall, Lasar Segall, and Jankel Adler. Charlotte did not appear surprised, rather almost oddly relieved, Julian thought, as he carefully watched her. She stared at the painting, almost lovingly.

The abstract artwork depicted a woman clothed in a transparent dress. At first glance, the woman appeared naked. But Engel was too clever.

A closer look revealed the subtle swish of sheer fabric accentuating a curvaceous body. Her long, unruly hair was the color of hay; her eyes were semi closed so that only hints of blue peeked through thick lashes. Engel never gave away too much. The woman's lush red mouth was uncharacteristically vibrant; she was smiling with teeth just barely visible. How strange, Julian thought. He had never seen Charlotte smile in any pose, even for René. How different this playful image was from Fricke's omnipotent goddess hanging in the House of German Art. Each artist believed his muse to be true. But the real Charlotte, Julian reflected as he turned to leave the gallery, was a lie. She was indeed a muse, but one who simultaneously inspired and destroyed, who reduced brilliant artists to mere men.

He stole a backward glance at the real Charlotte and saw a tear rolling down her cheek. She quickly wiped it away, as though sensing Felix coming toward her. Julian followed the direction of her gaze, and he felt the familiar energy of Felix's angry stride. He held his breath. *This is it.* But Felix strode right past him, seeing nothing around him but Charlotte.

Heaving a sigh of relief, Julian quickly exited The Jew Room. He moved swiftly through the building, and then stopped in his tracks beneath the doorway of the last gallery.

A lovely watercolor hung crookedly alongside the entrance. It depicted a mother and child walking hand-in-hand toward a country house. There was nothing about the composition that could have been construed as degenerate. Then he noticed the signature and felt sick: Max Kruger's name was scripted in the lower right-hand corner. Kruger had been right. He, too, had been labeled a degenerate. No wonder his source in the Nazi culture department had stopped taking his calls. He was in trouble.

René.

Julian left the building and scurried down the street until he was out of eyeshot, and then he ran.

Julian quickly turned onto Ludwigsstrasse, toward Kruger's home. The skies seemed oddly dark for early afternoon. The closer he got to Kruger's residence, the harder he found it to breathe. And then he saw Kruger's house, up in flames.

Bystanders swarmed the street as Gestapo hauled stuffed sacks into their trucks. Julian began to choke as he slowly walked forward. His mind was blank, his body numb, too afraid to think or feel.

A body was carried past the crowd, covered with a sheet. Julian glimpsed the remains of a charred foot hanging over the side of the stretcher. He could barely stand, praying that the foot did not belong to René. *That had to be Kruger; René was much thinner than that.* Julian did not care who was watching him now. He moved in dangerously close. He had to know for sure that it was not René beneath that sheet.

"Where to?" called out one sweaty official, who was carrying two loads of Kruger's cameras and equipment.

"Fricke's office," another man answered.

"Poor Helga Kruger," a woman standing near Julian whispered. "I heard Max is so badly burnt that his skin is like ash."

Julian turned to her, trying to conceal the fear in his voice. He used his best German. "What happened?" he asked.

"A horrible fire. Max Kruger. The artist." She stopped speaking, as if wanting to say more.

"Was that Kruger?" Julian pointed to the body.

She nodded. "He was alone in the house. A tragedy. At least his family was spared."

Julian wanted to hug her. "Are you sure he was alone?" he asked.

She looked at him strangely. Julian walked away and quickly mixed in with another group of bystanders. He searched desperately for René.

Julian gazed at what was left of the house. Remnants of Kruger's canvases were flung across the neighbor's lawn, charred bits of once-vibrant oils. The photos of all the artwork Kruger had planned to save must have been burned to shreds. His files, the lists of paintings, the records, were destroyed or confiscated.

The neighbors began to filter away. Julian knew he should leave with them, but he could not think clearly—he was shaking. *Where was René?* He walked anxiously around the side of the house. He didn't care who was looking at him now. He saw something glimmering among the blades of burnt grass and bent to pick it up. It was the jar of yellow paint, cracked with oozing liquid.

He felt a tap on his shoulder, but it was not a finger.

Turning slowly, Julian saw the long black cane tipped in gold, and he knew who it was even before he saw the man's face.

"You must be looking for René Levi. I'll save you the trouble." Friedrich Fricke aimed the cane in the direction of the street. "He is waiting for you in my car."

Chapter Thirty-Four

POTSDAM

René's face was stark white as they removed his blindfold. Julian thought it would have been better if they had been caught escaping Dachau; if the dogs had gnawed them apart bone by bone. Anything would have been better than coming out of the darkness to face the three men staring at them from a couch: the baron, Fricke, and Felix. The air around them stank, as if they were floating in a cloud of alcohol.

The baron coolly dismissed the guards, ordering them to wait outside. Once the guards were gone, the lights were turned off. Felix held a single candle as he led the four of them down a long, winding corridor, as if they were about to partake in some medieval ritual. Each door they passed was closed. The only sound Julian heard as they moved slowly across the hardwood floor was the scrape of René's limping foot behind him. Felix heard the sound too. He turned and stared at the leg. René glanced down self-consciously. Felix's cruel gaze met Julian's. He smiled slightly and then kept walking.

They entered a kitchen through a stone alcove. Julian's eyes gravitated toward the natural light filtering through a gingham-curtained window over the sink, the only sign of life outside this new prison. They stood in the middle of the kitchen and waited as Felix gathered glasses and filled a large sack with bottles of whiskey and schnapps. Julian stared at the liquor supply making its way into the bag, estimating that it would take them all at least three days to get through it.

A large loaf of black bread stood in the center of a wooden table. Julian's mouth watered as he imagined its doughy softness against his tongue; until he saw the long wooden knife handle sticking out from the bread and off the edge of the table like a guillotine, and then he felt sick.

Felix removed the knife from the loaf with two hands, as though raising an axe from the base of a tree trunk. He tossed the blade into the sack as well, and then unlocked a second door off the kitchen.

Julian held his breath, trying not to think about the knife as they descended into a damp basement. Color-coded wine bottles filled the long narrow corridor, a library of liquor. At the end of the passageway, a lone sliver of light crept out from a slightly opened door. It seemed to be the only opened door in the house.

As he was shoved inside the room, Julian knew he was going to die here.

Hours later, Felix, Fricke, and the baron sat around a small wooden card table sucking on plump cigars. Their faces were blurry. Beneath his swollen eyelids, Julian could barely make out the empty liquor bottles crowding around their elbows.

He and René were bound together with thick rope, their naked bodies pressed against each other. Julian's right eye was smashed into René's left cheek. He tried closing his lid to prevent drops of René's blood from dripping into his eye, but it was impossible to move. Julian knew he was dying, but not fast enough.

Felix moved toward René and Julian. "This, my friends, is what we call avant-garde," he announced to the others, his voice slurred. "Degenerate Art in the flesh." He indicated the two naked men. "They remind me of that horrific sculpture at the Munich exhibit, that bony monstrosity from Lübeck."

Julian yearned for death to free him from this torture. He wished Felix and the others would just slash his throat with the bread knife and be done with it. Instead, the knife glowed silently in the far corner of the room like a beacon of light. Why couldn't he have been set on fire, burnt to ash, like Max Kruger? Or, suspended from the rafters like Ernst Engel? One swift tug around the neck, and it would have been over. He pleaded for death to take him and René. But there was only the laughter of the three men moving thickly through the air, suffocating him. And then came the ice water crashing over them both. Gasping for air, Julian felt the stinging wetness wash over his broken body, taunting him back to life.

In his delusional state he saw his mother reaching for him. Her nightgown was unbuttoned at the top, revealing her neck and the top of her chest. Her long dark hair was disheveled, hanging loosely around her face. How he wished he could paint her like that—so hauntingly beautiful. She was still holding his drawing to her chest. His father was there too. His mouth opened wide, screaming that his only child had shamed him at the market, had robbed the pickle jar, had shaved his beard and sidelocks, and had chosen a meaningless paintbrush over an honest day's work and prayer. He waved an accusing meaty finger into the air: "You got what you deserved, Yakov." Grabbing the drawing out of his wife's hand, his father then stomped on it.

When Julian looked up, his father had faded, so had his mother, and hanging on the wall in front of him now was the last canvas that he and René had painted together just before they escaped Dachau. Even in his debilitated state, Julian could make out the false signature in the corner of the painting: *F. Von Bredow.*

Felix followed Julian's gaze to the painting. He laughed. "Does it bring back memories?"

René's pained voice cried out, "Where are my goddamn paintings that you stole from me?"

"You mean *my* goddamn paintings," Felix corrected him.

"My paintings, Felix. Where are my paintings?" René managed again through his delirium.

"Shut up!" Felix bent down and hissed into René's ear, "Your paintings now belong to me." He pointed to the signature. "I wanted you to see this, to know before we finish with you that it will be as if you never existed."

Felix eyed Julian, and then he slowly emptied the remnants of a bottle of whiskey over René.

René's screams electrified the room as the burning alcohol seeped into the lacerations on his body. It was unbearable. Julian prayed to a God he no longer believed in. *Just take him. Let him go.*

"Now, this is a true Degenerate Art pose," Felix announced calmly, as Fricke and the baron refilled their glasses. "And just think, René, I get to go home and fuck Charlotte," he taunted. "She is lying on my bed right now, those long creamy legs spread and waiting. That's all she does these days."

René passed out, just as Felix reached for the Bordeaux.

The concrete was cold against Julian's back. He tried to move, but his body had been strapped to the floor. He thought that perhaps they had finally left long enough for the two of them to die, and for that he was grateful. Then he heard moaning and a light touch at his foot.

"Are you dead?" René whispered.

"I think so," Julian answered. "Are you?"

"I hope so." René's voice was barely audible.

Neither of them spoke for a while. Julian listened to René's breathing, choppy and wheezy, sounding like Jacob's had just before he spoke Kruger's name. To Julian, it was the sound of death, and it was a welcome noise.

He tried in vain to see René in the pitch-black room. "They are going to kill us today," Julian said, feeling nothing as he spoke the words.

"Forgive me," René's voice cracked with pain.

An hour or more passed, as Julian concentrated on the light sound of the air moving, waiting for what would come next. Finally, he heard footsteps approaching from halfway down the corridor. He held his breath.

The footsteps amplified as they moved passed the wine bottles and head-ed toward the door.

Julian held his breath, praying that this time they would have guns to finish them off.

"It's not them," René said with certainty. "Listen closely."

The steps were soft and secretive.

"A woman, Julian."

The door opened, revealing the slim silhouette of a woman carrying a flashlight. The glare burned Julian's eyes. He could not make out her face. When she shined the light on René, Julian saw that she was carry-ing a pistol in her hand and had a large bag strapped over her shoulder. She moved her free hand over her mouth and averted her eyes. "My God—what did they do to you?"

They both stared at her in shock, as her face became clear. It was Helen Von Bredow.

Helen quickly looked away, scanning the room as if to muster the strength to enter farther. She then emptied the contents of her bag onto the floor. Shirts and trousers tumbled out, as well as a small knife. She moved swiftly, mechanically, avoiding eye contact as she cut through the thick ropes, freeing both of their arms and legs. Julian eyed the dangling ropes next to his legs, no longer enslaving him. But he knew better. Freedom was a liar and a thief, coming and going at whim.

"Put those on." She pointed to the clothes.

"Why are you here?" René asked weakly.

"Get up," she urged. "Please, we'll talk later. We have to get out of here. Now."

She watched them struggle to lift their heads. Neither could stand. She helped René up first, then Julian, and dressed them as if they were children. The trousers were too big, but Helen wrapped the ropes around their pants and tied bows at their flies. Barefoot and unstable, they leaned against Felix's mother as though she were a crutch. Julian pointed to René's palette knife on the floor. She picked it up, stuffed it inside her bag, and together they headed upstairs into the kitchen. Julian noticed the moonlight shining through the curtain over the sink. Before he was led out the door, he grabbed the loaf of black bread, which was left un-eaten at the center of the kitchen table.

Once outside they found themselves amid tall birch trees and dense greenery. Julian looked around quickly. No guards, no Nazis, just open space. For a moment, he felt as though he was back in Engel's woods, then he looked down at the brick walkway at his feet. The same white brick paved the driveway leading up to the Von Bredow schloss. He glanced over his shoulder and saw the kitchen door's gargoyle knocker, which identically matched the one at the entrance of the estate. They had been held at the baron's guesthouse all that time.

Helen Von Bredow's long, dark hair flowed down her back like a horse's mane. Her clear blue eyes were sharp and sparkling, her creamy skin stretched tautly against her pronounced cheekbones. She was a beautiful, softer version of Felix, thought Julian.

"I knew you were in there," Helen said quietly, and Julian could smell liquor on her breath. "I overheard my husband talking to Fricke and Felix. They are all drunk, asleep in the house now. We must move."

She looked away from their broken bodies, tears filling her eyes. "I knew your father well, René. I heard what they did to him, and I knew you were imprisoned on false charges. I should have done something sooner. But I was too afraid then." Helen wiped her eyes, and then pointed to a car hidden in the distance. "I cannot promise your safety. I cannot promise anything. But I am going to do my best to get you out of here alive." She combed her hand through René's blood-matted hair and looked sadly at Julian. "You both will get in the backseat of the car. One of you must lie on the floor, the other on the seat. I know you are hurting. It is a long ride. But we have no choice."

After a few hours, when Helen gave them the signal, Julian lifted the blanket off his head. He tried to sit up, but the pain was too intense. He looked at René in silence. They had made it across the border, out of Germany and into Austria, alive.

The sun was rising as they drove up toward a small peak. Julian was awed by the northern chain of the Alps and the Tuxor range to the south—red and white peaks, gold and emerald valleys, scenic from every angle. And for a brief moment he forgot the ordeal he just endured. Julian swallowed hard and fell back against the cold leather seat. *Ernst Engel would have loved it here.*

Helen Von Bredow drove slowly, taking a narrow path off the main road. Peering into the rearview mirror, she scrutinized René and Julian, who were now sitting up in the backseat. "We have a chalet up here. When the children were young, we vacationed here. It was a wonderful getaway for us. Since Hitler came to power, though, I am the only one who still comes."

"What if your husband finds us?" Julian asked. "By now, he will know we have escaped, and he'll know that you are not in the house."

"I'm trying not to think of all the consequences." She tightly gripped the steering wheel. "But I am leaving him, Julian. Wilhelm has become a monster. He has ruined Felix and has pushed away our daughter with all his Nazi ideology. He gave up our family for Hitler, and I can no longer be part of it."

"Where will you go?" René asked. "Your husband is very powerful. He'll find you."

"Yes, but he is not the only one with friends in high places. There are many of us who hate the Nazis and what they are doing to our country, to our families. Maybe I will go to Paris too." She laughed lightly, and the lines around her mouth tightened as she met René's eyes in the mirror. "I met your father in Paris a long time ago. It was at a Picasso showing." She sighed. "Jacob and I became lovers. Wilhelm found out. You were punished, René, because of me."

René shook his head. "No, I was punished because of Felix."

Helen's eyes watered. "My son used to be beautiful. He was a painter, a lover of nature. As hard as my husband was, Felix was soft. We were once extremely close. Now, Felix walks past me in my own home as if I am not even there. He has changed, and I don't recognize him. He has been brainwashed along with the rest of them."

She drove up to the chalet, a sprawling Tudor-style home similar in design to Engel's country house, but triple the size. "Wilhelm never cared for modern art," she continued, as she parked off to the side of the drive. "Everything that was the slightest bit abstract made him uncomfortable, but not Felix. He was like me, free and Bohemian at heart. Before he left for Paris, he and I used to go together to the avant-garde exhibits. It was our secret."

She pointed to the magnificent gold-capped mountains behind her home. "Modern art in Germany has seen its last days. The Nazis have no intention of stopping there, though. Wilhelm and his friends are busy building vaults on the outskirts of Germany, Austria, and Switzerland. And they have already begun digging salt mines in the Alps for storage. I have read through my husband's documents in the library, and it is frightening. He and his friends have arranged for select castles and villas strategically located throughout Europe to be used as storage depots to protect what they consider to be the most valuable artwork." She pressed hard on the brake and turned around. "Do you have any idea what all this means?"

Julian and René looked at each other in silent acknowledgment.

"A full-scale rape of Europe's most important art," Helen affirmed, turning off the engine and opening the car door. "Germany first, then Austria, Poland, and France. The Nazis' goal is to confiscate every major piece of art throughout Europe and incorporate the collection into what they call a 'Greater Germany.' They will destroy all art that does not conform to the Aryan ideal." Her eyes filled with hatred. "My husband is convinced that only he has the power to choose what is art. We are in the most dangerous of times."

Julian felt chilled. This was what Ernst Engel had feared the most: The mass funeral of Europe's modernists.

Helen slammed her door shut, then helped René and Julian out of the car.

"Helen," René asked softly, as he leaned against her. "I need to know something. While I was in Dachau, Felix made me paint for him at gunpoint. He stole my paintings." He looked down at his bandaged hands but refrained from telling her how they got that way. "I will never paint again. Those paintings are all I have left. Do you know where they are?"

She lifted René's chin toward her. "I know nothing about your paintings. I only know what happened to mine. I kept all of my treasures hidden in the basement of our estate. I had collected abstract art for years. I have my own family money. So Wilhelm never knew about my purchases, but Felix knew everything. When he moved back to our home, Felix showed my husband where the paintings were hidden, and they took everything away from me."

She held René's bandaged hands inside her own. "My son stood there like a ghost next to his father, watching as they hauled away my treasures. Years of collecting, nurturing, and loving the most beautiful artwork of our time, are all gone, René. And so is my son."

Gathering her strength, Helen pointed to a smaller house attached to the chalet. "I must leave now. I have work to do. You will enter through the servants' quarters over there. There is an older woman inside waiting. Anna. She is a nurse. A saint. She won't ask questions. She will take care of your wounds, prepare your food, give you money, and then you will be taken by her son to Paris in his car." She looked at both René and Julian, tears starting to form in her eyes. "I am so sorry for everything, for what my family did to you. You are safe here."

Julian looked at her intently. "You have helped others like us, haven't you?"

Helen smiled sadly without answering. Her bright blue eyes glimmered beneath the morning sun. They were the same mercurial shade as Felix's, colors that rapidly changed with his mood, his clothing, and his drink. She hugged them both goodbye, handed Julian both her gun and René's palette knife, and then turned to René. "Go home, but be careful." Her tone was unyielding. "And stay away from your father's gallery. My husband and son took that too."

WHITE

"Look at light and admire its beauty. Close your eyes, and then look again: what you saw is no longer there; and what you will see later is not yet."
—Leonardo da Vinci

Chapter Thirty-Five

PARIS, 1937

Julian and René entered the busy café off the rue La Boétie. Julian was worried about being recognized, but René did not seem to care. They sat at an outside table, their presence obstructed from the entrance by a large potted plant. René tapped the floor with his foot. He did not look at Julian, nor did he speak. Julian ordered two coffees and watched the street.

Passersby walked briskly, busy with their lives, their thoughts, having no idea what the two men had endured. Julian sighed deeply, his breath cutting sharply against his throat. Paris, the City of Light, had thrived and gone on without them, not noticing that their lives had been snuffed out almost completely.

A group of young artists, laughing as they entered the café, carelessly tossed their overstuffed portfolios onto an empty chair. Julian stared at them with envy and pain, watching the life that should have been his.

He turned to René, who gazed back at him blankly, lost in his own thoughts. There was nowhere to look but down at the coffee mug in front of him. White, round-rimmed, simple—wash, rinse, full, empty—each day the same. How Julian yearned for sameness, for the ordinary—to savor the thrill of being a young artist in Paris again. But like the sediment of brown grinds lining the bottom of the mug, that life, that young man, had become residue. Julian pushed the cup away from him and looked over at René, who was watching the street intently. *Damn it.*

Not again. He knew exactly what René was contemplating, and he had to put an end to it.

"We are going to your mother's house," Julian said. "We will stay with her, find a good doctor, and then we'll figure it all out."

René shook his head. "You know I can't face her yet, or anyone else for that matter."

Julian squeezed the coffee cup, wanting to break it into a hundred pieces. "We are free, René. Finally. We are in Paris. Didn't you hear a word of Helen Von Bredow's warning?"

"Whatever Felix is doing in my father's gallery, I need to stop it."

Julian stood. He felt like throwing the mug across the pavement. Eyes were on him now, but he did not care. "Enough! Have you forgotten Sachsenhausen? Dachau? Munich? The guesthouse? Goddamn it, where does it end, René?"

René glared at Julian as if he were his foe. This was not about his father's gallery, nor was this about his mutilated hands. Julian understood. It was about the laughing, carefree artists over at the next table. That life, that innocence, had been stolen from René too, and he could never reclaim it.

"I'm going to my father's gallery, Julian," René said firmly. "They are using his name, his gallery, as some kind of art laundering center, I know it. And I will not allow it."

Julian remained silent. He knew that he should just stand up and leave and begin a new life. How many times had he followed René, knowing he was headed into Hell? Yet, Julian could not leave his friend. He could not abandon the memory of Ernst Engel. There was not a day that passed that he did not think about the one hundred paintings that never made it to safety the night of Finch's exhibition. Those paintings cost Engel his life. Julian knew that he was now safe, but he also knew that after everything that had happened to them, he, like René, would never really be free.

René stood. "Are you with me, Julian?"

~೨ ೧~

Julian's body ached from crouching, and he felt disoriented as they hid in the alley facing the back door of Jacob Levi's gallery. All evening, they had watched men transport large canvases in and out of the door.

It was nearly midnight when the last group of movers finally left. Everything was dark except for one lone light visible from Jacob's office on the second floor.

"Somebody is still in there." René was eyeing the window, then pointed to the back door. "That door has two or three locks on it. We'll never break in. But there is a tiny storage room to the side of the building where my father used to keep his tools. I would hide inside there as a kid. There's a small window. The latch was always broken, but no one could tell. My father never bothered to fix it. Let's check it."

Julian grabbed René by his sleeve. "There could still be guards inside. Let's wait, René, and stake out the gallery at least until morning, just to be sure."

René's gaze softened. "You are always protecting me, Julian. What have I done for you?"

Julian opened his mouth, but no words emerged. René turned without waiting for an answer and walked toward the storage room window.

Once inside, René leaned over to touch the cold, hard basement floor of his father's gallery, tenderly, mystically, as if a prayer had been answered. He was home.

Against the far wall was a row of paintings waiting to be packed and removed from the gallery. René went over to them. "Those are from the David-Weill collection," he announced authoritatively. "Those belonged to the Bernheim-Jeune family. And those are Sterns'. Those over there once belonged to Miriam de Rothschild." René's composed veneer fell away and his voice filled with rage. "Those paintings all belong to my father's clients, and those bastards are stealing them!"

Walking around the large room, he examined each painting as if he had all the time in the world. He tenderly ran his hand over the faces, the colors, and the images, as Max Kruger had in his secret room. Tracing without touching, as though assembling the invisible pieces of his former life.

René then pointed toward a tiny room, the size of a closet. "That was my best hiding spot, Julian. My father would search all over, but he never could find me when I was hidden in there." He entered the small room, then stopped mid stride in front of a frameless painting. "Julian, come quickly! Look!"

Julian hurried toward him. It was René's painting—Julian's favorite—that had been showcased at René's exhibition at the Charles Ferrat Gallery. It was the oil of an old man drawn in charcoal, surrounded by a vivacious café crowd. The man's dark despair contrasted sharply with the carefree existence of those surrounding him. It was so simple, Julian thought, yet one of René's most powerful pieces. Jacob must have bought it and stowed it away before he was taken to Germany.

René whispered, his voice shaking, "My painting."

René picked up the canvas and pressed it lovingly to his chest, as though it were a kidnapped child who had been found alive. He began to cry as he traced his signature on the bottom right-hand corner of the canvas. Julian cried too, witnessing his friend's overwhelming joy. The painting was all René had left of Paris, of his old life, of the artist with magical hands, of his father's love for him. René was now like that old man in the painting—somber, damaged, isolated—when he had once been the ringleader of the colorful café crowd, toasting the immortality of youth and infinite possibility. Felix had destroyed *that* René, but at this moment, it was irrelevant.

René looked at Julian, rejuvenated and victorious, but his face changed abruptly, resuming the former crazed expression. He whispered, "There must be more."

Julian stared back at him and knew the truth. One painting couldn't save him, one alone wouldn't satisfy. It was not enough. René would never rest until all his paintings were rightfully recovered.

René gently placed the painting back inside the closet and directed Julian to the door leading up to the gallery.

"We will come back for the painting. Let's go up, Julian. Take out the gun."

Julian climbed the stairs nervously, clinging to the pistol Helen had given them, expecting a confrontation on the other side of the door, but there was no one, just silence—which was worse. Julian didn't trust silence. A storm always followed.

He held his breath as they tiptoed side by side down the hallway leading to Jacob's office. A sliver of light peeked out from the bottom of the closed door. They looked at each other. Someone was definitely inside. Julian squeezed the gun tightly as René signaled for him to open the door.

They entered the room and both stopped as they saw Françoise sitting at Jacob's desk.

Her lips barely moved when she saw them. Her voice was barely audible. "They told me you were dead."

She stood up and walked slowly around the desk. She looked completely different from the last time Julian had seen her. Gone was the drab dress, the stringy hair, the sallow skin of someone who had not slept in days. This Françoise was still paper thin, but now she was fashionably attired in a tailored pink suit, her makeup perfectly applied, her hair longer, thick and shiny. She looked expensively coifed. She quickly locked the office door and walked unsteadily back toward them, eyeing the gun in Julian's hand.

"Look at you." René's voice sharpened as he took in the pale pink lipstick, the exact shade of her clothes. "You are one of them."

Françoise went to the window, closed the curtains, and turned around. "You don't understand how it is," she said defensively.

René laughed. The sound was grating and unnatural. "I know exactly how it is." He held out his deformed hands as evidence. "Do you have any idea of what I went through while you sat in my father's chair and did business with the Nazis? All those paintings in the basement. How could you?"

She squeezed her eyes shut. René's voice was detached. "Felix Von Bredow, your new boss, shot my father dead in front of me and had his body thrown out with the prison's garbage."

"They blackmailed me." Françoise fought back her tears. "They lied."

"They always lie," René said, walking toward her. "What about my mother? My sister? Did they get to them too?"

"They are in the South, hidden with friends. I smuggled them out of Paris," she said quietly. "They are safe."

René sighed heavily and backed away from her. "Tell me, Françoise, what is left?"

"Some money and a few paintings that meant something to your father." She turned to Julian and pointed a manicured nail. "Damn you for taking Jacob to Germany."

"I had no choice."

"Neither did I," she responded bitterly. "Jacob gave me some documents just before he left—details about our clients and their collections, an inventory of Rohan-Levi, as well as his personal bank records. I was on my way to his lawyer, but they followed me and stole everything."

She moved toward René with an outstretched hand, but he turned away. "There was an emergency fund that only I knew about. I gave most of what was in it to your mother."

"And the rest of it?" René demanded.

"Untouched. But everything else is gone, René. Your family's home, the art, the house in the country. They cleaned out Jacob's life as if he never existed. And yours as well."

"What about my father's friends? Where the hell are they?" René demanded.

"They have been blackmailed, their families threatened. Our friends and clients are all too aware of Jacob's disappearance. And yours. They are fearful of coming to the same fate. So they are keeping their mouths shut and safeguarding what they can. Some are sending major artwork to the United States, Lisbon, wherever—just out of France."

"And my father's so-called friends in the government?" René shouted. "Are they afraid too?" He put up his hand as she opened her mouth to speak. "Don't even answer me. How are you getting away with this? Where are the police?"

"Don't you get it, René?" she countered. "Everyone—police, politicians—they are all preoccupied. All eyes are focused on Germany. Many are betting that the Nazis will eventually attack France, and they want to be on the winning side. Right now, huge profits are to be made off modern art, because that seems to be a Nazi priority."

Françoise looked away, wiping her tears on the sleeve of her jacket. Wiry lines of makeup absorbed into the raw silk material. She eyed the stains with satisfaction, as though justice had been done.

René ignored her crying. "But you stayed too, Françoise."

"I stayed because I had nowhere else to go," she whispered. "This gallery was my life, *is* my life. I was with your father so long, since just out of art school. The gallery was my only link to him, and I had to protect it. I did what they told me to do because they said it would keep Jacob alive. I knew they were lying. But I still had hope." Her voice cracked. "I stayed, René, so I could monitor the whereabouts of Jacob's art collection, and help our clients. I am overseeing everything, making copies of every transaction."

Julian looked at her suspiciously. "Just like Max Kruger."

She stared back at him defiantly.

"Then tell me," René continued, "if you know everything, where are my paintings?"

She broke away from Julian's gaze, looking surprised. "What paintings?"

"I painted day and night in prison for Felix. He stole everything. You must know where they are."

Françoise stared at René's bandaged hands. "Nothing has passed through these doors that I have not seen first." She paused. "Except for Felix's own artwork that he had sent here from Germany. At least fifty paintings or more."

René glanced quickly at Julian. Both recalled Felix's forged signature on René's painting in the Von Bredow guesthouse. Julian read René's mind: *Françoise is not to be trusted.*

"Well, then, where are Felix's paintings?" René asked slowly.

"We had them sent directly to a bank in Zurich." She looked from one man to the other. "I signed the delivery papers myself, but all the account information is with Felix."

René's hands fell limply to his sides. The hope, the possibility—all gone.

Françoise's eyes watered again. She reached up to touch René's cheek. "Your face, your body, your hands. They destroyed you."

Julian could see that René was trying desperately to maintain his composure. "Where is Charlotte?" he demanded. "I said, where is she?"

"In town," Françoise whispered fearfully. "For a few days."

"You will arrange for me to see her."

"No, you won't." Julian grabbed René's arm, so fragile and bony that it seemed almost breakable.

"Charlotte has become an important woman in the Reich," Françoise stammered. "And your old art instructor—"

"Léon Dubois?" René's mouth dropped open. "I don't believe this."

Françoise nodded. "Yes, she uses Dubois, and he follows her orders blindly. He would do anything for her." Françoise reached for a cigarette. "It is all too risky, René. Stay away from them. Please, let me help you."

"I'll take my chances." René headed toward the door and signaled Julian to follow.

Damn your stupidity, Julian shouted silently at René's back.

"How will I reach you?" Françoise called out softly. "Where are you staying?"

"I haven't had time to make reservations," René said sarcastically, facing her. "I will find you."

Julian dug his foot into the rug. "No, René. We're leaving Paris, now. Forget Charlotte. Françoise can arrange for us to get out of here safely. Let's go South to your mother, get some rest, and then we will figure out a good plan. We'll get help. Let's do this right."

"Yes, Julian, that's exactly what we will do." René's gaze was distant, blank. "But not just yet."

Chapter Thirty-Six

Julian and René sat in the café on the corner of the rue La Boétie and waited. Françoise had said she would be there with Charlotte at two o'clock. It was almost two twenty. At two forty-five Julian heard familiar voices in the distance. He looked up from his coffee. Walking toward them was Françoise, blinking rapidly, a signal that Charlotte was close behind.

A waft of lilac ambushed the table as Charlotte walked by without noticing them, and Julian felt dizzy. He glanced at René, whose eyes had become disturbingly luminous. Her familiar scent seemed to have engulfed him too. Julian glimpsed Charlotte's unchanged profile with hatred. Still beautiful; untouched by time or Germany.

Charlotte wore a black suit with shiny gold buttons, a chiffon scarf knotted loosely around her neck. Her dark sunglasses were oversized, emphasizing the subtle flip of her new bobbed hairstyle. As she sat down several tables away, Julian could hear her laughing at something and that was when he detected the real change. The sound of her voice was deeper, hearty, less girlishly seductive, more authoritative. Though Charlotte's back faced them, Julian could hear everything.

"I said ten paintings by Friday, Françoise." Charlotte's tone was comfortably arrogant, as if she were accustomed to giving orders. "They are expected in Munich by Sunday. And don't forget that the Léger and the Miró are being auctioned in Bern in two weeks. I saw the frames you chose—cheap and gaudy. Change them."

René stood.

"Where are you going?" Julian asked. This was not the plan.

"Isn't it obvious. Look at her. Goddamn it, Julian."

Before Julian could stop him, René walked over to Charlotte's table and stood behind her.

Charlotte snapped her fingers crisply in the air at a passing waiter, still focused on Françoise. "Café au lait for me, and no milk for you, right, Françoise? Why are you staring at me like that?"

René ran a finger along the exposed skin around her neck. "Hello, Charlotte."

She lifted her sunglasses, turning around slowly. Her eyes widened with shock at the sight of René, and she mumbled something incoherent.

"Don't look so disappointed." He walked around the table, and their gazes locked.

A minute passed, and Charlotte glared at Françoise. "You set this up."

"Françoise had nothing to do with this," René said sternly. "I held a gun to her head."

Charlotte put her sunglasses back on, then scanned the café. "Julian too," she whispered meeting his gaze then looking away, frozen. Tears began to leak out from beneath her sunglasses. "You need to get out of here, now," she said. Each word seemed to shake.

"Aren't I safe if I am with you?" René responded coldly. "According to the Reich handbook you are now untouchable."

Charlotte gripped the edges of the table and stood. She looked at Françoise. "Go back to the gallery now and cover for me." Her voice trembled. Turning to René, she said, "Meet me at the Hotel Louise. You remember the place. It hasn't changed." She clutched her designer purse with both hands. "There will be a key waiting."

"I don't want a key," he said angrily. "Just information."

Charlotte tightened her scarf, forced a polite smile at the maître-d, and exited the café.

～つ ～

By late evening, René still had not returned to the tiny cheap hotel room that he and Julian rented in the Latin Quarter. *Damn, where is he?* René had promised he would be gone no more than an hour. Julian glanced at the wall clock. Three hours had passed. He was angry with himself for letting René go alone to see Charlotte. *What if it was another trap?*

The peeling paint on the ceiling seemed to be closing in on Julian as he waited, his mind envisioning every possible scenario René might have gotten himself into. But there was no one to contact. He had to wait.

When the doorknob finally turned in the middle of the night, Julian sat up, gripping the headboard.

"Julian," René called out into the grainy darkness. "It's me."

Julian did not move. His voice was anesthetized from disuse and from paralyzing thoughts. "You were supposed to have been gone an hour at most, René, not a goddamn lifetime."

René touched Julian's trembling arm. "I am sorry. I knew you were worried. But there was no way to reach you."

Julian smelled the wine-stained breath and pushed René's hand off of him. "Bordeaux, or is it Beaujolais? Is that why we stayed in Paris? One last fuck?"

René sat beside Julian on the bed and stared up at the splotchy ceiling, focusing on the largest and darkest stain directly over their heads. "She married Felix."

Julian knew that must have killed him. "But she still slept with you, right?"

René pursed his lips. "Of course. Charlotte is a whore. She hiked up that skirt of hers, spread her long legs, and waited for me to get snared."

"Which you clearly did."

"Not right away." René mopped his face with the sleeve of his jacket. "I wanted to leave."

"But you didn't," Julian said accusingly.

"I wanted to tell her to go to hell, Julian. I should have killed her right there. But I froze. Can you understand that?"

"Here's what I understand." Julian reached over and lifted up his friend's shirt and pointed to the raw pink burns across his stomach. "Did she appreciate your body décor? Did you tell her the gory details about our stay in the guesthouse, courtesy of her husband?"

René turned away. "Yes, I told her. She kept kissing me, touching the burns, my hands, and crying. I fucked her when she was crying, Julian. I closed my eyes and pictured her as she once was, not who she is now. But at least I left with answers." He stood with his arms folded. "I got what I came for, Julian."

Julian shook his head. He could not even look at René.

"She agreed to help me trap Felix."

"Trap him?"

René nodded. "You think I am moving on with what's left of my life without my paintings? Without killing Felix?"

Julian blinked in disbelief. "Killing him is not going to change a damn thing. I promise you, he won't get away with what he did to us, your father, and Engel." Julian stood. "Remember, he is the criminal, not us."

René paced the floor. "Here's how it's going to go, Julian. I want Felix's blue blood staining my father's gallery floor. It's more than just my paintings at stake. I'm going to destroy him for taking everything from me."

"I can't believe Charlotte agreed to this." Julian walked over to the cracked mirror, took a quick look, and walked away. His face was ravaged. He looked like a skeleton.

"She doesn't know what she agreed to," René said. "But she owes me, Julian."

Julian drew in a deep sigh. "We will never be able to leave Germany behind, René. But we can start over on *our* terms. We can expose what happened there. We have friends. We know people—journalists, writers, and others who would take up our cause. We can get our revenge without killing anybody. You and I have already been in prison. Let's be smart, strategic. We can do this the right way."

"I have a plan, Julian," René said with conviction, hearing nothing.

Your plans have nearly killed us, Julian wanted to say, but didn't. "You owe it to yourself to get your life back," he said instead, searching René's eyes for some sign of sanity, but found nothing.

Chapter Thirty-Seven

"Dubois! Dubois!"

Felix, dressed casually in a loose white shirt and gray trousers, climbed the stairs of the Rohan-Levi gallery two at a time, springing forward like a panther. Julian hid behind a marble column on the second floor and watched him. He visualized Felix falling back down the stairs, the wounds opening on his face. Wrapping both hands around Helen Von Bredow's pistol, Julian used all of his self-restraint not to pull the trigger right there. It would have been so easy, but this bullet belonged to René. The plan was first to get information on the paintings, and then they would take care of Felix.

Dubois, sweating at the temples, dashed out of Jacob Levi's office. Julian was shocked by his appearance. He looked so old. His plain dark suit hung loosely against his much thinner frame, and his aged skin seemed doughy, as if he never ventured outside. His whole demeanor was weak, altered.

"Forgive me, Felix. I was on the telephone," Dubois said nervously. "A dealer in Frankfurt screaming about his cut from the Buchet collection. He said we cheated him out of ten percent."

"I'm not interested—deal with it, Dubois." Felix eyed him disdainfully. "There was no guard at the entrance. The door was left open. How many times do we need to discuss the importance of maintaining absolute secrecy here?"

"I was told to let everyone off for the afternoon," Dubois said meekly.

"Off for the afternoon?" Felix shouted. "Damn it, Dubois, you know better. Anyone could walk in. Who gave you this ludicrous order?" Felix's arms were crossed, and his tone was spiteful. *Payback for all that abuse in Dubois's studio,* Julian thought.

As if on cue, Charlotte walked toward Felix and Dubois wearing a black dress. A large amethyst sparkled at her cleavage. "I did," she said, as Felix moved toward her and took the jeweled necklace between his fingertips.

Dubois's face tightened as Felix traced the visible mounds of Charlotte's breasts in front of him.

"You have not worn this necklace since I bought it for you," Felix said quietly.

"Today is special. I told everyone to leave because I have a surprise for you." She tilted her head slightly. "I did not want us to be interrupted."

"You know I hate surprises," Felix grumbled.

"Yes, but this is different."

He touched her face with the back of his hand, and then held her chin tightly. "I like to come into this gallery with everything in place, not to find you dressed for the opera in the middle of the day wearing a necklace you hate. These things make me uneasy."

Charlotte's shoulders fell. She gestured toward Jacob's office. "Well, do you want to see it or not?"

"Dubois," Felix said without looking at him. "You will be joining us."

"That's not necessary," Charlotte said firmly, but Felix dismissed her with a flick of his wrist, signaling Dubois to follow them. *Just like a dog,* Julian thought, recalling a time when all Felix wanted was Dubois's approval.

Charlotte led them to the threshold of the office, making sure she was the last to enter, purposely leaving the door ajar as René had instructed her to do. Julian remained behind the column until he saw René's head peek out from the side stairwell door. They met in the middle of the corridor, walked silently together toward Jacob's office, and waited. Julian peered through the gaps between the door hinges and made out the three easels covered by large white sheets. As Charlotte moved toward the display, preparing to unveil her surprise, Julian handed René the gun, noticing how shaky it was in his friend's left hand, with only two good fingers to hold it. René had insisted on carrying the weapon despite Julian's reservations.

Inside, Charlotte ran her hand along the edge of the sheet. She hesitated then dramatically pulled it off. There stood three renderings of Charlotte by Felix, Julian, and René from the first day she had posed for them in Dubois's studio. Julian remembered the tattered peach robe she had worn and the lustful expressions on both René's and Felix's faces when she dropped the garment to the floor.

"This is your surprise?" Felix eyed the paintings angrily. "Dubois, what the hell is this?"

Dubois stammered, "I—I—Charlotte told me to bring those to the gallery. They were stored in my studio."

"You imbecile!" Felix yelled at him. "Get out of here."

As Dubois headed for the door, René entered the room with the gun aimed. "I'm afraid nobody is going anywhere."

"René?" Dubois stopped in his tracks.

"Yes, Léon. Surprised?"

Felix paused only for a second to collect himself and reach for his pistol, but René shouted, "Drop it!" His voice was steely. "Stand against the wall near the desk." He gestured behind him. "Julian, take his gun."

Julian emerged from the doorway, and Felix waved scornfully when he saw him. "And what do you know? There's Julian Klein." Felix turned fiercely toward Charlotte. "Did you bring them here?"

Charlotte stepped forward, her blue eyes blazing. "René, you promised there would be no violence. You swore you just wanted to talk to Felix, and then you would leave."

"I am keeping my promise." René kept the gun aimed at Felix. "This is only for insurance purposes. You know all about insurance, right, Felix?"

Felix ignored him. "So, Charlotte, you have already seen René behind my back?"

"It wasn't like that. I—"

"Goddamn you, quit acting." Felix could not conceal the hurt in his voice. "The dress, the jewels, the paintings—the whole display—how could you do this to me?"

Before she could defend herself, Dubois's voice rang out from the far corner of the room. He was holding his own gun, and it was aimed at René's back. "Put it down."

Felix, leaning against the wall, applauded. "Well done, Dubois. I underestimated you."

"So did I," said René, refusing to put down the gun, keeping it aimed at Felix. "Who knew that an artist who preached German Expressionism could be such a traitor to the movement? How can you live with yourself, Dubois, destroying the art you once loved?" He gestured toward Charlotte. "For her? Was she worth it?"

"Please, René," Charlotte whispered angrily. "Stop this. All of you put down the guns."

"And tell me, Dubois," René continued, as he met Julian's gaze—*I'm buying time,* his eyes told Julian's—"how can you sit here in my father's office, destroying all that he worked for his whole life? My father was the only art dealer in Paris who defended you after everyone else dropped you. You disgust me even more than Felix, Dubois, because you know better."

"Léon, give me your gun, now," Charlotte demanded, walking slowly toward him.

Dubois's hand shook as he pointed the gun at Charlotte.

"You would shoot me to defend Felix?" Charlotte laughed scornfully. "Well, this is a twist."

Ignoring the gun, Charlotte stood before Dubois. He tried to look away, as though Charlotte were a ray of hot sunlight in his eyes, but he clearly could not resist her, and she knew it.

"You married Felix, and that was unbearable!" Dubois cried out. "Now you are willing to risk everything we have built here together for René Levi. Why, Charlotte? Why nothing for me?"

"Nothing was ever for you, Léon," Charlotte said numbly. "You took me out of the whorehouse and made me a model, but I paid you back plenty."

Dubois's fixed stare never left her as the gun fell limply from his hand. He backed out of the office. Julian did not hesitate. He lunged for the gun, but Felix got there first.

Felix quickly pressed the pistol to Julian's head. "This is a fun game we're all playing here, isn't it. Everybody gets a turn. Now it's Julian's. Drop your gun, René."

René did not hesitate. He dropped the gun, and Felix closed in on him. But Charlotte ran in front of René. "Don't, Felix. It's enough. You have done enough!" she cried out. "I agreed to this meeting only because René had said he wanted to end the conflict between you two, and I believed him." Her eyes were wide with fear. "I didn't tell you René had contacted me, because I wanted you to come here today. I brought those paintings, Felix, to remind you that you are all artists, no matter what happened in Germany. That you were all once friends who worked together, loved one another." She pointed at Julian. "Look at them, Felix. They are destroyed. You won. You have me. Please, just let them go."

"Nice work, Charlotte." Felix pressed the gun harder against Julian's head. His gaze moved accusingly from Charlotte to René, his face turning dark red. "A reunion? You fucked him, didn't you? I should have killed them both a long time ago."

"But you didn't," René said, unable to restrain himself. "Otherwise, you would not have had my paintings to steal, to claim as your own. That's what you really wanted. It was never about Charlotte, was it?"

"Enough!" Julian shouted, his eyes begging René to stop.

"I am afraid it is too late to save him this time, Julian," Felix hissed inside his ear.

René pushed Charlotte aside. "You've taken everything from me, Felix. I will never paint again. I just want back what is mine. Where are the paintings?"

Felix shook his head with feigned pity. "Your paintings are worthless. I destroyed them."

René drew in a heavy breath, and Julian knew there was no holding him back now as he walked toward the three canvases.

"Take a good look, Felix," René said, pointing at Felix's inferior artwork, his blatant lack of skill. "You tell me whose painting is worthless."

Felix could not help himself. He turned and saw his painting sandwiched between Julian's and René's canvases. They all stared at the images, and Julian thought how time had passed but nothing had changed. Felix's face reined in tightly, as it had that day at the lake, that night at Finch's gallery, that afternoon in René's prison cell in Sachsenhausen, and the day he destroyed René's hands in Dachau. Their combined talent illuminated Felix's inadequacy, reminding him that with all the power in the world he could never have what they possessed, what he desired more than anything. René was right. Julian closed his eyes.

It was over.

Charlotte moved in front of René to shield him, but Felix's bullet got there first.

"No!" she screamed as René fell to the floor, clutching his chest. Julian charged toward René, but he felt a sudden, sharp pain seer through his back and down both of his legs. He held on to the edge of Jacob Levi's desk for support as Felix came toward him. And then everything became a blur—the ethereal blue eyes, the pockmarked cheeks, the dark slicked-back hair, the neck muscles straining through the skin. The face that haunted him went from gray to white to nothingness. He heard more bullets being fired, and then someone shouting René's name. Julian remembered thinking that it was his own voice as he, too, fell to the floor.

ORANGE

"We all know that Art is NOT truth. Art is a lie that makes us realize truth . . . "

—Pablo Picasso

Chapter Thirty-Eight

BEAULIEU-SUR-MER, FRANCE, 1938

When Julian finally awoke, he knew even before he opened his eyes that he was among the living. The room felt too sterile and too cold to be heaven. The pungent smell of disinfectant reminded him of Dachau, except that now he was lying on a real bed. He glanced down and saw that his right arm and both legs were wrapped in casts. When he looked across the room, he noticed Françoise sitting in a chair, watching him.

"You want to know where you are?" she said softly.

"Yes," Julian mustered. His voice felt parched and unused.

"You are in a hospital, in Beaulieu-sur-Mer, in the South of France." She paused, shifting her position on the uncomfortable-looking wooden chair. "Three bullets were removed, Julian. It's a miracle that you survived."

He wanted to laugh. Two young men escaping imprisonment, salivating dogs turning away—those were miracles. This, Julian wanted to shout, was not a miracle. This was a curse.

"You are safe here." She rose slowly, her eyes never leaving his as she walked toward the curtained window and opened it.

"Shut it!" he tried to yell, but barely any sound emerged. With his good arm, he shielded his eyes from the brutal sunlight. Françoise quickly closed the curtains and sat next to him on the edge of the bed. He turned away from her and stared at the bleached white ceiling. "René is dead," he whispered.

Françoise nodded, folding her hands together as though in prayer. "Yes, Julian. He is dead."

Julian noticed how her fingers were quivering slightly. He eyed her squarely. "Where is his body?"

Her hands unfolded, and she squeezed the edge of the bed. "Felix thinks that I had René cremated. That his ashes are floating somewhere along the Seine." Françoise's dark eyes blazed. "But I had him buried, Julian. In a small Jewish cemetery just outside of Paris."

"And me?" Julian managed. "What was my fate?"

She stood and walked to the foot of the bed. "They believe you died of your injuries."

"How convenient."

She averted her eyes, focusing on the curtains. "You really could use some light in here."

"Where are Felix and Charlotte?" Julian demanded.

She turned toward him, looking guilty. "Back to business."

"And you," he challenged. "Are you back to business?"

"That's not fair." Françoise began to pace the tiny room. "I work with them, but I work against them."

"And just how are you working against them? Remind me."

She stopped. A weighty silence passed between them. Her hands rested tightly on her slim hips. "You have no reason to trust me, Julian. But I will tell you this. I have evidence." She pointed her finger at him. "Photographs of all the artwork that they sent from Paris to the Reich. All the contracts, the trades—all the activity to and from the gallery." She took a deep breath. "They will not get away with it."

Julian laughed, and his whole body ached. "Too late. They have already gotten away with it. Felix is alive, and René is dead. The paintings are gone."

"You are wrong. They will someday pay for all of it." Her expression was fierce, and Julian recalled how girlishly pretty Françoise had been the first time he had met her in Jacob's gallery. Now, despite the perfectly applied makeup, her eyes were heavily bagged, and she looked years older.

"And what if *I* want to get away?" he asked coldly. "How will I pay for it?"

She exhaled deeply. "You need to heal first, Julian. And then you will leave here, secretly, and go back to America, go home."

"What if I decide to leave now?"

She shook her head sadly and sat down on the lone chair in the room. "You are paralyzed, Julian. But they believe it is only temporary. With therapy, you will walk again." She paused and said firmly, "You will stay here until I see that you are ready to leave."

"And who the hell are you to make that decision for me?" He tried to lean forward but his body resisted.

She pressed her lips tightly together. "I saved your life."

"What life?" He glared at her.

Her eyes became misty, the tough demeanor falling away. "Please, let me help you."

Tiny knives began piercing at Julian's legs. The pain was unbearable, and he was so tired. She was right. He was going nowhere.

Leaning back against the pillow, Julian squeezed his eyes shut, trying to ride out the pain. He was aware of tears rolling down his cheeks. He could sense that Françoise's hand had suddenly appeared, stroking his face, cupping his chin, promising that he would be okay. And she stayed with him like that until the nurses came with their silver carts and long needles, until the pain subsided, and he finally fell asleep.

Hours, days, or perhaps only minutes later, Julian opened his eyes to a woman's face that did not belong to Françoise. This one was lovelier. He had held it before, maybe even kissed it. He remembered its rosebud mouth sliding down his body, and its velvety skin pressing against his.

He managed to say, "Adrienne."

"Juliangelo." She smiled, attempting lightness.

He looked away to avoid seeing Adrienne hovering over him. The casts were now gone, but his body was pale and shriveled, and he felt ill. "Don't call me that."

She bit down on her lip. "Françoise told me that you were here. She said you had been asking for me. So, I came."

"Where is here?" Julian asked. "Forgive me. They keep telling me, but I forget when they stick needles in me."

"A hospital."

"Am I crazy?"

"Yes, sort of." She laughed. He remembered that sound and the way her freckles clustered together on her cheeks when she laughed. But the joyous giggle ended too quickly and her face stopped moving.

"René," she said under her breath, "is dead."

"Yes." Julian focused on the white wall across from him. "Felix killed him."

"What went on in Germany?" Her shoulders were trembling.

"It was the art. René was too talented, so Felix destroyed him." His voice cracked. "Jail, Nazis, torture—so dark, Adrienne, even you could not have painted it."

They did not say anything for a long while. Julian lost himself in her almond eyes, diving eagerly into the pools of honey brown liquid and not wanting to ever surface.

"Why didn't you leave Felix and René?" she whispered finally. "Theirs was an old story. A rivalry that had started even before you arrived." She walked around Julian's bed, her lovely face pinched with anger. "You were the middleman from the first day you arrived in Paris. They used you, pulled you. But you didn't see it. And you couldn't fix it, Julian. Damn you for your stupid loyalty."

Her words began to swim in his head as he studied her. *And I was stupidly loyal to you too, Adrienne.* She was even more beautiful than he remembered. The small lines around her eyes were more defined, the cheekbones had become more pronounced. She looked less like a girl, more like a woman. Who had she loved while he had been gone? Who had loved her back?

"Are you married?" he asked. He had to know.

"No." She studied her bitten-down fingernails. "But there is some-one."

He could feel something sharp jabbing at his heart. "An artist?" he asked. It hurt him just to say those words.

"No. I could never do that again." She eyed him painfully. "Bernard is a businessman, a widower with a young son. We live together."

He stared at her, hurling silent accusations: *Did this Bernard touch you the way I did that night? Did this Bernard paint your body over and over again in his head? Did he hear your voice in the deep of night, or when death was so close that it was only your face that kept him alive?* Julian fought back the tears. *Don't cry. Don't let her see you break.*

"Julian." She looked frightened. "Are you all right?"

"Did you ever think of me?" he whispered. "After that night?"

She seized his hand. "I never stopped thinking of you."

Her fingers intertwined his, but she quickly changed the subject. "There is a war going on, Julian. It is only a matter of time before the Nazis invade Paris. Word has it that we artists must fear for our lives. And perhaps we Jews even more so."

"Yes," Julian said, sitting up slowly, achingly. "They hate us." He could not remember the last time he had sat like this, or wanted to. His back muscles felt new and hot. He stared at the sheets around him, faded white but crisp. "I want to get out of here, Adrienne. Can you help me?"

She patted his hand gently. "They say you are not ready."

"How would you know what they say?" he lashed out, yanking his hand away.

She eyed him fearfully. "You are right. I wouldn't know."

Julian reached for her again. "I am so sorry."

The brown pools began to glisten. Adrienne touched Julian's face, and his mind began to travel. He suddenly remembered the evening when he picked her up for René's exhibition. He could see her now, just as she was, coming toward him, the form-fitting black dress wrapping her lithe body like a gift.

"You need to know something, Julian," she began slowly. "That night that we were together was not an accident, nor was it a means to get back at René." She touched her chest. "I felt it too. I felt it whenever you looked at me in Dubois's studio. I *wanted* you to look at me. I felt something for you from that very first afternoon that we spent together at the café." Her tears flowed easily now, but she didn't move to stop them. "When you left after that night, it was *you* that I thought of—not René. You." She smiled at the distant memory. "Do you hear me, Julian?"

Every part of him was on fire, knowing that Adrienne had actually loved him back. Perhaps she could again? He leaned toward her. "And now?"

She shook her head sadly. "There is no now. Only then, what was. My life has changed. I have changed. But that night, Julian, will always be ours."

He yearned to take her in his arms, to demand that she leave this Bernard and stay with him forever—but he was too weak, too tired, too damaged. He held on to the frayed edges of the blanket, embarrassed. "I wish you never saw me like this."

"You are alive," she said gently. "That is all that matters."

Emotion overwhelmed him as she removed her shirt and pulled him to her chest, wrapping her strong arms around his gaunt torso. He felt her small pert breasts against him. Her touch sent shivers through him. He closed his eyes, remembering the intoxicating scent of this woman as she stroked him gently, crying while telling him that he was still beautiful. How he yearned to believe her.

They lay together until darkness filled the room. He dreaded the moment when their oneness would end. Her body shifted and he felt the empty space as she disconnected from him, her breath tingling against his ear as she whispered that it was time for her to leave. He begged her not to.

She gently wriggled away from him. "I must."

She pointed to the door. He followed the direction of her hand and saw a white, slim, rectangular package leaning against the wall.

"It's for you," she said, as she rose from the bed. She quickly dressed, then picked up the package and unwrapped it. She walked back toward him and held up the artwork for Julian to see. He was stunned. It was his painting that he had left behind in Paris—the image of a painter at work in his studio. When he had left for Germany, the painter had been faceless. But this version had a face, a determined expression, a satisfied smile, as though the painter had finally achieved what he had set out to do.

"You painted it." He could barely speak.

"Yes. When you did not return, I went to your apartment. I took the painting, and I finished it. I painted it with you in my mind. You are the painter, Julian," she said tenderly, her eyes bright. "You can be that painter again."

Suddenly, everything seemed to hurt him at once. "No, Adrienne. I will never be that painter. I am the other one. The faceless artist."

She set the painting at the side of his bed, trying at first to hide her anger, and then exploding: "Damn you, Julian! You were as talented as René. You just never saw yourself—only his work, his brilliance. Felix was nothing, but you . . . " Her words trailed as she got up and moved toward the door.

"Adrienne, wait!" Julian called out with his strength. She stopped and turned around.

"Take the painting with you," he said. "Keep it. Remember me as I once was, or what I could have been. Not as I am now."

She went to the bed and knelt next to him. "Don't you see, Julian? It doesn't matter what happened to you in Germany. They can strip everything from us—our humanity, our ability to love, our innocence, but not the brush from our hand. You will paint again, because you, like me, have no choice in the matter."

She gazed at Julian as she had that night in Paris, and the connection between them felt overwhelming. He pulled her up to him this time and kissed her hard on the mouth, feeling her lips, her teeth, her tongue pressing fervently against his. She tasted of coffee and of mint, of the Paris that had once belonged to him, and to her, but was now as dead as René.

They held each other for what they each knew would be the last time. Her eyes told him that she had moved on, not because she wanted to, but because she had to.

Let her go. Not for you, but for her.

He released her gently, and her glistening eyes thanked him for setting her free. Inhaling deeply, Julian saw the door open and the hesitant sway of Adrienne's tight gray skirt as she picked up his painting and exited his room, but not his heart, not his soul.

Chapter Thirty-Nine

Françoise flung open the curtains, letting in the morning sunshine, and Julian welcomed the warmth against his face. She sat down next to him on the hospital bed as she did every Saturday. Smiling brightly, she said, "Happy Birthday, Julian."

"My birthday," he laughed, noticing how pretty she looked. She usually wore solid colors, but today her dress was yellow and gauzy, patterned with small red roses, as though she were going on a picnic and not stuck spending the day with him in a mental institution.

"Yes, you are twenty-six today," she said.

"I don't even know how old I am anymore. I feel like eighty-six," he said.

"I have something for you. A special surprise." She went to the far corner of the room and returned with a canvas. She turned it around slowly, and Julian's breath caught in his throat.

It was Engel's painting—*Women Bathing*.

Julian gazed with awe at the piece, at its brilliant colorscape that only Ernst Engel could capture. He recalled seeing the painting for the first time in Jacob Levi's gallery. He glanced up at Françoise, so overwhelmed that he could not speak.

She laughed with joy. "I bought this for you at an auction in Lucerne, courtesy of Charlotte and Felix, although they have no idea." She leaned the painting next to the bed and sat close to Julian. "After all, I do the books."

Julian looked up at Françoise, and he had a strange urge to kiss her. She had become everything to him over the past eleven months of recovery: mother, sister, and friend. But instead of kissing her, he took her hand inside his and examined her palm. The skin was so fair, almost translucent. "Why did you do this for me?" he asked.

She was watching his fingers lightly trace her hand. "I did it for you, and for them—Jacob, René, and Ernst Engel." She paused, her softness suddenly dissolving and the determined businesswoman taking over. "It was my small revenge." She smiled slightly. "The first of many."

Françoise walked toward the window, her back facing Julian. She stared out at the grounds below, seeing not the shimmering turquoise of the Mediterranean, rather the serene Lake Lucerne, where the auction had taken place. She started to speak, slowly, "It was not just any auction, it was *the* auction." She turned around, her delicate features twisting with anger. "How the Swiss pride themselves on their 'neutrality.' Liars, Julian! Everyone attending that auction had feigned innocence, but knew exactly what was about to take place."

It was nearly three o'clock, and at any moment the auction would begin. From her corner seat in the opulent salon of the Grand Hotel National, Françoise glimpsed Lake Lucerne through the arched window. It was tranquil and inviting, stretching as far as the eye could see. She stared at the idle movement of the water, recalling a landscape she had seen with Jacob at an exhibit in New York years ago by the American artist Albert Bierstadt. It was entitled *Lake Lucerne* and considered his greatest early work. Turning away, Françoise knew that the scenery, like everything in this room, was simply a façade.

Nearly three hundred and fifty well-dressed guests from around the world crowded the large hall. She could tell who was French, German, Swiss, Italian, Belgian, or American by their clothing, expressions, and mannerisms. Françoise had learned everything she knew about people from Jacob. She recognized many of the art dealers milling about—some had been colleagues of Jacob's, some friends, most competitors. Today, they were representing clients who wished to remain anonymous, to purchase valuable stolen art without anyone knowing the identity of the buyer. She was there to represent Felix and Charlotte, who had instructed her to purchase three paintings: Modigliani's *Portrait of a Woman*, Matisse's *River*, and Gauguin's *From Tahiti*.

Those paintings were among the 126 important works on the auction block by Modern Masters that the Nazis had expropriated from Germany's museums and private collections. Everyone in the room knew exactly what they were bidding on, and knew exactly where the money was going. And everyone was talking about two particular paintings: Pablo Picasso's *Absinthe Drinker* and Vincent van Gogh's *Self Portrait*.

Françoise glanced at the auction catalog. The works of art were listed in order of the lot numbers, then described by artist, title, date, and provenance *before* the sale. She wondered where these stolen artworks were headed, what would be their provenance *after* the sale? She was determined to record everything she saw at the auction, particularly the names and descriptions of those bidding on the work. No matter how long it took, one day, she vowed, everyone playing a part in destroying Europe's modern art, or stealing it, would be held accountable.

It was the least she could do for Jacob.

The Swiss auctioneer, Ivan Krebs took his place at the front of the room, announcing that the auction would be conducted in English, German, and French, but the bidding was to be only in Swiss francs. As he announced the format, he looked nervous, as he should, Françoise thought angrily. She heard that he had been specifically plucked by the Nazis to oversee that the stolen art would be sold to secretly benefit the Reich.

Françoise quietly made her bids on the paintings for Charlotte and Felix. She wore a hat and kept it low over her face, and she bid until she was successful. Charlotte had instructed her to depart immediately after she had purchased the artwork, but Françoise was not leaving the room until she got exactly what she had really come for.

At approximately six fifteen in the evening, the auctioneer stood, his voice sharp and clear as he announced, "*Women Bathing*, by the German artist Ernst Engel."

Françoise inhaled deeply as Krebs pointed to the painting being showcased behind him. The lake was pinkish, the sky yellow, the naked bodies free-flowing with maroons and splashes of indigo and cobalt. How she yearned to touch the painting. She could smell the colors, feel the art come alive.

Bidding cards were being raised swiftly into the air before Krebs had even finished describing the piece. Françoise counted ten other bidders, but it did not matter. The painting was going to be hers.

"I have an order bid of 132,000 francs," Krebs announced in German, English, and French. "The painting is sold."

Closing her briefcase, Françoise smiled to herself, satisfied.

Julian glanced at the painting and then at Françoise. "You did it for Max Kruger too—didn't you, Françoise?"

She met his gaze. "Yes."

He had known all along, but never asked. "You were his contact in Paris, weren't you?"

"Yes," she admitted. "Max was caught by the Nazis while sending a message to me." She looked away, as if pained by the memory.

Julian shook his head. "He also sacrificed Ernst Engel."

"And there was not a single day that Max did not blame himself for Engel's death. It ate him alive." She gestured toward the door. It was time for his morning walk.

Julian stood and stretched. Françoise looped her arm through his, and they walked slowly together out of the room and into the hospital corridor. They passed other patients in the hall, but Julian waved to no one. Françoise led him toward the large opened window at the far end of the corridor, their favorite spot in the hospital. From there, they could view the sea below, watch the white-capped waves crash against the large rocks.

"So beautiful," she said vacantly.

He nodded, waiting. He knew Françoise too well. Something was bothering her.

Her eyes darted around the corridor, checking if anyone was within earshot. Sighing deeply, she whispered, "They are leaving Paris."

Julian could see the strained muscles in her face. "Leaving? What are you talking about?" he asked.

"Felix and Charlotte are going to Zurich at the end of the month, and from there, they are moving to America to start a new life." She paused nervously, waiting for his reaction.

Julian did not respond, though. He could not believe what he was hearing.

"Come, let's go back to your room and discuss this privately," she said quickly. But he remained frozen next to the window, staring vacantly at the crashing waves below.

She came up behind him, her breath thick against his ear. "They are leaving Paris just as the Nazis are coming in. They plan to take their money, their paintings, and run." She tugged at his shirt. "Please, Julian, let's go back to the room and talk about this."

Julian's thoughts were spiraling out of control as she led him back to the room.

Once inside, she closed the door. "Julian, I know what you are thinking. I—"

"You are letting them get away," he said angrily. "Goddamn it, Françoise, why?"

She went over to the nightstand and began rearranging the flowers.

"Look at me, damn it!" he shouted at her back, knowing every word was ripping her apart. "You probably planned their entire escape itinerary."

The vase fell to the floor, and neither moved to wipe up the mess.

"Why, damn it?" Julian demanded.

"If I expose them now, then everything that I worked so hard to build will fall apart." Her eyes were begging him to understand. "They made *me* head of Paris operations. Do you realize the position I will be in, Julian? All the art that I can save? Right now, I have colleagues secretly taking inventory in the Louvre, the Jeu de Paume, working day and night just to take preemptive actions before the Nazis steal everything of value. Felix and Charlotte are a small sacrifice for the bigger picture. But when this war is over, I will have enough proof to expose them, wherever they are." Her voice rose. "They will not get away with this."

"Just like Ernst Engel was a small sacrifice." Julian walked to the window and looked out. The sunshine that had earlier felt warm and comforting now felt invasive. He turned to her. Françoise was staring down at the puddle of water, the broken glass, and the fallen flowers at her feet. "How long will they be in Zurich?" he asked.

She hesitated. "At least a week."

"What exactly will they be doing there?"

"They have meetings at a bank," she said uneasily.

"The same bank that is storing René's paintings." He felt the rage inside him rising. "The same bank that stole all of Jacob Levi's assets out from under him."

"You have just started walking again, Julian," she pleaded. "You have come so far." She fell back onto the chair. "I know what you are thinking, but you don't understand how it is."

"Oh, I understand perfectly." He seized Françoise by the shoulders. "I want their itinerary, all the information."

"Please, Julian." She looked frightened. "You are in no shape for a chase."

He tried to blot out the familiar pain that shot up his legs when he stood too long. "Bring me documents, money, and clothes," he said coldly. "I promise I will return here in one week."

"Don't ask me to risk my life, yours, and so many others," she said. "There is too much at stake right now. Please, let me handle them my way."

"You do what you need to do, Françoise. And I am going to do what I have to do, with or without your help."

She nodded, stood, and gathered her belongings. She turned, stopping in the doorway, bracing herself against the peeling white doorframe. The roses on her dress seemed to wilt as she stared back at him with dread. How he wished he could paint her like that—her mouth open, her eyes wide with fear, her pale creased forehead.

She sighed painfully. "There is something else, Julian."

He stared at her in disbelief. "What else could there possibly be?"

Françoise's voice shook. "They have a child now. A daughter."

Julian stopped breathing. "Why didn't you tell me?"

"I wanted you to heal."

"You are lying."

Julian watched her melt under his intense, unrelenting gaze. He knew the power he had over her. He was Jacob and René rolled up into one ball of guilt.

"Yes," she said, walking over to him. "I lied."

He searched her face. "Why, Françoise?"

She took his hands inside hers and squeezed them tightly. "The baby looks exactly like René."

Chapter Forty

ZURICH

The documents that Françoise had smuggled to Julian in the hospital were impeccable. She packed him up, brought him clothes, put Engel's painting and his other personal belongings in storage as though she knew he would be gone for a long time, or perhaps never come back. She drove him to Paris to catch the early afternoon train to Zurich. Neither spoke.

They stood together on the platform. It seemed so long since Julian had glimpsed the city he had once loved that he avoided looking around. He closed off his senses, refusing to embrace the reunion. Paris, which had once held in her elegant hands such promise to an idealistic young man, could not possibly love him now. Instead, he focused on the empty train tracks as Françoise slipped a wallet stuffed with money into the breast pocket of his overcoat.

They stood in silence, their arms looped, her face worried. Tears filled her eyes as the train approached in the distance.

"Be careful, Julian," she said to his unmoving profile, then handed him a package. "Everything you asked for is in there. I will see you back at Beaulieu-sur-Mer in one week."

He saw the watery flecks of emotion in her eyes, as though she did not believe her own words. He pulled her toward him and held her close, smelling her subtle yet musky perfume. He felt the softness of her shiny hair against his cheek, recalling once again the overpowering sensation of a woman, but never forgetting, even for a moment, that this woman's heart was still with Jacob, and his belonged to a woman he could never have. For Françoise, Jacob was present in everything she did. And Julian understood that more than anyone. He slowly, reluctantly, pulled away from her.

"Julian," she whispered quickly. "If anything should ever happen to me, I have left you enough money to live on. I've left you important documents. Everything is with the hospital director. She is an old friend. She can be trusted."

Before Julian could respond, Françoise pointed to the train and pushed him lightly forward. "Be careful, and please, come back."

The bank located on Bahnhofstrasse in Zurich's business district looked as imposing as it had years earlier. The same stoic marble busts at the base of the wide steps seemed to scrutinize Julian disapprovingly. It was as if they knew exactly where he had been, and where he was headed.

He had planned to be at the bank at least an hour prior to Felix and Charlotte's scheduled arrival so that he could assess the surroundings. He glanced at his watch: fifty-nine more minutes, right on schedule.

Fifty-five minutes later, the banker Herr S. Holstrom, the one man whom Julian thought he would never have to lay eyes on again, walked past him in the lobby, his polished leather shoes squeaking as he moved across the bank's glossy black marble floor. Holstrom did not appear to recognize Julian, whose face was swollen from the drugs he had been taking. His once muscular physique had also diminished. Thankfully, the dark, conservative suit that Françoise had given him blended perfectly into the bank's stuffy atmosphere, not drawing anyone's attention, particularly Holstrom's.

The banker's presence brought back the raw pain of the day Julian had sat before him as Holstrom signed Jacob Levi's assets over to Felix. Julian could still recall the fancy pen, the man's cold precision, the carnivorous way his beady eyes had scanned each document. Julian remembered Holstrom's wooden nameplate with the shiny gold border.

Holstrom quickened his step and moved toward the entrance. Any minute now, Felix and Charlotte should be making their way inside. Leaning back into the lobby's cushioned black leather chair, Julian hid behind a newspaper as the couple finally entered the bank.

Felix wore a gray tweed coat and black fedora, and Charlotte wore a long belted camel-colored coat with a colorful scarf bearing large, geometric shapes, reminding Julian of a Kandinsky painting. They were not touching at all, separated by a clear-cut border of air. Felix shook Holstrom's hand firmly as they paused in the center of the lobby.

"I have been looking forward to meeting you, Herr Von Bredow," Holstrom said. "Your father speaks often about your accomplishments."

Holstrom offered Charlotte a sanitary smile and frowned slightly when he noticed the scarf, as if it were an eyesore. "A pleasure."

She exaggerated a return smile, and Felix shot her a dirty look.

"Well, let's not waste time," Holstrom said with a clap of his hands. "We will stop in the director's office, deal with the transfer of the paintings, and then get down to business."

Julian watched them turn left down the corridor, and then out of view. He checked his watch again, rose, and exited the bank.

He waited for Felix and Charlotte at a small newsstand directly facing the bank. He imagined them signing release papers for all of René's paintings buried in the bank's vault. A good hour and a half passed before they emerged from the bank, walking in his direction.

As they approached, Charlotte appeared angry. Julian picked up his newspaper again, shielding his face as they passed him and stopped at the corner, several feet away from a parked black Mercedes.

Charlotte pointed at Felix. "You are absurd to entrust our lives, our safety, to that wet-lipped banker." She laughed mockingly. "And our new identities. Me, a fashion designer, and your new credentials could rival Leonardo da Vinci's. I can only imagine how much that cost us."

"Shut up, Charlotte," Felix replied callously. "How the hell could you embarrass me like that in front of Holstrom? Do you have any idea of his importance to the Party? Was that little act for my benefit?" Felix's voice rose. The newsstand's other customers were staring as he began to lift his hand threateningly. Julian moved to the far side of the kiosk and watched.

Felix's hand fell to his side. "I have no time to fight with you. Go back to the hotel and start packing," he told Charlotte as the chauffeur held the car door open for her. "I still have a few loose ends to wrap up with Holstrom, and then I will see you and Olivia back at the hotel in a few hours."

Olivia. The baby. Don't think right now, just act.

Once Charlotte slipped inside the Mercedes, Julian saw his opportunity and took it. He waited until Felix crossed the street back toward the bank, then he got into a waiting taxi. He instructed the driver to follow Charlotte's car without being obvious. He dropped triple the fare on the seat, and the driver knew better than to ask questions.

Several blocks later, nearing the end of Bahnhofstrasse, the Mercedes stopped in front of a posh hotel located next to the Schanzengraben Canal. Julian told the driver to continue one block further. He threw more money onto the man's lap and jumped out, then hurriedly made his way back to the hotel.

Entering the lobby, Julian felt his damaged arm tingling from all the activity. He stopped suddenly when he saw Charlotte waiting in front of the elevator. As she entered it, Julian inched closer and watched the numbers over the elevator pause at three, as he expected, and then return to the lobby. She would be heading to room 312. He waited another five minutes, then entered the elevator.

He paced the corridor near Charlotte's room, walking slowly toward her door. He heard the sound of bath water running. Knocking loudly, he held his breath.

Charlotte opened the door wearing a bathrobe. She held a pistol at her side. Her voice was calmer than it should have been. "I saw you at the newsstand, Julian."

"If you knew I was behind you, why did you let me come this far?" he replied, equally composed.

She eyed him icily. "Curiosity. I was told you were dead, and I wanted to know why you were walking the streets of Zurich."

Julian gestured to her gun. "Do you mind?"

She followed his gaze, but did not move. "What do you want from me?"

"Answers," he said quietly. "And then I will leave."

She turned and ushered him into the room, closing the door behind him. He looked around but there was no sign of a baby. She carefully placed the gun on the nightstand and sat on the edge of the ornate canopy bed in the center of the room, watching him as he took in the expensive antique furniture.

"How could you, Charlotte?" He turned to her accusingly.

"How could I what?" she said, betraying no emotion.

"How could you have watched René die and still be here with Felix?"

She looked away. "After what happened, I did what I had to do to survive."

Julian made a panoramic sweep of the room, then gestured to the clothes on her bed which were neatly arranged, glittering like jewels. "Furs, dresses, hats. This is not just survival, Charlotte. This is power, position—pure Von Bredow wealth."

"Felix is my husband."

"From what I hear, you take your vows seriously."

"Leave now."

Julian did not move. She had helped to destroy his life. She did not deserve to live hers so easily. "Why are you stealing René's paintings? Haven't you taken enough from him?"

"René is dead," she said coldly. "His paintings will survive the war."

"And what about the Matisse, the Gauguin, the Modigliani? And who knows how many other works you and Felix have stolen. They don't belong to you!" Julian accused, his composure leaving him.

"I bought those paintings!" she replied firmly. "And I am in every one of those damn paintings of René's in some shape or form! They all belong to me." She got up from the bed and moved toward him. "And how do you even know about those purchases? They were bought anonymously." She stared at him. "Françoise."

Julian remained poker-faced, but his heart beat rapidly. He had just betrayed his friend.

"Was it Françoise?" Charlotte demanded.

"No," he said. "No one knows that I am alive. Just you."

"Just me." She laughed mockingly. "I am not stupid, Julian. You have always known that."

"You're not stupid, but you are a fool," he said spitefully, thinking about Françoise. *How could I have been so careless?*

"You are a bigger fool for coming here," she said, her eyes flashing with hatred.

His gaze matched hers. "Felix will somehow use the paintings to his advantage. And you are allowing that to happen, Charlotte. How quickly you have forgotten that night in Johann Finch's gallery."

"René is dead!" she shouted, her cool veneer falling away. "Dead, Julian. And you know what? It was those goddamn paintings that killed him. Killed all of you."

"They don't belong to you!" Julian repeated, as he began pacing around the room. He noticed that the water had run over the edge of the bathtub and onto the floor, but said nothing.

He turned angrily, pulling out the only card he possessed. "If you don't find a way to get me those paintings, then I will tell Felix that your daughter is René's child, not his." He paused. "I assume, knowing you, that Felix has no idea the child is not his."

She blinked rapidly, and Julian saw genuine fear in her eyes. She quickly lunged for her gun and aimed it at Julian. "You wouldn't dare tell Felix. You and I both know that if you tell him the baby is René's, he will do nothing to me, but I can guarantee he would hurt the child." Her eyes gleamed dangerously. "Are you prepared for that, Julian? To destroy René's only legacy?"

Julian felt the urge to destroy the porcelain beauty of her perfect skin, to crack its undeserved smoothness into tiny, jagged pieces. One bullet, he thought, eyeing her gun, but he knew he was too weak to wrestle it away from her. He began sweating so profusely from the pain in his legs and from hating her that he could practically smell the salt on his skin. He knew she was right. He could never do anything to hurt René's child.

"Just remember," Charlotte repeated threateningly, "if you try to ruin my life in any way, at any time, it is René's daughter who will pay the ultimate price."

"You cold bitch. She is your daughter too," Julian cried out.

"Yes, she is mine, and so are the paintings," she spat, pointing the gun at the door. "Now get out! Go find your own life and stop living René's."

Julian retreated toward the door, unaware of his feet moving, then he stopped abruptly in his tracks. Visible under a pile of folded clothing on a chair was René's notebook. He recognized it immediately, with its faded blue cover, its thick yellow pages.

His stomach growled. He hungered for the feel of it. He could practically smell the ink drawings. Inside that notebook was Dachau, the Box, the Pit. The notebook was René's art, their life—all that was left of the truth. Charlotte had stolen everything from René. She could not have that too.

With his back to her, Julian quickly snatched the notebook, stuffing it inside his pants, and closing his overcoat. He looked up and saw her reflection in the mirror: icy and triumphant. As he turned the doorknob and left the room, his whole body ignited with the realization that she had not seen him take the book—*their Bible of Proof.* As usual, Charlotte had been looking only at herself.

They now knew he was still alive, Julian thought as he exited the building. But worse, they also knew that Françoise was not to be trusted. She had lied to them about Julian's death and had told Julian about their illicit art dealings. Julian felt sick. He had ruined everything for her, putting her life in jeopardy, while accomplishing nothing. He had to warn Françoise somehow. He would go back to Paris tonight.

Walking briskly along the bustling Bahnhofstrasse promenade, Julian barely noticed the sweet smell of the Linden trees lining the street, nor the numerous lush private gardens filled with red geraniums in full bloom. He stopped briefly at the Burkliplatz, the point where the Limmat River emptied into Lake Zurich. He neither saw the beauty nor heard the group of tourists asking him to please move, that he was obstructing their view of the lake. It was as if time had stopped and his senses had gone dead.

He kept walking until he found himself in front of the Kunsthaus Art Museum. Standing before one of Europe's most prestigious cultural institutions, he thought of all the paintings that would never make their way through its venerable doors.

His mind flooded with images. He recalled the meeting at the Von Bredow estate where the groundwork was laid for the destruction of modern art. He pictured the Degenerate Art Exhibition, and Helen Von Bredow risking her life to save him and René and other young artists. He envisioned Max Kruger in his final moments, burning alive with his treasured paintings. He thought about the auction in Lucerne that Françoise had attended. All the modern masterpieces that had landed in dishonorable hands, so many works whose true histories would be forever buried with the rest of the Nazis' secrets.

Julian thought of how he had once been a young man brimming with conviction; a rebel who had traded in his prayer book for the freedom of a paintbrush. He had followed his heart and his hands, willing to pay the ultimate price. Anything just to paint. But he had lost everything. His freedom, his friends, his passion.

But not his life. Not his ability to tell the truth.

Pressing the notebook to his chest, Julian stared back at the museum defiantly. Finally, he understood that what was at stake was greater than René's stolen paintings.

Julian Klein is both naive and easily convinced. Felix had been right.

He buttoned his coat, lifted his collar. *Not anymore.*

YELLOW

"I have no fear of making changes, destroying the image . . . because painting has a life of its own."
—Jackson Pollock

Chapter Forty-One

THE ART INSTITUTE OF CHICAGO, JULY, 1960

It had been twenty minutes since Julian had locked himself inside the museum's cramped bathroom stall. Twenty minutes. Twenty days. Twenty years. It didn't matter. It was all the same, a series of moments leading up to this one. Stretching out his legs, Julian glanced at his watch, then stood and exhaled deeply. *It was time.*

Removing his dinner jacket from the door hook, Julian walked slowly across the linoleum floor, pausing briefly at the oval mirror. He glanced at the face he knew so well but no longer recognized. Only his eyes, a penetrating shade of green, remained the same, unchanged by Paris or Germany or all that came after. *His mother's eyes.* Shaking off his reflection, Julian turned and quickly headed into the gallery—not to attend the Art Institute gala, but to crash it.

As he entered the packed room, few people took notice of him. It was probably the jacket, he thought. Rented for cheap. The white had a slight yellow sheen. This crowd, with its designer gowns and tailor-made tuxes, knew the difference. By the vacant, dismissive looks he received, Julian was aware that he was instantly deemed not one of them. It was better that way. He walked quietly to the back of the room and waited. And then she walked in.

Olivia Broussard arrived at the gallery alone, as Julian had expected. Her long black hair fell across her slim shoulders like a cape. Her olive skin was flawless. She had ebony eyes, full lips, and high cheekbones.

Julian braced himself against a nearby chair. Olivia looked so much like René that it was almost unbearable.

Smiling warily for the waiting cameras as though she were used to the attention, Olivia kept walking, offering a polite wave to those who called out her name. The photographers closed in, took the few shots they needed, and looked over her shoulder, knowing that her famous parents would be just moments behind.

Suddenly, the art world chatter waned to a faint buzz as Felix and Charlotte Broussard entered the gallery. Felix brushed past the usher holding up a purple velvet rope, slowing down only when he saw the media clamoring for his attention. He pivoted to the left, guaranteeing that they captured his best angle. He served up a pearly, capped grin.

The spotlight magnified Felix's face, shining into his large blue eyes as a television reporter asked him about the importance of this exhibition.

"It's about line, form, and color," Felix explained, gesturing toward the wall of paintings in front of him. "It is about expression and movement. The images are nonrepresentational, which means no actual objects are exhibited—rather the emotion the image invokes is what you will see on the canvas. My work is the quintessential fusion of European training and American influence."

The magnified sound of Felix's voice, the guttural German-accented English, after so many years, seared through Julian. He felt lightheaded listening to the lies that tumbled effortlessly from Felix's mouth, knowing that he was probably the only one in the gallery who could see through Felix's charade. He was the only one in the room who knew that Felix's name was a fake, that Von Bredow had been carefully buried back in Zurich.

Julian turned toward Charlotte, the secondary attraction, who was already busy working the other side of the room. She tilted her head with its swept-up, still-blonde tresses toward those photographers who really mattered: society and fashion paparazzi. She seemed to want to ensure that they focused on the plump sapphires dangling from her lobes like overripe fruit. Julian saw the enamored faces surrounding her and marveled at how she still managed to bewitch the unsuspecting viewer.

Julian watched her slow, practiced strut. That walk had not changed in twenty years. As Charlotte sluiced through the circles, she managed to keep her silk-clad back to her daughter at all times. Olivia, too, steered as far away from her parents as possible, as though seeking refuge in the farthest corner of the gallery, close to where Julian was standing. She practically leaned against one of Felix's paintings as she plucked yet another drink off a waiter's tray. Her black dress was tight and backless. She looked overexposed and Julian yearned to place his cheap jacket over her bare skin to protect her.

Olivia was undeniably beautiful but seemed lost. She repeatedly looked over her shoulder as if expecting someone to come to her rescue. From where he stood, Julian could read the urgency in her dark eyes: She was ready for him.

He had been aware of this since last year, when he attended the opening of Olivia's art exhibit at New York's Guggenheim Museum. Her work was among a collection of paintings by emerging young artists. Her paintings of abstract body parts were mesmerizing. As he stared at the convulsing black swirls, torrents of red entangled with violently purple appendages, he saw the whole story inside the images. She was her father's daughter. Julian could barely breathe. He yearned to shout out the entire story, to tell Olivia the truth right there in the middle of the crowded museum. Instead, he stood near a large thigh-and-breast rendering and said nothing.

Julian had viewed her exhibit five times that week. On his last visit, Olivia had touched his shoulder gently and told him that she had seen him studying her paintings, and did she know him? He had shaken his head, mumbled something about her impressive work, and had walked into the next room. He wasn't ready. *Twenty years to prepare for this*, he had scolded himself as he stood behind a large sculpture, *and you're not ready?*

He straightened his shoulders. *Not this time.*

The overhead lights began to flicker, and Julian waited patiently as Felix's guests charged the ballroom, a stampede of black ties. Two young men grabbed Olivia's arm, vying to escort her, but she shook them off and turned in Julian's direction. Beads of sweat rolled slowly down his back as he met her curious gaze. He moved toward her courageously, no longer afraid of the consequences, having nothing left to lose.

"Have we met?" Olivia's voice, like her mother's, was laced with sultry confidence.

Julian tried to keep his voice steady. "I saw your exhibit last year at the Guggenheim."

She scrunched her nose, staring at his face. "Strangely, I remember. Yes, the 'Rising New Artists' exhibition. It was a joke." She laughed.

"On the contrary," Julian said, "I thought it was quite good."

"You mean quite entertaining. I was lumped in with a bunch of NYU students who could barely hold a paintbrush." She stood back, assessing him. "You didn't have a mustache then."

"Nor did you."

She laughed again, and Julian smiled, the muscles feeling sore from disuse.

"What do you think of Felix's retrospective?" she asked, making a panoramic sweep of the gallery. "And forgive me, what is your name?"

"Julian." He extended his hand, pointing to the canvas behind her. "Monstrosities. That painting must be fifteen feet high."

"Eighteen to be exact."

"I much prefer the earlier works," Julian said carefully, gesturing toward the collection of artwork hanging on the walls under the heading "Felix Broussard: The Early Years"—René's paintings. "Those paintings have meaning. The others are childish, the paint appears slapped on, sloppy."

Olivia inched closer to him. "You are the only one here who would dare say such a thing." She eyed Julian with large, intense dark eyes—eyes that he felt he knew so well. "You were not invited, were you?"

Julian looked down at his suit. The cheap white dinner jacket was a giveaway. He decided not to lie. "I came to see you."

Olivia scanned the room nervously. By now, the cocktail area had nearly emptied. Everyone who mattered was already in the dining room.

She sucked in her breath, as if she were searching for something. Julian jiggled the loose change in his pants pocket to put some noise between them.

Olivia suddenly looked scared. "I am sorry, but I think I'd better go. I'm late. Nice to have met you." She gave him a close-lipped smile and headed toward the dining room. Julian called after her, but she kept walking.

"René Levi," Julian shouted desperately at her back. "His name was René Levi."

Olivia stopped moving, and he quickly walked toward her. They stared at each other until Olivia's eyes became glassy. The few remaining guests standing around the gallery began to notice. He knew he had to leave the exhibition before Felix discovered him.

"Who is René Levi?" Olivia's voice was barely audible, yet Julian detected some longing.

He glanced around the room anxiously. "This is not the place."

Olivia's dark eyes flashed. "What do you want?"

"Nothing more than to talk with you." He chose his words carefully.

"Say what you have to say right here," she said firmly.

Julian glanced over her shoulder. The dining hall doors were now closed. He knew they would be looking for Olivia.

He paused. "I need to speak to you privately. It concerns your family. Things I believe you should know."

"How would you know what concerns my family?" She continued to eye him suspiciously.

"Because I was there," he said quietly. "Where things happened."

Olivia said nothing, but did not make any attempt to leave. He quickly handed her a note with the name of his hotel and the address. It was warm from the heat of his pocket. "Meet me tomorrow night at my hotel, seven o'clock. I will be in the lobby waiting for you. But please, it is crucial that you keep this between us."

Olivia glanced at the paper, front and back, then took a few hesitant steps away from him.

Chapter Forty-Two

Julian stood at his hotel room's lone window and wrapped its faded chenille curtain around his chest. He stared down at the empty street. *Why did I tell Olivia seven o'clock? Why not this morning, or even last night after Felix's exhibition? By now she's had too much time to think, too much time to decide not to come.*

He glanced at the clock on the nightstand. Six forty. He picked up his jacket and headed down to the lobby.

He sat at a corner table in the small bar by the window, nursing an orange juice. It was seven thirty, and Olivia still had not arrived. He stared out the window and waited. An hour later, a lone taxicab pulled up to the stoplight directly across from the hotel. He knew that it was her before the car door even opened.

Julian braced himself against the chair as Olivia let herself out of the cab, crossing one leg languidly over the other. She stood on the sidewalk and faced the hotel. Her leaning posture, the way she cocked her head slightly as if studying a painting, looked so much like René that it was almost painful. Julian felt his heart beat in sync with Olivia's footsteps as she approached the building. She crossed the street quickly, and his heart began a drum roll. She entered the hotel lobby, and for the first time in years, since the day he had confronted her mother, Julian realized that he was afraid.

Julian stood as Olivia walked toward his table. Her ebony eyes appeared tired, taut with anxiety.

"Thank you for coming, Olivia." He gestured toward the chair next to his, but she remained standing and did not bother to apologize for being late.

"I was awake all night, debating whether or not to come here," she said nervously, glancing around the empty lobby. "Or, whether to ask my parents about you. I spent hours walking along the lakeshore today, trying to decide if it would be better just to leave things the way they are."

"Better for whom?" he whispered, gesturing her again to sit down.

"Perhaps I should leave," she said, stepping backward.

"No, please stay."

She began to retreat into the lobby.

Julian realized that he must seem frightening. He felt all the emotional build-up of the past week as he walked toward her, trying to keep his voice even. "Please, don't go, Olivia," he said gently. "I know this is all very strange for you. I am sorry if I have offended you in any way."

She pursed her lips together and tugged at her ponytail like a teenager. Julian sighed with relief as she returned with him to the table and sat down.

Her voice was low and accusatory. "Who are you, really?" she asked. "Is your name even Julian? Your mustache is a fake. Look at it—it is practically falling off. I thought about that thing all day and wondered why you were wearing it."

"I didn't want to be noticed last night at the exhibition." He paused, feeling the intensity of her gaze. "My name is Julian Klein."

She seemed nervous. "Well, then, Mr. Klein, I could use a drink. I function better with a little wine, and then you can tell me who you were hiding from at my father's exhibition." She looked around the room. A waitress appeared, and Julian asked her to bring a bottle of wine. He remembered the numerous drinks Olivia had downed the night before. In some ways, sadly, she seemed to be Felix's daughter too.

She then dangled a pack of cigarettes in the air and took one out. Julian picked up the hotel matches on the table and lit it for her. She inhaled deeply. The nicotine seemed to sedate her, making her instantly chatty. "You have a slight accent," she said. "Yet, you are American, aren't you?"

"I was born in Chicago, not too far from here." His voice wavered. He could not make small talk about his life—it had not been small. "I have lived in and around Paris most of my life, though."

"Where is your family?"

Julian shook his head. He had no plans to go there.

"I have a right to know with whom I am dealing." Olivia's tone regained its hostile edge.

"I last saw my family when I was barely nineteen," he began. His voice was distant, as if telling the story of someone else's life. "I left home for Paris, planning to become the next Picasso, but the war got in my way."

"So, you are a painter." She smiled slightly, and then lit another cigarette before stubbing out the first one. "Well, you are here now. Are you going to visit them?"

Running his palm over his dry lips, Julian said, "My family thinks I am dead."

Olivia blew smoke toward the ceiling then eyed him squarely. "Well, are you?"

"Dead, or going to visit them?" They both laughed. Her laugh was full and throaty, like Charlotte's. His laugh seemed to belong to a stranger. It was a sound he had not heard in a long time. "I would rather my family remember the young man I once was than meet the man I have become."

Olivia began opening a pack of cigarettes. "Well, then, how do you know my parents?"

Julian exhaled deeply. His words emerged slowly. "I met them both in Paris in the thirties."

"Funny, they never mentioned you."

He looked at her intently. "I'm sure they didn't." He paused. "Felix and I studied art together and became close friends. Inseparable, actually."

Glancing briefly out the window, Julian hoped to find external strength. Outside it was dark and quiet. He had held this conversation with Olivia hundreds of times in his head, but suddenly everything that he had wanted to say to her seemed to slip away. How could he reveal that René was her real father, that Felix was a murderer and a fraud, that her mother was a whore and a thief, without destroying her? She was just twenty-one, not much younger than he was when René was murdered. How could he tell her all this without tearing her young life apart?

Suddenly he wanted to know her, not just as René's daughter but also as a woman, a painter. He leaned forward. "How long have you been painting, Olivia?"

"I have always painted," she said, eyeing him intently. "Just like you, Mr. Klein."

He said nothing.

"It is in your hands." She touched her own palm. "The way your fingers curl when you speak. As if you would rather be painting your words."

She was sharp, like her mother. Julian glanced at his once promising hands, and then looked up. "And you?" he asked.

"I paint because it is the only way I know how to function. It is like eating and drinking for me; it is how I survive." She drew out a long, heavy sigh. "You have to understand, painting is not a hobby for the Broussards—it is our way of life. We do nothing but paint."

"Charlotte does not paint."

Olivia raised an eyebrow. "That's right. But my mother understands art better than anyone I know. Even my father respects her opinion above all others. To this day, he refuses to show a single painting until she approves it first."

Julian smiled wanly, remembering when Charlotte had said that Felix did not possess an original stroke. "And what is your opinion of Felix's work?"

"Let's just say that I agreed with your assessment at the museum. I see decadence in his work." Olivia laughed painfully, then looked away. "Believe me, my opinion is not appreciated."

She poured herself another glass of wine and sat back. "Now, tell me, why exactly am I here?"

Julian swallowed hard. There was no going back now. "At the exhibition last night, it seemed as though René Levi's name was familiar to you," he said slowly.

She nodded hesitantly. "Yes, I'd heard it before. There were several times when I was a child that I pretended to be sleeping, and my mother would come into my room and stare at me, whispering that name."

"Did you ever ask her about it?"

"I did once. She said René Levi was an old boyfriend from Paris who died very young of an illness and that it was an extremely painful loss for her. She warned me never to discuss him, especially in front of my father." Olivia focused her gaze over Julian's shoulder, as if the memory of that conversation were being projected against the faded gray wall. "After that, I never heard his name again. So, I stopped asking."

"René did die young," Julian said carefully. "But not the way you think."

Her eyes widened. "Was it suicide? Is that why she didn't tell me?"

"He would never have killed himself." Julian remembered the mural of hope that René had painted inside his Sachsenhausen cell, his fierce determination to survive. "But René was young when he was murdered in Paris."

A long silence passed between them both.

"Who killed him?" she asked softly, her lovely face twitching with anticipation.

Julian's throat tightened, as if two large hands were wrapped around it. This was all coming out backward. "There are things you need to understand before I tell you."

"Oh, I see. I am here so you can 'show me the light.'" Olivia got up from the chair and stood in front of him. She looked so young in her faded jeans and turtleneck. "I don't play games, Mr. Klein."

She was tall, practically his height. Julian stood too, and her eyes met his evenly, just as her mother's always had. He whispered, "This is not a game. There is no light here. Just plain dark facts."

She stepped backward, as though pushed by the force of his words. "You don't have to tell me about dark facts," she said defiantly. "I paint them."

"I know," Julian said anxiously, not wanting her to leave. "I saw the rage in your paintings. The furious, broad brushstrokes—swirls of darkness everywhere. I saw Felix and Charlotte's faces buried inside your work. I knew then ... " His voice faded.

"Knew what, goddamn it!" Olivia's face was flushed, her voice accusing. "How is it that you are the only person who sees my parents inside my paintings? And why do you see anger in my work, while the so-called experts call it passion? I don't even know you." She looked away, facing the window, but her feet were planted. Julian could see tears forming in the corners of her eyes.

"You tell me who is right," he said gently. "I watched you in New York. You never knew René Levi, but he was an immensely talented painter. Like you. Olivia, look at me."

She turned toward him.

"I came to Chicago not to visit my family, not to attend Felix's big gala, but to tell *you* the truth about your parents' past. I have been planning this conversation, this meeting, for a long time. So many times I wanted to contact you over the years but didn't, perhaps because I was afraid. And now you are finally here with me, and I don't know how to approach this without hurting you."

Something in Olivia's tough demeanor seemed to melt. Her shoulders trembled slightly. She slowly sat down. So did Julian. She leaned forward, her face just inches from his. "You need to understand, Mr. Klein, that from my perspective there was no past. I never met any relatives. There were no cousins, no doting grandparents. Our home in Bedford was cold and silent, a prison with three inmates. Painting—art—has been our only way of communicating. Other than that, there is nothing."

She paused, sat back into her chair with her arms protectively hugging herself, and Julian longed to comfort her, but he held back, too afraid he would scare her off again. "Nothing, except secrets."

"I'm so sorry, Olivia."

She stared down at her shiny cowboy boots, like a little girl trying to see her reflection in their polished surface. "You have no idea what they were like."

He shook his head. "I'm afraid that I know exactly what they are like."

She reached for the pack of cigarettes and lit up two at once. She did not ask whether or not Julian smoked as she handed it to him. He took the cigarette—anything to hold onto, anything to keep her there.

"How was Felix as a father?" Julian asked. He had to know before he went any further.

She seemed to be searching for the right words. "We were never close. He treated me as if I were his competition, not his daughter." Her gaze intensified and became misty. "As if he somehow needed to conquer me because of my talent."

Julian eyed her squarely. "Olivia, this may be very painful. Are you ready for the truth?"

She did not back away this time. "Yes."

"Then come with me."

When they entered Julian's hotel room, he ushered Olivia toward the imitation Louis XIV chair in the corner. He watched as she scrutinized the room, and he felt embarrassed by its cheapness, but it was the best he could do with what was left of Françoise's money.

"I am going to leave the door open, Olivia. You can leave at any time if you don't feel comfortable here," he said. "I will be right back."

He entered the bathroom, shut the door, and leaned against it, trying to collect himself. He turned on the faucet and stuck his head beneath it, then shook out his hair. Looking up, he studied his reflection in the mirror and saw the familiar stranger, the remains of a man who had once been handsome. His eyes looked haunted, and his cheekbones protruded against his sallow skin. No wonder Olivia was afraid of him.

His shirt was wet with perspiration. He took it off, grabbing the tan sweater he had worn the previous day that was hanging on the door hook. He stared again at his reflection, at his bare chest, and the endless, ugly scars, remnants from the Von Bredows' guesthouse. He shook his head sadly as he put on the sweater. There was so much that Olivia could never know.

He paused before opening the bathroom door. She was standing by the window and turned when he entered the room. He forced a small smile. "Well, you're still here."

"Yes," she said. "I am not leaving."

He slowly pulled an old newspaper photo from his wallet that Françoise had given him. It had been taken at René's exhibition at the Galerie Ferrat. His friend's lips were closed, his face pensive, as he stood alone in front of a wall filled with his paintings.

"This is a photograph of René Levi," he said, handing the picture to Olivia, waiting for her reaction.

She stared at the image, then brought it close to her face as if to smell it. When she pulled the paper away, tears filled her eyes. "If I cut my hair, it could be me. Who is he, Julian? Who is this man to me?"

He handed her a handkerchief. "René Levi is your father."

Silent tears began to stream freely down her face. "I have always known there was someone else. Damn it. Why did you wait so long to find me?"

Julian looked away. He did not want her to know that he had spent years in a mental institution, that he had traveled relentlessly throughout Europe collecting incriminating evidence against her parents and others who had used the war to steal and destroy modern art. He had finished off the work that Françoise had started. But right now Olivia needed to hear his story to believe him, not to see him for what he had become: a man consumed with vengeance, carrying the torch that Ernst Engel had handed him.

Shrugging, he replied simply, "I am here now, Olivia."

The handkerchief trembled in her hand. Julian briefly closed his eyes, still seeing Olivia's face as he spoke. "Those paintings that begin Felix's exhibition, those brilliant pieces he supposedly painted during the war years—they are not his. They belong to René." He could feel the heat of his own breath against his face. "Felix built his name on René's work, René's blood."

She stared at him without blinking. "I have seen my father paint for days straight without sleeping before an exhibition," she argued. "And I have seen him receive acclaim for those particular paintings."

"I don't have to tell you how the system works," Julian countered. "Once Felix established himself as America's premier abstract expressionist, he became immune to criticism. So, by the time he ran out of René's paintings and produced his own inferior artwork, no one held him accountable. Charlotte knows everything. She was part of all this."

"Part of what?" she demanded. "Damn it, Julian, who killed René Levi?"

Julian tried desperately to maintain his composure. "A Nazi. And not because René Levi was a Jew, but because he was a painter."

"I don't understand. Why would a Nazi kill him for being an artist?"

"The Nazis killed many artists," Julian explained. "They went after the artists before they started murdering Jews and others. But this particular Nazi had eyes only for René, because René was more talented than he could ever be." He paused, and what he yearned to shout out sank around him like quicksand, his voice barely audible. "So, he needed to conquer him."

Olivia's eyes dilated as she waited for the inevitable.

"You know who killed him," Julian said quietly.

Neither of them moved. The air felt suffocating.

"Where do you get off making that kind of accusation about my father?"

"I was there." Julian paused. "It is the truth."

Olivia's eyes became wildly defiant. "First, you say this man, René Levi, whose name I heard but a few times when I was child, was murdered and that I am his long-lost daughter. Then, you say my father is the Nazi who did him in. What next? Is my mother Eva Braun?" she spat. "Tell me, what does all this make me?"

"Innocent. Just like René Levi." Tears filled Julian's eyes.

Olivia shook her head. "My mother may be superficial and aloof, but she is not a thief or a Nazi." She waved the photo of René. "Yes, he looks like me. So what. Maybe he is my biological father. Maybe my mother had an affair with him and hid the pregnancy from my father." She pointed a finger at Julian. "Maybe that's what all this is."

Julian shook his head. "You have no concept of what it was like back then. Deals were cut. High-ranking Nazis bought forged identities from sympathizers."

"Oh, now my parents are high-ranking Nazis."

"They were Nazi royalty, Olivia," he said firmly. "Anyone who had any connection to them is now dead, buried with the rest of their past and secrets."

He turned away and allowed himself to think of Françoise, who had disappeared just after his visit to Charlotte in Zurich. Julian blamed himself. Françoise's death was his fault alone. If only he had not gone to Zurich, she might still be alive today. He imagined that his friend's ashes were floating somewhere along the Seine. He glanced over at the large suitcase near the wall. At least Françoise's legacy—the evidence she collected against Felix, Charlotte, and so many others who had betrayed modern art—had survived the war. Françoise's life's work was in that suitcase.

After Françoise's disappearance, he had gone back Paris to find Adrienne to see if she knew anything of Françoise's whereabouts, only to discover that Adrienne, Bernard, and the boy had been sent to the Drancy Deportation Camp during one of the Nazis' roundups of French Jews shortly after she had visited him at the hospital. He learned that the three of them were later gassed to death at Auschwitz. Julian stared down at his shoes. The pain of losing Adrienne, even now after so many years, was devastating.

Olivia interrupted his thoughts. "Tell me, Julian, what prevented you from going to the police about this murder years ago?"

Julian looked at her incredulously. "What police? It was Paris on the verge of war."

"What about later? After the war?"

"There was no after. Thousands of French Jews were killed, and the French were too busy celebrating their Resistance heroes." He tried to control his rage. "No one gave a damn about one more dead Jew."

Olivia threw up her hands. "Yet, you are alive. You seemed to have witnessed everything. Why did you wait so long to come forward? He is the legendary Felix Broussard, after all—man with the golden stroke; God's gift to art-kind. You could have had the media eating out of your hand." Olivia clutched his arm. "Give me something more, Julian. Anything to back up your accusations."

Breathing heavily, Julian pulled away from her and moved quickly toward the closet. He dragged out the leather suitcase filled with incriminating documents. But first, he removed a large rectangular package from its lining. The package was covered with light pink tissue paper. Unwrapping it, he caressed the notebook, as he had done thousands of times before. The jacket was torn, the pages curled and yellow, but it was dust-free. Holding René's notebook against his chest, Julian said, "These are the sketches René drew in Dachau, where we were held as prisoners. Each page will match a painting that was shown last night at Felix's exhibition. Inside each painting, you will find René's name hidden within the composition. René never knew if he would survive Felix's war, but he was determined that his name—his art—would. I was there, every day, every night, with him in Dachau. I saw him draw each one of these sketches, Olivia. I have held onto this book for years. Now, I want you to have it."

He slowly handed Olivia the notebook, then pointed to the suitcase filled with Françoise's evidence and his own collection of documents that he had spent nearly a decade tracking down. "All the proof is in there. Records, photos of looted art, contracts with Felix's and Charlotte's signatures, photos of your parents in Germany and in Paris, documents concerning their illicit business dealings." Julian paused. "And not just their dealings, but evidence against many others as well."

"What do you plan to do?" she asked fearfully, as she stared at the suitcase.

"I plan to take the information to the authorities." Julian's eyes blazed. "But, I wanted to talk with you first. I wanted you to hear the truth from me and not read about it. It was the least I could do for René."

He gestured to the notebook. "I came here to tell you the truth about your real father, and his artwork. I owed René Levi that. Felix stole his paintings, but you are René's living legacy. All of those paintings belong to you, Olivia," Julian said forcefully. "Not to Felix, not to Charlotte. I will not rest until I know René's work is safely in your hands and his name is honored."

He gauged Olivia's reaction; the frozen face. René might have painted her like that, her beauty so terrified and momentous.

"They are still my parents, Julian." She squeezed her eyes shut. He had clearly pushed her to a place where she did not want to go.

"Why did you become a painter, Olivia?" he whispered.

"I did not become anything." She opened her eyes wide, throwing back her raven hair defiantly. "I was born painting."

Chapter Forty-Three

BEDFORD, NEW YORK

Olivia hesitated, then walked slowly toward her mother, who was gardening in the backyard. Charlotte's swanlike neck was tilted as she assessed whether the hedge was even. Her blonde hair was pulled back with a loose green ribbon.

"It's even, Mother," Olivia called out, taking Charlotte by surprise.

"Why, Olivia, what brings you here? I've been trying to reach you for three days. I thought you had left town."

"I did, actually. I went to the beach house."

Charlotte smiled demurely. "With someone?"

"Alone."

Her mother stood and wiped her hands on her grass-stained shorts. She studied Olivia's face. "You're not feeling well, are you?"

Olivia met her gaze. "I am fine."

"You look pale." Charlotte gestured toward the house. "Your father is busy in the studio. Let's have a cold drink on the porch."

They entered the house through the side door. Charlotte carried on about Olivia's appearance. Surprisingly pale, she added, for having spent a few days at the beach.

"Graciela," Charlotte called into the kitchen at the housekeeper. "Fix us iced tea with extra lemon and bring the drinks out back."

Charlotte sat down on a daisy-patterned lounge chair and waited for her daughter to speak. After a moment Olivia leaned forward and said bluntly, "I want you to tell me exactly how René Levi died."

Charlotte's sun-kissed cheeks turned instantly white. "I'd rather not discuss that," Charlotte said, looking away. "You know how it upsets me."

"Well, we will discuss it, even if you are upset."

"I don't appreciate your attitude, Olivia, or the way you are looking at me. What does it matter? He was a friend who became sick and died in Paris. It was dreadful, and so long ago."

Olivia crossed her arms. "You're lying."

A nerve in Charlotte's still-beautiful face twitched. She stood, elegant but angry. "How dare you."

"Sit down, Mother." Something about Olivia's commanding tone caused Charlotte to sit back against the daisy pattern; her face remained controlled.

"You and I both know that René Levi did not die of an illness. Although that would have been lovely compared to what really happened to him. My father—" She paused, as if uncertain what to call Felix—"killed him. He murdered René Levi in his father's gallery. You were there."

Charlotte's mouth dropped open. "Really, Olivia, you look like you have not slept in days. And that color you are wearing does nothing for you."

"I don't give a damn what I look like!" Olivia shouted.

"You have no right to shout, Olivia. Where are you getting this absurd story?"

Olivia stood and circled her mother's chair. "This happens to be the story of my life—about my *real* father, René Levi. Let's start with the lies, since there seem to be so many."

Charlotte was silent as Olivia slowly recounted what Julian had told her. Her mother tried to control her facial muscles, but she could not mask her eyes, which were becoming a paler blue with each of her daughter's accusations. And then Charlotte began to cry.

Olivia took a few steps backward, stunned. She had been prepared for more of her mother's lies, not her emotion. She had never seen Charlotte cry. She watched her mother's tears with fascination, and for a moment she yearned to wrap her arms around her, to protect her.

"Did you even love René?" Olivia asked softly. "The risks you took so Jacob Levi could see him again. It had to have meant something." She searched Charlotte's tormented face.

"Julian Klein," Charlotte said under her breath. "Julian Klein found you."

Olivia heard the name, but ignored it. "Yet, you stood by Father's side, gloating at every exhibition, knowing damn well all those paintings belonged to René Levi."

"Who the hell do you think you are?" Charlotte demanded, suddenly overflowing with bitterness. "How could you even begin to know why I did what I did? You were raised with everything. So much money and comfort you never had to think twice about what you were going to eat, *if* you were going to eat at all. I had to survive, that was always my first thought. Everything else came second."

"Including me, Mother?"

They stared at each other. Charlotte's face was wretched and tender. She reached out to Olivia, but recoiled in anger when her daughter stepped back. "It doesn't matter that Felix claimed those paintings," Charlotte said. "The important thing is that René Levi's artwork survived the war and is celebrated."

"Did you even love him?" Olivia demanded again, knowing the answer, having had years of practice reading her mother's eyes to decipher what she was really thinking even though she always kept her true feelings so tightly sealed.

"Yes." Charlotte stared at the pattern of daisy clusters beneath her and began to stroke the cushion as though it were René lying next to her. "But René is dead. Do you know what it means when the only person you truly love dies?" She leaned forward, her face taut and angry. "When he died, I died. That is the entire story. The rest of it doesn't matter."

"It matters," Olivia whispered as she lit up two cigarettes. "You know, more than anyone, just how much it matters."

They smoked together in silence. It was the first time Charlotte had ever opened up to Olivia. It was the first time Olivia had ever seen her mother as human, as fallible, as a woman who had truly loved and lost. But the feeling only lasted for a few passing moments.

Charlotte stood, lifted her head high, and ground out her cigarette. Her eyes resumed their permanent vacancy, and Olivia knew that the intimate feelings her mother had exposed were now once again buried. She stared longingly at Charlotte, yearning for a deeper bond, wishing they could share more, but she knew it was impossible. Her mother was untouchable. Olivia nodded painfully, ground out her cigarette, and turned to go.

Charlotte did not call her back.

Olivia walked through the garden, her long legs moving rapidly across the manicured lawn. She ascended the wooden staircase leading up to Felix's studio. With each step, the familiar smell of turpentine sharpened. Felix was painting in his signature uniform: white T-shirt, black bandanna tied loosely around his neck, baggy workman's pants splotched with paint.

"Your mother never mentioned you were coming," he said as Olivia approached him, standing before his canvas.

"She didn't know," Olivia responded. "I thought we could talk."

"I am busy, Olivia. Give me two hours and I will meet you back at the house."

She cleared her throat. "I'd rather we speak now."

Felix put down his brush and moved toward her. "What have you got there?"

"A notebook."

"A notebook," he repeated thinly. "Yours or someone else's?"

"Someone else's." She could not hide her nervousness.

"Is that meant for me?" Felix asked in a gruff yet guarded tone.

"No, it was given to me."

"Who gave it to you?"

She remained silent, knowing better than to reveal Julian's name.

Felix growled. "I told you, I am extremely busy."

They both breathed hard, the thick choppy sound between them impenetrable.

"I know everything," Olivia said finally, breaking the silence.

"Everything?" Felix laughed scornfully. "Are you still on drugs?"

"No, I'm clean." Olivia paused, resenting his condescending tone. "But perhaps you're not."

Felix's face darkened. "Who the hell do you think you are, walking in here and speaking to me like that?"

"I just want to talk."

"There is nothing to talk about." Felix turned away from her and continued painting.

"For once, don't shut me out." Olivia stood behind him, watching him paint with those broad brushstrokes. *Slapped on, sloppy.*

Felix stopped painting mid-stroke and turned to face her. His eyes were burning with anger as he stared at the notebook. "Who the hell have you been talking to, Olivia?"

She tried to conceal the tremor in her voice, but after all these years his temper still terrified her. "It doesn't matter. I just want to hear the truth from you about your past."

"The truth?" he mocked. "What makes you think there are lies?"

Olivia said nothing. She noticed the beads of perspiration collecting at Felix's temples. His eyes were wide open and his breath was heavy. "Do you know who I am, Olivia?" he asked.

She nodded.

"Then you would know better than to waste my time with this frivolous inquisition when I have an important exhibition coming up."

"I know you," she said slowly, mustering courage, "but I could never comprehend why you tormented me all these years." She took a deep breath. "Until I learned about René Levi."

Her confidence grew as she watched her father shrink before her. The palette in his hand began to shake. "Did you resent me because I am really his daughter?" Her voice rose boldly. "Was it because I became a painter? Or, because my mother never stopped loving him?"

"You bitch!" Felix shouted, hurling down the palette and grabbing Olivia by the shoulders. "You were half of him. You were all of him. The way you look, the way you paint. In my face every goddamn day to remind me."

"Get your hands off me!"

"Who the hell have you been talking to?" he demanded again, shaking her.

Olivia pushed him away. "You once told me that the Broussards owed everything to art," she said accusingly. "Now, we owe the truth to art. I have to know: Did you steal René Levi's artwork and claim his paintings as your own?"

Felix laughed, and Olivia hugged her body as if to protect herself from his patronizing sound. "You want the truth, Olivia. You used *my* artwork, my name, to get where you are," he told her. "You think they would exhibit your pathetic paintings at the Guggenheim? Without me, you would be nothing. Don't forget that."

"Without René Levi, you would be nothing." Olivia's voice hardened. She knew her father had always hated her, but she had never understood why, until now.

"Nothing? You see that painting in the corner?" Felix stormed over to a large unfinished canvas. "Even if I never complete that painting, there are hoards of people willing to pay hundreds of thousands of dollars for my signature alone."

He made a panoramic sweep of the studio with his palette. "Take a good look around you. Next month, the first lady, the governor, and every important modern artist living in the United States will be honoring my life's work at the Museum of Modern Art—you call that nothing!"

Felix's T-shirt was drenched, plastered to his chest. She had never seen him like this. She realized, suddenly, that he was afraid. She recalled the contents of Julian's suitcase filled with incriminating documents. "Felix Von Bredow," she began, but he cut her off.

"Von Bredow is dead!" He kicked a fold-up chair next to him, and it went flying. "You cannot change the past."

"But you can change the future. Start over. Do it right," she pleaded. "Before it is done for you."

He lunged toward Olivia, and his eyes were blazing. "And who is going to do it for me? You? Is my own daughter going to betray me?"

She lowered her gaze.

"So, this is what I get after everything I have given you, done for you?"

The sheer force of his voice seemed to be filling every crevice of the room. She eyed the staircase, thinking she should run now, but her feet felt heavy, rooted to the floor.

"Your mother and I sent you to the best schools, you know all the right people. You have closets full of designer clothes and a monthly allowance that could feed a Third World nation." His face was now inches from hers, and she could smell the alcohol on his breath. "Doesn't family loyalty mean anything to you?"

Olivia felt dizzy. It was true. She had been given the best of everything from her parents, yet nothing of substance. They had never seemed concerned about the things that had mattered to her friends' parents: whether or not she did her homework, with whom she was hanging out, and if she was experimenting with sex and drugs. Felix had ignored all of it, and so had her mother, who was too preoccupied with her society friends to notice that Olivia's grades had been well below average, that she had slept around, and that she had done more than her fair share of drugs.

Her father cared about only one thing: *her* artwork. His interest was obsessive—a constant interrogation from the time she was a teenager: *What was she painting? How long did it take her? What size was the canvas? Where was she buying her supplies? Who had seen her paintings?* Nothing else about her life had ever interested him. Even now.

"I'm leaving," she said finally, turning toward the staircase.

"Wait, don't go just yet," he called out almost too calmly, as he pointed to his unfinished canvas. "You have to understand that I am under enormous pressure to finish that painting. I have not slept in three days. I am not thinking straight." He mopped his face with his bandanna. "What do you really want, Olivia?"

She recognized the controlled complacent tone of voice, and it set off an internal alarm. It was a ploy, a fake. He would use that tone with her mother, with his art dealers, with her whenever he wanted something. She despised that false sound, despised him, but he was still the man who had raised her. She had to give him the chance to own up to his past. She whispered, "All I want is for you to tell the truth."

He bowed his head and gazed deeply into her eyes. "Yes, but first you must tell me where you got your information, so I will know how to handle this problem properly."

Olivia swallowed hard, wanting desperately to believe him, but she knew better. "I can't," she whispered, and then said firmly, "I won't."

Felix dropped the bandanna. Instantly, the simulated calm gave way to a familiar recklessness. He stomped across the floor. His hands became meaty fists pounding at his sides, his jaw clenched, and his nostrils flared. It was a hideous look that had frightened Olivia since she was a child; a look that would cause her to run into her bedroom and lock the door.

"Damn you, Olivia. I have had enough!" He slapped her hard across the face. "You will tell me."

She touched her bruised cheek. "I hate you!" she cried out, then ran toward the stairs.

"No, you hate yourself," he shouted after her. "Now, get out of my studio!"

Olivia clutched the notebook tightly against her like a shield and bolted to her car.

Breathless, she got into the vehicle and locked the doors. She gripped the steering wheel tightly and began to sob. Neither of her parents seemed to feel remorse for lying to her about their past.

She glanced down at her slim lovely hands, a gift from her real father. He was murdered because of his talent, because of his hands. Trembling, she turned on the ignition and quickly drove away from her parents' home and back to the city, where Julian Klein was now staying. He was in danger. She had to warn him before Felix somehow got there first.

Chapter Forty-Four

THE MUSEUM OF MODERN ART, MANHATTAN

Julian glanced at his watch. It was nearly seven-thirty in the evening. Olivia had been inside the museum for just over an hour, as they had planned. He walked through the lobby wearing an expensive suit she had bought him that he would never wear again. He looked almost as though he belonged. Julian laughed to himself as he proceeded to the gallery. He would never belong.

He wondered how she was doing. He had neither seen nor spoken to Olivia in the past two weeks since they had made their plan and he had gone into hiding, staying with a friend of hers in SoHo. He thought back to the night when she had banged on his hotel room door. She had just confronted Charlotte and Felix, and her face was tear-streaked with thick lines of black mascara. She fell into his arms, crying, and he consoled her. They had spent the entire night talking. She told him about her childhood, her fears, and her art. And much later, she reached for his hands and asked him about his past. This time, he did not hold back.

He told her about his parents, about the pickle jar filled with money that he had never paid back, about his cousin Sammy, and about Adrienne, René, Engel, Kruger, and Françoise. He told her about Sachsenhausen and Dachau, but not the guesthouse, not the scars on his body, just the ones on his heart. Instead, he spoke of the old Felix, the young man he once knew and loved in Paris. He described Charlotte's great beauty, her bravery, and her instinct for survival, even her love for René.

He had wiped the tears from Olivia's eyes and said that despite every-thing René had endured, he had never stopped loving her mother. Julian sensed that Olivia needed to hear that her parents had a good side. Her confrontation with them had broken her. It had been too much.

When she finally fell asleep, Julian sat in a chair next to the bed and watched over her. When she awoke several hours later, her eyes were clear and her voice unwavering. "In two weeks my father is going to be honored for his work. Everyone important will be there, and so should you," she said, reaching again for his hands. "It is time, Julian, for you to come out and present all of the evidence you spent your life gathering. No more hiding."

Exhaling deeply now, Julian smoothed his dinner jacket and clutched his suitcase tightly. After two decades of living in the shadows, tonight would be his debut, his reunion with Felix.

Julian quickly cut through short empty corridors until he saw the sleepy-eyed usher waiting at the entrance of the main gallery. Julian flashed his invitation and avoided direct eye contact. The man gave Julian a quick once-over.

"You are late," the man said, scratching the back of his neck, sounding bored. "Cocktails started nearly an hour ago."

"Traffic," Julian answered curtly, and he pointed to his suitcase. "I have to catch a plane late tonight. Where can I store this?"

The usher gestured toward the coat check in the corner of the room, then handed Julian a complimentary book of Felix's paintings. Julian stared at the thick glossy book with Felix's photo on the cover. He was scowling and craggy-faced, wearing his signature black bandanna and splotched overalls. He held a paint-crusted palette and was applying paint to an almost finished canvas of a woman with an anguished ex-pression. The thickly applied brushstrokes were horizontal blotchy reds, with slashes of black and triangles of white. The edges of the painting were rendered in a pale flesh color, as though the woman were self-destructing into fragments. The image was both dramatic and deeply disturbing. Julian had read somewhere that that particular painting had sold for more than six million dollars.

"Keep it." Julian declined the book, checked his suitcase, then walked quickly toward the ballroom. He stepped inside just as Felix was taking the microphone on stage. Behind Felix stood a large covered canvas. Julian waited near the door as Felix cleared his throat. Seeing an empty chair against the wall, Julian quickly sat down, scanning the room for Olivia. *There must be more than five hundred people here paying homage to Felix,* Julian thought angrily.

Felix put on his glasses and began to read a list of those who had supported the evening's festivities, including the first lady and the governor of New York. Over his tuxedo shirt, he wore not a jacket but a black silk cape, which shimmered under the spotlight. Charlotte was seated to his right, watching the adoring crowd with a fixed smile. Her gold sequined dress sparkled beneath the lights, momentarily blinding Julian. She was still beautiful, if not even more so, Julian thought. Her cheekbones were more pronounced, accentuating her full lips and eyes. She posed on the stage like a queen, assuming the role she had prepared for her entire life.

"My friends and colleagues, I welcome you." Felix raised a glass, his voice resounding through the gallery. "Tonight, we celebrate Abstract Expressionism, the New York School, a movement of artists who set out to create an environment where art is freedom and freedom is art—and who succeeded. I am deeply honored to be here representing my colleagues, whose brilliant works have made New York City the center of the art world."

He nodded at the head table, where a dozen prominent artists were seated. "Our movement is divided into two groups: those of us whose works are exemplified by action, images that are physical in context; and those of us whose primary focus is to explore the effects of pure color on canvas." He gestured toward the still-covered painting behind him. "Tonight, I am donating my latest painting to the Museum of Modern

Art. I consider it one of my most important works because it fits into both categories of Expressionism—movement and color. I call it *Man on Fire* because it explores the concept of rage, which I believe to be the most powerful of all human emotions."

He stepped to the side of the podium and signaled a slim young woman to come forward. She quickly walked toward the painting and dramatically unveiled the artwork.

The audience gasped, and Julian thought he was dreaming. It was *his* painting—his masterpiece—from the last night he had painted in Engel's studio.

My painting. My name. My rage. Not yours, Felix. Not yours.

Julian yearned to scream out the truth but his breath, his body, everything seemed to fail him at once.

Felix stood on the stage, smiling with closed lips as the audience gave him a standing ovation. *My ovation,* Julian thought. He felt a tug on his shoulder, but he could barely turn around. From the corner of his eye, he saw the familiar long dark hair and ebony eyes.

"It's mine," he whispered without looking at Olivia.

"Julian, look at me," she said firmly, pulling him around to face her. "What are you talking about?"

"That is my painting, Olivia." He pointed to the stage. "My only canvas to survive Germany."

Olivia looked shocked. "Stand up and say something now."

"No, it's over. Don't you see?" Julian felt he was withering and blooming simultaneously. "What matters is that Felix knows the truth. They are clapping for him, but deep down, he knows that the applause is for me."

Julian recalled the night of René's exhibition at Johann Finch's gallery, when Felix and his thugs had stolen René's and Engel's paintings from Engel's studio but ignored Julian's work, as though his paintings were not worthy of being stolen or defaced. Yet here, tonight, Felix had saved the best for last—displaying Julian's painting as his most important piece, representative of an entire movement of art.

"Listen to me, Julian." Olivia shook him out of his trance. "He can't get away with this. Stand up for yourself. Do it now."

But Julian was frozen, staring at the painting. He barely noticed that Olivia had remained standing as the ovation died down and the guests resumed their seats.

Felix returned to the podium and saw Olivia standing alone, staring at him, arms crossed. He and Charlotte exchanged worried glances, but he kept his focus on the other side of the room, as he continued to speak. "My friends, this is truly an honor. Lastly, I would like to thank—"

"René Levi." Olivia's voice rang clearly through the ballroom. "You would like to thank René Levi, who is dead, and Julian Klein, who is here right now, very much alive."

"No, Olivia," Julian pleaded. "Not like this."

At first there was a stunned collective silence, then the room flooded with whispers, as Olivia pointed to Julian. She gestured him forward.

When he finally stood, he met Felix's shocked gaze as Olivia continued speaking: "This man standing next to me, Julian Klein, is an important artist and should be on that stage tonight." She pointed at Felix. "That painting—that work of genius that Felix Broussard calls *Man on Fire* was painted by Mr. Klein in Germany years ago and stolen by the man I call my father." Her voice began to crack. "You must understand, this is extremely difficult for me. Felix Broussard stands before you tonight being honored as a leader and founder of the Abstract Expressionist movement when he, in fact, spent the early years of the war in Germany destroying artists—young Expressionists like Mr. Klein." She pulled Julian close to her; their arms were now linked. "There are more than fifty paintings in this exhibition that were not painted by my father. The evidence, I'm afraid, is tragically overwhelming."

Tears began to roll down Olivia's face, and Julian held her hand tightly. He felt a renewed sense of strength and purpose.

Suddenly Felix's larger-than-life presence began to diminish in front of all those who had celebrated him. His face, his skin, his clothes were all converted into fugitive colors, rapidly losing pigment under the sharp illumination. He stood, bent over the microphone, silenced and exposed.

"Finally," Julian whispered, the tiny sound of justice echoing throughout his body.

But then Felix's thundering voice belied his shrunken stance. "Security!" he shouted, pointing at Julian. "That man is a criminal!"

Felix turned to the man seated next to him at the podium, who looked too shocked to move. "What are you waiting for? You are in charge. I said get him out of here!" Felix faced the audience. "That man wants money. He is blackmailing my daughter to get to me."

A young reporter ran over to Julian and shoved a tape recorder under his nose. "Is that really your painting?"

Julian hesitated, knowing that he, too, would now be under a microscope. All those years spent at the institution would be smeared over the man's newspaper. Suddenly, it didn't matter that *his* past would be exposed too.

As four guards took hold of him, he recalled Ernst Engel and Max Kruger asking him how far would he go for art. Julian glanced briefly at the head table seating America's leading contemporary artists—those who believed that Felix walked on water—and Julian knew that tonight he would go the distance.

"Leave him alone!" Olivia cried as they began to drag Julian from the room.

It took only seconds before the pack of reporters jumped up, leaving their foie gras untouched. They ran after Julian, surging forward, notebooks in hand. Questions were shouted out at Julian from all sides of the room, but he did not respond. His eyes met Charlotte's, and they remained locked.

Her blazing stare pierced Julian's gaze, then blew out like a faulty light bulb. Julian realized that she knew it was only a matter of minutes before the life that she had so carefully crafted would fall apart.

~◦ ◦~

Outside the ballroom, the four guards released Julian, and he now stood next to Olivia, both surrounded by reporters. She slowly retold Julian's and René's story, as though their lives had become hers. When she finished, she opened Julian's suitcase and spread out the evidence across the black-and-white nametag table. The reporters sifted through Françoise's meticulous documents recording Charlotte's and Felix's illicit activities and eyewitness reports given by employees of the Louvre and the Jeu de Paume, detailing thousands of paintings the Nazis had confiscated from their museums. Julian had collected hundreds of testimonies from German Expressionists, German and French museum curators, and Holocaust survivors who described in detail how their private art collections had been seized from their homes, never to be seen again. The evidence was astounding.

"Julian Klein was a man possessed," a reporter remarked. "The research is exceptional. We should hire him."

"This could be the story of the century," exuded another journalist, pointing to photos of famous paintings by Picasso, van Gogh, and Klimt that had been stolen and were now hanging in some of the world's most prestigious museums. "Heads are surely going to roll."

Julian watched the event unfold until, over Olivia's shoulder, he noticed Felix slipping out a side entrance, alone. It was his cue. He began to walk away when Olivia grabbed his arm.

"Where are you going?" she asked.

"You will be fine," he assured her.

"Don't go," she pleaded accidentally into the head of someone's microphone.

"Go where?" the reporter demanded.

Olivia whispered, this time directly into Julian's ear, "Let it be. Please, Julian."

Julian took her lovely hands, René's hands, inside his, holding her and his friend once again. He reached inside his pocket and handed her a sealed envelope. "I was going to save this for later," he said softly. "But take it now."

Just in case, he added silently, as he watched Olivia tuck the envelope inside her purse.

As he turned to go, the reporters started to follow but stopped once Olivia began to reveal the contents of René's notebook. *Their Bible of Proof.* Then, Julian was completely ignored.

Julian watched Felix scurry down a side street. His shoulders were slumped, his hands lost inside the folds of black fabric. He was sure Felix must have heard his approach, because without turning around, Felix quickened his pace. But Julian was faster. He ran as though he were a young man again, and he easily grabbed Felix's arm, pulling him to a halt.

Standing perfectly still next to Julian, Felix looked past him, his voice nostalgic. "Remember Paris, Julian? The laughter. How hard we laughed back then."

"I remember the guesthouse, Felix," Julian responded coldly. "And your laughter there. The rest is gone."

"Such freedom we had."

"You were free, Felix. I was tied up and tortured."

Felix turned to Julian, his eyes ablaze, but his voice, by contrast, was surprisingly tender. "You were too trusting."

"All I ever wanted was to paint," Julian said simply.

"That's all I ever wanted too."

"But you never saw your own canvas, Felix—only René's. You never believed in your own hands. So you had to destroy René's."

"I was afraid then," Felix said quietly.

Julian was suddenly flooded with memories of the hammer, the blood, and the screams in Dachau.

"Afraid of what?" Julian demanded.

"Of being exposed for what my hands could not do."

"And now, Felix," Julian taunted. "Tell me what you are afraid of now."

"There is no now. There is only yesterday, when everyone believed these fingers were golden." Felix held out his hands in front of him. "You have taken it all away from me."

"It was never yours to begin with."

"You have been waiting for this day, Julian, until I rose so high that no one could touch me. Only you."

Julian nodded. "Yes, but I waited too long. You have enjoyed too much."

"And you?" Felix sneered. "Look at you—pathetic. You have taken on René's cause to make yourself feel better. It allows you to hide behind the truth. You have accomplished nothing."

Julian laughed mockingly. "And tonight, you hid behind *my* painting as your greatest work. Who are you to talk about truth? You never wanted me to believe that I, too, had talent, from that first night in Paris. See, it wasn't just René's hands that you were afraid of, Felix. You were afraid of mine as well. If only I had known."

"You are a nobody! I paint every goddamn day of my life!" Felix shouted. His breath was heavy. Julian smelled the Bordeaux. "Look at you. Half a man. What the hell have you been doing all these years?"

Julian looked away, then met Felix's gaze evenly. "I was left for dead, remember? I spent years following your trail, and your father's. I collected all of Françoise's files. After you and Charlotte had her murdered, I met with her friends, her colleagues, anyone who had information, until I got everything I was looking for—all of her meticulous documents describing your crimes and the crimes of others. I then tracked down many artists and collectors—those who had survived the Nazis—but not Adrienne, Felix. Your friends killed her."

At the mention of Adrienne's name, Felix looked away.

Julian continued, "I am no longer 'naive and easily convinced.'" He moved in closer, just inches from Felix's face. "Your sick story is just one of hundreds. Yet, you alone, Felix, have achieved the highest level of celebrity with your lies." Julian shook his head. "But not anymore."

Felix stretched his arms wide, as if Julian were supposed to fall in and reclaim a long lost embrace. "Well, then, what are you waiting for?" he asked. "I can never go back now. Finish the job. This is why you came."

Nodding, Julian removed René's palette knife from his coat pocket. Felix stared at the rusty tool and laughed. "Do you plan to slice me up like bread?"

Turning the knife front and back, Julian explained, "Every day in Dachau after René painted the pictures you stole from him, he gave up his meals to dig us to freedom with *this*."

Felix stared hard at the small knife. When he finally looked up, his eyes were misty. "You think I have everything, Julian. But I have enjoyed nothing."

Tears began to roll down Felix's face, and Julian was taken aback. "My own daughter betrayed me tonight. Despite everything, I loved Olivia. We barely spent a moment apart when she was a little girl." He looked away. "Until she started painting. Just like him. The way she held the palette, how she eyed her canvas, the tongue pressing against her cheek—just like him. It was as if he were there, rising before me. By the time Olivia was twelve, she could paint better than I could on my best day. And that's when it started." He wiped his face with the cape. "It was then that I began to hate her for possessing what I could never have."

"Your jealousy has ruined everything for you, Felix," Julian said, turning the knife over. "And because of it, you destroyed everyone around you, including yourself."

Their eyes joined like magnets. Julian watched the unnatural blue of Felix's anger freeze in place. "Just do it," he begged. "My life is over."

Julian grazed the knife along Felix's expectant throat, and then pulled his hand away. Felix's eyes flickered with surprise. "For years, Felix, all I wanted was for you to fall, to die," Julian said slowly. "I dreamed of killing you after I exposed you. But now, I want you to live, to be a witness to your world crashing around you. There is no better punishment."

Raising his hand high into the air, Julian paused, allowing Felix the moment to escape, and he took it. Julian watched his stride, long and fearful, until all that remained of Felix was the frenzied flap of a vanishing cape.

Julian slowly began to walk back to his hotel. He realized that Felix had lived like a king and had also lived in hell, tormented by his own demons. For the first time in too many years, Julian felt pity for Felix.

He glanced at the knife still in his hand. He stopped, held the knife briefly to his chest, and then tossed it into a garbage bin on the street. He no longer had use for it. Gazing up at the charcoal sky, Julian felt a strange tranquility envelop him.

"Juliangelo." He seemed to hear the familiar voice beckoning from high above, as it had so many times before.

"Yes, René, I am here." Julian pictured the young man whose scarf swept loosely off his shoulders, whose jet-black hair fell rakishly over his eyes. "Remember what you said in Dachau? Other people—like Felix—were born to live, but you and I were born to paint. I believe you now, my friend."

The image seemed to be smiling down at him, buoyant and proud, and then it slowly, peacefully faded. In its wake, the stars shimmered brilliantly against a dark canvas, and Julian knew that René was painting.

PURPLE

"The only time I feel alive is when I'm painting."
—Vincent van Gogh

Epilogue

BEAULIEU-SUR-MER

Olivia detrained three stops east of Nice. Signs around the station trumpeted the town's star attraction, Kérylos, the seaside Greek villa with breathtaking views of the Mediterranean. None of the signs revealed the coastal village's well-kept secret: the small, sequestered mental institution perched high on a hilltop also overlooking the sea.

She arrived a half hour early, sat on a bench, and waited for her ride. A group of backpackers were off to the side of the road examining maps, and an elderly British couple holding umbrellas complained to each other about the heat. They saw her and stopped mid-sentence, lowering their voices. Even with her large sunglasses and hat, Olivia had been identified.

The story had hit the dailies, the weeklies, and the television shows like an unending explosion. Olivia had been quoted everywhere. Her paintings, to the delight of her dealer, were showcased next to photos of René Levi's paintings and accompanied by stories of how the famous artist Felix Broussard had passed off Levi's brilliant artwork as his own. Sordid tales of Felix's early wartime activities took on a new life.

Charlotte, who had never taken an unflattering photo, was pictured in a wide array of past society events. Yet, the words next to each photo had destroyed any dignity Felix and Charlotte might have had left. The picture of them heading inside the police station for questioning had been reprinted everywhere. Charlotte wore black Hollywood-style sunglasses and a charcoal Chanel suit; she clutched an oversized Gucci purse as if to protect herself from the swarm of reporters. Felix wore dark sunglasses and a plain gray suit, his hands loosely gripping a thick black briefcase, his expression blank and stoic as if he had nothing to fear.

Everyone seemed to have his own take on Julian Klein, the obscure artist who had brought the great Felix Broussard to his knees and exposed the dubious histories of many important contemporary paintings. Because of Julian's evidence governments, major international museums, socialites, financiers, art dealers, and others would now have to come clean and show accountability for their secretive art purchases. And many destroyed families across Europe, whose paintings had been seized from their homes by the Nazis, would soon have their day in court.

Olivia smiled to herself. Everyone was talking about the painting called *Man on Fire* and demanding to see more work by the elusive Julian Klein.

And René Levi's paintings now belonged to her. She had spent the past month ducking from the media, locked in her studio, painting over Felix's name and signing her real father's name to each of the stolen canvases. She and Julian planned to showcase a traveling exhibit of René's work at galleries around the world.

But the price of truth had been great. As she continued to wait for her ride, Olivia stared into the midday sun, thinking about her parents. Charlotte had passed Olivia in the police station as though they were strangers. Olivia had tried to say something, to make a connection, but Charlotte had turned away, her freshly cut blonde hair swinging freely. Olivia had glimpsed her mother's face: her eyes were vacant, as always. She knew her mother would never forgive her. Olivia had felt a deep sense of loss as she watched Charlotte moving past her and down the hallway toward Felix. Her parents had exchanged a few quiet words, their voices becoming a united murmur, their hands joined. Olivia knew at that moment that no matter what, her mother would always stand by Felix's side, sharing a past that only they understood, and she, as always, would remain the intruder, the outsider. She had betrayed her parents by exposing them, and she would always have to live with that. But now there were no more secrets, no more lies, no more shadows. Now, she could live with herself.

The British couple finally left. The hitchhikers, caring nothing for world events, offered her water. Then, they, too, departed from the train station. Olivia removed the envelope Julian had given her from her purse and read the note once again:

All for you, Olivia. In memory of René Levi—your father, my friend.
—Julian Klein

Beneath the handwritten message were two typed addresses: The first, a cemetery on the outskirts of Paris. Beneath it, a name and phone number of an institution in Beaulieu-sur-Mer. Julian had refused to tell her what the note meant. He was determined that Olivia see everything for herself.

Peering out at the deep blue coastline, she recalled the tiny, dilapidated cemetery on the outskirts of Paris that she had visited the previous day. She had found the grave that bore René Levi's name. She sat in front of the small gravestone for hours, holding a bouquet of flowers. Before leaving, she placed the bouquet on someone else's grave and pulled out a small notepad from her purse and sketched a bouquet. When she finished her drawing, she signed it and placed in on her father's grave. The caretaker gave her two large rocks to hold down the paper.

She stood and cried.

When Olivia arrived at the institution, the director was waiting for her on the front lawn. The woman appeared to be in her early fifties, more attractive and less stiff than she had sounded on the telephone. Her hand was outstretched even before Olivia exited the automobile.

"We heard what happened, Miss Broussard," the woman said. Her hands were warm and calming to Olivia, who nodded and followed the woman inside the bleached white building.

"Julian Klein spent more than ten years here, on and off. He would come and go as he pleased. Sometimes a year or two would pass before he would return, and yet he always came back. We never turned him away. He was . . . " the director hesitated, "unreachable. But he was considered a model patient, special." She smiled, revealing coffee-stained teeth.

Olivia stopped. "He was here that many years?"

"You look shocked."

"I knew he had spent time in an institution—but not a decade."

The director shook her head and said quietly, "This place is not a prison, more of a rest home, a respite from the outside world. Many of our patients are war victims. In here, they feel safe, protected." The director pressed her clipboard against her chest.

As they walked together down a long corridor smelling of disinfectant, they passed by several paintings. The director pointed at two large oils on the wall. "Those are Julian's."

Olivia scrutinized the artwork. The seascapes were indeed lovely, but mundane, she thought, disconnected, revealing nothing of the man she knew. They kept walking.

The director opened the door to her office, moving past a secretary who did not look up from her typewriter, and unlocked a large conference room door. She gestured inside the room. "Julian contacted me before you arrived and asked that I set this up for you. He was very specific."

She tried to usher Olivia inside, but Olivia stopped at the threshold, not believing what was before her eyes: an entire room filled with paintings, anticipating her arrival like ladies-in-waiting.

So, Julian had been painting all along. She entered the room slowly. She had never seen anything like this before. Julian did not just paint. He *was* the paintings.

Dozens of canvases were propped on easels around the room—her own private exhibition. She started at the beginning, in front of an abstract oil of a woman posing next to spoiled potatoes in a market. Olivia could practically taste the dull rot of the potatoes, and she could almost feel the smooth, creamy brush strokes embellishing the woman's face. She was a princess, the painting shouted, not a peddler.

Olivia moved on to another painting depicting a group of young, bright-eyed artists at a café, laughing with carefree innocence. Olivia knew it was them—Felix, René, and Julian—at the height of their friendship. Moving down the line, she viewed a beautiful young woman with almond eyes lying naked on a bed with the sun rising behind her. Adrienne, she thought, that must be her, *that* night. Olivia went on to a horrifying image of dying men in a box, and then to a wretched portrait of a young man crying as he stared helplessly at his mutilated fingers. Thick splotches of blood engulfed him. Olivia stepped back and hugged herself. She began to cry when she came upon a brutal murder scene, a body whose disfigured foot lay at the base of a large desk. It was the death of her father.

She spun around, dizzy with emotion and completely overwhelmed. The paintings were aggressive, passionately executed, in blinding hues and lashing brushstrokes, with chaotically colored backgrounds. Olivia knew she had entered the tempestuous world where *Man on Fire* had existed, and she did not want to leave.

"Mr. Klein requested that we number these for you," the director interrupted. The tremble of her voice belied her self-assured stance. She whispered, "It is his life, isn't it? It is what happened to him, why he was so silent. Miss Broussard, do you hear me?"

Olivia responded absently, "Yes. His life, and others who meant everything to him."

The director cleared her throat. "He was afraid that the paintings would be stolen or destroyed if they were discovered, so we hid them here all these years." She paused, then whispered, "I have been waiting for the day that I could finally bring his incredible work to light."

She gestured toward two carefully wrapped canvases leaning against a wall. "He specified that those particular paintings be shown to you last and separate from the others."

Olivia felt faint. She needed air. She glanced at a second door leading to a patio. "Would you mind if I opened the paintings out there, alone?"

"Not at all." The director unlocked the door.

Olivia went out to the patio, quickly moving past the wrought iron furniture and the manicured bushes. She walked until she reached the edge of the cliff, then looked down at the isolated beach: an alcove carpeted with sand, surrounded by rocks against which the powerful waves crashed. She pictured Julian painting down below and decided to head toward the narrow path and open the packages there.

The air was salty, inviting. The closer she got to the water, the easier she breathed. Stepping onto the sand, she kicked off her sandals and began to unwrap the first package. She ripped the paper recklessly, like a child opening a birthday gift, not caring that she was littering the grounds while the director watched her from the conference room window.

It was a vibrant painting of nude bathers by the brilliant artist Ernst Engel. A painting that Olivia knew had meant everything to Julian. She smiled to herself as she opened the second painting.

She noticed his signature first. It was the only painting in the series that Julian had actually signed. It was his first name only. The *J* was inflated like a bubble, a dominant, confident swirl. She eyed the painting slowly, taking in its richness, then ran her hand gently over the canvas, caressing its detailed texture.

A slim teenager with long, dark hair stared into an oval gilt-framed mirror. Her clear, olive skin was accentuated by a sleeveless white dress. Her profile was lovely yet shadowed, overcast with pain and longing. The reflection of a smiling young man with the same raven hair and ebony eyes gazed back lovingly at the girl from inside the mirror. It was her and René Levi, her father, face-to-face for the first and only time.

Olivia touched the painting's slim blond frame and held it close to her, embracing all that Julian Klein had given her. She had once been the girl in the painting—locked and lonely. Not anymore. Julian's art—his world—like a boat lost at sea, had become hers to save. And, in turn, it had rescued her.

She was determined to bring Julian back to Paris. Together, they would visit René Levi's grave and then find a quiet place to paint. She had much to learn from him. He would teach her not to see color, but to *feel* it.

She glanced at the beautiful young man in the painting and smiled. Yes, she thought, her father would like that.

Walking toward the shore, Olivia dug her toes into the grainy, doughy wetness where sand met water. She watched the powerful turquoise waves envelop the golden beach. Drops of saltwater sprayed into her mouth, and she licked her lips, tasting the splendor surrounding her. Flexing her fingers eagerly, Olivia felt revitalized as her mind began to paint.

Acknowledgments

Fugitive Colors is a work of historical fiction. I researched extensively and interviewed dozens of experts for background information about Paris in the 1930s, Nazi Germany, the history of modern art, and specifically "Degenerate Art." I would especially like to tip my literary hat to Lynn H. Nicholas for her masterpiece, *The Rape of Europa: The Fate of Europe's Treasures in the Third Reich and the Second World War*, and to Stephanie Barron, curator of the powerful exhibit and book *Degenerate Art: The Fate of the Avant-Garde in Nazi Germany*, shown at the Art Institute of Chicago in 1991—simply brilliant.

Many thanks again to the Hollywood Film Festival's Opus Magnum Discovery Award for recognizing and honoring my manuscript. A girl never forgets her first . . . prize; or her first published short story. *Hadassah* Magazine, you brought to life "The Painting" years ago. That moment, that stunning cover artwork, meant everything to me—it was the prequel to *Fugitive Colors,* and where Ernst Engel first made his appearance.

To the *Jerusalem Post* and *Moment* magazine: Thank you for the incredible opportunities you gave me, to edit and report on the most fascinating news, which not only landed on paper but also deep in my soul.

To all those who suffered for their art, their passion—artists whose canvases and brushes were plundered and stolen from their hands. Your legacy lives on, I hope, through Julian Klein's voice; your story was told . . . and your truth.

And to those who have graced my life and my work:

Liza Fleissig of the Liza Royce Agency—the incomparable feisty agent with a laugh that could be heard from New York to Chicago—discovered my manuscript and took *Fugitive Colors* the distance, and to Ginger Harris-Dontzin. Julie Matysik, my brilliant editor at Arcade, who can magically spin an ordinary word into gold.

To the editors along the way: Lisa Eisen, a woman who wears many hats in my life; my beautiful soul-sister *and* bad-ass editor with a wicked red pen, the incredible Sally Arteseros, the talented Nathan Englander (for his insightful suggestions on character development); to super-strategist Daniel Kim (whose advice I *never* pass up); and to all those who read my novel and threw their suggestions my way, especially the "Deerfield Moms," who demanded to know more about Julian's childhood. They suggested including a prologue from his past (hope I did you proud, Ladies). A personal note of gratitude to Sam Harris, president emeritus of the Illinois Holocaust Museum and author of *Sammy: Child Survivor of the Holocaust*, who read *Fugitive Colors* and gave me the greatest of all compliments: "I'm proud of you. You got it right."

To the women who make me a better woman: Beth Richard (your voice is music to my ears, Sistah), Lisa Newman, Julie Kreamer, Rebecca Fishman, Randi Gideon, Ellen Katz, Leslie Kaufman, Amy Klein, Bonnie Rochman, Malina Saval, Dina Kaplan, Sharon Feldman, Staci Chase, Paula Goldman, Julie Gorden, Marnie Wilcox, Leslie Golub, Terri Frydman, Revital Frydman, Susan Barr (mother-in-law extraordinaire), and Bonnie Schoenberg (who proves over and over that "forty-plus" is really *two* twenty-year-olds dancing inside one woman—Amen!).

To my Support Squad. I am blessed with a large family who deserve a few shout-outs: Jonathan Frydman (for always keeping me grounded), Jimmy Frydman (my "bookend"—for always showing the logical side to an emotionally charged Big Sis), Jason Frydman, Richard Barr (my number one fan and book distributor), Steve Schoenberg, Jason Richard, Suzanne Cahnmann, Leonard Cahnmann, and Joseph Frydman. And to the next generation: Josh, Jonah, Jacob, Tommy, Ben, Tamar, Ziv, Zohar, Danielle, and Sabrina.

To my inspiration: Grandpa Ephroim Frydman (nearly 102 and still the handsomest guy in town), and Grandma Rachel, who taught me the meaning of life, love, and survival—I can picture you now serving up God's favorite dishes in Heaven's Kitchen (HE just better clean his plate . . .).

A special thanks to an amazing cousin and friend, Gary Lincenberg, for his brilliant legal mind and warm heart, and for using his talent and skill when I needed him most.

To my mentors: Sue Chernoff (best boss ever), Sherren Leigh, Steve Leibowitz, Mitch Pilcer, Joel Weisman, Hershel Shanks, and Suzanne Singer—for teaching me the ins and outs of journalism. Never take "No" for answer.

To my *GIRLilla Warfare* team, especially my incredibly talented designer Dave Stepen. And to Marcy Padorr for putting my work on the map and just being so damn wonderful.

To Solomon Schechter Day School for encouraging me to write, write, write . . . and to *always* ask questions.

To my fabulous baristas: Without my daily dose of "Grande Extra Hot Mocha" and "plugging" into my local Starbucks (home-away-from-home), none of this could have percolated.

And to my Happily Ever After: Davey Babe, Noa, Maya, Barski, Chloe, and Izzi—you make the journey so much sweeter, the drama stronger, our home so much warmer. Loving you is the best chapter of all. *xoxo*

About the Author

Lisa Barr has been a journalist for more than twenty years. She served as an editor for the *Jerusalem Post* for five years, covering Middle East politics, lifestyle, and terrorism in Jerusalem. Among the highlights of her career, Lisa covered the famous "handshake" between the late Israeli Prime Minister Yitzhak Rabin, the late PLO leader Yasser Arafat, and President Bill Clinton at the White House.

Following the assassination of Prime Minister Rabin, Lisa profiled his wife Leah for *Vogue* magazine, and they maintained a friendship until Mrs. Rabin's death. She later served as managing editor of *Moment* magazine based in Washington, DC, which was co-founded by Nobel Peace Prize winner Elie Wiesel. Most recently, she worked as an editor/staff reporter for the *Chicago Sun-Times* covering lifestyle, sex & relationships, and celebrities. She earned her master's degree in journalism from the Medill School of Journalism, Northwestern University.

Lisa has contributed to numerous publications worldwide. Her manuscript for *Fugitive Colors* won first prize at the Hollywood Film Festival for "Best Unpublished Manuscript." Her website and blog, *GIRLilla Warfare: A Mom's Guide to Surviving the Suburban Jungle* (www.girlillawarfare.com) launched in spring 2012.

Her greatest joy is raising her three beautiful daughters, and "coffee time" with her husband David Barr. She lives in Chicago with her family, two dogs, and lots of girl drama—fodder for her next novel.